Tour To Midgard

The Forgotten Land

Keith McArdle

Also by Keith McArdle

<u>The Unforeseen Series</u>

The Reckoning: The Day Australia Fell
Aftermath

National Library of Australia Cataloguing-in-Publication entry:

McArdle, Keith, 1978- author.
 Tour to Midgard : The Forgotten Land
 978 0 9925 6572 5 (pbk.)
 1. Australia. Army 2. Special Air Service Regiment--Fiction.
 3.Time travel--Fiction. 4. Adventure stories.
A823.3

Cover design by Eloise Knapp, EK Cover Design
Printed and bound in Australia by IngramSpark on 50lb white paper

Connect with Keith online:

Website: http://www.keithmcardle.com
Facebook: https://www.facebook.com/KeithAuthor
Twitter: https://twitter.com/KeithAuthor

for Simone

PROLOGUE

Thousands were dead, or dying. It was a disaster! Following September Eleven, the United States determined to capture the mastermind behind it all. A man whose name the world would never forget. Osama Bin Laden.

Somalia, Afghanistan and Pakistan saw large numbers of U.S. troops deployed in search of the rogue. The President had at his disposal an army of faceless, nameless men and women who fed information and advice from around the world. Within ten days of the atrocity at the Twin Towers, the President's advisers thought it likely Bin Laden had fled to Iraq. Seven hours later Iraq was under increasing scrutiny and within twelve, the President had given the go ahead to begin operations.

Rather than send more troops into Iraq, the American Department of Defence chose to offer funds to the Kurds, asking they hunt for Bin Laden.

If they ceased their search, even for a day, the funds would stop. Kurdish Peshmerga Forces began purchasing high-tech weapons from America in large quantities. That was when the trouble started. The Kurds were persecuted ever since Iraq had become a country. Saddam Hussein was unrelenting in keeping with this historical "tradition". During the Iran- Iraq war, thousands of Kurds were gassed under Hussein's orders. The Kurdish people wanted revenge and it came in the form of US greenbacks. Fierce urban warfare erupted in the streets of every major town and city. The Iraqi Army fought well, but was on the back foot from the beginning. In almost every firefight, they withdrew before the ceaseless Kurdish onslaught. Within four weeks, the Iraqi Army was no longer a cohesive force. Pockets of Iraqi soldiers continued to fight, but they were overwhelmed. Iraqi civilians found themselves cornered in the streets and slaughtered. Then the fleeing began. Tens of thousands of people streamed from the cities, piled onto trucks, walking, travelling any way they could to escape the new threat. Some convoys drove into well-organised ambushes and slaughtered without mercy.

Iraq was falling apart. The United Nations announced it would restore peace and stability, but they knew if they moved in, they would not be a peacekeeping force. They would be a peace-making force. A sobering realisation that opposed the reason for the creation of the UN.

It was the only way to regain some semblance of order in Iraq.

CHAPTER 1

GENEVA

"What can America offer this peace-keeping force?" the chair of the UN spat, looking at the representative for the United States of America. The chair's voice was distinctive, with its heavy French accent.

"Unfortunately, we have carrier groups tied up in support of troops in Afghanistan and Somalia. We are way beyond our budget as it is, so are unable to help in this matter."

The American representative leaned back in her chair; it was obvious America did not want to help. They wanted Bin Laden and by stopping the Kurdish uprising, they would be hindering themselves.

Cameron Eves, a well-spoken Australian, almost smirked as he watched the chair hold back a rebuttal. A tall, stocky man, Eves was clean-shaven with dark curly hair, his eyes glinted with intelligence but his face gave away nothing. He wore a black business suit, a mobile phone resting near his left hand and a glass full of water stood by his right. In plain clothes, enjoying his weekend with his wife, he looked like a typical surfie.

Few people knew he attended United Nations meetings, representing a well- established western country. Even fewer would think someone who preferred to wear board shorts and old shirts on his days off could have that many letters after his name. Cameron knew as well as any of the representatives there, that America's military budget was a bottomless pit.

America deployed half a million soldiers, thousands of strike planes and attack helicopters into Iraq in the early 90s. The cost was somewhere near several hundred billion dollars.

"So far we have several generous contributions, but we need more ground troops. Especially Special Forces," the chair turned towards a mahogany lectern. A well-built soldier was making his way up the dais as the chair continued, "I'll leave that to General Billiar to explain."

"Good morning," the General began his accent one of a well-educated Englishman. What was also immediately recognisable, were the medals worn on his jacket. There were enough of them to sink a small battle ship.

"My name is General Billiar. Now, we have a situation here in Iraq and a serious one I might add. A minority group, the Kurds, persecuted for many generations now have state-of-the- art weaponry… a lot of it." The General's eyes rested on the American representative for a moment before he looked away. "The Iraqi Army lies defeated and the Kurds, trained and led by Kurdish Peshmerga Forces, are now killing or shooting at any Iraqis. The whole country has become destabilised and the civilian death toll lies at fifty thousand. That figure's rising by the day, in fact by the hour."

"What we need are specialist soldiers, Special Forces if you like, who can get in close and observe. If the situation becomes volatile and there is no civilian activity in the area, they will rectify it as they see fit. A peacekeeping mission will not work, we need to take a tough stand, but we also need to be careful. We know the Iraqis will dislike our presence, yet, we have no idea how the Kurds view us. If they see us as an enemy or a threat then we have two opponents with which to contend. It could get messy."

"Once our special forces on the ground relay to us exactly what is going on, our next goal is to re-stabilise the country. Move people back into their homes and try to establish a good relationship between the Iraqis and the Kurds. It's going to be a tough and lengthy operation. Now what we need from you are Special Forces soldiers, trained in desert warfare. We need to observe hostile activities first to get an idea of what is going on. We've heard the rumours, but we need them substantiated. The Special Forces soldiers will be our eyes and ears."

Several representatives raised their hands. The chair made a note of the number of hands and which country they represented.

"Now we need to befriend the Kurds," continued the General, "offer them something that will subdue their urge to kill every Iraqi on the spot. An Iraqi officer by the name of General Muhammad Al-Hazareen is responsible for the majority of atrocities against the Kurds. If we capture him and bring him to trial then this may be enough to appease the Kurds. We will need to make the trial public too, perhaps with regular pamphlet drops over Kurdish territory with updates on the trial. After all not everyone will have a TV."

"As far as our intelligence and sympathisers can gather, Al-Hazareen's moving to a small town called Barzan for his protection. The town is in northern Iraq near the Turkish border. There is usually a strong Kurdish presence in this area, but currently most of these people are in the southern areas of Iraq creating havoc. Kurds in or around Barzan think Al-Hazareen is a Kurdish commander secreted there to avoid capture by the Iraqi Secret Police who want his head. Clever.

"We need a small Special Forces unit to go in, capture Al-Hazareen and bring him out. The danger of this mission will be significant and if not planned, the soldiers will come back in wooden boxes no matter how good they are. I want to make that clear. It is a dangerous mission, but one that is important to the United Nations' involvement in this area. We need a representative to put soldiers forward."

Several reps grabbed their mobile phones and talked hushed tones. One by one, they hung up. For a moment, there was silence in the large room. The General's eyes moved over the representatives.

It seemed to General Billiar that no country would offer their soldiers. It was quite understandable given the task they were to perform. However, unknown to anyone there, Cameron Eves was still on his phone. When he hung up, he looked at the General and raised his hand.

"Sir, I believe we can do it," Cameron Eves's Australian accent broke the silence.

"Special Air Service Regiment?" asked the General. "Yes, Sir," replied Eves.

SASR had gained an impeccable reputation during their involvement with anti-terrorist forces in Afghanistan. In particular Operation Anaconda. The Australian SASR had played an integral part in the success of the operation, including calling in air and artillery strikes.

The General nodded. "Excellent. That is all, thank you ladies, gentlemen and Mr. Chairman for your time today."

The General took up his papers and left.

* * * * *

Steve Golburn was relaxing in the afternoon sun, turning sausages and watching his two children play. Kathy, his ten-year-old daughter, was teasing her younger brother, Brent, with a beach ball. Brent was two, with brown curly hair like his father and determined to get his hands on the ball.

"Kathy, stop teasing him. Let him have the ball," Steve said. The sausages were almost done and the sizzling smell wafted through the air. There were three other barbecues around them, all overlooking the beach. It was the perfect place for a Sunday afternoon family outing. The distant laughter of children lingered on the soft breeze. Five or six kids were playing in the sea.

Steve was a well-built, fit man who walked with a confident swagger as if he was without a care in the world. He loved being with his family, after all he was away almost eleven months of the year with work.

"Almost done?" Judy asked as she put the tomato and barbecue sauce on the table.

"Pretty much," Steve looked across at his wife. They had forgotten to take the sauces with them when they parked the car. Judy had walked back to get them and looked like she needed a drink. Steve poured her a glass of chilled white wine from the esky. She smiled as he handed it to her.

"Dad this is no fun," Kathy said, sitting with her legs crossed and her chin on her hands. Brent was giggling as he kicked the ball, running after it and kicking it again.

"Watch out Manchester United," chuckled Judy.

"Why don't you go and kick the ball with him," said Steve. He got up and took a gulp of his VB.

"Ah, that's better," he said.

Judy's mobile phone rang.

"Hello?"

"Are the sausages done, Dad?" Kathy asked as she placed the beach ball on the ground nearby and sat on it.

"Ah, okay," Judy sounded disappointed.

"Yup, almost," he said turning the sausages once more, before arranging them on a plate. "In fact, they're ready right now," he added.

"Err, yes he's right here," said Judy passing the phone to Steve. She did not look happy. "It's work," she said.

He stopped himself from swearing. "Steve Golburn here."

"Sergeant, it's Corporal Miller here. Sorry to disturb you, but something's come up. It's urgent. We need you in here within the next hour for a quick brief."

"This ain't any exercise is it?" Steve asked looking down at his wife.

She looked away at this and shook her head.

"No mate, this ain't no fucking exercise."

Their marriage was already under stress and this was the last thing Steve wanted to happen. It had got to the stage where Brent thought that Steve was just a good friend who came to visit every now and then. Kathy enjoyed seeing her father but she could survive without him and had done since she was born. None of this seemed to bother Steve, but Judy knew it hurt him, even if he didn't show it.

They packed up the plates, wrapped up the sausages and left, their Sunday afternoon in tatters. When they got home, Steve saw them to the front door, kissed the children and then hugged and kissed Judy.

"I shouldn't be too long baby," he kissed her once more.

She was trying hard not to cry. "How long will you be gone this time? Two months? Six?"

Bloody hell, here we go, Steve thought, but he knew it was just as hard on Judy looking after the kids by herself as it was for him on operations. He took a deep breath.

"Don't do that, not now honey. Listen," he took her hand, "I'll be back as soon as I can," he said and pulled her to him. He kissed her and then left.

Judy took the kids inside. She sat down on the couch. She could not believe this was happening. Steve had only been home three days after a two-month exercise.

"Mama, I hungry," blurted Brent, putting a hand on her knee.

"Don't worry Mum, I'll make him a sandwich," said Kathy, leading Brent to the kitchen by the hand.

Judy buried her head in her hands and sobbed. Kathy came in to see her mother sobbing on the couch. She ran up to Judy and hugged her. "Don't cry, Mum, please don't cry."

Brent stood in the doorway, a sandwich clutched in one hand and honey dripping onto the floor. He looked on with confusion. The world in which he lived was tearing itself apart and he was still too young to realise it. Judy clutched onto Kathy and rocked back and forth. She wiped her tear-stained cheeks. Would he come home this time?

Judy closed her eyes and tried not to think about it.

* * * * *

Steve sped down the outside lane of the highway towards the centre of Perth. He did not know what the mission was about, but from the sound of the phone call, it sounded like he might have another wartime deployment. It was every trooper's dream to go on at least one war deployment, but more than one was better than excellent.

He guessed it had something to do with Iraq. The Kurds had become a powerful force, killing all Iraqis in their sights. It had been all over the news for the last fortnight.

He had enjoyed his time with his family, he always did. But Steve was one of the uncommon men who found themselves in the ranks of the Australian Special Air Service Regiment, the elite soldiers of the Australian Defence Force. The SASR was one of the most elite units of any force in the world. America had some excellent elite outfits, but they were on equal ground with the SASR.

Steve had been in the SASR for almost fourteen years now and was one of the more experienced men in the regiment. At thirty-seven, he could still cover fifteen kilometres on foot in less than forty minutes. He pulled into the barracks and drove towards the guard at the gate. He pulled out his identification, wound down his window and stopped next to the "slot machine" as some called it. He slipped the plastic card into the machine and slid it downwards. The machine would read the barcode on his ID and check its authenticity. This all took the space of less than a second. The barrier came up.

Once he had parked outside the operations room, Steve walked up the small flight of stairs and made his way to the briefing room door. He could hear muffled voices inside. Sweeping his eyes across the room, Steve smiled. They were all old faces.

He had worked with these men on many occasions. So much so that many soldiers in their squadron dubbed the small group "The Usual Suspects".

Dave Hill had a face like it had been chiselled from a rock face, the telling sign that he was a desert specialist. Not a man for small talk, he only ever spoke when there was something to say.

Will McDonald was a well-built man of twenty-five, and easily the youngest on the patrol. When something had to be blown up, his eyes lit up like a child's. Consequently, he could set up some deadly booby traps for the enemy to stumble on.

Scott Gillman was rough as guts, with tattoos covering his arms and back. He had a mouth like a sewer and spent most of his money pissing against a wall each weekend.

Matt Russell, at twenty-eight, was short and balding. He had the look of a slow man old well before his time. However, he was in fact incredibly fit and built like a bull terrier; his bright green eyes were alert, missing nothing. All the soldiers present were trained medics, but Matt was a qualified field doctor and sniper.

Sergeant Steve Golburn was the most senior soldier in the room. He was the team commander and looked upon almost like a father by the other soldiers. He had been commander every occasion this small group had worked together.

"Well, well, look what the fuck'n cat dragged in," Scott said, chuckling. "Good to see ya mate."

"Good to be here," replied Steve. "So what's the go?"

"Dunno yet," Will said. "Ben just got a call as he was about to fill us in."

Corporal Ben Miller was one of the intelligence soldiers, or "spooks" as they were often called. If they needed maps, satellite images or weather reports he was the man to see.

"How's the missus and kids going?" Dave Hill's deep voice broke the short silence.

"Yeah, they're going really well, mate. Although they were a bit cut when Miller phoned me and told me to get stage side."

"With you gone it'll give her more time to get to know her new boyfriend," Scott laughed. No one else thought it was funny. "Shut up Scotty," said Dave.

"Just trying to lighten the fuck'n mood. Feels like some prick's just died," said Scott taking out a packet of cigarettes.

"Not in here mate," Will said. "The room's a bit small to be filling it with shit-flavoured smoke."

"If you want to smoke go outside mate," Steve said, taking a seat.

Scott sighed. "All right, all right, point taken." He put the cigarettes back in his pocket.

"I'd assume with all the coverage Iraq's been gett'n, we might be heading for the Iraqi desert," Matt said looking at the members of the group.

"I hope so," said Dave. He had not yet passed up an opportunity to undergo desert work. "Although it won't be much of a desert this time of year."

"A desert's a desert," Scott said, with a matter-of-fact manner.

"No, it's not dickhead," said Dave. "It's summer here in the Southern Hemisphere, so up there it's winter. You're looking at hot days and bloody freezing nights. It's not uncommon for it to rain, sleet and sometimes snow in the desert in that part of the world during the winter months."

Scott shrugged. "Ah, we'll be right, a few electric blankets, a couple o' wood stoves and a few heaters should see us through."

"Smart arse," said Will with a smirk.

"Righto, sorry about the delay fellas," said Ben Miller, closing the door behind him. "Steve! Great to see you. Right, now that we're all here I may as well get straight into it."

Miller moved to the head of the table and laid out more maps, satellite images and other pieces of information.

"Now, if you've been watching the news, you'll all know that Iraq is in a world of shit, it's falling apart by the day. The United Nations wants a peacekeeping force in there immediately. They've already started sending advance troops into Iraq, mostly Special Forces who are observing and communicating with the UN. As you guys might know, the Kurds got their hands on multi-million dollar equipment and weapons from the Americans. They're now killing any Iraqi soldier or civilian they come across. The whole country is quickly turning into a disaster area. Not a good situation, obviously. To begin with, America refused to help the UN. However, since then, they have offered one carrier task force group which is two days from commencing operations, some transport planes, about one hundred special-forces troops, five squadrons of attack helicopters, namely Apaches and two squadrons of F-16 fighters. Okay so that's where the country stands at the moment."

"Now that we all know what's happening in Iraq, we'll move onto the why. Quite simply, America wants Osama Bin Laden and from the reports written following interrogations of his high-ranking officers, they seem to think he would have fled to either Somalia or Iraq. "America as you know from CNN moved into Somalia with force some weeks ago.

"So the hunt began, spearheaded by the extremely motivated Kurdish Peshmerga Forces.

Having said that, the Iraqi Army has pretty much been decimated. That's how the country started falling apart. Therefore, your mission is one of propaganda. There is an Iraqi officer, General Muhammad Al-Hazareen, who has been responsible for Kurdish atrocities for almost twenty years. If you can observe him, move in and then capture him, the UN can put him on trial for crimes against humanity in a very public court appearance. The UN is hoping this will quell the Kurdish uprising somewhat and give them some room to move. The next mission for the United Nations will obviously be to try to establish a good relationship between the Kurds and Iraqis. Your mission is going to be hard and incredibly dangerous, which is why you have been allotted ten days of planning time before you depart."

"Ten days!" blurted Scott. "Fuck's sake, my arse has already gone to sleep and it's only been about ten minutes!"

"I'm afraid it's ten days or you don't go," Ben said, "Colonel Bracker, the man who will be helping you to plan your mission does not want, in his words, 'a fuck up'."

"That's a very basic run down on your mission. I'll leave the planning of the mission to yourselves and Colonel Bracker, who'll be here," Ben looked at his watch, "in about half an hour."

The room was silent. They had only met Colonel Bracker briefly on a handful of occasions. An SASR trooper during Vietnam, Bracker had worked his way up the ranks, before applying for, and receiving, his commission as an officer in the Special Air Service Regiment. He had seen an unbelievable amount of action and the men were honoured that such a man would take time out to help them with their mission.

"Bloody hell, so we finally get to meet the big man," said Will softly.

It had not been a question and the others remained silent, still stubbed that they were about to meet the most highly decorated soldier in the history of the SASR. The man had seen operational service in Vietnam, Korea, Borneo and a two-year attachment to the British SAS meant he had seen service in The Falklands War. Once he had returned to the Australian SASR, Bracker saw action in the First Gulf War, Somalia, Cambodia, East Timor, Afghanistan and the Second Gulf War. He was literally a living legend, and when he retired would probably have enough travel experience to work as CEO of Lonely Planet.

"Righto," Ben stood up. "I'm off, if anyone wants to contact me for any reason, my number and extension is up on that board over there." He pointed to a pin board behind Steve, which had various pieces of paper attached to it, one with two phone numbers circled in red ink pen.

"Not a problem mate," said Steve. "Thanks for straightening everything out."

Ben left and the guys started shooting the shit, catching up on each other's lives. What they had missed, what they had heard and what they thought about each other. After a while and a lighthearted argument between Matt and Scott, the powerful hum of a V8 was heard outside, before the engine fell silent. They could hear someone walk up the stairs and move into the foyer. Steve stood as the door opened.

"Glad you could make it, Sir," he said by means of welcome to Colonel Bracker.

Bracker was a tall, fit looking man. The sandy coloured beret, a famous trademark of the SASR sat on his head like it had been designed for him. His pale blue eyes were cold and penetrating; his face seemed hard and unforgiving.

"Thank you Sergeant Golburn," said Bracker. His voice was deep and authoritative. He sat in the seat where Ben had been sitting and looked at each soldier in turn.

"So *you're* the usual suspects they all talk about!" The Colonel said.
"Let's start shall we?"

CHAPTER 2

"I'm not going to take too long here today," said Colonel Bracker leaning back in his chair.

Fuck'n hope not, Scott thought, playing with a pen.

"Now before we start, we need to determine our worst case scenarios. It's always the smart soldier who plans with the worst in mind."

Colonel Bracker leaned down and pulled five books out of a bag at his feet. He began to distribute them to each of the men. Steve was not familiar with the title. On the cover of the book was a colour photograph of the sun rising up over the flat, arid plain of the Iraqi desert. Above the image were the dark yellow words Iraq: The Forgotten Land.

"Every man is to read this book," the Colonel said as he passed a copy to Scott.

"Not a problem, Sir," replied Scott as he began flicking through the pages. "It might be for Will though. Too many words and not enough pictures!"

The Colonel jumped in before Will could manage a response. "Let me just say that this is not a fucking book club!" He paused for a moment shooting a couple of well-aimed glances at Scott and Will. "This is a dangerous time of year to be working in Iraq. The temperature can range from hot to cold within a few short hours. Understanding the terrain and the winter weather conditions will help you before you disembark."

Bracker tapped one of the books on the table. "One thing that is not mentioned in here is the town of Barzan itself. There are many strange stories and a hell of a lot of mythology that surround the town and indeed that particular area of Iraq. Something about strong magic imbued in the land. If what the stories say is true, then a group of Gods took mortal form in, or near, Barzan."

Scott sniggered. "Yeah I know it's a bit hard to swallow and we all know it's a lot of bullshit. But if you ever mingle with the locals, just bear in mind they consider the land sacred, so don't offend them!"

"How long have we got to read it?" asked Steve.

"Three days," the Colonel answered. "I am being generous because I don't want you buggers skimming through it." Stretching down once more, Colonel Bracker produced five notebooks, each with a pen. He dropped them onto the centre of the table and gestured towards them. "Take notes you might think pertinent to the mission."

"So it is a fuck'n book club then!" muttered Scott.

"Except that your exam is a practical exercise and not a fucking essay, soldier!" Bracker retorted. Bracker stared at Scott. "Any questions?"

The men indicated the negative. Colonel Bracker stood up. "Right," he said, walking towards the door holding his bag. "I'll see you all back here in three days, ten hundred hours sharp. Make sure you're here," he said over his shoulder. His footsteps faded as he strode away.

Steve stayed on base that night and began reading Iraq: The Forgotten Land. The author, Simon Nite, was a British freelance journalist based in Iraq. Simon had reported for most of the major media organisations in the West over many of decades. The book was claimed by most as one of the definitive works documenting both the country and its people. It was also amongst the recommended textbooks at universities and institutes across the world. Nite was a well-known anti-war activist who would be shocked to learn his work would have military application. There was more to Iraq than Steve had thought. It seemed most lived in a society that possessed technology that rivalled that in western countries. However, it was the locals and their history that interested Steve most of all. Living in small communities out in the country, keeping to themselves and owning no real high-tech items were the Bedouin. Steve learned that a Bedouin obliged to accept, feed and water any man or woman who approached their dwelling, even if they were a sworn enemy. If they were a sworn enemy, the Bedouin were unable to pursue them until the food and water they had given their guest had passed through their system.

Eight hours was usually the agreed time. A visitor could stay with the Bedouin for three days before they could even ask the visitor's name. They had some strange customs, but they sounded like a tough but friendly people.

Steve also discovered the Kurds had been persecuted by the Iraqi military from time immemorial. During the eight year Iran- Iraq war, thousands of Kurds were gassed, Hitler style. Entire Kurdish villages wiped out by scud missiles attached with chemical warheads. It was little wonder that the Kurds were so angry and vengeful towards the Iraqi people. The book covered tourist attractions, culture, history and religion.

Steve did not sleep that night. He continued to read and take notes. By midday the next day, he had read the book, taken pages of notes and was bone weary. He drove home and spent the rest of the next two days with his family. As was the policy within the regiment, he was not to tell his family where he was deploying. But the families of members of the SASR watched the seven o'clock news and were aware of which hellhole their partners were likely deploying.

The day before he was to deploy Steve took his family to Cottesloe beach. The sky was a deep blue, made more so by the thin wisps of cloud that stretched to the horizon. The ocean surged and swelled, waves breaking onto the shore, advancing across the sand with a soothing hiss before fleeing back. He loved the beach, and so did the kids. He smiled as he watched them frolicking in the shallows. Judy sat on a beach towel watching them, their picnic lunch stowed away in an esky beside her.

"Careful," Steve chuckled as Brent was bowled over by a wave. He leaned down and picked his son up out of the water.

The toddler wiped his face and giggled. Steve walked out further so the ocean crashed about his thighs, Brent tucked under one arm giggling and squirming.

"Ready, Son?" grinned Steve, as he lowered Brent into the water, but keeping a firm grip on him. When the next wave was almost upon them, he threw his son into the air and caught him. The boy screamed with excitement.

"Ready?" he chuckled as Brent waved his arms in the air. He lowered his son into the water so that only his head was above water. The wave coming towards them must have looked huge from Brent's perspective. At the last moment, Steve threw him up into the air again. After fifteen minutes of this game and growing tired, Brent asked to join his mum. Carrying him up to Judy, he placed his son onto his mother's lap, before heading back into the water to join Kathy.

"Race ya, Dad!" called Kathy, readying herself to catch an incoming wave.

"You're on!" Steve smiled. Waiting until the wave was almost upon him he threw himself forward and began swimming until he felt the water surge around him. Increasing his speed, he could feel his body swept along and kicking forward, thrust his arm out in front of him. With the power of the wave behind him, it felt like he was flying through the water at incredible speed. As he neared the beach, the power of the wave subsided and he felt the sand beneath his feet. Standing up he noticed Kathy had beaten him.

"You'll have to do better than that, Dad!"

"I was just warming up," he replied, pretending to stretch his arms.

"Yeah right!" Kathy said.

"Now I'll try again, for real this time," he said, with a wink.

Kathy beat him again.

"Takes us oldies a few goes to warm up," grinned Steve, "give me a few more waves and I'll put you to shame!" "Okay, you're on, Dad!"

Again, Kathy won.

Steve came spluttering to the surface and climbed to his feet.

"At least I don't cheat!" said Steve with a grin.

Kathy gasped. "I didn't cheat," she called, throwing a piece of seaweed at him. The seaweed splattered across his head, giving him instant dreadlocks. Kathy burst into laughter. He threw the seaweed aside with a grin.

They caught waves together for another half an hour, Steve winning only a handful of times, his daughter beating him easily. After they had tired of the game, they walked hand in hand up the beach to where Brent and Judy waited.

As the water dried upon his skin, Steve could feel the salt crystals forming, and rubbed them from his shoulders. He accepted a ham, tomato and cheese sandwich from Judy with a smile.

The family ate together in silence, watching as the waves crashed against the beach with soothing rhythm. The tide was coming in, and within twenty minutes, the sound of the ocean escalated as the water reached closer.

"Want to go back in?" asked Steve.

"No thanks, Dad," said Kathy. She was lying back on a towel, a hat covering her face from the sun. Brent was asleep on a towel. Judy had covered him with a thin blanket.

"What time are you leaving?" Judy asked.

"Early," replied Steve. "About five."

"Going to say goodbye to the kids this time?" Judy asked.

Steve sighed. Here we go again, he thought.

"I do every time. Just because they are asleep most times doesn't mean I don't say goodbye."

"Then I have to deal with their questions in the morning, trying to explain where their dad has gone and for how long, when I don't even know?"

"Bloody hell Judy, do you want me to shake them awake and tell them I'm going away for seven months and that they might not ever see me again? How does a child process that? Not well is my guess."

"You could at least wake them up and tell them you'll see them soon!"

"I kiss them on the head and tell them I hope to see them soon," said Steve looking out to sea.

"That's not the same thing!"

"Isn't it?" Steve asked, turning to face her. "Are you sure about that? Because where I'm going the best I can do is hope to see you again. If I promise more than that it's nothing but a lie!"

Judy turned away. Her shoulders shuddered as the tears came. She cried, trying not to disturb her children.

"I'm sorry babe," Steve said pulling her to him. "I'm sorry," he said again, kissing her hair.

The family drove home in silence.

That night they watched Shrek together, and although Kathy had seen it several times before, it was the first time Brent had seen the film. Whilst the kids and Steve giggled together, Judy huddled against her husband.

In the morning, he woke early and walked into the kitchen to make himself breakfast. Judy appeared in her nightgown bleary eyed.

"I'll be ready shortly," she said.

"Okay," he said with a smile.

At 06:30 hours, Judy drove Steve into the base. He leaned down next to the driver's side window, an overnight bag containing some belongings slung over his shoulder. "We'll be here for another six or seven days before we leave. I'll see if I can get home again soon," he said. Judy nodded her head but didn't reply. She was too busy trying to hold back tears. Steve smiled and kissed her before turning and walking in the direction of the briefing room.

"Take care Steve, I love you," she called, her voice shaking. He did not hear her. As it was each time this scene played out, her body was numb and the familiar, doubtful feeling of whether she'd ever see Steve again filled her mind.

He turned back and waved as he continued walking backwards.

"Love you babe," he said as the doors to the building swallowed him up. He stopped to watch Judy through the small window in the door as she turned the car around and drove out towards the front gate.

Steve opened the briefing room door and stepped inside to see the disgruntled face of Scott Gillman. Will McDonald was behind him, clutching a cup of coffee and chuckling.

"Ya dickhead," Scott blurted. "I asked for coffee, two sugars and milk. Never heard of the NATO standard cup of coffee? Christ, if ya want something done, do it yourself."

"Sorry Scott, I could have sworn you said black tea," smirked Will.

"Dickhead," Scott repeated as he poured the tea down the sink. "Steve, how ya going mate?" Will said.

Scott looked around. "Hey mate," he called.

"G'day boys," Steve greeted them, slinging his bag onto a chair.

"For Christ's sake!" Matt said, throwing the Army newspaper he had been reading down on the table. "Our frigg'n union team just got flogged again, that's twice in a row!"

"Who'd we lose to this time?" asked Will, taking up the paper. On the front cover was a picture of a young soldier who was abseiling down a cliff. A physical training instructor was above him, standing on the ledge and urging him on.

"We lost to those poofters in the RAAF," replied Matt. "That's twice they've beaten our team this year."

The disappointed medic looked up, "g'day mate," he said to Steve.

"Where's everyone else?" Steve asked.

"Dave said he's held up in traffic. Should be another twenty minutes or so."

"Bullshit," chuckled Scott Gillman with a fresh, steaming cup of coffee in his hand. Everyone knew that if Dave were going to be late, he would ring them on his mobile and tell them he was held up in traffic. He had even had the gall to do it on exercise last year out in the Woomera desert. The truth was he had rung them as he sat reading the paper at a petrol station outside town, with a sandwich and a coke to keep him company. He had told them he would endeavour to get the 4 x 4 Land Rover back to them as soon as he could. Dave was a solid soldier, but like many of them in the SASR, he had a colourful sense of humour.

Dave arrived in the briefing room ten minutes later, followed shortly afterwards by Colonel Bracker. The group launched into planning their mission, beginning with what they had extracted from the book. The planning of a mission was the most important part of an operation. Success or failure relied on thoughtful and meticulous planning that incorporated most scenarios. In that way, if a problem did arise, the patrol could react immediately.

The planning of a mission by SAS soldiers was far different to the regular army.

They would then go ahead and collectively plan the mission. Some soldiers, who preferred the old "This is the way I want it done and that's the end of it", did not look upon this type of open floor planning kindly. Both methods had their pros and cons.

Over the next six days, Colonel Bracker and the soldiers worked on the planning, starting early and finishing late. They could leave nothing out. It was draining work, but they knew just how important it was. They discussed the rendezvous point for resupply. If they needed to stay longer than necessary, they would need more water, food and fuel for their chosen vehicle. This would be brought in by helicopter upon radio request.

Finally, on the sixth day, Colonel Bracker wrapped it up. "I think we've just about finished," he said, taking a sip from a steaming cup of coffee. "I intended for the planning phase to be ten days, three days studying the book and seven on the mission planning, but there's only so much we can plan for. Take tomorrow off, which is Friday if my brain hasn't abandoned me. Tie up any loose ends you might have, say goodbye to friends and family, and for fuck's sake don't be late on Saturday morning. It'll be your fuck'n arse if you are!" he said, looking at each of the men in turn.

"Go out and have a good time tonight, enjoy yourselves, but stay out of trouble."

"Thanks for helping us out, Sir," Steve said, extending his hand.

Bracker shook his hand and nodded. Each of the men took their turn to do the same. Afterwards, he gathered his things and made his way to the door. He turned as he opened it. "Best of luck with your mission men. I hope you nail that bastard."

"Right," said Scott. "It's beer o'clock, time to get shit faced."

Steve held up his hands for silence. "Okay fellas, go out tonight and have fun, but do not be late Saturday morning. I repeat do not be late Saturday. Because if you are then it's not only your arse, it's my arse too. Right, get out of here and enjoy yourselves."

"What, you're not coming with us?" asked Will.

"No, I'm taking Judy and the kids out to dinner and a movie," replied Steve.

"Ah, doing the old man thing," said Dave, nodding, dodging Steve's retaliation with a chuckle.

"I don't get to see much of them," Steve said. "So may as well make the most of it. Who knows, I might even get lucky," he said with a wink.

"That's fair enough. I think we're all hopin' to get lucky mate," Scott called from the briefing room door.

"Which movie are you going to see?" asked Matt, slinging his bag over his shoulder.

"I saw the ad for Ice Age 2 on the TV the other night. Looks like a funny movie," replied Steve.

"Go and see that movie," Matt said. "That is one of the funniest movies I've seen in a bloody long time. Christ, it cracked me up like you wouldn't believe. I went with Tanya and she wanted to take her son with her, so we couldn't go and see an action packed 'I'll be back' movie. I thought it'd be a boring kid's movie, but man was it funny. Good choice mate, go and see it."

"You've talked me into it," said Steve with a grin.

"Anyway, we'll leave you to it," said Matt. "Have a good time."

"Say g'day to Judy and the kids for me," said Will, as he followed Matt and Scott out the door.

"Will do mate."

"I'll see ya Saturday, Steve," said Dave, waving from the door. "In the meantime, don't strain yourself old man," he said.

"Get out of here, Sunshine, before I whip your arse," Steve threw a scrunched up ball of paper at Dave.

Steve cleared the table, straightened the chairs, grabbed his gear and left. This was the only time off he would have with his family for some months, and he was going to make the most of it.

CHAPTER 3

At 0900 hours on Saturday, the soldiers, Land Rover and equipment were ready to leave from RAAF Base Pearce, just outside Perth. The vehicle was a 6x6 Long Range Patrol Vehicle, built from the ground up for the Australian SASR. On the bull- bar were attached six small smoke mortars. If the patrol came into heavy contact, could dispense a smoke screen and allow them to withdraw. There were also infrared headlights for night driving. The roof and roll bar were absent as was the windscreen. A .50 Calibre mounting ring sat high in the middle of the vehicle upon which was a .50 Calibre heavy machine gun.

The vehicle was armed in a way that if contact ensued, the patrol had enough firepower to either overcome the enemy, or break contact and withdraw. A Mag 58 machine gun was mounted in front of the forward passenger to cover the immediate front. Unlike the .50 Cal, this machine gun carried smaller bullets. The mount could only swivel from the two o'clock to the ten o'clock position. Between the Mag 58 and .50 Cal, the Land Rover could pack a punch.

The Rover also carried six 25-litre Jerry cans full of fuel; not to mention camouflage netting.

They were able to take more warm weather gear, food, water and ammunition than if they had been on foot with packs, weapons and webbing.

The Land Rover would do little to ward off the elements, but then it was not designed with comfort in mind. Steve and Will carried M4 carbine assault rifles with M203 grenade launchers attached beneath the barrel. The rifles sported suppressors, which reduced noise and flash. If a soldier happened to be lying prone, the suppressers reduced the amount of dust kicked up when he fired a shot.

Dave and Scott carried the Minimi light machine gun. Having ACOG sites fitted meant they could engage targets out to 600 metres with accuracy. The Minimi they carried was a 'para' version, much shorter than the Minimis carried by the infantry Battalions.

Matt, being the sniper of the patrol carried an M-110, which was a semi-automatic sniper rifle that fired the 7.62 mm round. The weapon was accurate out to 1000 metres.

One piece of equipment they should have been issued was a Javelin anti-tank missile launcher. The Q-store had none left in their armoury. More were on backorder, but this did not help Steve. Instead, they were issued a handful of M-72 Light Anti-Armour Weapons (LAW), which fired a 66 mm unguided anti-tank rocket. Not as effective as the Javelin, but it would have to do.

A C-130 Hercules would fly in from RAAF Base Richmond at 0930 hours, refuel, then load on the Land Rover as well as the soldiers.

This was to be the beginning of their long, uneventful journey towards the United Arab Emirates and Iraq. The half-hour wait gave the men time to go over everything again. They checked their equipment, weapons and the vehicle. It was important they had the correct supplies and that the equipment they had was undamaged.

As they finished their inspection, a strong English accent broke the silence.

"Righto lads, gather in, gather in there!"

Steve grinned as he watched Pete Massicks stride out towards them, with a large camera around his neck. Pete was a civilian contracted by the Australian Defence Force as a photographer and was beyond exceptional. He had been a Royal Marine Commando during the Falklands War. Although he had been a soldier, photography had always been his passion and his forte.

On occasions in Bougainville, Somalia, Bosnia and East Timor, he put himself in danger to snap authentic photographs. Steve had a feeling that he did it for the rush.

Pete waved the five soldiers into position in front of the Land Rover. "Righto, machine gunners on the outside. You riflemen kneel down in the middle there. That's it. Good." Pete took several photos before sitting down and chatting with the men.

At 0926 hours, the loud, high-pitched roar of the C-130 drifted towards them from the other end of the runway. It was an H-model, the camouflage paint and the emblem of the rearing stallion on the tail plane indicated that it was a 36 Squadron Herc.

The soldiers inserted hearing protection. It was a simple matter of rolling the foam-like cylindrical material between forefinger and thumb to condense it. Once in the ear, it would re-expand to its original size. It was an effective and cheap means of hearing protection. The Hercules lumbered off the runway and taxied towards the marshaller.

The beast came to a halt less than twenty metres from the waiting soldiers. After half a minute or so, the roar of the engine began to fade.

Once the aircraft was refuelled, the Land Rover was loaded, the soldiers boarded and before long, they were airborne. They touched down in Dubai after what seemed an eternity, with several stops to refuel. The soldiers had slept some of the way, the rest of the time they read or played cards. The next day they were flown to Qatar, where they stayed for four days before departing again.

* * * * *

The next leg of the trip would be another lengthy journey. Their flight, this time by United States Air Force Hercules, would take them over Jordan and into Turkey. It would only be a few hours' drive from there to their mission at Barzan, across the border.

"She's not any old Herc," boasted the American loadmaster as he walked with the five soldiers across the tarmac.

"What d'ya mean?" Steve asked.

"We're trialling an airlift element of the 160th Special Operations Aviation Regiment." The loadie pointed at the C-130. "This is one of them."

The cargo door began to open and within moments was touching the tarmac. The American loadmaster stepped aboard and picked up his helmet from one of the seats, a 9mm Glock holstered to the outside of his right thigh.

He gestured for them to form a semicircle around him before he squatted. The soldiers moved around him, put their weapons and equipment down and knelt. "Okay, there's been a change of plan," the Load Master had a strong Texan drawl. "Our ETA at Colemerik coincides with a multi-national sortie being flown out. Refuelling tankers, fighters, bombers are outward bound around the time we are scheduled to arrive. We can't afford to circle around waiting for them to finish their deployment; we have a VIP and his vehicle to pick up at Ercek." He held up two fingers. "You guys have two choices. You can either make a high altitude, low opening five kilometres from the airbase and we'll be on our merry way. Or you guys are welcome to wait for the next airlift to Colemerik, which will be sometime tomorrow morning, around 0145 hours. What do ya wanna do?"

"That's gotta be a rhetorical question," grinned Scott. "How 'bout a LALO?" Will asked.

"Yup," the loadie nodded. "We can do a low altitude, low opening."

"What about our vehicle," asked Steve.

The loadmaster nodded. "That is the problem, there isn't enough time to rig parachutes to it, so we can't drop it out the back."

"Well I don't wanna go without our vehicle mate," said Steve.

"Want us to unload?"

"No, we can drop you guys out the back, do our next mission then come back to Colemerik and drop the vehicle off for you. The air traffic should have cleared by then."

"We've got weapons, equipment and supplies on board that vehicle, mate. We're not gunna let it outta sight."

The loadmaster shrugged and was at a loss.

"Your riggers, how fast are they?"

"Pretty fast," replied the loadmaster, "but not fast enough to get it done before we are due to takeoff."

"So, take 'em with us," said Steve. "Waddaya mean?" asked the loadmaster.

By this time, the Captain had joined them to see the cause of the holdup.

Steve shrugged. "Bring 'em aboard and let 'em rig the vehicle in flight."

The loadmaster nodded. "Not a bad idea," he admitted. "I'll contact the riggers' supervisor and see if he'll release a few of 'em for the day."

"Sounds good. Let's go then," Steve said. There was no way he was leaving an Australian vehicle in the hands of an allied force without being there himself. Now that it looked like the Rover would be parachuted in, he was happy to continue on the next leg of the journey.

The riggers arrived within twenty minutes. They unloaded the huge parachute packs and skidboard. Once they finished, the loadmaster signalled everyone to form a semicircle around him.

"Okay, I'm sure you guys know the drill, but this Herc's a little different from the one's you've experienced. Stay seated and strapped in during takeoff, I'll signal when you can unbuckle and move around. If you don't strap in for takeoff, you will end up with injuries. Don't fuck with me on this one. There are parachutes for you on board and once I've given you the all clear to unbuckle, you can begin your jump prep."

The soldiers nodded and walked aboard as the first engine whined into life. Moments later the propeller began to spin. They could smell the strong aroma of aviation gas carried on the strong, warm wind.

The second engine started and within minutes, all four propellers were beating the air with ferocious power. The loadmaster signalled for them to strap on their seat buckles. He took his helmet and placed it underneath one of the seats. There was no need for him to wear it inside the plane. Instead, he wore a headset to maintain communications with the pilot and the second loadmaster.

The Hercules was no different to any other in which they had travelled, thought Steve. The familiar red seats, the armoured panels lining the floor and the first aid kits were hanging above the seating, as they should be. As far as they all could tell, the C-130 that was beginning to taxi towards the runway was the familiar old Herc they had grown to know over the years.

The loadmaster stood by the cargo door as it closed. Once the large metallic door had sealed with a dull clunk, he joined the soldiers and strapped himself in.

The men felt the Hercules turn before coming to a slow halt. It was almost a minute before a thunderous roar rose above the noise of the engines and Steve glanced out the small porthole. He watched two British Tornadoes thunder into the sky in close formation. Their landing gears tucking themselves out of sight. The Tornadoes did not need much distance to take off so they used a short runway that intersected the main one. The Hercules would need to wait until the sortie had taken off. Another roar drowned out the C-130 and three more Tornadoes screamed into the sky to join the first two. The Herc rumbled out onto the main runway and turned into the wind. From this angle, Steve could see that a USAF Star Lifter had stopped where they had been moments before, waiting for them to take off. Taxiing behind the Star Lifter was another USAF Hercules. In the distance, two Apaches rose into the sky and moved off towards the west at low altitude.

The engine pitch rose and the Hercules lurched forward. Scott slid sideways before his seat buckle stopped him from travelling any further.

Steve felt the seat buckle dig into his side, stopping him from sliding towards the rear of the plane. It might have looked like an average Hercules to the soldiers, but they had never been in a transport plane this powerful before.

"Fuck'n Jesus," mouthed Scott in disbelief.

Before they knew it, they were travelling into the sky at what felt like a 45-degree angle. Their stomachs were in their boots. After about five minutes, and once they levelled out, the loadie unbuckled and stood up. He signalled for the men to unstrap the seat restraints. The riggers jumped up and secured the parachute packs to the vehicle in preparation for the drop. They rigged the chutes in a way that the Land Rover would not descend nose down. During the flight, they moved the vehicle onto the skidboard. Built into the skidboard was shock absorbing material, which would reduce damage to the vehicle once it landed. The American riggers moved with a fluid precision that instilled confidence in Steve. The last thing he wanted was to be without a vehicle. Steve prepared his parachute, pack and weapon for the jump. They wanted to jump a low altitude, low opening and hoped the pilot would oblige. They would only be 1, 000 feet from the ground when they stepped out the back. Once they were free falling they would wait two seconds before pulling their ripcords. When their parachutes had deployed they would be between 60 and 90 feet from the ground.

From the time they left the aircraft to feeling solid ground beneath their feet, only 10 or 15 seconds should have passed. It was not Steve's intention to break any records today. The LALO jump was an opportunity for his patrol to hone their skills.

Scott kicked Steve in the side. He looked up and saw Scott was strapped back into his seat, wearing a set of headphones. "Five minutes to jump."

Steve told the others who did not have headphones. The soldiers began donning their gear. It was a surprise that they had covered the distance so fast. Steve calculated that the C-130 must have been travelling more than 1,000 km/h.

The loadie had strapped on a harness and clipped himself onto the side of the plane near the cargo door. He had also plugged the communication lead into the comms panel so he could hear information or commands from the pilot. When the cargo door opened, it was his job to ensure that it opened without malfunction. The harness would stop him falling from the aircraft should anything go wrong.

Meanwhile Steve and the others checked their harnesses, backpacks and webbing. It was important to check, re-check and re-check each other. Any loose gear or open pockets meant that equipment or weapons could be lost in the jump. If it were a real combat situation, losing gear or weapons could compromise not only the mission, but also their lives.

Steve and his men braced themselves as the C-130 went into a steep dive. They dived for almost half a minute before straightening out at what Steve assumed was 1,000 feet. They felt the aircraft slow and grabbed onto hard points to steady themselves. The cargo door began to open and a blast of air entered the aircraft. The loadie watched the door as it opened, the wind whipping his uniform. After the cargo door had opened, the loadie turned to the men and held up two fingers. Two minutes. The five soldiers made their way to the open door and the yawning landscape below. The loadie passed them each a set of clear goggles that would protect their eyes from the wind on the way down. The men placed the goggles over their eyes and secured the elastic straps. The loadie held up one finger.

The men re-checked each other once more before moving into position. Dave and Scott, who were the gunners and had the greatest amount of firepower, would be the first on the ground. Matt, Will and finally Steve would follow them.

Steve tapped Dave and Scott on the shoulder. "Dave, I want you at 12 o'clock," he shouted. "Scott, you go to six, we'll form up on you two." With a machinegun at 6 o'clock and 12 o'clock, the patrol was well protected. If the soldiers were jumping into a combat situation, the order of jump would be no different. If the jump was mistimed even by a second, Steve knew someone would die. But then they were not cheap thrill seekers in search of adrenalin, they had all practiced this jump many times before.

The American riggers had released the chains holding the skidboard down, before giving the thumbs up. They pushed the skidboard towards the end of the ramp. Gaining in speed, the skidboard, attached to which was the Land Rover, tipped over the edge and within a second had disappeared from sight. Steve hoped to Christ the chutes had opened.

The loadie turned to the soldiers, held up five fingers, then four, three, two, one. Dave hurled himself out the back of the aircraft, followed by the others at intervals of two seconds.

Steve watched Will disappear out the cargo door, counted to two and then stepped out into thin air. Warm, fume-filled air and the roar of the engines hit him as he fell. A moment later the smell of the fumes and the noise of the engines were replaced by the thunder of cold air in his ears.

"One," he counted to himself.

He could see that Dave was already on the ground and was sprinting into position, Minimi in hand. Scott's parachute was open and he watched as Matt's chute bloomed into life.

Scott had landed and unclipped his chute, which floated to the ground behind him. He sprinted into the 6 o'clock position, throwing himself to the ground. Will's chute flared open beneath Steve.

"Two," Steve counted, pulling the ripcord. He grunted as the parachute opened above him, slowing his rate of fall. He felt the sudden pull on his parachute harness telling him that his drop line, with his pack and webbing had deployed. Steve was about 30 metres from the ground.

Leaning back, he looked up making sure the parachute had opened. He counted the parachute lines, satisfied that none of them had twisted. Glancing back, he could see the Land Rover shrouded in parachute silk in the distance. It was impossible to tell from this distance if the vehicle had sustained any damage.

He watched as Matt ran into position, going to ground in the 3 o'clock position. Steve looked up and over his right shoulder watching the

C-130 above them as it banked, vapour trails streaming from the wing tips.

When he looked back again, he saw Will had landed, unclipped his weapon and was running for the 9 o'clock position. The ground came up to meet him and Steve rolled as his feet hit. He detached his parachute mid-roll, unclipped his weapon as he came to his feet. Releasing the drop line, he sprinted into the middle of the circle going to ground.

"Nice," said Steve, climbing to his feet. The others also stood up, adrenalin glinting in their eyes as they grinned like children. It was only then that the noise washed over Steve. He turned towards the airbase. The whine of turbo prop engines mingled with the roar of jet engines and the juddering power of helicopters. He could not see the runway because a long hedge of trees blocked his view, but he could smell the AVTAG. Whatever mission was outbound was huge. Drowning the combined roar of aircraft was a new sound: a powerful scream vibrated the ground. Ten seconds later he watched four British Tornadoes streak above the trees in close succession. Following was a twin propeller Eagle Eye; a large, flat circle fixed above the fuselage indicated it was a fighter control aircraft.

The noise of the five departing planes gave way once more to the thunderous roar of the numerous aircraft awaiting take off from the airbase. A low-pitched shriek filled the air, putting the noise at the base to shame as six Euro-fighters cut the sky in close formation. They appeared above the thick trees that concealed the airbase from Steve's sight. The aircraft climbed to altitude and within minutes were tiny specks against the sky. Another roar grew, drowning out the mixed noise. Two air-to-air refuellers lumbered into the sky, a light brown smudge of burned fuel streaming from their huge jet engines.

"Someone's about to get their arse kicked," chuckled Scott from beside Steve.

"Tell me about it," shouted Steve as the loudest roar he had ever heard thundered across the sky. He could feel the power vibrating through his chest. Scott said something else, but it was lost in the noise.

The perpetrator showed itself, a B-52 heavy bomber cut the sky, on its way to deliver a payload of devastation. Three more B-52s took off and as their size diminished in the sky and their noise faded, the airbase, which had emitted a dull roar, was now a soft burr. Steve watched as sixteen Blackhawk helicopters departed, followed by seven Chinooks. Leading the convoy were nine Apaches and five Cobras.

With the main event now over, the noise from the airbase was almost non-existent. The soldiers packed their gear away and walked to the Land Rover. As he pulled the parachutes away, Steve could see no obvious damage to the vehicle. Detaching the vehicle from the skidboard, he climbed into the driver's seat and turned the key. The vehicle started first time.

"Nice one," said Dave.

As the engine was left to warm up, the soldiers detached the parachutes, packed them away and placed them in the back of the Land Rover. They would drop them off at Colemerik where the parachutes would make their way back to the American riggers in Qatar.

They drove towards the airbase at a sedate fifty kilometres per hour, giving the British soldiers guarding the gate plenty of time to see them. The last thing they wanted was the British to think them a threat and open fire. Coming to a gentle stop near the gate, Steve nodded at the nearest guard.

"G'day mate," he said.

"Afternoon, Sir. May I see your identification please," the guard was aware the soldiers before him were not British. He kept one hand on the SA-80 assault rifle slung across the front of his body.

"Yeah no worries," Steve held the ID card up for the guard to inspect. The others followed suit.

"Thank you, Sir, which unit are you with?"

"We're with the Australians," answered Steve.

"Oh okay," replied the guard, who was not aware there were any Australians on the base. In truth, there was only a token Australian force in Colemerik. The majority of them, including six Australian FA-18 fighters, their pilots and ground crew, had not yet arrived.

The guard nodded at the other British soldiers, who raised the boom gate to let the vehicle pass. Steve drove through with a nod of thanks. One kilometre to their right was the flight line, where huge numbers of aircraft were lined up in neat rows. There were fighters, fighter control, transport, bombers, and helicopters. Steve saw most of them originated from NATO countries.

The Australian area was miniscule compared to the other forces inhabiting Colemerik. It was called Camp Linacre, but with only an advance force populating the area, Steve and the others had plenty of room to relax for the night. They met some of the Australians at the mess that night and made small talk over dinner. The SASR soldiers did not talk about why they were there or when they would leave, but the other Australians knew who they were. They also knew that before long Steve and his soldiers would be in circumstances far more dangerous and far less comfortable.

CHAPTER 4

As a deep blue tinge gave the eastern sky a touch of light, the Australians were returning from the mess after breakfast. Colemerik was quiet all but for the burr of a C-130 Hercules as it rumbled into the sky, delivering supplies or bleary-eyed troops somewhere in Iraq. Within twenty minutes, as the sky turned a dull pink, the soldiers were under way. They had shredded their identification cards and burned them. Nowhere on their person did they carry any rank or identity. It was common practise in case of capture. They drove for ten minutes, passing two other vehicles, before they reached the southern gate, guarded by four soldiers.

"Thanks fellas," Steve said to them as he drove through the raised boom gate.

They nodded and watched with interest as the Land Rover headed south towards the border. By the little he could see of their uniforms in the poor light Steve thought they were Danish soldiers.

By sunrise, they had driven almost an hour and a half. They were keen to cross the border without drawing attention. By mid-morning, they had driven over the border and into Iraq. They kept clear of roads or populated areas, instead driving on low ground making sure they were not silhouetted against the skyline.

Around lunchtime, Steve stopped and watched a drove of distant goats with interest. He turned the engine off. A young goat herder was walking behind them, hitting the nearest goats with a stick and driving them onwards to some unknown destination. The boy seemed bored. Watching in silence, the Australian soldiers had their weapons ready. Priority dictated that their secrecy and anonymity were more important than the boy's life. If he noticed them, he would die. They watched the boy and his goats until they had disappeared from sight.

Engaging the ignition, the engine sprang to life and Steve accelerated, keeping to a sedate pace to avoid kicking up too much dust. Three more times they either stopped or deviated from their route to evade goatherds or villages.

"Hold it!" hissed Scott at one point, flicking off the safety catch and swivelling the fifty-calibre machinegun to bear down on a smudge of dust. Steve stopped the Land Rover. The dust was growing closer and the sound of an engine came in intermittent burbles as the gentle breeze blew towards them.

Within minutes, an old, decrepit looking truck of Russian origin came into view.

"One occupant," spoke Will, as he stared through the binoculars.

Matt brought his weapon up resting it across his knees in a way that looked unthreatening, almost complacent. But he could react lightning fast if the situation turned sour.

The vehicle came to a screaming halt beside the Land Rover. An Iraqi man with a full beard grinned out at them, his arm resting on the door. The grin vanished as he saw the foreign weapons and he became wary.

The Iraqi spoke in an agitated tone. Scott replied.

Nodding, the man continued to watch them.

"What'd he want?" whispered Steve.

"Wants to know where his son is, he should have herded fifty head of goat back home by now. The monthly markets are the day after tomorrow," replied Scott.

"You tell him we don't know?"

"Yup."

"So what now?" whispered Steve.

"What now? He thinks we've either kidnapped or killed his son. Matt get ready to drop him."

"Way ahead of ya," replied Matt.

The Iraqi's face was solemn now, even angry decided Steve. The newcomer shouted at them, his eyes betraying his anger.

Scott shouted back, his hands splayed out before him in a gesture of innocence. He was trying to defuse the situation, but failing. The man climbed out of the vehicle, an AK-47 clasped in his hands. The Australians held their fire. Scott continued to try to dissuade the man. The Iraqi spat a comment in reply and with a snarl raised the weapon to his shoulder. A single rifle crack broke the moment. The man dropped to the ground in a lifeless heap. Matt lowered the M- 110 sniper rifle from his shoulder.

"Fuck it!" snarled Scott. "Stupid bastard should have listened to me!"

"Yup, he should have," said Steve and accelerated away. They left the abandoned Russian vehicle idling where it stood. And a corpse lying face down in the sand.

They drove fast now, blistering along at up to a hundred kilometres per hour when the terrain allowed.

Steve did not want to risk the gunshot being heard by local inhabitants who might be curious enough to go and investigate. When they were twenty kilometres from the site of altercation, Steve slowed to a sedate pace. They drove without seeing another soul for what seemed an eternity.

"If I was a God, there wouldn't be a chance in hell I'd take mortal form in a shit 'ole like this," Scott grinned, looking at the others. "Give me surf, sand and hot chicks any day of the week."

"Well you've got plenty of sand, mate," chuckled Steve.

The sun began to retire throwing a blanket of dull orange to the west. As hues of deep pink began to outweigh the orange, they came upon the distant village of Barzan. Parking the vehicle in a deep, protective wadi hidden from view, the soldiers donned their packs and walked closer to the village. When they had covered close to five hundred metres, which took almost an hour of slow patrolling, they decided to set up an observation post. Dave was sent forward to select an area for the OP. Having spent most of his SAS career in deserts worldwide, Dave did not pull any punches when it came to his incredible knowledge about the desert. Once he had chosen the perfect location, the rest of the patrol advanced and began digging a wide depression out of the sand. A desert camouflage net over the observation post gave them concealment. When the sun rose in the morning, no one would be the wiser that the Australians were there, keeping watch over the village.

Intelligence said General Al-Hazareen was hidden in the village, but whether he had arrived yet was still not confirmed. The half-moon was still high in the sky, but when early morning arrived, it would have slid beneath the horizon. It was then that Scott and Will would go on a recon patrol into the village in search of the General. It was their task to find out if he had arrived, and if so, where he was and how well guarded.

"You blokes hit the sack, I'll keep watch for now," said Steve unslinging his weapon and dropping his pack in the sand beside him.

"Matt, you're up next, I'll wake you in a couple of hours."

"Yup, righto."

As the others settled down in their sleeping bags, Steve lay down on his stomach. Bringing the Minimi into his shoulder, he looked out towards Barzan. The Minimi light machinegun was always used as the weapon of choice during piquet. The rising moon was bright, making the need for night vision almost unnecessary. But the leader of the SASR patrol was not willing to take any chances. The pale light of the moon played tricks on the eyes, making something appear where there was nothing, or hiding someone from view.

Steve scanned the horizon, keeping his ears open for any unusual sounds that could mean their situation was about to take a turn for the worse. As the minutes ticked by, his mind turned to his family. He missed Judy and the kids. If he were not careful, before he knew it his children would be adults with their own lives. His marriage was under stress and he knew that if he did not spend more time with them he would not have a family. He was due for five weeks leave and was considering taking it when he got back.

Judy wanted him to quit the army and re-join the civilian world. Steve was opposed to the idea and the couple had argued about it at length. The SASR came first and family second. That had always been the unwritten rule within the ranks of the Special Air Service Regiment and always would be. Although he loved his family, he was dedicated to the regiment. It was a mentality that many wives and loved ones had a lot of trouble understanding. For this reason, the divorce rate within the regiment was high. Steve knew if he did not begin spending more time with his wife and children, he would be divorced.

Nor was it his immediate family that suffered. He had not seen his parents for almost three years. Two and a half years had passed since he had spoken to his brother, let alone visited him. But then it was the price one paid for entering a unit such as the SASR. And it was a price that he and many of his colleagues were willing to pay.

* * * * *

At 0100 hours Will, followed by Scott, moved out of the observation post and made their way towards the distant town of Barzan. Few lights shone in the small township, but in the little light thrown by the stars, the outskirts were still visible to the naked eye. With the night vision goggles on, Barzan was visible to both soldiers. No residents were moving around and all looked quiet.

These were ideal conditions for the mission Will and Scott intended to undertake. As they moved closer, the challenging bark of a dog broke the silence, the sound echoing out into the stillness of the night.

Without taking his eyes from their destination, Will signalled for a halt and both men went down on one knee. The dog barked again, this time sounding a little unsure. The sound faded into silence and both soldiers waited for a few minutes, before rising to their feet and continuing towards the town.

Apart from their weapons, the soldiers hoped they would pass as Iraqi locals. They were hoping that any enemy that they might come into contact with would take little notice of their weapons. But they were hoping that in such a small town, few people would be awake at 1:00am.

It took them almost an hour of slow patrolling to reach the outskirts of the town. Once they had travelled into Barzan, Will moved away into the shadows of the buildings, crouching low. He continued to patrol parallel to Scott who had slung his weapon and tucked his night vision goggles out of sight. Will was Scott's cover man should he get into a tight spot. If a sleepy Barzanian resident were to glance out the window, they would just see an Iraqi man out on a night's stroll. It would look more suspicious were they to see what looked like two Iraqi militiamen armed to the teeth.

Scott was careful not to put any buildings or objects between himself and Will as he moved. They were closer to the building within which they had been told General Hazareen was, or would be staying. It was their mission to infiltrate the house, find out if he was there and then leave. Tonight would not be the night they grabbed him; it was an intelligence gathering patrol. The more information they had with which to work, the better their chances of success.

A dog padded out of a nearby house and made a beeline for Scott.

Will went down on a knee and brought his weapon to bear, sighting it at the animal's thin body. Scott held out his hand and let the dog sniff it. The animal moved forward, sniffed his outstretched palm, wagged its tail and moved closer. Scott patted its head then continued. The dog was statue still, watching the departing man, its ears cocked. It stood without moving for a minute, before turning and trotting out of sight behind a nearby house.

Will rose and moved on. Scott was standing with his hands on his hips with his back turned to his advancing comrade. He gazed at the stars with feigned interest. In reality, Scott was waiting for the patrolling soldier to catch up with him.

Without looking around, Scott continued strolling towards their destination. They were much closer now. The pair moved on for another ten minutes before they rounded a corner. Will saw movement ahead. It was a man with his back to them. The acrid aroma of cigarette smoke drifted through the air. Scott immediately changed direction towards the Iraqi. Will almost chuckled as he realised that Scott wanted nothing more than to steal a smoke off him. But he had not seen the man as fast as Will's night vision eyes had. In such a small town, it would be suspicious to ignore a person, even at such an early hour of the morning. The man coughed and spat, before turning towards Scott as he heard him approach.

"As-salaam alaykum," Will heard Scott speak, waving at the man.

"Peace be with you," Scott said in Arabic, waving at the man as he advanced.

The Iraqi man responded in kind.

"I arrived yesterday afternoon visiting my sister who has just moved here," Scott began. "I'm so excited to see her again that I could not sleep. I haven't seen her for ten years now, would you believe? Excuse my poor manners, I am Ahmad Dhabi," said Scott smiling, his face hidden within his shamag. He could not remember whether Iraqi people shook hands when introducing themselves, so he fell silent.

"Yes, family is important, ten years is a long time my friend! I am Adil Abu," the Iraqi responded, holding out his hand. Scott took it and was surprised at the strength of Adil's grip.

Meanwhile Will had moved forward until he was twenty metres from the men. Close enough that a single accurate shot could be taken on the Iraqi, killing him. Will lay down on his stomach and sighted the M4 at the Iraqi's chest. A gunshot would attract attention, but it would guarantee a kill. Will had a bayonet with him, and even though killing a man with a knife was quiet, it was not as easy as Hollywood made it look.

When a person wielding a knife murdered someone, they were usually stabbed more than fifteen times. One single shot from a safe distance would kill an enemy and re-establish Scott's safety if it were compromised.

"What is your sister's name?" asked Adil. "I might know her."

"That is the reason I am visiting her," said Scott pausing for a moment, having side stepped the question. "She has only just moved here herself. She is staying with someone over the other side of town. She was a journalist in Baghdad, but fled when the Iraqi army started rounding up Kurds in the city. She wanted to live in a small town somewhere far away from all that. I have helped her move what little belongings she had here. We arrived yesterday afternoon. I might stay another week or so, before I head back home." Scott smiled, hoping to Christ the man believed him.

"Yes, the violence has not been good. Still America have given us justice against the Iraqis, we are only repaying them for generations of oppression. It is not good that your sister was forced to flee her career, but she will be safe here. The Kurdish Army has kept the Iraqis at bay and we have seen no violence here yet."

Scott nodded. The Kurdish Army, he thought to himself. The situation was far worse than the UN realised. The Kurds' only intention was to murder Iraqis on mass.

"Do you think you could spare a cigarette?" asked Scott.

"But of course, my friend," responded Adil, reaching inside his clothing.

Will's finger took the first trigger pressure as he watched the Iraqi reach into his robe. The hand came out holding a packet of cigarettes and Will released the pressure on the trigger.

Scott pulled a cigarette from the packet and placed it in his mouth.

"Have you got a light?" he asked.

Scott had a lighter on him, but it was one he had bought in Perth and had English writing on it. He was not willing to risk being compromised should the Kurd see the foreign words even in the dim light. Adil held out a lighter and ignited the cigarette. Scott nodded his thanks and took a long drag. It was the first cigarette he had smoked in a while. He inhaled and stopped himself from coughing. It was the worst cigarette he had ever tasted. But he opted for the bright side, it was a cigarette.

"I've heard that we're not the only ones to have arrived," spoke Scott. "Thousands are fleeing from the cities."

"You are correct in this," replied Adil. "I know of four different families who have joined our community in the last month alone." Adil became animated. "And we have a celebrity joining our town! An officer in the Kurdish Army has been sent here for protection, away from our Iraqi enemies." Adil leaned towards Scott. "I am one of his guards." Adil pointed behind his house. "He's staying just around the corner from my home!"

"You must be honoured to be hand chosen for such a task," responded Scott. "It must be pleasing to be the guard chosen for this great officer."

"No, no, it is not just myself. There are thirty others."

"I wouldn't mind meeting this man before I leave. I go in a week, do you think I will get a chance to see him?" Scott inquired.

"Oh yes, of course. If what we have been told is correct, he should be arriving sometime later in the morning or this afternoon. We are all excited to see him."

"Yes I'm sure you are," Scott replied.

The men continued to talk for almost ten minutes while Will lay on the cold ground, his crosshair never leaving the Kurd's chest. Adil bid the man he knew as Ahmad Dhabi goodbye and disappeared into his house. Scott walked on moving around the side of the house, following the road east towards the target building. He continued to lie there for another five minutes, making sure the Kurd did not reappear. Having decided the man had gone to bed, he rose. His weapon was trained on the entrance to the dwelling and his finger on the trigger. Moving past Adil's entrance, he turned eastward, following Scott. After he covered another twenty metres, Will stopped, scanning his surroundings. On the other side of the road, crouched in the shadow of the houses was Scott, who now had his weapon in hand and was wearing his night vision goggles. He was staring back at Will. With his left hand, Scott pointed at a house in front of them. A mansion stood almost one hundred metres distant and was situated on a slight rise. The house was built in such a position that the road came to an abrupt halt at the front door. It looked new and well built, constructed with the comfort of someone important in mind. As far as the intelligence they had been given was concerned, it was intended for General Hazareen. Will nodded and the soldiers rose and moved forward.

They stopped often, to look and listen for noises or indications they were being observed. In the case of a compromise, Scott would lay suppressive fire upon an enemy target with the Minimi. Will would sprint back and cover Scott as he in turn withdrew. It took fifteen minutes for the soldiers to reach the house and conduct a slow, thorough perimeter search to locate any guards. With no indications of any piquet, the men entered the dwelling. Two rooms were seen to the left of a steep stone staircase, which led to the second floor. What was immediately clear to the men was the smell of fresh paint. To the right of the stairs was a large open area that looked to be a living room. Scott indicated that he would search upstairs while Will was to search the rooms downstairs.

Will, weapon in shoulder, moved towards the open doorway of the first room, while Scott disappeared up the stairs. The first room was empty, apart from two sets of bunk beds one against each wall. The second room also contained two bunk beds and on the bottom bed of each slept a soldier. He scanned the room. Leaning against the wall were their AK47s, both of which seemed well cared for. There was a small cupboard against the wall near the entrance. Will moved to it, careful not to touch the half open doors in case they created unnecessary noise. Peering in he saw an ironing board, iron, and hanging up were the uniforms of the sleeping Iraqi soldiers. It was hard to see accurate details, but the uniforms looked well ironed. On the floor of the cupboard were two sets of boots, both of which seemed polished and well kempt. This spoke of discipline and pride. Contrary to the belief instilled in most westerners by the media, these soldiers appeared to be professionals.

Turning back to the beds and moving closer, Will bent down by the closest bunk and looked into the face of the soldier. He would have knelt had his left knee not cracked. Using the photograph of General Al-Hazareen that he had burned into his memory, he compared it to the face of the sleeping Iraqi. The result was a negative and he moved to the second man, bending down so that he was a foot from the man's face. He held his breath so his exhalation did not disturb the man's sleep. This was also a negative and with a last, silent sweep of the room, Will left. He moved out into the living room, looking for anything that might give them a clue about when the General might be arriving. As it was unsafe for either of the soldiers to talk, Will did not yet know what Scott had gleaned from his conversation with Adil. He searched the small alcove behind the stairs, found nothing and made his way to the front door.

It seemed to Will that the General had not yet arrived. The mansion to be Al-Hazareen's was guarded by a small contingent of soldiers assigned to protect him. If the bunk beds were anything to go by then there would be at least six to eight Iraqi soldiers guarding the General. He assumed the rest of the soldiers would arrive with the General himself.

It took Scott another five minutes. As he descended the stairs, he shrugged and shook his head. Their mission complete, the soldiers departed the house, making their way back to the observation post. Not wanting to risk coming across Adil again, they made their way back via a different route. Will once more crouched in the shadows as Scott, his weapon and night vision goggles out of sight, strolled down the road.

✳ ✳ ✳ ✳ ✳

The sun broke the horizon, painting the few clouds that dotted the sky a vibrant pink. A bird's call echoing in the distance. Scott yawned. He was sitting on the ground, leaning against his pack for comfort. The desert camouflage net just above his head, hid the culvert from view.

"Okay," he began in a half whisper, skimming over the notes he had written after they returned from Barzan. The writing was messy, sentences running almost diagonal to the page. But then it was difficult to write when the only light available came from stars.

"Here's what went down last night," he shifted into a more comfortable position and cleared his throat. Matt was lying on his stomach looking outwards, the Minimi pulled into his shoulder, watching for movement. He would hear the same brief after he was relieved from sentry. The others were sitting in a tight circle, listening to Scott.

"As you know, me and Will carried out a scouting mission into Barzan last night," he spoke so his voice did not travel far. "The goals of the mission were to enter the town without compromise and locate the house where the target will be staying. The mission began at 0100 hours this morning and the objectives were completed."

"We had a possible compromise not more than ten minutes after we entered Barzan," he continued. "There was a Kurdish villager out having a durry, so I approached him. Will was giving cover. Given the situation, it would have been more suspicious of me to ignore him. I spoke to him for some time, I stress that our situation and task was not compromised in any way. Now if what this man said is correct then it sounds to me like thirty local village men have been paid to protect the General during his stay here.

The local Kurds think that this Iraqi General is actually some hero Kurdish leader. Clever concealment by the Iraqi Army. I'm not sure if the yanks have provided them with weapons. He was pretty excited he was one of thirty local militia posing as the General's guards. He also stated that the General would be arriving in Barzan either this morning or this arvo. Either way, General Hazareen will most likely grace us with his presence bloody soon."

Scott took a sip from his water bottle before continuing. "We dribbled shit for ten minutes or so before he went back to bed. Will and me continued towards our target and made a successful and unchallenged entry into the house. It is a two-storey joint, or to be more accurate it's more like a fuck'n mansion. Upstairs I found a private bath, shower and toilet. Alongside this was a master bedroom, with a pretty fancy looking king-sized bed. I mean fancy, the kind that would have disappeared if we had a fuck'n removal truck at our disposal."

Scott fell silent and gestured to Will who took over.

"Throughout the scouting mission into Barzan, I covered Scott. When we entered the target building, Scott searched upstairs while I conducted a recon in the lower story of the house. There were three compartments to this area of the building. The first was a large open area, which seemed to be a living room. I have the feeling that the furniture for this room hasn't arrived yet. It might turn up with the General himself. To the left of the staircase was a short hall, which had two rooms leading off from it, one to the left, the other to the right.

The room to the left, contained four beds, in bunk bed style, one set against each wall. Apart from that, the room was Spartan. Within the second room slept two Iraqi soldiers. Their weapons, the AK47, were leaning against the wall nearby. The rifles looked to be clean and well maintained. The soldiers' boots and uniforms were in immaculate condition. An iron and ironing board were located in the room. It'd seem the Iraqi government has sent eight soldiers as a bodyguard for the General. No doubt they'll disguise themselves as Kurdish Army, as will the General himself. The first two of these eight are part of an advance party, protecting the house from break and enter by locals."

"This poses a problem. When the time comes to infiltrate and take the General with us, we're most likely gunna face eight professional soldiers with AKs.

There is no way, unless we drug him somehow, the General will want to leave. He will wake the soldiers on the lower level. If a contact follows, it'll alert the thirty militiamen sworn to protect Hazareen. As you can see, it could turn nasty fast, so our preparation needs to be solid. We need to be able to react immediately to any situation."

Will tore a page from his notebook and handed it to Steve. "Having said that, this is a rough hand drawn map of the house, using information gathered from the recon of the target building."

Steve and Dave copied the map in their own notepads. It was important that they know the layout of the house. When the time came for the group to make a move on their target, each man needed to move fast within the building. Matt would also copy the map down once relieved from sentry.

"Are there any questions?" Scott asked, looking around at the group.

Steve and Dave remained silent. They knew that within 48 hours they would be walking into a possible death trap. It had all the elements of a grand cock up, as the Poms would say. But in Steve's experience, anything could be done if it was planned.

"Right, we've got the heads up," said Steve. "Now we'll go into the planning phase. I want opinions and thoughts, no matter how stupid you might think they are. Believe me, if we bugger this one up then we'll get to push up daisies from the inside of a pine box under six feet of cold dirt. I want everything covered, everything."

With that, the soldiers began their plan that would see them capture an enemy officer and escape by vehicle without detection. Either that, or capture an enemy officer and fight their way out before escaping by vehicle perhaps losing several members along the way. It was going to be a challenge, but it was not impossible.

As the sun rose, heating the bone cold air, five members of the Australian SASR planned their upcoming mission.

The Iraqi government had no idea that had General Al-Hazareen been left in Baghdad, he would have been safer than he was in Barzan. Much safer. Why would he be safer in Baghdad than in the sleepy little town of Barzan, hundreds of miles from the violence?

The answer was a small hidden observation post on the outskirts of that little town.

CHAPTER 5

The morning was chilly, the sun giving off no more warmth than an electric heater in a snow blizzard. According to the American spooks, it was heading for one of the coldest winters in Iraq. Although it had already snowed, the soldiers knew they had not yet seen any real winter weather. With dark grey clouds closing in from the north, they knew they were in for more snow. It was almost time to move in and capture their target and the men were eager.

Steve cocked his head as he heard the faintest sound of a strained, whining engine in low gear. The noise faded and returned with the cold breeze but continued to grow louder. It was the engine of a four-wheel drive and it was heading in their direction. Scott turned himself to face the sound and brought the Minimi up into his shoulder. He stared down the ACOG sight, waiting. The others remained silent, covering their arcs. Was it a local farmer? Soldiers? Could it in fact be the General?

Growing louder, the white Toyota Land Cruiser came into sight. It strained up over a wadi and disappeared into its depths, the engine pitch rising as its speed increased. The vehicle began to strain again as it climbed up over the opposite lip of the wadi and continued on. It was heading parallel to them, to the right of their position, which was cause for some relief. But the Toyota was only about thirty metres away. This could not be Hazareen, as the vehicle was heading south. Hazareen would be coming from Baghdad, which was the opposite direction. Could they have doubled around the village to come from the opposite direction? It would reinforce the story of the heroic Kurdish General seeking safety in Barzan. Possible, thought Steve.

They could hear the loud voices of the people inside, talking and laughing. Looking through his scope, Steve counted four people, the driver, one passenger riding in front and two in the back.

The passenger riding in the front turned his face towards them, hawked and spat out the window. He coughed another one up, hawked and spat that out the window before looking away. For a moment, Steve thought the man had seen them. At this range, it would be difficult but not impossible to see the desert camouflage net that covered their observation post. Steve tensed. The passenger who had coughed his lungs up whipped his head around again and was staring in their direction. He must have issued a command to the driver because the Toyota came skidding to a halt. The man was pointing and with the engine now idling it was possible to hear him speaking.

"Scott what the hell's he saying?" hissed Steve.

"Can't make it out…he's talking about a dog…for fuck's sake. That mongrel dog's right out in front of the cam net," Scott swore. "We should have killed it when we had the chance," he hissed.

The dog that investigated Scott during their patrol of Barzan now stood less than fifteen metres from their position. It was looking back towards Barzan. The occupants of the vehicle were laughing at it. One of the rear doors of the vehicle flew open and a soldier ran out towards them, grinning and firing his AK47 in the air. The animal tucked its tail between its legs and ran ears flat to its skull. They laughed harder, cheering the man on in loud voices. The soldier was still coming towards them fast, firing short bursts above his head as he approached.

Steve lay still and kept his crosshairs on the man. The dog was long gone and the man was about the same distance from their position as the animal had been moments before. Unfit, he was puffing hard but still grinning. He waved back at the Toyota and shouted something at which the other men laughed. Steve noticed he wore the uniform of an Iraqi. Although the rank slides, corps badge and cap made him look more like Kurdish Peshmerga. It was possible then that one of the occupants of the vehicle was the General himself.

Steve hoped the Iraqi would turn around to his right before making his way back to the vehicle. In this way he would present them with his back as he turned, making the chances of him spotting the Australian observation post slim at best. If he turned to his left, he would be facing their OP. Steve maintained the crosshairs over the man's chest, waiting, watching, silent. The Iraqi soldier took a deep breath and let it out, his AK47 now slung and his hands on his hips. He looked out towards the direction the dog had fled, chuckled, shook his head and turned around. He turned to the left.

Stopping mid stride, the grin on his face vanished as he saw the cam net and the soldiers within it. His eyes widened. Scrabbling for his AK, he caught hold of it and – Steve fired two shots into the soldier's chest. The man crumbled to the ground.

"Contact," roared Will, pushing his M4 through the cam net, taking aim and firing a grenade at the motionless vehicle. Several of the Iraqis were shouting as doors opened. But before they had time to dismount the vehicle, the projectile zipped in through the open rear door the now dead man had left open. It exploded with a loud crescendo that shattered the silence of the chill winter morning. Scott opened up with short bursts from his Minimi, the bullets slamming through the front and rear doors of the vehicle. If the grenade had not killed the three men inside, then the Minimi had.

"Let's go! Let's go!" shouted Steve. Dave, Minimi in hand, pushed his way out the small opening in the cam net. He sprinted back, going to ground to cover the six o'clock position. Scott followed him, running forward, diving to the ground covering the twelve o'clock position.

Will was up. He tore out the pegs that held the cam net in place, tied them together and shoved them in his pack. While he did this, Steve gathered the cam net, rolled it and tied it to the outside of his pack. Matt was on his guts in the middle of the whirlwind of activity taking place around him. He had a radio handset pressed his ear.

"Zero Alpha, this is Bravo One, over."

He paused. Nothing. "Zero Alpha, Zero Alpha, this is Bravo One, this is Bravo One, over."

Another pause . . . more silence. "Shit!" He changed radio frequency to the alternative frequency, brought the handset to his lips. "Zero Alpha this is Bravo One, over."

Nothing. He would have better luck with the more powerful antennae attached to the Land Rover, but he could not wait that long. He changed frequency to the American radio frequency. The Americans only had one frequency, which was easy to memorise.

"Any call sign this is Bravo One, over."

"Roger Bravo One, this is Black Dog, go ahead." The American accent was thick. It was music to Matt's ears.

"Black Dog, this is Bravo One, we are a ground call sign, we are compromised. Enemy follow up imminent. Need help, over."

"Copy that Bravo One, we have two birds of prey on the tarmac. If you get in a tight spot, give us the word."

Will tapped Matt on the shoulder, it was time to go. Both men stood and moved back to the waiting soldiers. The pace was quick as the soldiers made their way towards the Land Rover five hundred metres away.

As they moved, Matt continued. "Black dog, appreciate that, grid 2649 1720, read back, over."

"Roger Bravo One, I read back 2649 1720."

"Black Dog, will keep you informed as our grid changes, over."

"Copy that Bravo One. This is how it's going down: these birds are going airborne. They will wait at the border. Will cut down air support delay if air support required. Do you copy?"

"This is Bravo One, acknowledge your last. Appreciated. Out."

The American airbase at Colemerik in Turkey was at least 140 kilometres from Barzan in Iraq. By fast air that represented a delay of several minutes, which was nothing to worry about. But Black Dog was concerned about delay. The air support would be helicopter gunships. An Apache would cover that distance at battle speed in about 21 or 22 minutes. In a firefight, anything could happen in that time. Having the choppers waiting at the border, ready to go, would mean a delay of several minutes before they arrived.

The five soldiers were making a beeline towards the Land Rover that had been left at the bottom of a wadi the night before. They were moving at a force march speed, around eight kilometres per hour.

They had covered almost five hundred metres and were beginning to move up a steep incline in the terrain. It was the last hill before they reached the flat ground that led to the hidden Land Rover. Will, bringing up tail-end-charlie, turned mid stride as a powerful diesel engine was heard in the distance. It was a long way off, but it was fast becoming louder.

"We've got a follow up," he shouted to the four soldiers in front of him. Steve glanced over his shoulder as he walked. An old truck travelled towards them from the town, a thick trail of dust behind the vehicle. This was not good. At best, the air support was still 17 or 18 minutes away. The vehicle must have been alerted after the shots earlier. The truck was moving towards them at close to 80 kilometres an hour. A murderous speed considering the wadis and rough ground. The good news, Steve decided, was that apart from the driver, the vehicle might be empty. He doubted it though.

"Let's prepare a welcoming committee!" shouted Steve.

Without hesitation, the five soldiers sprinted in an extended line, finding cover behind trees or rocks. Dropping their packs, they waited. Matt pulled his pack towards him. The radio was attached to the front of the pack by several quick release clips. He unclipped the radio and pulled it out. It was stored within its own smaller pack that could be slung onto an operator's back. Matt pulled it onto his back and attached the hand piece to the front of his webbing for easy access. If a firefight started, their packs would be left, but the radio would be taken with them.

Luckily, they were near the border of Iraq and Turkey and not only was it mountainous terrain, it was also fertile. The hill they had been climbing was covered with vegetation, trees and tough native grass that concealed them. They could have kept moving away from their pursuers, but movement increased the risk of being spotted. The soldiers kept at least ten metres from each other. If a grenade exploded amongst them, only one or two of them might die rather than the entire patrol.

Will and Steve pulled out the rocket launchers they had stored under the top flap of their packs. The 66 or light anti-armour weapon was a short, round tube that fired a small unguided anti-armour rocket. It was a one-shot, throwaway weapon. To fire the rocket launcher, it had to be extended to its full length, after which an aiming sight popped up at the front and rear of it. Matt and Will pulled the 66s open ready to fire and engage the approaching enemy.

The men could not see if the truck was carrying troops, but it would be naive to assume a vehicle would approach without carrying armed men. The soldiers assumed the worst as the truck came closer. The engine was straining as it moved across the terrain, bouncing and rocking on its old, worn suspension. Startled birds took off into the sky. The vehicle came to an abrupt stop beside the white Toyota. The passenger flung his door open and ran to the stricken vehicle. He peered in through the driver's side window before turning round and gesturing towards the idling truck. He was shouting something, but the hidden Australians could not hear what he was saying.

Three Kurdish militiamen jumped from the back of the truck, proving the Australians' fears correct. One of them approached the corpse of the first disguised Iraqi. While the other two jogged towards the Australians' observation post. All that remained of the OP now was an empty depression in the desert. As the Kurds stepped down into the depression, they kicked the sand looking for clues. Meanwhile, the five Australians went over the actions they had taken as they prepared to leave the position. Had a wrapper fallen out of a pocket? Had they left anything behind that would provide evidence about them? No, not that any of them could think of . . . apart from their footprints.

None of the SASR soldiers were concerned. Given the situation and time they had to escape, there had been little opportunity for them to cover their withdrawal completely. The soldiers watched as the Kurds climbed back into their truck. The vehicle began following the trail left in the sand and moved towards them.

Steve kept his eyes locked on the vehicle. "I'll trigger the ambush if it's necessary."

The vehicle edged closer. Steve brought his binoculars up. He could see three men sitting in the cabin, one driving, one passenger and the other sitting between them. He could not see into the back of the truck, but it was becoming clear that there were soldiers in the back. If they were unlucky, they would soon find out how many.

The Australian soldiers did not want to fight. A firefight would result in a heightened possibility of capture. They wanted to slip away unnoticed and head back into Turkey. But soldiers had been killed and the five men of call sign Bravo One knew their enemy would not give up. It was more possible that within five minutes, they would find themselves in a firefight.

The vehicle crawled closer, slowing as it came to the base of the hill. It was no more than two hundred metres away now and the smell of diesel drifted up to their position. With a roar, the truck surged forward and for the first twenty metres, climbed the incline well. But it was an old truck and was not designed for mountain ascents. Soon the wheels began skidding. The momentum of the truck slowed and then stopped altogether. Refusing to give in, the driver put pedal to metal and the diesel motor roared. The wheels skidded and slid. Small rocks spat from the wheels and flew into the trees behind it.

The soldiers could hear the Iraqis now, although their words were obscured. The passenger was shouting and gesturing to the driver who shrugged his shoulders.

"What does this prick think he's driving? A fucking V-8 turbo Land Cruiser?" Scott whispered.

"Alright knock it off," chuckled Steve.

Steve continued watching them through his binoculars. The Iraqi passenger turned to the driver and said something, before leaning out of the window and shouting a command to the back of the vehicle. He banged the side of his door with his hand. The engine dropped to an idle and the vehicle slid back several metres. The driver was quick to pull on the hand brake before the backward momentum increased.

"Oh Christ, here we go," muttered Dave as Iraqi soldiers spilled from the back of the truck.

There must have been close to forty soldiers. Half of them spread out to the right, the other half to the left. Eight of the soldiers posed more of a concern. Most of the Kurds wore civilian clothes, and carried AK-47s, which meant they were local militia with no formal training. But a small number were dressed in neat, dark green military uniforms, which spoke of discipline. They appeared to be the soldiers in charge.

It was possible they were Republican Guard, but their rank, corps badges and caps had been altered. There had been just two soldiers stationed in the house last night, so the other six must have arrived that morning from the opposite side of Barzan. It was now a distinct possibility that Hazareen and his personal guard had died in the first contact. If a contact was to take place these eight soldiers were the ones to drop first.

The truck, now free of its load, began to crawl once more up the hill towards the waiting men. The enemy were little more than 100 metres away and were visible. For the most part, their faces were tense and they had fear in their eyes. They knew that enemy soldiers had taken out the Toyota and killed the men inside, including the General who they had sworn to protect. As for the eight disguised Iraqi soldiers, if they lived they knew Saddam would not be pleased with them. They also knew that their enemy was around the area somewhere.

The militiamen were patrolling forward alongside the truck. Steve was thankful it was not an APC. If it had been, the small patrol would have been up shit creek not only without a paddle, but also without a canoe.

The pursuers came closer. Christ, thought Steve, if they continued on this course they would be on top of them within minutes. Sooner rather than later, Steve would have to start the contact and he knew it.

Slowing as it came to a steeper part of the incline, the wheels skidded and, for a moment, the truck stopped. The man at the wheel stamped on the accelerator, the engine roared, the wheels span again, spewing out churned earth and rocks. The vehicle lurched forward, continuing to defy the hill.

Steve dipped his head so that he was staring down the ACOG scope. He fixed the crosshairs over the driver, exhaled, and fired a short burst. The windscreen shattered and blood sprayed in a fine mist, which tinted the windows claret. The soldier who had been driving sat up in the seat with a grimace before sliding to the right. His head slammed into the side window. The two Minimis barked into life and three Kurds were down before any of them could react.

The militiamen were screaming at one another now, in panic or confusion. They began firing from the hip. It was clear they did not know where their enemy lay. A thundering BOOM resounded and a 66 rocket tore through the air, slamming into the engine block of the immobile truck. The explosion that followed sent a shock wave through the five hidden soldiers. For the Kurdish militiamen standing closer to the truck, it must have been much worse. As the smoke settled, it became obvious just how much worse. Several were down. The ones who had been closer to the explosion were dead. One was decapitated, another was missing a leg as well as half his face and another had a large hole where his chest had been.

Many Kurds were on the ground writhing, screaming or moaning. The dull, metallic thunk of a 40mm grenade launcher added to the chaos. The grenade sailed through the shattered windscreen of the truck and exploded inside the cabin. The passengers, who had been wounded by the rocket, had been halfway out of the vehicle before the grenade exploded. Life was torn from them in a murderous roar of fire and shrapnel.

Some of the militiamen were now running away from the Australians, sometimes turning to fire. Others were running forward and being dropped by the murderous Minimi and M4 fire coming at them. Meanwhile the eight disguised Iraqi soldiers had gone straight into an ambush drill and were fire-and-moving off to the right.

It was a textbook manoeuvre and they knew what they were doing. They knew an enemy in front of them had ambushed them somewhere on higher ground and they were attempting to outflank the Australians.

Dave saw the threat. "Get those bastards!" he screamed, firing the Minimi from his shoulder in long bursts. Two Iraqis went down. The rest, seeing Dave's position, returned fire but continued their rapid movement off to the right. Dave threw himself to the ground as bullets zipped, whizzed and cracked over and around him. His face was cut as small splinters of wood exploded from a round slamming into a tree nearby.

Some of the militiamen had also seen Dave kneel up and aimed their fire towards his position.

"I see 'em," yelled Will. He brought his rifle to bear and fired off a 40mm grenade. It travelled towards the Iraqi soldiers at 90 metres per second, impacting with a deep boom.

Another of the soldiers was down before the remaining men disappeared into dead ground off to the right.

"Withdraw!" roared Steve. "I'm moving, cover me!"

The firing from the Australian position intensified as Steve got to his feet, sprinted back and threw himself to the ground. The air around him came to life as hot lead shrieked past, thudding into tree trunks or earth.

"Two and three, go!" yelled Steve.

Will and Dave sprang up, sprinted back and dived down. The Kurds were running up the slope towards them now, firing from the hip and shouting. Some were kneeling to take aim, but few took the time. Most of the bullets zipping past the withdrawing Australians were inaccurate, fired in haste and without care.

The fire coming down at the Kurds from the Australian patrol above was creating devastation. Half the men who had dispersed from the truck were down and several had fled towards Barzan, their rifles dropped and forgotten.

The Australian soldiers continued to conduct a fighting withdrawal. One or two of them at a time moving back while the rest gave covering fire.

Steve lined an advancing Kurd up through the holographic sight and fired two rounds. One round ripped through the Kurd's chest, the second went through his throat, spattering the foliage behind him with blood. The man dropped to the ground motionless.

Steve took a deep breath and fired a short burst at three advancing Kurds. He stood up again and sprinted back. Throwing himself to the ground, he grunted as a rock dug into his pelvis. The burst had wounded two men: one in the arm, the other in the leg. Both were down, screaming their pain to the sky. Steve had landed in tall grass and could not see the third enemy. He leant up and saw the Kurd kneeling down beside his two wounded comrades. He was shouting at them, as if being shot was their own fault. Again, he started firing at the withdrawing Australians. Steve took aim and sent a short burst that ripped through his chest. The man dropped motionless beside the two screaming men. Several other militiamen had seen where Steve had fired from and directed their assault towards him. Bullets zinged past him, one thudding into the ground just two metres to his left. He kept his head down until the incoming rounds found interest elsewhere. Steve looked up again, took aim and shot another Kurd who was running towards them, shouting and firing his AK47. He sprayed the weapon from side to side as if he were playing a leading role in The A-Team. The round took him full in the face and he dropped without a sound. Steve ripped out the near empty magazine, shoved it down his shirt and pulled out a fresh one before slapping it into the weapon.

The dull roar of a 40mm grenade exploded, sending up a thick cloud of dirt and acrid, dark smoke. The distinctive bark of the Minimis continued as Dave and Scott poured a murderous barrage on their pursuers. The firefight was so intense that it was difficult to hear the shots of individual weapons. The noise was a continuous roar of violence.

Steve saw four Kurds dart behind a thick tree for cover. The ear-ringing BOOM of a 66 ripped through the air as the rocket sped towards its target. The explosion sent a shock wave through the ground.

Smoke covered the scene for several seconds. Moments later, two of the Kurds stumbled out, one with his face a mangled mess. The other militiaman had blood pumping from his arm, his shirt was ripped, his chest was bleeding and his face was cut to bloody ribbons. He had left his weapon behind and was staggering around in confusion. Bullets ripped into both men and their torment ended before their bodies hit the ground. The two remaining Kurds who had taken refuge behind the tree must have been torn apart.

"Stoppage!" roared Dave. He cocked his machinegun and flicked it open to inspect the ammunition belt. Stoppages occurred if dirt, grit or rocks were stuck in the working parts.

"Get that gun up!" shouted Steve, as Matt sprinted back and dived to the ground, providing covering fire for the next man to move back.

The Kurds were still in the fight. Several militiamen kept up a sustained rate of fire from behind the destroyed truck.

"Almost up!" Dave yelled, flicking out a piece of bent belt link that had caught up in the working parts. Dave's machinegun burst back into life, ripping into the chest of a Kurd running towards a tree. The man went down. His face planed into the earth and the forward momentum sent his body skidding a metre before it came to a limp halt.

Steve sprinted back, threw himself down and kept his head down as several rounds hissed past him. Another round cut the air near him with a loud WIZZ, another zipped by cutting a sapling in half. If they did not take out the Kurds or withdraw far enough for their enemies to give up the chase, it would only be a matter of time before the patrol was killed.

The Kurds were fire-and-moving well, but they had one weakness. Steve knelt up, took aim through his 40mm grenade site and pulled the trigger. The hollow, metallic THUNK sent the small projectile cutting through the air towards its target. Steve dropped as the air around him once more came to life, with bullets zinging and zipping past. He did not see the grenade's flight, but he heard it explode. Kneeling up, Steve fired three short bursts in quick succession, covering Scott and Will as they sprinted back. The churned dirt, thrown up by the grenade was still falling to earth and black smoke drifted up into the treetops. Steve saw with grim satisfaction that the explosion had killed three Kurds. The Kurds' weakness was that they were too close together, as Steve's grenade had just proven.

The five men of call sign Bravo One took up a total ground area of over 50 metres across their axis of withdrawal. Whereas the four or five remaining Kurds intent on advancing towards the Australians took up less than 20 metres. They were bunched up and unless they spread out and were good, they would be dead within the next – BOOM.

An ear-shattering explosion ripped chunks of bark from nearby trees. The limp body of one militiaman somersaulted through the air, landing with a dull thud. Will lowered his weapon, reloaded his 40mm grenade launcher and sent a second grenade into the Kurds moving towards them. It exploded bringing their advance to a halt as it ripped the life from the only man to survive the previous explosion.

With most of the enemy either dead or wounded, the Australians fired at the militiamen behind the truck.

The five Australians had fallen back during the firefight and were now over three hundred metres from where the ambush had begun. The men of Bravo One fell back but continued to pour a ruthless barrage of firepower upon the destroyed vehicle below.

* * * * *

Bullets thudded into, and around the truck, kicking up dirt, puncturing tyres and ricocheting off the thick metal hood. One man had his head in his hands and was screaming his fear into the dirt. His AK47 lay beside him as bullets screamed and whirred by. One of them leaned out from behind the safety of cover and fired a long burst from a rifle. A fine spray of blood erupted from his leg and he fell back, clutching the limb. Before his comrades could pull him back into cover, more bullets stitched his chest and he fell limp, his dead eyes staring up at the dark grey sky.

The remaining two screamed at one another, yelling, arguing. A faint whistling cut the sky and grew ever louder. Deciding that it was best to move from cover and retreat to Barzan any way they could, the first peered around the side of the truck.

All he could see was the green of the forest and dead comrades littering the forest floor like scraps of paper on a street pavement. Although the air was still thick with enemy bullets, there was no sign of the men they had been fighting. It was almost as if they were fighting ghosts or wraiths from days long gone. But one thing was for sure: if they did not move, they would be dead within minutes.

The whistling was more a dull scream now. With a shouted word of encouragement to his friend, the first man launched himself into the open and began sprinting for the distant town. The second man followed eyes wide with fear. With a whistling shriek, the 40mm grenade round slammed into the ground, exploding between the two men, cutting them down.

* * * * *

The roar of the firefight subsided, until only the screaming of the wounded and the shouts of the hidden remained. Sometimes an AK barked into life, but the few Iraqi militiamen who were still able to fight were petrified. They knew they would be dead within seconds if they stepped into sight. The Australians continued to withdraw, firing at possible enemy positions or into the wounded left in the open.

Within seven or eight minutes, the firefight was over. The Kurdish militia who had sat in the back of the truck only quarter of an hour before had been massacred. What was of concern to the withdrawing Australians,

49

were the uniformed men who had deployed alongside the militiamen. They had not shown themselves. Steve's gut instinct told him that they had not withdrawn but had moved into a point of ambush further up the hill.

The soldiers patrolled towards the dead ground. Will was sent forward to scout the area, and when no enemy were spotted, he signalled for the others to advance. The group moved down into the dead ground, leaving the moans and screams of the enemy wounded behind them.

Keeping their spacing, they patrolled, listening and watching for the enemy. Each soldier patrolled their arcs as they moved. Watching one's arc meant a soldier's weapon was pointing where he was looking. The angle of arc ranged from 3 o'clock to the right, all the way through to 9 o'clock to the left.

Will, who was lead scout, stopped and held a hand up to halt those behind. He took a knee and pointed his thumb towards the ground. It was the signal for enemy. He could see the enemy through a small gap between two shrubs. One of them had been wounded during the previous fight and lay motionless on the side of the ridge. Will watched him for a long time through the ACOG sight, but could see no chest movement to show he was breathing. The ground around him was soaked with blood. Another two were lying nearby. One clasping his leg with blood streaming between his fingers. The other was still, his dry, dead eyes staring up at the sky.

Two others were close by. One was writhing in pain and clutching his thigh. Shrapnel had entered his leg. The other knelt over him clamping a hand on the wounded man's mouth so he did not cry out.

The Australians opened fire almost at the same time. Bullets tearing into yielding flesh and ripping life from bodies. The wounded man was silenced forever. But the unwounded Iraqi fired an instinctive burst before a bullet tore through his throat, others shattering his skull. The burst he fired caused a terrible toll.

"Dave's dead!" called Matt, with an edge of disbelief in his voice.

"He's dead, man!"

From where Matt lay, Dave appeared to have taken a 7.62mm round through the face, which had taken half his head with it. He lay in a bloody heap to Matt's left.

Matt sprinted towards Dave, diving to the ground beside him. He rolled him over and checked his breathing. Nothing. He checked his carotid pulse, again out of instinct more than anything. Nothing. He swore. Matt pulled Dave's weapon from his dead hands and slung it. He tucked the spare belt link into his own webbing and ripped free Dave's dog tags, placing them away in a pouch.

"Christ!" snarled Steve. "We'll come back for him, let's move!"

As scout, Will led the way out towards the Land Rover, followed by Scott, Steve and Matt, who brought up tail end charlie. They patrolled fast enough that they did not make too much noise. Each man was at least fifteen metres from the next, giving each other plenty of space. The small group had almost reached the top of the hill where they knew the ground would flatten.

Just another hundred metres beyond that would be the wadi where the Land Rover was hidden. Within a minute, the soldiers were in the wadi. Will and Matt moved to the Land Rover while Steve and Scott provided cover from the 12 and 6 o'clock positions on the lip of the wadi. Will and Matt moved fast. They walked round the vehicle, checking the tyres and the equipment. Matt lay on his back, pushing himself under the vehicle to check the underside, while Will checked under the hood.

It was important to check the vehicle for booby traps before mounting and heading off. It had been left here unguarded for 24 hours and the enemy could have placed anything on it during that time.

"We're clear!" called Will.

Steve sprinted down and climbed into the driver's seat. Matt and Will also mounted the vehicle. Scott would continue to provide cover until the engine turned over and they were ready to drive off.

Will moved into position behind the forward-facing gun, ripping off the canvas cover and cocking it. Matt jumped on the .50 cal, making it ready to fire.

"We've got company!" called Scott from the lip of the wadi.

Steve froze, his right hand on the ignition key, his left foot pressing the clutch to the floor and his left hand resting on the gear stick. He cocked his head and heard the faint, familiar noise of a diesel engine, before it faded again in a light breeze. Regardless of any enemy, he was not going to leave one of his soldiers behind.

"We'll grab Dave first, then we'll piss off!" he called, turning the key and revving the engine. "Right, Matt, get off the 50 cal and let Scott on.

I want you to get on the radio and call in some air support. We're in the shit and we're sinkin' deeper by the second. If we don't get support soon we're gunna be stuffed."

"Got it," Matt said, sliding over into the rear passenger seat while Scott climbed up onto the .50. Steve dropped the Land Rover into first and planted the accelerator. The vehicle lurched forward, the wheels skidding for the first few metres before finding their grip. Within seconds, the Land Rover was moving up and out of the wadi.

Steve did a U-turn, skirted around the edges of the wadi and accelerated towards Dave's body.

They covered the ground and came to a skidding halt beside Dave. His skin was mottled and almost purple in colour. The ground around him stained with blood. Scott hauled the body across to the Land Rover and lifted it into the rear of the vehicle, before climbing back up onto the .50 cal. Blood and brains were oozing out of the bloody hole in Dave's head. Matt pulled out a ground sheet and laid it over the corpse, tucking the edges under the body to prevent the sheet from flying away while they were driving.

"You right?" Steve looked over his shoulder at Matt.

"Yup," replied Matt.

The shock of Dave's death had not hit any of them yet, but Steve knew it would. Dave was a big loss. Working in small units for long periods built up a rapport amongst soldiers, so much so that they were not just good mates, but brothers. Dave's years of training and experience, had been snuffed out in an instant because an enemy soldier had taken a random shot.

Steve stamped on the accelerator. He turned around and headed back the way they had come. They had 6 kilometres of rough terrain before they reached a dirt road leading north towards the steep mountain ranges to their right. Beyond the mountains was Turkey.

Steve worked up the gears, as the vehicle sped across the landscape towards freedom. He accelerated to just under 130 kilometres an hour, which was about the Land Rover's top speed. The ride was rough and Steve was not particularly careful about avoiding small holes or rocks. He swerved around wadis or deeper holes, careful not to allow the rear end to slide out of control. They had not yet seen the vehicle in pursuit of them, but Will and Scott were eager to give it a warm welcome with the machineguns.

Matt was crouched down behind Steve's seat trying to get some cover from the wind so he could use the radio. He had also clamped one hand upon Dave's body so that it did not bounce or slide out of the vehicle.

"Black Dog this is Bravo One, we need air support now, over!" "Roger Bravo One," responded the strong American voice, "the birds are on their way, ETA to your previous grid about five minutes. Do you want them at your previous grid?"

"Acknowledge that Black Dog, send them to previous grid. We have vehicle in pursuit and they should see it from that posi—"

"ENEMY!" shouted Scott and the .50 cal roared into life. Hot, empty cartridges spat out of the ejection opening, some spilling out over the side of the vehicle, others rolling around on the floor. Steve flicked an empty cartridge that had landed in his lap over the side of the vehicle. Will's gun opened up moments later. Both weapons were pointing out towards the left, barking at something Matt could not see.

"Black Dog contact, wait out," Matt shouted over the noise. He looked up at Scott.

Scott pointed and continued to fire. Matt shifted into a position where he could see beyond Scott who was firing long bursts from the .50 cal. They had driven beyond the forest, which hid them from view and out onto elevated ground looking down on a flat plain that rolled towards Barzan. A white four- wheel drive Ute was tearing across the lower plain straight towards them. It was returning fire. It looked like there was a .50 cal gun mounted on the back of the vehicle, as the gunner was standing in the tray of the Ute. Trace rounds from the enemy gun seemed to hang in the air for several seconds before accelerating towards them. Firing from a moving vehicle was difficult, but Will and Scott's fire was accurate. Their bullets either zipped close to the pursuing vehicle, slammed into the ground in front of it sending up showers of dirt or hit on target.

The Ute was still about 800 metres behind them but it was closing the distance. Luckily, the operator behind the .50 cal seemed to be inexperienced and was overexcited. The closest the Australian soldiers had come to being hit was a tracer, along with seven or eight bullets that passed metres above their heads.

"Black Dog, this is Bravo One, where's our bloody air support?"

Matt was yelling over the noise of the guns.

"Roger that, ETA about 2 minutes, meantime hold on, the cavalry's comin'."

"Acknowledged, we are in a camouflaged Land Rover, travelling north. We are being pursued by a white four-wheel drive Ute."

"Matt how's that air support comin'?" shouted Steve. "Two minutes!" he responded.

Steve slammed on the brakes. Scott almost slid from the gunner's seat, Matt slammed into the seat in front of him and had the wind knocked from his lungs. Steve sent the vehicle skidding to the right and brought it around onto the dirt road they had been aiming for. He began accelerating north towards the mountain ranges, to Turkey and to their escape. Matt grunted as he tried to pull Dave's corpse back into the Land Rover. The body had half slid over the side and Dave's legs were dangling close to the road below them. With one last heave, Matt hauled the corpse back inside where he arranged the ground sheet over the pale body and tucked the edges back in.

Scott continued to send lethal volleys towards the chasing vehicle.

Will's gun could not swivel beyond the 10 or 2 o'clock positions and so the Mag 58 sat silent, steam rising from the red-hot barrel. The chasing Ute was about five hundred metres behind them now and still closing.

Matt grabbed Scott's Minimi and turned around, burying his knee into the soft cushioning of the seat to steady himself. Bringing the weapon to bear, he fired the Minimi in short bursts. It was almost impossible to fire with accuracy, but it was better than nothing.

A popping sound came from behind Matt and he watched the 40mm grenade arc into the air. Dropping down in front of the vehicle, it exploded on impact. He turned to see Will reloading the grenade launcher, smoke coming from its barrel.

"Fuckin' hell!" shouted Scott.

Matt's heart sank as he looked into the distance at Barzan. Speeding out of the small town were four armoured personnel carriers. There had been rumour of a large surface-to-air missile pad some distance outside Barzan. It was well protected to stop Kurdish militants from infiltrating the area. It had been placed in Northern Iraq to take out allied fast air flying in from Turkey. Each APC would carry around ten to fifteen men and this time they would be trained soldiers, not just inexperienced militiamen. They looked like the Russian-made BMP, a reliable armoured vehicle. The APCs were still a good two or three kilometres away, but they were giving chase.

Although 80 kilometres an hour was beyond the top speed of an APC, if the Land Rover was damaged and could no longer travel, they would have to move on foot. The armoured vehicles would then be on them in minutes.

The Land Rover was sitting on 120 kilometres an hour, but the faster Ute was closing the distance and was almost three hundred metres behind them now. The .50 cal machinegun boomed with fury.

"A Javelin would be handy right about now!" shouted Will.

"Tell me about it! I didn't think we'd need the 66s, let alone a Javelin!" yelled Matt.

"Lucky he's a useless shot!" roared Scott, before returning fire in a long burst.

Matt was trying to shoot out the tyres of the enemy vehicle, but at that distance, it was almost impossible. Another popping sound rose over the loud rattling of the .50 Cal and a grenade arced over Matt's head, travelling towards the Ute. The chasing vehicle swerved as the grenade exploded to its right. The driver almost lost control of the vehicle as the back end started to slide out, but he regained control.

Matt threw the Minimi back onto the floor of the Land Rover and picked up the radio.

"Black Dog, this is Bravo One. I have an addition. We now have four armoured vehicles in pursuit, over."

"Roger that Bravo One, hang on, we're coming."

"Thanks, out."

"Gotcha!" roared Scott, sending a long burst towards the chasing Ute.

Matt picked up the Minimi again and turned to see why Scott was shouting. He watched the vehicle do something he was sure the driver would regret for the rest of his life. He brought the four-wheel drive to a skidding halt.

Matt thought Scott had hit the driver, but he realised the .50 cal had gone silent. Without a gunner, the vehicle was nothing more than a target. The white Ute was beginning to turn around and head back to Barzan when Scott and Matt opened up at the same time. The Minimi and .50 cal rounds tore through the thin metal skin and through soft flesh beyond.

Another metallic pop came from behind them. This time the 40mm grenade had found its target in the rear tray of the Ute and exploded. The smoke from the impact drifted away and they saw the white vehicle rolling away from them, its occupants dead.

The APCs were still coming towards them in an extended line, with dust streaking behind them. The Land Rover had dropped to about 80 kilometres an hour now, as the engine strained to climb the steep mountain ranges. The sky was still a dark, dirty colour, the threat of snow only about half an hour away.

A white blur flashed overhead followed by a zipping shriek. Scott on the gun facing rearwards was the only one to see it. The APC on the right flank exploded, flipping into the air through a wall of black smoke and flame. It was almost like a toy an angry child had thrown. The APC slammed into the ground, cartwheeling several times across the arid plain before coming to a rest on its roof. Then the sound of the distant explosion hit them; it was deep and powerful, like a mighty god striking a giant bass drum. The Apaches were there somewhere firing on the APCs, but had not shown themselves.

Scott missed the second flash that shrieked past them at almost 5,000 kilometres an hour. Neither Scott, Will nor Matt missed the destruction of the second APC. The armoured vehicle disappeared in a mix of dark smoke, flying dirt and orange flame. One of its tracks was ripped away by the explosion and sailed through the air like a girl's hair ribbon caught in the breeze. The vehicle ploughed into the ground nose first, its tail end on fire, its body broken and twisted. The sound of the second explosion came to them, followed by the deep booms of the 20mm cannons that were mounted on the two remaining APCs. It was strange that they had only started firing on them now.

"They're firing at us!" called Scott.

"No they're not!" responded Steve.

Scott turned to Steve and was about to ask what he was talking about when he saw them. The two Apaches were no more than 50 feet from the ground and were coming towards them fast. Dark fumes were blasting into the air from the exhausts on either side of the engine. They had a threatening, demonic look about them. A bright flash came from the side of one of the Apaches and another missile streaked through the sky over their heads, slamming into a third APC. The air erupted with noise as the 30 mm chain gun on the second Apache boomed into life, bullets tearing into the stationary white Ute.

The choppers roared overhead, high-pitched turbine engines adding to their threatening presence.

They watched as the Apaches split up, one banking to the left, spraying one of the stricken APCs with armour- piercing 30mm rounds. The other Apache fired on the fourth APC, destroying it with violent ferocity. It hovered over the flaming, smoking shell spraying it with 30mm cannon fire. The flame coming from the gun mounted on the underside of the helicopter was a metre long and awesome to watch. Steve kept his eyes on the road.

The choppers moved towards each APC, firing down on them with 30mm cannons. With this completed they flew towards Barzan, scouting for any other enemy activity.

The soldiers lost the Apaches as the Land Rover moved higher up into the hills into thick woodlands. The trees cut off any view of the town as well as the helicopters that hovered near it. The vehicle climbed higher, and for a second Matt got a glimpse of the Apaches. They had split up and were heading back towards them. It seemed they were looking for any other enemy in the general area that might threaten the soldiers' escape.

It was incredible the amount of firepower the gun-ships carried.

They had taken out four APCs, laden with armed soldiers in less than a minute. Something cold struck Matt's face. He looked around at Scott, who was still on the gun facing the rear. He assumed Scott had spat in the wrong direction, but he had not. Another snowflake landed on Matt's cheek.

Within the space of five minutes, the snowfall had thickened to the point where they could only see about forty metres ahead. Steve had dropped the speed back to about 60 kilometres an hour and they prayed no other enemy had decided to follow them.

The Apaches would experience difficulty operating under current conditions. Chances were they had headed back to base. The snow was falling thick and fast and the soldiers pulled on their shamags, keeping their faces warm. Although the temperature had plummeted, the snow would also provide good concealment for them. It would be a long, cold drive home.

CHAPTER 6

They made slow progress for half an hour, before the snowfall thickened into a white curtain blocking vision to ten metres. They were forced to make the decision to stop and find cover. The soldiers were freezing and the snow was not going to clear any time soon. If they did not find suitable cover, hypothermia, that silent assassin, would begin taking them.

They put canvas covers over the machineguns to protect them from the weather. The weapons would be cleaned once they found shelter. It was clear the enemy was no longer following them and the guns would no longer be needed. Steve's teeth were chattering as he drove. The others leaned forward in their seats, arms crossed, heads bowed, shamags pulled about their heads and faces. Each soldier wore camouflage fatigues over thermal vest, woollen jumper over fatigues and shamag over head and face. Thick woollen gloves protected their fingers. Still the cold cut through them like a knife.

Steve continued to drive for five minutes before they rounded a corner in the road, only visible when they were almost on top of it. Another hour of steady snowfall would blot the road from view and driving would be impossible.

"What's that?" Steve shouted over the wind. For a moment, the wind dropped and they could detect a large, dark oval shape carved into the side of a mountain.

Will looked up, and Steve noticed the faintest tinge of blue in his lips. He was already becoming hypothermic. "I dunno," Will mumbled. "Might be a cave."

"I reckon it might be too. You all right, mate?" Steve asked Will with concern. Will nodded then bowed his head against the freezing wind and driving snow.

Glancing back, Steve noticed the remaining two soldiers were in no better condition. He accelerated towards the cave opening that was about three hundred metres in the distance and about thirty metres off the road on the left.

He aimed the Land Rover towards where he thought the cave had been before the snow swirled across the sky and blotted his vision. He blinked snowflakes out of his eyes and felt the warm comfort of hypothermia not far away. He tried not to let it cloud his thinking.

If it was a cave then it seemed to lead into the side of an ominous looking mountain. But he did not raise his hopes. It may also have been a trick of the eye.

He pulled off the road, hoping the snow had not become too thick and ploughed towards where he thought the cave had been. He changed down a gear, his fingers having lost their dexterity. Steve heard one of the soldiers groan behind him but did not have the energy to look around. The vehicle lurched as it growled over a fallen trunk hidden by the blanket of snow. The snow was close to a foot thick, but not thick enough to impinge their momentum. But if the snow continued to fall, the vehicle would be useless in twenty minutes. If they did not find shelter soon, death would claim them. Steve swerved around a tree that appeared out of nowhere. He swore as the vehicle clambered over another unseen fallen log and changed back into first gear as they mounted a steep incline. The Land Rover was moving at a snail's pace now. The skin on Steve's face was numb and when the wind blew, he could feel the hollow of the sinuses in his skull.

Something caught his peripheral vision and through the thick snow downfall, he saw the faded outline of the cave. He turned towards the cave, too tired and cold to let the others know. As he closed the distance, the opening of the cave became darker and more defined. Finally, he drove into the cave mouth, relief washing over him as he gained some reprieve from the onslaught of the snow and freezing wind. The cave was much larger than he had expected. In fact, it was colossal. Parking the vehicle, Steve rested his head against the steering wheel, trying to summon the energy to climb out of the vehicle. The other soldiers were not moving. Steve could feel sleep enveloping him, comforting him, taking him into its warm embrace. He was home, he could rest. Finally he could rest. But realisation called to him from some frozen area of his brain and convinced him to awaken. Anger washed over Steve. He did not want to die like this, in some unknown cave, beaten by the cold.

With a snarl, he climbed out and banged on the side of the Land Rover, "Let's go!" he shouted. "Out!" Steve could hardly force his lips to form the words.

There were grunts and groans from the other men, but none of them moved.

"Get out! Out!" Steve roared. This time his words were as clear as day.

It took several minutes, but the others bundled out of the vehicle.

"Okay, we need to get warm. Get your hexamine stoves out and get some warm food and drink into yourselves." Even as Steve was speaking, the men were hauling their packs from the Land Rover, grabbing cooking stoves, tins of food and drink satchels. Except Matt, who had curled up in the foetal position on the ground near the vehicle.

"Matt!" called Steve. "Oi, Matt!" He knelt beside the soldier. "Matt!" Steve shook him hard. Nothing. He checked Matt's radial pulse, but it was absent. Matt's carotid pulse was slow, but strong, a good sign.

Steve slapped the soldier hard on the face, "Matt!"

Matt groaned and muttered something incomprehensible, but did not move. The others, realising Matt was deteriorating, set up their hexamine stoves, started their water boiling and went to help. Matt's clothes were drenched with melting snow. With some cursing, they managed to pull the clothes from him and dry his skin a little. Steve and Scott then carried him to the Land Rover. Will opened the bonnet of the vehicle and spread a sleeping bag out over the warm engine. They lifted Matt into the sleeping bag and zipped it up. Within minutes, the others were standing around the bonnet of the vehicle, preventing any wind from reaching Matt. With hot drinks in their hands, they started chatting about the firefight.

"I bet ya Hazareen was in the first vehicle we took out," said Scott. "You might be right," agreed Steve, "Still, we'll never know." He brought the cup of hot chocolate to his mouth, savouring the warmth as he felt each sip descend into his core. "God that's good," he muttered.

"Well, good to be out of the snow at least," said Will staring out into the blackness, listening to the raging storm outside.

"With a bit of luck, Black Dog has informed our unit of what's gone down," said Steve. "At least he should have done."

"We going back in?" asked Scott, almost hinting that the patrol should move back into the area of Barzan to complete their mission.

Bloody hope so, Will said to himself.

"Don't know yet," Steve took a gulp of the hot drink. "We'll see what the orders are when we get back to base."

"Fuck it, we should go back in," Scott said looking out into the storm, his eyes giving away his anger.

They might have accounted for themselves, but at the end of the day, the mission had failed. Steve was furious about that. Dave's death also played on them all. He quelled his anger. Fucked as it is, what happened out there happened, learn and move on, Scott thought. Steve reached towards Matt, pushed his hand into the opening at the face of the sleeping bag and checked for a carotid pulse. Matt's skin was warm and the pulse was faster and stronger than before.

"Piss off!" Matt muttered.

"Back in the land of the living, eh?" smiled Steve. "Thank Christ for that," he said under his breath.

Steve went to make another hot drink and was back shortly with a steaming cup. The soldiers helped Matt into a sitting position. Despite his reluctance, Steve forced Matt to drink until the cup was empty and then allowed the soldier to lay back and rest on the warm engine block. "This is about as comfortable as lying on a bed of rusty razor blades for Christ's sake," complained Matt.

"Just hang tight there, mate, we'll get you some dry clothes to put on," said Steve.

"Dry clothes?" asked Matt. "Hey I'm bloody naked in here, man! You bastards stripped me?"

"You can thank us for savin' your life later," chuckled Will.

Finally, with three layers of dry clothes on, Matt stood before them, hands on his hips.

"So whose bright idea was it to friggin' strip me?" asked Matt.

Scott wiggled his little finger. "Dunno how you keep your missus happy."

"Get stuffed man!" Matt grinned. "It was cold outside."

"Cold? That's an understatement," said Steve, passing another hot cup to Matt. "Drink that."

Steve walked back to the vehicle and pulled clear another twenty-litre container of water so they could refill their water bottles.

Sadness washed over him as he noticed that a section of the tarpaulin had lifted and part of Dave's face was showing. Ice had formed in the hair of his eyebrow and closed eyelashes. His skin was a deep purple now and rigor mortis had set in.

Steve pulled the sheet back over Dave, before moving away and preparing his own food and drink.

Half an hour later, with warm food and drink in them, the soldiers were more comfortable. They were huddled together around the bonnet of the vehicle that still emitted some warmth. It would be a long, cold night, but with luck, the snow would stop falling and they would be able to leave by morning.

Even though the snowstorm showed no hint of relenting, and no sign of enemy, they were in enemy territory and compromised. Regardless of the weather, they needed to remain alert and ready to fight. The soldiers stood guard in rotations throughout the night.

Whoever stood guard would move around to the rear of the Land Rover facing the cave entrance with a rifle in hand and night vision goggles on. He would wait and watch for any sign of enemy movement. The snow continued to fall, hour upon cold hour, until the early hours. The cave entrance had been all but blocked with snow.

If the weather did not improve, there would be little chance of them leaving the shelter next day. The sun was beginning to rise as the sky had turned a coffee colour. He took off the night vision goggles and turned them off. The snow continued to fall. By 0700 the next morning, snow still fell, covering everything that came between it and the ground. The snow had given the patrol welcome reprieve by covering their tracks and providing excellent camouflage. Steve knew it was a safe bet that while the snow fell they would not be found.

The cave was now dark and little could be seen outside until the snow across their exit was either cleared or melted. The latter was improbable. Steve turned on the headlights of the Land Rover to provide some light so he could check food stocks. If they portioned their meals, they would have enough to last them another eight to ten days. But they still had to cross the Turkish border soon.

As the soldiers sat cleaning their weapons or preparing breakfast, Steve prodded the snow blocking the opening.

"I don't think this is too thick!" he called out. "A couple of entrenching tools and we should be out of here within three or four hours.

Scott sat chewing on his meal with the headlights glaring into his face. He pointed his spoon in Steve's direction. "You just need to be careful, mate, a lot of snow has fallen overnight. You don't wanna go starting an avalanche."

"True, true," Steve replied continuing to prod the wall of snow. "But it still feels pretty thin. Even if there were an avalanche, you'd think we'd be safe in a cave. Plus the snow'll melt. We may as well give it a shot."

"Who dares wins, man," said Matt with a grin as he cleaned and oiled his rifle barrel.

"You wanker," replied Will with a smirk.

It was important to stagger their routines, so that as Matt cleaned his rifle, Scott was eating. Will was checking the fluid levels of the vehicle, the tyres and fuel, making sure it was ready to drive.

When all weapons had been cleaned, two of them slung weapons, retrieved entrenching tools and began shovelling snow. Once there was enough light flooding in, the headlights were switched off to conserve the battery.

"Come on man, I'm putting you to shame," said Matt, throwing another load of snow clear.

"Conserving my energy, mate, the rabbit and the turtle, remember who won that race?"

"Conserving energy? Is that what you call it? Where I come from it's called bloody lazy," grinned Matt.

Will threw a spade full of snow at Matt, who batted it aside as if he were swinging a baseball bat.

"What's this?" Matt asked.

He had noticed a strange, rectangular obelisk near the wall of the cave mouth. It seemed to have been buried into the earth, but the stone itself rose out of the ground at least five feet. Etched over the surface were ancient looking symbols. It was not English and none of the soldiers could read the strange script, but that it told a story was obvious. Many of the letters were faded and weather worn.

"No idea," shrugged Will, passing a hand over the surface of the stone.

After an hour, Steve and Scott took over the shovelling duty. The exit was now only half blocked.

"Jesus Christ!" exclaimed Will from the rear of the cave.

Steve stopped and glanced over his shoulder, sweat dripping from his forehead. "What?" he asked.

"Come and have a look at this!" called Will.

Steve and Matt walked over to Will, while Scott continued to dig. Will gestured towards a tall, but narrow, opening at the rear of the cave, which they had missed the previous evening. The opening was pitch black and it was impossible to say what lay beyond.

"Grab the NVG, Will," said Steve, keeping his eyes on the tall, narrow slit in the rock. They could smell a damp, mustiness issuing from the blackness and guessed there must have been a slight leak in the ceiling beyond the opening.

Will handed Steve some night vision goggles. He stepped into the opening, pushing forward, forcing his body through.

"Christ!" Steve's voice echoed throughout the cavern. "This is a squeeze. There's a pathway that looks like it's man made. It leads down to the right."

Meanwhile Scott grunted as he threw another shovelful of snow out of the entrance. As he bent down to drag out another shovelful, he heard a faint, but powerful engine that seemed to be growling towards them. Throwing the entrenching tool behind him, he dropped to his stomach, unslung the Minimi and flicked the safety off. The entrenching tool landed with a clatter and Scott held his breath as the owner of the deep grinding noise rumbled into view about 200 metres away.

"Stand to!" he yelled.

The others instinctively hit the ground, crawling into firing positions.

It was a medium battle tank and the light machinegun that Scott was pointing at it would be of no more use against it than a peashooter. It would be the only kind of vehicle the Iraqis had that would make it up the mountain after the heavy night of snow. The tank gunner was in a high position and could see over the half-blocked cave entrance and the Land Rover within. The 100 mm gun turret swung round to bear with a dull whine that was only just audible over the grumble of the tank's engine. The elevation of the 100mm gun descended as the gunner took aim.

"Cover!" yelled Scott, levering himself up and sprinting back to take cover behind the vehicle. The loud boom of the gun broke the morning silence.

Steve was still inside the inner cave and well protected. They heard the shrieking scream of the shell an instant before the loud, muffled explosion upon the slopes of the mountain above. The gunner had fired in haste and the shot was inaccurate.

"Get in here!" roared Steve to the other soldiers.

Matt and Will were running for the narrow entrance at the back of the cave before Steve finished his sentence. Matt snatched up his radio and first aid pack on the way past. Scott ran to the Land Rover and delved into the equipment and stores. He grabbed whatever he could. Slinging two 66 rocket launchers over a shoulder, he grabbed a link of Minimi ammunition and draped that across his neck.

Pulling three ration packs towards him, he hefted them into the crook of one arm. Turning, he saw the gun lowering its elevation in preparation for a second shot. This time it would be accurate.

Pulling gun into shoulder, Scott brought the weapon to bear and the loud, distinctive bark of the Minimi echoed in the cave as he fired a long burst. The bullets slammed into the ground five metres in front of the tank, kicking up white puffs of snow. Several bullets hit the armour of the tank but ricocheted with loud pinging whines.

Scott ran for the narrow opening at the rear of the cavern as the second boom exploded outside. The loud scream of the shell hit Scott as he threw himself to the ground. This was it. He was going to die. The shell hit the top of the cave entrance. The explosion that followed shook the ground, sending chips of rock cascading from the ceiling.

A loud high-pitched ringing was all Scott could hear as he managed to climb to his feet. He could feel the ground beneath his feet vibrating and assumed the tank was advancing towards the cave mouth. He did not bother to watch it turn the Land Rover into a sardine can as it approached. He took several faltering steps towards the opening through which the others had disappeared. He reached it and threw the rockets, food and ammunition into the blackness. As he pushed one leg into the narrow cave entrance, he looked back expecting to see the tank almost on top of him. Instead, he watched the cave entrance disappear in a flurry of falling snow. All light left the cave and he was sure the blackest pit of hell would look no different. They were trapped. The tank had caused an avalanche that had buried them in a tomb under the mountain.

Digging their way out of the snow was one matter, digging out of an avalanche was something else. The entrenching tool was definitely not up to the task.

Scott squeezed his way through the narrow opening and stood. He could see nothing, although he could still hear the incessant ringing in his ears. Tinnitus, that was the word for it, he remembered. Strange what things you remembered, Scott thought. He assumed he had done permanent damage to his ears.

"Is that you Scott?" called a muffled voice from a distance.

"Yeah," he replied.

"Mate, we're only here, no need to yell!" replied the voice. It sounded like Steve.

"What happened out there?" asked Matt.

"It was a fuckin' avalanche! Unbelievable!" replied Scott.

"Right let's see if there's a way out of here," said Steve, knowing that there was still a tank outside. They were still not clear of danger and to become complacent was to be caught, or worse.

The four men moved off in single file. Steve led the way in his night vision goggles. The others grabbed hold of the webbing on the soldier in front.

They were forced to walk in an uncomfortable half crouch through the narrow, low tunnel. Running his hand along the wall as they walked, Will could feel that the stone was uneven and there were small chip marks in the rock. It seemed to be manmade. The chipped rock reminded him of a bridge he had once seen in Tasmania. Convicts had built the bridge sometime in the 1800s in a small town called Campbell Town. The stone, from which the bridge was made, had been shaped by the prisoners with hand picks and could still be seen in the rock today. This stone felt much the same.

"Watch your footing!" said Steve. "We're about to descend."

The party slowed down to a half walk before descending a set of worn and uneven stairs. Someone lost their footing and hit the ground, the sound echoing around the cave.

"Careful," said Matt.

"Yeah I'm right," shouted Scott.

"Shit, man, no need to yell," said Matt.

"What?" shouted Scott. "You're gonna have to speak up!" "Holy crap, man, he's as deaf as a door post," chuckled Matt.

The tunnel levelled out once more and the men continued to move forward.

Steve stopped five minutes later. "Hang on."

"Urgh!" It was Matt's voice. "He said stop! Christ, man!"

"Huh?" Scott yelled.

"He said stop!" shouted Matt.

"Righto," roared Scott.

Steve shook his head and chuckled. Then he turned to the fuzzy green view before him. If what he saw was correct, then the small tunnel was about to come to an end and led out into a huge cave, three or four times the size of the one they had slept in. It seemed monstrous.

With night vision goggles on, it was hard to tell the size of the cave. Steve's view was two-dimensional, so what appeared to be a large cave could have just been a huge stone. But it was worth investigating. He had a feeling they were close to discovering a section of the catacomb that would lead the patrol to safety.

"Okay, you guys stay here," Steve said. As the only one with night vision, Steve was the only one capable of clearing the rocky entrance beyond. Even though it was a cavern and any animals did not inhabit it, it paid for them to move with caution. The locals would know about this tunnel system and where it came out and so they could stage an ambush.

Moving forward and lifting his rifle to his shoulder, Steve stepped out into the cavern. The silence was almost deafening, and made the hairs on the nape of his neck stand on end. There was something about a silent, untouched place that made him uneasy. He crouched and looked around him, listening for noises and movement, but all was still and the only sound was his own soft breathing. Back on his feet, he walked around the left wall of the cavern, stopping often to listen and look. After twenty minutes, and having detected nothing, Steve moved back to the others.

"Okay, this is the deal. The cave beyond that entrance is bloody huge. I've never seen anything like it. There is only one exit, so there will only be one point of defence. That makes things easier. We will stay down here for a day or two and let things settle on the surface. Then we'll try to get out of here and with a bit of luck back into Turkey. Questions?"

"Can you speak up?" shouted Scott.

Will grabbed him. "Shut the hell up," he growled. "Want to get us killed?"

There was silence for a moment.

"Sounds good to me," whispered Matt.

"Yeah, me too," agreed Will. "Right, let's go," spoke Steve.

Steve stood up and the others held onto each other's webbing as they made their way into the cave. A large rock jutted out from the ground towards the rear of the cavern, which was where Steve planned to place the sentry. In that way, if contact with the enemy were made, the rock would provide cover.

He led them to the rock and then passed the night vision goggles around, so each man could survey the cave and where they were located in relation to the exit. Each of them now had a rough map in their mind. Even in the blackness after, they would know which general direction the exit was, should they need to make an escape.

Scott lay down in the prone position and pulled the Minimi into his shoulder. Using the night vision goggles, he directed the weapon towards the exit, prepared for any enemy wandering into the cavern. The other soldiers sat down with their backs against the rock and rested.

Scott's ears had improved. Although the incessant ringing was still there, it was fainter and he was beginning to be able to hear the others talking.

As Steve closed his eyes, exhaustion washed over him. Images of his family passed through his mind's eye like a slide show. Judy all dolled up on the day of their wedding and the birth of Kathy. Kathy at nine months, snuggling into his chest and falling asleep. Kathy, as a toddler, running along the beach and laughing with a plastic bucket and spade in one hand and a towel in the other. Steve smiled to himself. The birth of their son, Brent. He had screamed the house down when he had been born. Brent kicking the beach ball the day Steve had been called about this mission. Steve sighed. He missed his family, and with each passing year, he missed them more. Perhaps it was time to retire. Otherwise, he faced a broken family for sure.

* * * * *

There was a loud crack and Steve found himself in the midst of a blizzard on a narrow path. To his left was a sheer drop and to his right the huge wall of the mountain he had to descend.

He had no idea where he was and the snow was already ankle deep.

"Why is it that you have come?" The voice was deep and exuded authority. Less than ten metres away stood a tall man dressed in a way he had never seen before. His long white beard and silver hair were whipped and buffeted by the fierce storm. The man wore a thick cloak held together at the neck by a large wooden brooch. He wore a long sleeved brown shirt and faded brown trousers tied at his waist with what looked to be rope. The man's piercing blue eyes were as cold as the snow and wind and they chilled Steve to the core.

"Why?" The man asked again before falling to his knees, with his, hands together in prayer. His eyes now showed either fear or respect, Steve could not tell which.

"Could you be the Tuatha? Are they returning to the world? Oh please let it be so, Father God," the man said, turning his face to the skies. "Let it be so."

* * * * *

"Steve." A hand shook him by the shoulder.

"Yeah," Steve muttered, his mind filled with the strange dream.

"Your turn for piquet." It was Matt's voice.

"Okay," he said, taking the night vision goggles. He put them on and winced against the bright green light. His eyes began to water. Lying down, he took up the Minimi and stared down the sights towards the exit.

A voice echoed in his head. It was a deep voice filled with suppressed hope and excitement. "Could you be the Tuatha?"

The dream made no sense and left him curious. He had only ever dreamed with such vividness as a child and he felt it strange he should do so now after all these years. Who, or what, was the Tuatha? Who was the old man?

Steve decided it was a dream brought on by exhaustion and stress. There was no point wasting energy analysing a meaningless dream. He cast an eye over his three motionless comrades sprawled on the ground as sleep held them in its warm embrace.

Looking back to the exit, Steve caught a glimpse of a small rectangular shape shimmering to his right. Through the green haze, he could not make out what it was with any clarity.

He did note there was some sort of markings above the shape. Steve walked towards the small, shimmering object.

What Steve found strange was rocks only appeared through night vision as black objects. But this rock was beaming with light brighter than the moon, or at least it seemed that way. He could not believe how he had missed it on his first scout of the cavern. He took off the goggles but could see nothing. The curtain of the cave's blackness closed around him, so that although he thought he knew where the exit was located, he could not be sure. Putting the goggles back on, he once again saw the light the rock seemed to emit. Kneeling beside it but continuing to point his weapon towards the exit, he picked it up and rolled it around in his hand. It was a crystal, not a rock.

The crystal was as long as his hand and about half the width of his palm. Its edges were rounded and the light coming from it seemed to pulse, almost as if it had a life of its own. Its own heartbeat. Steve checked the exit, but saw and heard nothing. He turned and looked at the wall near where he located the crystal and saw a deep impression in the rock the same shape and size as the crystal. Below the indentation were inscriptions in a language he had never seen before. The letters were composed of jagged, straight strokes, with no curves. They seemed primitive yet artistic.

Tossing the crystal in the air and catching it Steve got to his feet. A frown creased his face as he looked at the shaped crystal in his hand. He moved back to his position and lay down, pointing the Minimi once again at the exit.

CHAPTER 7

"What the fuck is it?" asked Scott the next morning, switching on his torch. There was no sound all night and the soldiers were confident their enemy would not be able to hear their voices from this deep underground.

"Oh, for Christ's sake, man, bit of warning woulda been nice!" said Matt wincing against the sudden light.

"Sorry, mate," said Scott turning to shine the torch into Matt's face.

"Piss off," Matt laughed, pushing the torch away.

"I dunno," replied Steve. The torch was now directed back to Steve's open palm, which held the jet black, rectangular crystal. It was polished to a high sheen and the edges were rounded. The crystal seemed to absorb the light thrown from the torch, rather than reflect it.

"Turn the light off mate," Steve said. "All right, who's got the gogs?"

"Me," replied Matt. "I just put some new batteries in."

"Put 'em on."

There was a pause and then a click as the goggles powered up.

"Shit!" Matt said. "How the hell? Shit, pass the gogs round, have a look."

In the pitch black of the cavern, no one could see anything, but with goggles on, the crystal in Steve's palm emitted a powerful glow. On closer inspection, the light thrown from the crystal was pulsating, almost like a heartbeat.

They switched the goggles off and Scott flicked on the torch. The crystal was once again black, although it continued to absorb the torchlight.

"Where'd you find it?" asked Will.

"Over there. Come and have a look at this." Steve led them to the etchings in the wall.

"Seems it'll fit into that indentation?" said Scott. There were no chip marks or gouges in the indentation to suggest how it was made. It was smooth, flawless, perfect, almost as if human hands could not have made it.

"Wonder what this says?" asked Will, passing his hand over the strange, letters. Steve spotted what appeared to be an 'R' amongst the sentence, but even this letter had been cut with straight lines. The letters had a runic look to them.

The soldiers fell silent as they looked at the unfamiliar lettering that looked to have come from another time. Historical artefacts always fascinated Steve. Something about this seemed almost magical. But there was something else that he had missed. Below the indentation were some other letters that appeared to be Arabic.

"Well let's see what happens," said Steve with a shrug. He placed the crystal into the indentation in the wall.

"No don't," said Scott, in mock fear.

Steve pushed the crystal into place and took his hand away, expecting the rock to fall. There was a grinding sound, a click and then the crystal slammed into the wall with a dull thud so that it was flush with the wall. The jet-black object looked more like a tile on the face of the cave than the crystal it had been moments before.

"That was….kind of fuckin' creepy," muttered Scott, holding the torch beam on the motionless crystal.

"You're tellin' me," said Steve.

"This is like something out of Indiana Jones," said Will.

"Indiana," Matt's voice trailed away. "This is some weird shit, Will, I'm on edge here, mate. What made that crystal slide into the wall?"

"Want me to read you a story snookums?" asked Scott. "Come on," he slapped Matt on the shoulder. "Grow some balls, mate. Time for breakfast."

"None of you bastards are taking this serious, are you?" asked Matt.

Scott shrugged. "A crystal slid into the wall and made a bit of a noise. Shit, you're usually as calm as a brain surgeon in theatre, man, what's gotten into you? Forget it Matt, we'll deal with anything that comes up."

"Yeah, guess so," muttered Matt, grabbing the torch from Scott and shining it at the silent, unmoving crystal.

Steve sat down and took out a packet of dry biscuits he kept in his pocket. The biscuits had been crushed into tiny pieces, but he ate them anyway.

"I've got cheddar cheese for breaky," announced Will. "Oi, Matt, slip out and cook us some bacon and eggs, mate."

"Half your bloody luck," replied Matt. "Muesli bar for me."

Most of their rations, apart from several small snacks, were still in the Land Rover. Scott had managed to salvage two single man ration packs, and that would last four of them two days if they were careful. After breakfast, they would have to try to dig their way out to the surface and make an escape. If Lady Luck held them in any regard, the enemy had assumed they were dead. Steve did not relish the thought, but there was only one way out and that was the way they had come in.

After breakfast was eaten, Steve took a tiny LED torch and tried to lever the crystal out of the wall with a pocketknife but it would not move. He shrugged and turned to the others.

"While you guys eat, I'm goin' to have a look at the Land Rover. I might bring some more stuff down," he said. Holding his weapon under the crook of his arm, he set off towards the exit with the torch. He was about to make his way up the steep incline, when there was a deep, reverberating explosion that shook the cave. Small chunks of rock and streams of dirt fell from the ceiling. Steve was thrown to the floor; the torch crashed to the ground and went out.

The sound echoed into silence and the cave became still once more. It had sounded like a bass drum, amplified a hundred fold.

"You right, mate?" he heard Scott ask.

"Yeah, you?"

"We're okay," Matt replied. He had shrugged into his first aid pack and was tightening the straps on his shoulders. It was better to have the pack with him so he could immediately access it if someone was injured.

"What the hell was that?" Will asked. "It sounded like a friggin'—"

The cave shook again, but this time the noise did not fade. Their surroundings continued to shake and shudder. A chunk of rock the size of a man broke from the ceiling and slammed into the ground, smashing into pieces. Pulling the rifle into his shoulder, Steve lay prone. He clicked the safety catch to fire and directed the barrel towards the exit. Behind him, his hand groped around for the torch and found it. He tapped it against the ground. The bulb flickered and died before beaming back into life and flooding half the cave with light. Pointing it towards the exit, he could see nothing remarkable. The violent shaking and deafening noise continued and dust and chips of rock streamed from the cave ceiling.

"Bloody hell! Look!"

Steve looked around. The crystal was glowing a dull, powerful blue and the inscription carved into the wall burned bright red. The shuddering noise of grinding stone filled the cavern and then silence followed. The light thrown from the crystal and inscription faded away. Steve could hear someone breathing close by, but otherwise the cave was once more silent and still.

"Everyone all right?" asked Steve. "Yup," was the response.

Steve knew that the other soldiers were in the same mindset as him. They were lying prone with their weapons ready to fire. Something was happening and the men were not sure what it was. Whatever would happen next, they were ready. Or so they thought.

A sudden cold breeze blasted around the chamber and was gone just as fast as it arrived. Steve's torch failed. Then it happened. Steve suppressed a gasp as his stomach lurched into his throat. It seemed the floor had given way. They were falling, falling, with cold, bitter wind lashing at their clothes. He tried to look around but could see nothing, everything was dark and apart from the blistering howl of the wind in his ears, he could hear nothing.

The skin of his hand stung as something slapped against his palm. His fingers instinctively closed around the object. He had pushed the crystal into the wall! It was warm now, almost hot.

Then came a voice, distant and muffled, as if it came from inside a cardboard box. "—public in general that forces have commenced combat and combat support operations."

Hang on, thought Steve. That's John Howard isn't it? Steve tried to yell out to the others but nothing came out. He tried again. His mouth opened to form the words, but no sound came out. It was as if he was living inside a nightmare. He continued to fall, concerned that the other members of the patrol had been either injured or worse.

"This aggression will not stand." This time it was George Bush Senior's voice.

"—can do for you, but what you can do for your country!"

Then came a strong British accent. "We shall fight on the beaches. We shall fight on the landing grounds. We shall fight in the fields and in the streets, we shall fight in the hills; we shall never surrender—"

The falling sensation stopped and all returned to what seemed normal.

"You guys okay?" It was Will's voice.

"Yeah I'm fine," replied Steve, relieved that at least one of the others was still with him. He tapped his torch but nothing happened.

"These night vision goggles must be broken," said Scott.

"Mum?" It was a child's voice. "I'm scared." The accent was British, it sounded like a London accent.

"What the fuck you doing here, kid?" Scott's voice boomed and it was obvious to Steve that the soldier was frightened. He suppressed a smile.

"It's okay, love." This time a woman's voice. "It's okay."

He noticed a faint wailing sound, a siren he realised, and in the distance, the deep burr of many engines. They sounded like hundreds of planes.

"What's happening?" asked Matt.

"Dunno, mate, but my trigger finger's starting to get pretty itchy," replied Scott in a shaky voice.

The roar of the engines was almost all they could hear. Intermingled with the noise was the dull thudding of, of what? Machineguns! No not machineguns, anti-aircraft guns!

Boom, boom, boom, boom, an anti-aircraft gun nearby had started firing skyward. Steve still could not see anything, but he thought he could detect distant shouts of a gun commander, giving elevation and fire control orders. It sounded like a 20mm gun judging by the methodical lack of speed at which each bullet was shot skyward.

He could hear the child crying and immediately thought of Judy, Kathy and Brent. Instincts overcame him and he wanted to find the child and comfort her.

"It's okay," he heard the mother say, fear strong in her voice.

The floor opened up once more and Steve fell. All went silent and the cold wind buffeted and pulled at him.

"Damn colonial bastards," the voice had a posh English accent.

"How many do we have against us?" "Near 30,000 French knights, Sire." "30,000!" The voice faded and Steve continued to fall. Once again the sensation stopped. Everything was black, but he could hear a quiet crackling noise. An image flashed through his mind of an ancient castle with torches in brackets on the wall. The torches' flames crackled and gave weak light to the room, where a large group of men stood. Most of them were soldiers wearing polished silver chain mail and their helmets reflecting the light thrown from the torches like a mirror.

Amongst them stood a man, with long brown hair. He was dressed in rags and he looked dirty. Blood was seeping from a wound at his temple. The prisoner, for it was obvious that is what he was, had been cuffed and wore a blindfold around his head. The man was tall. Wait, thought Steve. No, he was only about six foot one, whereas the others around him averaged at about five and a half feet, if that.

They all stood before a man dressed in a flowing black silk robe. He wore a dark hat that moulded itself to his skull and which gave his pale eyes a complete lack of emotion. The man was sitting in a booth five feet high. A small set of stairs led up to where the man sat.

The image disappeared and once again, Steve found himself in the dark.

"Anyone there?" he asked. "Yeah," said Scott.

"Still here…I think," replied Matt.

"This is crap," said Will. "What the hell's happenin—"

"What have you to say for thyself?" The deep authoritative voice cut Will off.

Silence followed as the Australians listened. Steve thought it would have been good to be able to see something. Then another image appeared in his mind. The tall prisoner looked up towards the man in black, who nodded. The blindfold was ripped from the prisoner's face.

"Thou art a traitor to thy king and thy country!" continued the judge. "Thou hast broken thy allegiance to thy king! Thou hast killed his soldiers and sacked his cities! Thou hast plundered churches and dealt death to ministers of religion like some Viking pirate!"

The judge paused, and then held up a large, old, yellow piece of paper.

"Here before me do I have a scroll upon which thy name shall appear. This scroll, upon the morrow, and well after thy death I should add, shall be sent forth to the king." The judge pointed at the prisoner. "Thy king! It is a scroll asking for pardon from him. If thy name should appear here," he continued to hold the scroll up. "Then thy death shall be swift and just. Else it will be slow and painful." The judge smiled. "Excruciating let me assure thee."

Almost as if in a movie, Steve watched the view pan around so that he was now looking into the face of the prisoner. His eyes were a deep green. Hatred, defiance and pride were visible in the man's eyes.

A white scar ran down his face and another across his chin. There was a scar on the bridge of his nose from some minor scuffle.

Through gritted teeth and with hatred burning in his eyes, the man made his reply. "I cannot be a traitor for I owe him no allegiance." The voice was a strange combination of both Irish and Scottish. Steve had never before heard such an accent. "He is not my sovereign; he never received my homage; and whilst life is in this persecuted body, he never shall receive it. To the other points whereof I am accused, I freely confess them all. As governor of my country, I have been an enemy to its enemies. I have slain the English. I have mortally opposed the English king. I have stormed and taken the towns and castles, which he unjustly claimed as his own. If I, or my soldiers, have plundered or done injury to the houses or ministers of religion, I repent my sins. But it is not of Edward of England I shall ask pardon."

"Then it is set," said the judge, with a malevolent grin. "Take him away," he said with a flick of his wrist.

Silence followed. The image disappeared and again Steve felt himself freefall, with the familiar cold wind enveloping him as he fell.

CHAPTER 8

Steve cried aloud as his body hit the ground hard. He tried to roll to break the impact but failed. He was paralysed. A mighty crack exploded through the heavens, more powerful than any he had ever heard. He could not be sure, but Steve thought he had seen a bright blue streak across the sky that accompanied the blast. It was still dark. He lay on the ground, motionless and silent for almost two minutes before he felt a cold wetness seeping through his clothes chilling him to the bone. Steve could feel tingling in his hands and feet that bordered on painful, but with some effort, he was able to move. It is bloody pouring, he thought, wiping his face and sitting up. He picked up the rifle and put it across his lap. His master hand instinctively curled around the pistol grip. The crystal, still in his left hand, remained warm. Steve pushed the crystal into one of his pockets, feeling the warmth against his leg. He could hear the quiet hiss of the rain as it pattered upon the ground, turning the cold earth to slush. A flash of lightning revealed thick cloud covering the sky. The powerful thunderheads threatened flash flooding. A crack of thunder accompanying the lightning rolled through the heavens three seconds later. By his reckoning, the lightning had struck more than five kilometres away.

"Steve!" the voice hissed. "Steve!"

It sounded like Scott. Steve walked in a half crouch towards the voice, but lost his bearings. He stopped and knelt.

"Where are ya?" Steve called.

"Over here, mate," Scott sounded closer.

Steve moved forward and found the remaining soldiers huddled together under the protection of a small rock overhang.

Steve was forced to crawl on his stomach; it was so low to the ground. There was plenty of room once he was under cover though. The others had arrived in much the same way as Steve. Matt even thought he had broken a rib because he had hit the ground so hard.

Unlike Steve, the other three seemed to have arrived close together. They had found each other and then located to the closest dry area. The three soldiers estimated they had been there for the better part of an hour. That can't be right, Steve thought.

Only five minutes had passed since he slammed into the ground, but he knew when shock set in it was easy to lose track of time.

"We'll wait the storm out until morning and then go for a look around," suggested Steve.

Although none of the soldiers had spoken of it, they did not know where they were, or what had taken place in the cave. The main thing was they were alive and safe. For the moment anyway. When the cold glow of morning made itself known, they would scout the area for enemy.

* * * * *

It was a dark night, darker than usual. The chill air was warded away by the fire burning in the centre of the room. The flames cast long shadows. The stars, usually blazing, were not to be seen. The dark storm clouds were keeping their beauty from sight.

Tharkol sat before the fire, staring into the flames. Behind him, on the earthen bench that ran around the perimeter of the long house, were his wife and his wife's mother. They were talking in hushed whispers. His son lay beside them, deep in sleep. He was three summer's old and already showed signs of becoming a good man and a fine warrior. The boy filled Tharkol with pride.

Outside he could hear the distant, muffled sound of Thor as the Storm God went about his business. The village of Ulfor needed rain. In fact, it had not rained in a season, and the crops were in need of water.

A mighty roar of thunder exploded, louder than any Tharkol had ever heard. It was as if the sky itself had been split asunder. He jumped and touched the hilt of his sword as he felt the war spirit rise inside him and sweep away the cobwebs of lethargy. Around the edge of the closed door, Tharkol thought he saw a bright blue flash that accompanied the powerful thunder. Perhaps he had imagined it. The women were staring wide eyed towards the doorway. Perhaps he had not.

Tharkol strode to the thick, wooden door and the hinges creaked in protest as he swung it open.

He held his sword fast as he stared out into the dark night, but saw nothing. Something had changed. He saw nothing, and smelled nothing, but he could feel it, like a silent fog sweeping across the valleys. Something had changed. The stories of old told of Odin coming to earth to walk amongst his people. The earth shaking thunder and bright blue light foretold something. It was almost as if something, or someone, had entered the world.

Tharkol stood in the doorway for a long time watching and listening, but seeing and hearing nothing. Closing the door he walked back to his sleeping son, the women having long returned to hushed conversation. In truth, the sound of the storm outside pleased the farmer. His family would eat well this winter. Providing the coastal vermin did not venture inland. If they did, they would kill and steal what they could. Then they would take those they deemed satisfactory as slaves, either to keep as

77

their own, or to sell to the highest bidder. Last year had been a good year. Thinking of day-to-day happenings served to calm Tharkol, tearing his mind from the stories of the gods.

The inland community of Ulfor had only suffered one raid and that attack had been by young warriors who had never been a-viking. The attackers had been defeated. But two Ulfor farmers lost their lives in the skirmish.

Tharkol stared into the fire as he remembered Yarmok and Sven, both good men who had lived in Ulfor for nigh on twenty summers. Both men came from large families. The departure ceremony of the fallen farmers who had contributed so much to their way of life was a time of great grief. They had died as heroes and would dine with Odin for all time.

A hand shook his shoulder. "Tharkol!" It was his wife, Ulkeena. "You are growing deaf in your age. Come here!" she beckoned him outside.

He looked out into the darkness. The rain was heavier than before and was almost deafening as it hammered on the ground and hissed amongst the crops in the distance. He smiled as he looked up into the dark, cloud-filled sky, giving silent thanks to Thor.

"Look!" Ulkeena said, pointing into the darkness.

Tharkol followed her finger and squinted against the darkness. He saw a dark robed figure clutching a staff, making his way towards the chieftain's long house at the other end of Ulfor.

The figure walked with a slight limp and his hooded cloak was wrapped tight around his body against the cold. A chill passed through Tharkol as he realised it was Romeeros, the rune singer. Rune singers were magical folk about whom not much was known. But one thing Tharkol did know was that rune singers only ever appeared in times of trouble.

* * * * *

Berag threw another log on the fire at the centre of the room and turned to watch his daughter of thirteen summers sleeping in peace. Nearby his wife dozed. Rubbing his swollen shoulder, the chieftain sat down near his sleeping family and stared into the fire. Sleep would not take him. His right shoulder always swelled and pained him when a storm was near. Berag had taken a spear in the shoulder as a younger man during a conflict with a group of coastal warriors who had travelled inland a-viking.

It had been a terrible day, his father slain, his brother stabbed through the stomach, had writhed in agony for hours. The

Valkyries had come for him close to dawn the next day. With his sword clasped in his hand, the spirit of Berag's brother had been taken away to the halls of Valholla.

As chieftain of the Ulfor village, Berag cut a dominating figure. His hair and beard were grey with age, and his skin sagged with the years that lay upon them. But his bright blue eyes still shone with a cunning intelligence and his frame showed what it had once been. In his younger days, he had been a formidable man, massive across the chest and fit enough to run in full armour for most of the day. It was no secret in the village that he had served with the Varangian Guard for almost five years.

The Varangian Guard were a large group of warriors chosen from villages and cities all over the Northlands. Masters of the battle-axe, they had been recruited by the Byzantium king to serve as his personal bodyguard. The stories and history surrounding the Varangian Guard was legend.

Berag rarely talked about his younger days in the guard, but when he did, there was utter silence from his listeners. The chieftain was a living legend, particularly amongst the younger men of the village.

There were several thumps on the door and Berag groaned as he stood up. Wondering who could be calling upon him at such a time he walked to the door and swung it open. Stepping aside, he gestured for Romeeros to enter his home. The rune singer nodded and brushed past the giant old man, leaning his staff up against a wall. His cloak was soaking and Romeeros moved to the fire. Holding his hands out, he allowed the heat thrown from the bright orange flames to penetrate his cold skin.

Berag gave the rune singer time to warm himself. He sat near his sleeping family and watched as steam rose from Romeeros's clothing. The cloaked figure rubbed his hands together and cleared his throat.

"What brings you here, Romeeros?" asked Berag, not sure he wanted an answer.

Pushing the hood back from his face, Romeeros looked around and fixed his pale blue eyes on the chieftain.

"It is not good Berag as, I'm sure, you already surmised. Something dangerous has re-entered this world. Something deadly. And that something is here, near this village."

"What is it?"

Romeeros shook his head and did not reply. Instead, he looked into the flames and took a deep breath, letting it out in a long sigh.

"The Tuatha-Day-Dannan are here my friend. They have arrived."

Berag sat in silence with his eyes fixed on the rune singer.

"But how could that be any threat to us?" whispered Berag.

"You misunderstand," replied Romeeros. "It is not they who are dangerous, I, like you, am happy to see them in this world, but they carry something deadly. Something that should never have re-entered this place. I sensed it the moment they came here."

"What is this…this thing they carry?" asked Berag, his voice bringing a soft groan from his daughter, who rolled over in her sleep.

"At this moment, it does not matter what it is. What does matter is that a Kadark also sensed the Tuatha-Day-Dannan enter this world and he, like I, knows what it is they carry. More than this, the Kadark wants it. He wants it more than anything he has ever craved. As I speak these words to you, he is already rallying coastal warriors to him to journey inland a-viking.

He will do anything to get what the Tuatha-Day-Dannan carry and he will destroy anything or anyone that comes between him and what he seeks. At this moment, Berag, your village stands in his way."

Romeeros watched in silence as the Ulfor chieftain struggled for words. At last, he shook his head.

"Prepare yourself, my friend," spoke the rune singer, clasping a hand on Berag's shoulder. "Prepare your people, for there is a hard fight ahead of them."

For Berag the news came as a double blow. It was hard enough to accept that the Tuatha-Day-Dannan were here, near his village, let alone that his people would soon be under attack. The Norse children often fell asleep to tales of the Tuatha-Day-Dannan and the good they would reap throughout the land. Berag himself as a child had been told many tales by his father about the power of the gods of light. Never had he imagined that they would appear in his lifetime.

The Tuatha Day Dannan, the gods of light were here!

"How long do we have?" asked Berag.

"Nine, maybe ten days before the Kadark and his followers arrive.

Keep your best warriors here and send the women, children and older members of the village into the hills."

"But the older men will want to stand and fight. It would be a grave injustice and a great humiliation to send them away."

"I understand this," Romeeros replied. "But it is why you were chosen as chieftain. You must convince the elderly men to leave. As I said, it will be a hard fight. These warriors come inland not for loot, food or slaves; they come for the item carried by the gods of light." Romeeros sat down, sighing. "It is not a battle that you fight, but a war. You must prevail, or this," Romeeros swept his arm to encompass the home that Berag had worked so hard to create, "and everything you know will be gone. Be forewarned, if they succeed, not a house will be left standing. And not a person left alive."

"But why did the Tuatha-Day-Dannan choose Ulfor as their destination?" asked Berag.

"It matters not my friend," replied Romeeros. "What matters is that they are here and there is nothing to be done about it. You must prepare, for what approaches will be devastating if you and your people are not ready."

The two men sat staring into the flickering warmth of the fire as it devoured a fresh log.

"The wind speaks an ill omen," came a soft, deep voice.

Both men started and turned. The silhouette of a tall, well-built man blocked the doorway.

Berag ushered him in. "Come in Thormdall, it is a pleasure to have you here."

The warrior known as Thormdall ducked under the door and entered the dwelling. Without hesitation, Thormdall turned to Romeeros who was still seated. "Pray tell me rune singer, what is happening? I have never felt a message in the wind like this."

Romeeros looked up at Thormdall, who struck an imposing figure. Even as a rune singer looked upon by most as the wisest, Berserkers always filled Romeeros with a sick, spine chilling dread. He knew that Thormdall was not some young, witless man pretending to be a warrior of Odin. He was a true Berserker, a man chosen by Odin to do his bidding. He had never seen Thormdall in action, but he had heard the stories. The man was almost untouchable on the field of battle. He had only met Thormdall once when the warrior had been much younger, but even then, there had been something about him. He was calm and relaxed, regardless of the circumstance or situation. As cold as ice. It was disconcerting to the rune singer.

"What is it rune singer?" asked Thormdall.

Romeeros cleared his throat and told the newcomer the news he had given Berag.

"That is interesting," spoke Thormdall. He folded his arms in front of the fire. The orange light dancing on his face revealed the pale white scar that ran from his right eyebrow to his chin.

"What makes you think they will come here?"

"Because the Tuatha-Day-Dannan are here walking this land as we speak. What they seek is also here."

"You misunderstand me. Why would the Tuatha-Day-Dannan come here? Why this particular village? Vokthorp is only four days easy riding from here."

"I do not pretend to know the ways of the gods, Thormdall.

They will be here come sunrise, of that I am sure."

Berag coughed. "So what is it Romeeros? What is this thing they carry?"

"It matters not—"

"I believe I speak for Berag, myself and indeed the entire village when I say that I beg to differ. With due respect Romeeros, I believe it matters. If we are to come under attack because of this…this object, then we have a right to know what it is." Thormdall's piercing eyes stared unblinking at the rune singer.

Romeeros moved to the doorway. Glancing up into the night sky, he listened as the rain slashed through the grass outside and hissed into the crops only a stone's throw away. He let out a soft, deep breath. In the doorway of the neighbouring long house, he could see the dark shape of a young woman hugging a cloak to her. She peered in his direction wondering what business a rune singer would have with her chieftain.

Turning from the doorway, he shivered.

"It is a crystal of power. Some say it was a gift from the gods. The truth is nobody knows where it came from. But what we do know is that it has two qualities. It can bend time so that movement from one time to another is possible. It also has an influence-"

"Did you say it could bend time?" asked Berag.

"Yes, it is hard to explain, but it can move the person carrying it forward or back in time, as well as those within his direct vicinity."

"I am beginning to like the sound of this rock less and less," grunted Thormdall.

"As I was saying," continued Romeeros. "The crystal has an influence on others that emanates from within the carrier and magnified by the crystal. For instance, if the person carrying the crystal is a person of great anger, the people immediately around him will also become angrier. They will begin to view the world in the same way as the individual carrying the crystal.

"It is an item that would help, let us say, in the ruling of a kingdom, for instance, or a village. It will not make people do what the carrier wants them to do, but it will influence them so it is far easier for them to be persuaded as he wishes. It has great power and could have great political implications."

Romeeros raised his eyebrows. "And although it could be used for great good, in the wrong hands it is also capable of great evil.

This is why the Kadark seeks it. For if it was to fall into his possession, this whole land will slip under his influence and into darkness."

Romeeros watched the fire crackle and spit in protest at the damp log Berag lowered onto it.

"It is not a thing of nature," Romeeros spoke. "It is not of this world and should not stay here. When the Tuatha-Day-Dannan arrive on the morn bearing the crystal, we must make plans to move it far from here."

"Should that not prove easy?" asked Thormdall. "After all did you not say that it could move the carrier forward or back in time? If we moved it forward in time far enough that all that remained of the Kadark were bleached bones, would it not solve our problem?"

"It would, but we need to move it into the future and hide it so that it will never fall into anyone's hands, for good or for ill. Either that or find a way to destroy it."

"Sounds easy enough," spoke Berag.

"If only it were," responded Romeeros. "To move the crystal forward or back in time—"

"No, I mean it would be easy to destroy it would it not?" asked Berag.

"I do not even know if it can be destroyed Berag. But to move it, we need to get to a…gateway, if you like, that will allow us to do this. There are many of these gateways scattered throughout the world."

"My head is beginning to hurt, but I think I understand," said Berag, rubbing his eyes and yawning.

Thormdall nodded, but said nothing.

"Before either of you ask, there is only one main gateway in the world, the several hundred others are only minor gateways no longer in use. This main gateway often thought of as the first gateway ever created in this world, is far away in another country to the southeast. If we are to attempt to destroy or rid ourselves of the crystal then it must be to this gateway that we travel. It can only be reached on foot, hoof and longship. It will be a dangerous journey, but one that must be taken if we are to ensure the safety of our people, and future generations."

"In which country is this gateway?" Berag asked.

"I do not know for sure, but from the stories and half-truths I have heard, it is in Badawark territory."

"I know little of these people," spoke Thormdall, looking across at the rune singer. He waited for Romeeros to explain, but Berag broke the silence.

"The Badawarks invaded Byzantium thirty-two summers ago now. Ferocious fighters, they carry small round wooden shields covered in the skin of an animal they call a camel. They fight with spears and scimitars-"

"Scimitars?"

Berag waved his hand for silence. "Within two days they had fought into Byzantium. Thirteen villages lay gutted, animals either killed or set free. Crops burned, and food stolen.

"The Badawarks had carried out border raids many times, sometimes up to fifty raids in one year. But this. This was something that neither the king nor the Varangian Guard had ever seen before. It was a consolidated, disciplined attack upon the kingdom. It was obvious their destination was Byzantium and the throne.

"It took three days of marching before we were on them. The king went forward with his skirmishers. The guard was on all sides of the monarch within the skirmisher formation. I was close to the outside of the Varangian square so I saw a lot of the fighting. The Byzantium skirmishers are fine soldiers, some of the best in the world. Aggressive and disciplined, a rare but lethal combination. They fought hard but the Badawarks, no matter how many fell, just kept coming. It was not long before they were through and fell amongst the Varangian guard's ranks.

"We fought well and routed the Badawarks within the hour. But we lost a lot of men that day."

Berag stared out into the night, it was raining. His mind was full of the piercing clash of steel on steel and shouted orders. Swirling dust thrown up by the jostling feet of men and horses in combat, the sickly, sweet stink of blood drying upon skin. Above it all was the sound of screaming men, pain racking their dying bodies. An agony that often followed them right up until the moment of their death…maybe even beyond.

"We lost a lot of men that day," he said again. Blinking out of his reverie, Berag turned to Thormdall. "So you see my friend, what I am saying is that this crystal has to travel across dangerous territory. If it indeed is to Badawark that it needs to go to reach this supposed gateway. There is no guarantee that whoever goes will make it at all."

Romeeros stood up. "That is something we will think about tomorrow. Berag, when the sun reaches high noon, call a village meeting. I will be there. Then we may discuss how we go about sending this crystal on its way."

Nodding, Berag watched the rune singer lift the hood of his cloak over his head and face before disappearing into the dark night.

Thormdall clasped a hand on the chieftain's shoulder. "I will see you at the meeting my friend. Try to sleep."

With that, Thormdall ducked under the doorway and was gone.

"Can you not sleep?" It was the soft, sleepy voice of Helga as he stood warming his hands before the fire.

"I cannot," he replied, turning to her and smiling.

"You're no longer young, my love, you must try to get some rest."

"Thank you for reminding me," he chuckled sitting near her and pushing a hand through her silver-flecked hair.

"Are you feeling well?" asked his wife, concern entering her voice.

"I am well," he lied, stroking her brow. "Now go back to sleep, my love, tomorrow will be a busy day."

"Why so?" she asked closing her eyes and pulling the blanket tight around her.

"I just have a feeling," he replied. He closed his eyes against the piercing sound of clashing steel and the screams of the dying as memories from another time poured into his mind.

* * * * *

Steve rolled onto his side, shielding his eyes with his hands. As soft as the early light was, his eyes were straining after having been in darkness for so long. The rain had stopped, but the ground was still a quagmire. He could feel the comforting weight of his rifle on his back and his chest webbing pressing against his body. He brought the rifle around, clasped it in his hands and flicked the safety off. When he had become accustomed to the light, he saw the other soldiers were nearby.

Scott was lying face down with his head resting on his arm. Steve could see he was breathing. Matt was already up, he had his weapon slung and was kneeling over Scott, his first aid pack open beside him.

He was taking Scott's blood pressure, before rolling the soldier onto his side and checking for any obvious wounds or injuries. When none was found, Matt moved onto the next soldier.

"I'm all right," Steve said when Matt arrived by his side. "Still gotta check ya, mate," Matt said.

Matt relaxed once he had checked all the members of the patrol.

"What the hell happened?" Matt asked.

"I've got no bloody idea, mate, no bloody idea. I had a few mates back at school who used to do acid, and the stories they used to tell about what they'd seen or heard while they were stoned were unbelievable. I never did drugs, but Christ I reckon what we went through back there would be something like being stoned."

"You're not wrong, mate," said Matt. "I lost my radio, I can't find it anywhere."

Will had left the shelter and was kneeling on the other side of the circle of standing stones, staring down the ACOG scope attached to his rifle. With the light of the morning, it was easy to see they were on a plateau with a steep hill behind them, but lower ground was in front of their position. It was down into this lower ground that Will was watching. Scott was now in a half sitting position, squinting against the light. The stones themselves must have been half the height of a man.

"Oi, come look at this!" Will called, seeing Steve and Matt were awake.

Steve pushed himself out of the low shelter, and jogged over to Will, followed by Matt.

"We got a village down there. There is some movement. Several hundred people. Definitely not Iraqis. Dunno what's happened, mate, not even sure where we are. But there's people down there and they might help us."

Steve admired Will's mind, which had switched straight back onto the ball game as if nothing was amiss. Steve was still confused.

"Several hundred you reckon?" muttered Steve.

"Yeah, not your average Joe Blows either. I dunno what the hell's going on Steve, but these buggers are knocking about with swords strapped to their sides. They dress like they just stepped out of the thirteenth century."

Steve took a knee, brought his rifle up and looked down the ACOG scope at the huddle of buildings in the distance below.

"What the hell," he muttered to himself. As Will mentioned, the men wore sheathed swords by their sides. They dressed in long sleeved shirts and trousers that were dark green, brown or black. Many of the villagers also wore thick cloaks. Apart from the boys, all the men wore long hair and beards. The women wore their hair pulled away from their face, whereas the girls and younger women wore their hair loose about their shoulders.

"What the hell," Steve muttered again. He lowered the weapon and looked at Matt. "What the bloody hell's happened?"

Matt shrugged.

"Righto, where the fuck are we?" Scott shouted in the distance, he was sitting in a hunched position with his head touching the ceiling of the shelter.

Matt pulled a pair of binoculars from his webbing and stared down at the distant village.

"Bloody hell," Matt said.

"Yup, you said it," Steve replied, his weapon held across his body.

"Wouldn't have a bloody clue what's happened."

When Scott saw the village, his response was much the same.

"Well they ain't fuckin' Iraqi," said Scott flicking off the Minimi's safety catch. Steve thought Scott would open fire and moved to stop him, but Scott began pacing backwards and forwards, swearing to himself.

"I reckon we should go down there," said Steve. "Yup, agreed," said Scott.

"Ya can't," said Will turning towards them. "Ya can't be serious! Those bastards'll want to cut us up and feed us to the pigs!"

"Only one way to find out, I guess," said Matt as he stood up. "Get your arse in gear, mate, let's go," growled Steve.

Will joined the others, and the four soldiers made their slow way down the hill towards the village. Towards uncertainty.

* * * * *

The sun was warm as it rose over the distant mountains. Yet the wind was cool and gentle on Tharkol's skin as he stepped out of the house. He stretched, yawned and noticed that the sky was beginning to clear. The rain had passed and his corn crops seemed all the better for it. In the distance, it looked like heavy rain clouds were moving in from the north.

He turned as a shout broke the silence. Berag and his wife were standing outside their home in the distance. Their daughter, Tina, was jumping up and down pointing at four tall men making their way towards the village from Romhalf's Hill. They carried what appeared to be dark pieces of wood and dressed in a fashion that Tharkol had never before seen.

"Ho! We have visitors." It was Nyarl.

"Aye, it seems that way," the man responded, not taking his eyes off the distant newcomers.

Nyarl gestured as he came alongside Tharkol. "Let us go and greet them."

87

The two men started walking towards Berag, whose distant figure remained motionless. His hand was shielding his eyes from sun so he could better see the men who approached.

* * * * *

The whole village had noticed them. Some did not leave their homes, as they had decided to watch events in comfort and safety.

But many gathered around Berag, unsure who these men were. They had their weapons at the ready in case it was a Viking raid.

For Berag it was a tense time. He watched the figures, who he could only assume were the Tuatha-Day-Dannan, approach. These were not men visiting or looking for a home to stay the night before moving on. These were gods sent to earth by Odin.

They were tall and all wore strange, dark, identical patterned clothing. Each was bearded, with unkempt hair that protruded out beneath strange helmets. Each had an odd-looking piece of equipment fastened to their chest. Attached to this were compartments of varying sizes placed across their chest. They moved with care, but with purpose. In their hands, they held strange shaped items that ended in a round tube. It was possible that they were some sort of weapon Berag conceded. Their eyes were hard, but not cruel. They had toughness about them that young Viking warriors only developed after many battles.

"Who are they?" came a voice from the left of the gathered crowd.

Berag noticed it was Kettle, a young man who had not yet seen fourteen summers. Eager to see battle, his hand was clasped upon the hilt of his sword. It would be a good time, he decided, to explain that the men who approached were not enemy.

"Stay your hand, young Kettle!" Berag said. "These men will be welcomed into our village like long lost relatives."

"How do you know that?" asked Kettle.

Agnost, Kettle's father, slapped him on the back of the head. How dare he speak to the chieftain in that way!

"Trust me, my young friend," Berag replied.

* * * * *

"Hearts and minds," reminded Steve as the patrol moved down the hill towards the small village. The houses were narrow and long, and looked like old rowing boats that had been turned upside down. One enormous house, which dwarfed the buildings around it, stood in the

88

centre of the village. It must have been more than half a football field long. Crops surrounded the village, although he did not know what they were. In the distant background to the west stood an enormous mountain that dominated everything in the immediate vicinity. Each man was on instant, their fingers touching the triggers of their weapons.

What had happened, God only knew. But these people did not look Iraqi. Their clothes were different. They had swords and some of the men had what looked like round shields slung across their backs.

Maybe they were some kind of medieval re-enactment group. But if they were, what were they doing in the middle of the Iraqi desert in the middle of winter?

As they approached, a tall man, presumably the leader of the rag tag group stepped forward. He had put a lot of work into his costume, because it looked real, as did the massive axe he had slung on his back. The older man, his grey hair and beard making his piercing blue eyes even more intense, held up his hand in greeting.

"G'day there!" called Steve, waving.

The group of people immediately began murmuring amongst themselves. The man who had greeted them let his hand drop by his side and seemed unsure.

"What are you guys doing all the way out here?" Steve asked.

The four soldiers came to a halt before the old man who was staring with intense interest at the weapons.

The grey haired one smiled. "Veelak thengis," he spoke holding out his hand. He was trying to make the newcomers feel welcome.

The man pointed at Steve's weapon. "Was Baten Arkleerin mer daost see traagon?"

Steve looked at Scott. "Do you know what language he is speaking?

Is it some derivative of Bedouin?"

Scott shook his head. "My god," he said eyes wide in shock.

"Scott!" Will tapped him on the shoulder.

"No, it isn't Bedouin, it isn't any form of Arabic, it sounds Danish, but all fucked up."

"What do you mean?" Steve asked.

"Um, it's hard to explain….okay, you know how Shakespeare wrote his plays? The English is all arse about face and you have to think about the words to understand what the hell he's saying?"

Steve nodded. "Yeah sort of."

"Well it's the same with this, it definitely sounds Danish, but it's all muddled up and hard to understand. I think he wants to know what our rifles are. I think."

"Denmark," breathed Steve. "But how is that possible?"

Scott stepped forward. "Veepons," he said, holding his rifle up.

"Was sund eer naamon?" the grey haired man asked, eyeing Scott's rifle in such a way that it seemed he doubted such things could be weapons.

"I think he wants to know their names," Scott told the other soldiers.

"Our names?" asked Steve.

"No. The names of our weapons."

"Our weapons?" asked Steve bewildered.

"This is a fuckin' set up," chuckled Scott. "Sex machine!" shouted Scott holding the weapon high above his head, laughing.

The group of people flinched at the sudden noise and movement. There was a metallic hiss from the right and the old man roared at a young man, whose eyes were wide with fear. His sword was half unsheathed. The boy, who could not have been older than fifteen, sheathed his weapon, but kept his hand on the hilt. Steve noticed his knuckles were white.

"This isn't any set up," said Steve.

"Wartoz!"

A cloaked figure picked his way across the muddy ground towards them with a staff. As the figure approached, he threw back his hood. The man's eyes were pale blue, his grey hair and beard streaked with brown, telling of younger days.

* * * * *

Romeeros studied the four newcomers. They were tall, but one more so. The men did not seem frightened, he noticed, their eyes were more curious then anything.

Romeeros came alongside Berag.

"What has happened?" asked Romeeros.

"Where were you?" responded Berag, a touch of anger in his voice. "That matters not. What has happened?"

"Nothing. We cannot understand each other."

"I see."

Romeeros gestured for the men to come closer. Making his movements slow, he grabbed one of them by the wrist and led him back through the crowd, which parted to make way. The other newcomers followed.

As Berag watched them move off into the distance, Tharkol came to his side.

"What in the name of Odin is going on?" he asked.

"I know not," Berag said. "I know not."

* * * * *

"Where's he taking us?" asked Matt.

Despite being led by the wrist, Steve managed to turn to him. "I don't know, but if he makes a move put a bullet in him." He kept his tone light and friendly so as not to cause suspicion.

They entered one of the houses. Even up close, the house looked like an upturned boat. Inside was a large, long room, in the middle of which was a fire with a hole in the room for the smoke to escape. The room reeked of wood smoke, so the hole was only partly effective.

On the walls were shields of various colours and sizes. A huge axe, the haft of which must have been four feet long, was mounted on the wall above a primitive looking dining table. The preserved head of a bear, frozen in time hung next to the axe. Its face was snarling and revealed huge canines in its mouth. The beast must have been massive in life. Hanging near the bear's head was a large fur rug, presumably the bear's skin.

The house was split in two. The first, and largest part, was where the owners ate, slept and lived. The second part, separated with a four-foot high wooden wall and small lockable door, was where they kept the animals during winter.

As Steve's eyes adjusted to the darkness, he noticed a pig on the other side of the partition. It was pushing the ground with its snout and grunting. Nearby, a horse chewing on a mouthful of fresh grass looked up at the newcomers.

He could see some smaller animals moving around near the pig but could not make out what they were in the poor light. The smell of the animals mixed with the wood smoke but was not particularly repulsive. The cloaked man led them to the table and they sat down.

"Sujet lungaj spoten," he said.

"I'm sorry mate, we've got no idea what you're talking about," said Steve.

Realisation seemed to strike the man. "You speak Anglish?" he asked, his accent strong.

"We speak English, yes."

"Anglish," he whispered and remained in silent thought for a while. After a long pause, he spoke once more. "I will beckon our Chieftain here." With that, he was gone.

"This is a bloody set up," said Matt, his chair creaking as he leaned back. "These guys are those fanatical re-enactment type people. They were pretending to speak a different language when we arrived. Pretty impressive."

"Mate, I don't know what's going on," said Steve. "They don't look Iraqi and neither does the landscape look like Iraq, there's far too much rain."

"Look, it's this simple," said Scott. "Remember those protestors who wanted to become human shields just as the Gulf War broke out? It was organised by a Pommy guy I think. They hired a big double- decker London bus and made their way over to Iraq picking supporters up along the way. Remember? What if these people are a break off from that group? What if they are here to ruin our mission? I mean, so far they have done a pretty good job."

"You're not thinking, mate," replied Steve. "Where did all this rain come from? I mean this isn't a just a bit of rain and sleet, these guys have had a good three-hundred mil. Those mountains off to our west weren't there yesterday. And how did we get from a sheltered underground cave to being out here? Something's not right."

"I agree," said Will. "Something definitely ain't right here. It's almost as if we are in another time, but that's impossible."

A tall man ducked under the entrance followed by the cloaked man they had spoken to before. The older, taller man was the same who had greeted them at the start.

"Righto," said Scott. "Just what the fuck's going on here? We've got a job to do and we need to move on! I understand you don't agree with the conflict in Iraq but that's no fuckin' reason to endanger our lives. If you don't explain or let us go, we will shoot our way out of here."

"Scott!" said Steve, placing his hand on the man's shoulder. "Relax, mate."

"My name is Berag," said the newcomer, seeming to struggle with the language. "I am Chief of Ulfor, the village here. I do not understand all you speak. What is Iraq? And what is fuck? I do not understand these things."

Steve decided to introduce himself, his men, and their predicament.

"Listen Berag, our language doesn't matter for now. What matters is we don't know what's going on here. Something seems to have happened, and it happened after we came into possession of this crystal." He pulled the crystal from his pocket.

Berag sat wide-eyed and silent. He seemed fearful of the crystal in Steve's palm.

"I understand that you may be a little confused, but all will be clear soon," said the cloaked man. "I must apologise for not introducing myself sooner. I am known as Romeeros.

"Berag has called a council to discuss the situation with the rest of the village. The council is to be held in the Great Hall immediately. Please come with us."

CHAPTER 9

Berag and Romeeros disappeared through the doorway. Confused and unsure, the soldiers nonetheless stood and followed. The cold air bit into their clothing and their boots squelched through the wet, muddy ground. Steve could see the crowd outside had dispersed. Only a few remained, watching the soldiers and talking in hushed whispers.

They followed Romeeros and Berag along the muddy road that wound through the village. Steve noticed the villagers were flocking in the near distance. After a short journey, the huddle of dwellings was far behind them and the group was standing in open ground the size of a football oval. At the centre stood a huge longhouse with an entrance that was an imposing eight-foot high. The double wooden doors, attached by thick, steel hinges, were swung open and the villagers began filing in. Steve guessed the building was almost two hundred feet long. As they walked closer, Steve noticed intricate patterns carved into the great doors. There were also runes embedded in the wood under beautiful motifs of heroic warriors squaring up against mighty dragons. A huge serpent was carved around the edge of the doors, its mouth latched around a mighty looking helmed warrior wielding a great hammer. The woodwork was beyond skilled; it was perfect and spoke of the pride, patience and passion of the artisan who had created the images.

Steve was the first of the Australians to walk through the entrance. He felt dwarfed by the doors. He stopped and looked around the massive building. The roof was at least fifteen feet high and thick beams of painted hardwood held the roof in place.

"Looks cyclone proof," Matt whispered to Steve.

The walls were decorated with various polished weapons, helms, shields and animal hides. Most of the village people were now sitting around a long table that was almost as long as the building itself. They watched the soldiers with curiosity.

Romeeros approached the Tuatha-Day-Dannan.

"Welcome to the Great Hall," he said.

Berag lead the soldiers to seats on the right of the high backed chair at the head of the table. Romeeros sat down opposite them and gave them a reassuring nod. Berag sat at the head of the table but remained silent as he watched the villagers and let the burbled noise of voices and laughter wash over him.

The table itself had been crafted from oak. Steve admired the tiny creatures, warriors and runes that had been carved along the edge of the table lending character and life to the wood. They were beautiful depictions of great battles and heroic deaths, he thought.

"Welcome to the council," said Berag, clapping his hands. Silence followed.

"I speak in Anglish as this is the only language spoken by our guests." Berag spoke slowly so all could understand him. It was clear he also struggled a little with the language.

"Can someone please translate for those who do not know Anglish? I have called a council so we may all understand what has happened here."

It seemed to Steve that all the married men had been invited to the meeting, because their wives sat beside them. But there were no single people here, nor were there any children. Steve noticed one man who stood near the exit at the far end of the building. His piercing blue eyes sent a chill through Steve. The man's hand rested on the hilt of his sword and although he seemed relaxed, everything about the man spoke of controlled violence. This man had killed people, of that Steve was sure.

"Welcome people of Ulfor to this council. We are here today to speak of the Tuatha-Day-Dannan."

There was a gasp and all eyes turned to the four newcomers. It was the first time Berag had mentioned the Gods of Light.

"What's the Tuatha-Day-Dannan?" Will asked Matt. "Christ knows," Matt replied.

"No more games now, my friends," Berag said to the Australians. "Why have you come?"

"Berag," Steve leaned forward. "We don't know what's going on here. We found this," he said, placing the crystal on the table, "and the next thing we know, we are here. We were hoping you could tell us what's going on."

"What is he saying?" called a voice.

"Wait my friend," spoke Berag, holding his hand up. The chieftain leaned in towards Steve. "You mean you are not the Tuatha-Day-Dannan?" he asked.

"What exactly is the Tuatha-Day-Dannan?" asked Steve.

"They are gods, sent by Odin to the world of man when times turn ill. Legend says that they will come bearing the Crystal of Orises."

"I am sorry to disappoint you, mate, but we are not gods. We are men just like you."

"I've had enough of this bloody role-play shit," shouted Scott. "What the fuck's going on here?"

"Scott!" Steve hissed. "These people aren't re-enactors. And this isn't Iraq. As crazy as it might sound, I think we have come back in time. I know it sounds crazy, but I can't think of anything else. It's the only way I can explain what happened to us back in that cave!"

"That can't be right," said Scott. "We can't have gone back in time, it's impossible!"

"That's what I thought, but something definitely ain't right here." Steve turned back to find Berag and Romeeros talking in hushed voices.

Seconds later, Berag leaned back in his chair and looked at the soldiers.

"You are not the Tuatha-Day-Dannan?" asked Romeeros.

"No, of course not! We are just men, and what's more we want to get back to where we came from!"

"What is it you mean?" asked Romeeros.

"What is going on?" bellowed a deep voice from the other end of the great hall.

"Silence!" roared Berag. "All will be revealed."

"Well it seems to us," continued Steve, "that we moved through space and time after we took that bloody crystal." He pointed at the pitch-black crystal resting on the table before him. "But now we want to get back to where we came from!"

"You have travelled across the land?" queried Romeeros.

"Not just the land, but also through time. It seems we're from your future, and we'd like to go back. That's where we live. We don't belong here."

"You think we've come back in time?" asked Matt.

"It's the only thing I can think of," replied Steve.

"That's fuckin' impossible!" Scott's face was red with fury or fear, or both; it was hard to tell.

"We should never have stuffed around with that crystal," said Will. "What's done is done. We can't help that now. But we need to find a way back, otherwise we're screwed," said Steve.

"So what exactly is that thing?" asked Steve, pointing at the crystal.

"If you tell the truth and you are from our future then I can think that it must only be," Romeeros's eyes were fixed on the black crystal. "It can only be the magical Crystal of Orises. It was found in this village by Orises many hundreds of years ago. Orises was a great warrior who fought with the Yarmsklinga, as well as the Varangian Guard."

"Yarms what?" asked Matt.

"Yarmsklinga. There were a group of warriors who fought as mercenaries. They were well trained and turned more than one battle in the favour of their employers. In fact, Orises became leader of the Varangian Guard, known as the Host. He returned home when he heard of the death of his father. By the time he arrived back in Ulfor, almost two moons had passed since his father's death and he had long since been buried. Orises went out to the ship under which his father lay and dug a grave for himself. He made it known that following his death he would lie beside his father and would not leave for the afterlife until it was so. But as he dug, he came upon a crystal," Romeeros stopped for a moment and picked up the crystal. "This crystal," he said, holding it up for all to see.

"Even today it is possible to see the burial ships under which Orises and his father lie."

None of the soldiers understood what Romeeros was talking about. But they knew it was for the benefit of the village not just for them, so they remained silent.

"The Crystal of Orises was believed to have been a gift from the Gods. It was to become a talisman for each man who led the Varangian Host. Orises was the first leader and after he stepped down the next Varangian Guard chief was to take possession of the crystal. It was a sign of power and demonstrated who was in charge of the Host at that time."

When Romeeros put the crystal back on the table, Steve took it and put it back in his pocket. If the crystal were the key to their return home, he would keep control of it.

Two boys, who cannot have been more than twelve and who were the sons of one of the couples present, appeared in the doorway. They struggled to heave a large wooden keg into the room. Behind them appeared a teenage girl holding a large sack over her shoulder. A cheer went up and after the keg had been put in position, the boys waved and left. Swinging the sack from her shoulder, the girl delved into it and took out what looked a bull's horn. She opened the keg and submerged the horn. Then she handed the wet, dripping horn to the nearest man, who passed it on to the next, and so on, until it reached Berag.

The chieftain up-ended the horn and took a long drink. All eyes were on him. Berag held the horn in the air. "Some of the best I've tasted!" he shouted.

"Do not drink it all Berag, you are thirsty when it comes to mead!" shouted an older woman nearby. Good-natured laughter followed and the girl began handing out horns filled with mead until everyone had one.

"Go on, take a sip," said Berag to the four newcomers.

Steve took a sip and the others watched him to see his reaction. Up ending the horn, he gulped down the rest. Berag and Romeeros laughed.

Matt sipped the drink and was surprised by the sweet taste. It tasted like honey, but with a tang and slight bitterness that was irresistible. He finished his drink too. The empty horns were passed back down the table where they were refilled once more.

"Don't gulp this one down," Berag warned. "Otherwise your head will spin."

Romeeros called for silence. "As I was saying, the crystal became a sign of power. Yet, they did not know the Crystal of Orises radiated and enhanced what the carrier felt and believed to be right. If he was a man of malice and believed all those opposed to him should be killed, then his hatred influenced those around him. It is a tool for good or evil, depending on who carried it. If a Kadark was carrying this crystal, then the sentiment in this room would be dark, anger would flare and people would begin to bicker and fight."

"A Kadark?" asked Matt. "What's that?" he asked.

"Kadarks," said Romeeros, "are not of this world. They are ageless beings, or so it is said. I have yet to meet one, Odin pray I never do. If what you say is true, then you travelled through a portal to arrive in our land." Romeeros's English, or Anglish as he called it, was exceptional, although his accent was thick. He did not seem to struggle with the words as much as Berag.

"The portals are ancient. Elders whose bones were dust long before the eldest amongst us was born made them.

It was through these portals that the Kadarks were pulled. I say pulled, because they arrived through no intention of their own. When the portals on earth were created, the Kadarks were dragged from a different realm into this world, or so it is told. It is not known how many walk this earth, but all they want is to return to their land. They will do anything to do so, including murder and rapine. The Kadarks are evil beings."

Romeeros took a long sip from the drinking horn.

"They are not human," he said. "There are only three Norse priests that I know of who have come face to face with a Kadark and lived to tell the tale. Not one of them think the Kadarks are human."

"Not one," whispered Romeeros. "The Kadarks wear long dark, hooded robes. Their faces are filled with shadow and malevolence. It is believed the cloaks hide inhuman, demon-like faces of which Loki would be proud."

When Romeeros stopped speaking, the hall was silent. The villagers had heard the tales of the Kadarks since they were babes in arms. Steve noticed, the people of Ulfor continued to believe the story of the Kadarks.

"Let us pray we never encounter one here," said Romeeros. Steve noticed several people gesture across their chests with their thumbs as if to ward off evil.

"Alas!" continued Romeeros. "As I was saying, the crystal of Orises is a neutral force. Not of the light or of the darkness, but can be used for either. At the time the crystal was discovered, Orises did not realise this, nor did any of the other commanders of the Varangian Guard. But a Kadark did know the power of the crystal and gathered men to him willing to fight for his cause."

"It took the Kadark and his force three moons to arrive in Byzantium and gather even more men to him. This time they were not Vikings, but Badawark warriors. Savage men from the neighbouring land of Badawark, who had always been opposed to the presence of Byzantium. Using his powers, the Kadark and his followers entered the Byzantium palace and headed for the Varangian barracks. They slaughtered the chief of the guard in his sleep so the crystal was now in the hands of the Kadark." Romeeros shook his head. "With the crystal in the hands of a Kadark, our worst fears were realised."

Romeeros drained his drinking horn and nodded for a refill.

"Within a week, the Kadark and his men lay dead, victims of Badawark treachery. It was not explained how the Badawarks killed the Kadark. It is believed the few Kadarks who walk our earth are immortal and cannot be touched by the mightiest of blades.

"The Badawarks returned to their land, handing the Crystal of Orises to the Badawark king, a man of great anger and hatred. In the hands of the Badawark king, the crystal radiated the anger and hatred for the Byzantium Empire that he held. It was not long before the king and his Badawark army were marching towards Byzantium with the intention of conquering the nation. The outlying towns and villages were destroyed. Men killed, children slaughtered, women raped and murdered, livestock butchered. A Byzantium army marched out to meet them, and so began the ten-year war. It was a black time and many tens of thousands of lives were lost.

"Finally the Badawarks managed to breach the Byzantium capital Constantinok. The fighting changed from open warfare to street-to-street fighting. This did not last long before the Badawarks were pushed back over the border towards their own capital.

"A middle-aged Byzantium warrior-cleric of the Order of The Flame, a man called Mahaazad, was involved in this final battle. Both sides were weak and exhausted after the decade-long war. The Badawarks finally fled the field of battle. Many retreated towards the Badawark capital. But the king, still in possession of the Crystal of Orises, fled for the nearby hills to the north. Knowing what the king carried, Mahaazad gave chase and caught the Badawark king as he entered a cave high up in the mountains. The two soldiers guarding the monarch fought to protect him. Mahaazad killed them both, but in so doing received a deep wound to the chest. Even in a weakened state, Mahaazad killed the king and seized the crystal."

Romeeros placed the horn down on the table and continued. "Mahaazad was a warrior-cleric of incredible power and knowledge. Even today in Byzantium, the name of Mahaazad holds great power. As he was dying, Mahaazad worked his way through the cave system and found the most isolated place. It was in the bowels of the earth, hidden behind the back wall of the main cave. The tunnel led out into a giant chamber. There he performed an ancient rite to send the crystal many years into the future where it could not be touched.

"It is here the story grows sketchy. But it is believed that as he finished the ritual, he threw the crystal at the wall where its shape would be burned for evermore. With that, the Crystal of Orises was gone forever. We Norse people believe that the crystal will appear once more when the Tuatha-Day-Dannan comes into this world. The Byzantium people believe that Mahaazad will appear with the crystal when times call for it."

The hall fell silent.

"So is this the Crystal of Orises?" asked Steve, patting his pocket.

"Without a shadow of doubt. But there are still questions that I do not have the knowledge or wisdom to answer," replied Romeeros.

"But for now, relax and enjoy yourselves. I would like four families to volunteer to take one of these men into your home. Feed them and keep them warm and do not be afraid as they will not harm you, I know their hearts. You can trust me on this."

The council sat for some time afterwards drinking and talking. An elderly couple whose children had long since grown up took in Steve and all but one had left the village. One of their three sons was now a woodworker in a nearby village. Their daughter had married a farmer on the other side of the mountains and their youngest son killed in a Viking raid five years before.

Scott was invited into the home of a burly, loud man with a thick, untidy beard. His wife was a short plump woman who was a marvellous cook. That night he sat down to a steaming meal of venison and corn.

Matt stayed with a young couple and their two children. The boy would have been no more than four and the girl only twelve months old at best. They were a friendly family with a close bond.

Will was billeted with an elderly couple near the centre of the village. Their daughter, Heleena, who was twenty-three summers old, also lived with them. She was a stunning young woman and had refused every suitor, or so her father boasted. Will was speechless when he laid eyes on her for the first time. She had flowing dark hair, brown eyes and an honest smile. While her figure was not overweight, neither was she stick-thin. She was curved, as a woman should be. He tried to feign disinterest but found it impossible.

* * * * *

Romeeros walked to a small abandoned building on the outskirts of the village. It was where he always stayed on his infrequent visits to the village. Ignoring the cold, he sat inside the long forgotten dwelling and relaxed, closing his eyes. He felt the familiar warmth flowing through his body.

"Broanar," he spoke the name in his mind.

There was no response, but Romeeros held his concentration.

"What is it?" came a deep voice from inside his mind.

"I have some news for you. The crystal is here, yet the carriers are not the Tuatha-Day-Dannan."

"How do you know that?"

"Because they told me they were not," replied Romeeros in his mind.

"So, how do you know they are not?"

"I trust their word."

"But what if they do not even know it themselves?" asked Broanar. "They could well be the Tuatha and not know it."

"It is a possibility."

"It is more than a possibility my friend," replied Broanar. "A prophecy has been fulfilled this eve whether you or the carriers know it. I have read the stars and it has begun. You and I sensed the crystal enter this world as I am sure did the Kadark. As we speak, he will be gathering people to him. Before long he will come inland to the village in search of the crystal."

"What should we do, Broanar? I can see no solution."

"There is a man on his way to you, an Arab warrior-cleric. He can help you. He knows the history of the crystal and how to use its power. He also knows the location of the master portal. Although I cannot guarantee he will be there before the Kadark and his followers arrive. Prepare for battle for I fear blood will be spilt before his arrival."

"I thank you my friend," said Romeeros, the voice fading from his mind.

"I am losing your voice my friend. Hold strong, all will be well."

101

Romeeros opened his eyes and took a deep breath. The dull, silver light from the moon beamed through a window and shone on his face.

* * * * *

Will awoke early the next morning moving from the house as the family slept on an earthen bench carved into the wall. Only coals were left of the fire, but they still released a small amount of heat. It would only take some fresh kindling and a little digging into the coals and the fire would be revived.

He moved outside and relieved himself against a tree. Pulling up his zip Will noticed the same warrior who had been standing in the doorway at the meeting. The man was sitting cross-legged facing the rising sun. His sword was lying unsheathed across his legs and his head was bowed in prayer.

"He is greeting the sun and speaking to the Gods."

Will turned to see Heleena. She had a cloak pulled around her body, although he could still see the gentle curve of her breasts.

Clearing his throat, he asked, "He's a priest?"

"Priest? I do not understand," she said in a thick accent. A dark lock of hair fell across her face, which she brushed behind her ear.

"A man of god, if you like."

"Yes, Thormdall is a man of Odin," she replied with a smile. "He is a Berserker. A man chosen by Odin. Thormdall has done battle against Vikings who tried to plunder our village many times before."

"He is a Berserker?" asked Will. "Does that mean he goes crazy and hacks at everything he sees moving?"

Heleena stepped closer, the smile fading from her face as she watched the praying warrior in the distance. "No quite the opposite. The man sends a chill down my back. He is calm even in the heat of battle. But I do feel safer knowing that he is around. He has never been bested with a sword to my knowledge, so it is good for the village that he is here. Particularly in the autumn time when the coastal vermin come inland a-viking. They search for supplies and bounty for the winter months."

Thormdall rose and began walking towards the forest. He turned mid-stride and eyed them from the distance.

"I will be gone for some days," he called. "Inform Berag!"

Heleena waved and nodded.

"Sounds like you guys live a hard life," Will turned to her.

"It could be much worse. There have been villages, many days ride from here, that have been burned to the ground by raiders."

"Let's hope that never happens to you guys."

"What is guys?" she asked.

"Oh sorry, it means, uh, you people."

"I understand," Heleena chuckled. "I still find it hard to understand everything you say."

"I know, so do I," Will said with a smile.

"Come walk with me," Heleena said. "Where?"

"In the forest," she replied.

"Wait, don't you want to get something more comfortable to wear?"

"No," Heleena said, as she adjusted the cloak around her.

* * * * *

Steve stretched outside. The cold morning air moved around him, chilling him to the bone. He heard the sound of a woman's laugh and turned. In the distance, on a small hill that looked out over the village, he saw Will with an attractive young woman beside him. She held a blanket around her body and they were talking and laughing together. That they liked one another was obvious. Smiling, he turned away and noticed a man sitting cross-legged in the near distance. His sword was lying across his legs and his head was bowed as if he were sleeping, or perhaps praying.

"That is Thormdall, he is talking to the Father God. It is a Berserker ritual. They all seem to do it as the sun rises."

Steve turned to see Therfil in the doorway. The man was bald, but for a streak of white hair at the back of his head that reached down past his shoulders.

"I thought there was something different about him. Had a feeling he was a crazy."

"A crazy?" asked Therfil.

"Not of sound mind, I guess you could say."

Therfil shook his head. "Thormdall is one of the most level-headed men I know. Nothing mad about that man. If there's anything chilling about him, it is his absolute calm. I have not once seen him angry, even in battle."

As they spoke, Thormdall stood up, re-sheathed his sword and moved towards the forest in the distance.

"For all his level headedness he is still a hard man to read, which can be disconcerting," said Therfil.

* * * * *

103

"I've always thought Berserkers were crazy men who went into fits of rage," said Willl. He watched Thormdall disappear into the tree line.

Heleena laughed. "Who told you that? It is not true. The true Berserker is not fazed by anything, even in the thick of a sword fight. If you see Thormdall in action, and I hope you never do as it will mean you are in danger yourself, then you will see what it is that I mean."

"The men of your village seem pretty keen to fight. Why is that?"

"Keen?" Heleena asked.

Will was about to explain but she stopped him.

"It does not matter. Fighting is part of our culture. To enter the Hall of Heroes, our men must die in combat with a sword in their hand. It is why they never shy away from a fight. From what I hear in the village, it seems a fight will soon be upon us."

"It looks that way. As I understand it warriors from the coast are coming inland here to Ulfor."

"Warriors?" she spat the word. "They are no warriors, they are criminals who fight and kill to steal food, coin or slaves. They no longer believe in the Gods and so have no respect for them or their will. Instead they have been taken in by the lies of the Chreest men."

"Chreest men?"

"It is hard to explain, but I will try. The men who believe in this Chreest teaching say that there is only one God. They trick people into joining their ranks and giving them money and possessions. The Chreest men say it will pay for their entry into the afterlife. It is all a lie."

She was silent as they entered the narrow path leading into the dark, chilly forest. The smell of moss and rotting leaves enveloped them.

"But this Chreest religion," she continued, "has not so many rules as our own. In this way, they can kill a man and then repent in the knowledge that their God is all forgiving. It is not so easy with our people. If you kill a man, then you start a blood feud with his family, they will hunt you, and your family until justice is done. This is a much fairer system of govern. It forces a man to consider the consequences before he commits a wrong. The good thing about the Father God, whom we call Odin, is that once we are born into his world, we cannot leave. So these coastal criminals, these Vikings who think they have changed their religion, have not. Odin is still watching them and biding his time before he punishes them. And punish them He will."

"I am confused when you say Viking. Aren't you Vikings as well?" asked Will.

Heleena looked angry, and a threatening glint entered her eyes.

"No," she said. "You are new here, so I will leave your comment pass. Viking describes a raider. 'Vik' translates into Anglish as a creek or river mouth. The Norse longships are so light they can float in shallow water. The Vikings can row up narrow creeks or rivers to attack unsuspecting farms and villages inland. Vikings are not Norse warriors, they are Skeldings," she stumbled over her words. "Skeldings," she repeated. "Bad people, who are hung, exiled or locked away."

"A criminal?" asked Will. He could not help glancing at Heleena's moist lips; they were full and inviting.

"Yes, a criminal, I could not remember the word. We call them Skeldings in our tongue. Vikings are crinim…criminals, they have no honour and are disloyal even to their own people. Norse warriors might sail similar longships, but they bow to the old ways and honour the Gods. They live by the Norse lefskar….law. We are not Vikings, Will. We are Norse; different people."

Will nodded. He liked it when she said his name.

"Norse," he said nodding. "It sounds like these men are nasty bastards. I guess the people of your village'll be glad to deal with them."

"Yes, we will be, but if they bring too many men as Berag seems to think, then we could be in danger."

"I dunno, from what I've seen, I think this village'll be able to account for itself pretty well."

Heleena looked confused.

"Your people look like they can fight well."

"I understand now," she smiled. "Yes, we can fight well. Norse children are taught in martial law long before they learn to till soil and harvest crops. A Norse warrior is worth perhaps four Vikings."

They walked on some more before Heleena veered from the path.

"Come, follow me, I want to show you something."

Will had started to lose his bearings and was surrounded by thick forest on all sides. The forest canopy hid the sky and a dim gloom enveloped the pair. A strange, shrill birdcall broke the quiet. As their boots crunched through the thin snow a flap of wings suggested the bird had retreated to safety. Will lost his footing as he tripped on an exposed root and landed face first in the snow. Heleena laughed. Spitting snow and cold dirt from his mouth, he shook his head with a grin.

"Watch your footing," Heleena giggled.

Before long, they came upon a clearing where Will spotted a small cave in a rock face. It seemed to travel almost ten feet back into the rock face. The pair ducked into the shelter and Will saw a circle of large stones in the centre of the cave into which had been placed fresh, dry wood.

"This is a well-known shelter," Heleena said. "It is a custom to ensure that fresh wood is placed ready to burn. If a weary traveller is caught up in a blizzard or poor weather, this shelter is ready for them. This humble cave has saved many lives."

Will noticed runes had been carved into the ceiling at the rear of the cave.

"What does that say?"

"The markings?" she asked. "It says 'Thrain son of Bothrik sought refuge here'."

"Cool! Medieval graffiti!" Will laughed.

Heleena appeared mystified.

"Tell me of your home," Heleena said.

"My home? Not much to tell. I live alone, I rent a small house near the army base. It is not a bad life, although I hardly live there," he smiled.

"What is rent?" Heleena asked.

"Oh. It means that another person owns the home, but I pay them each week to live there."

Heleena frowned. "I understand what it is you say, but it is a strange idea."

Will understood that Heleena's village lived more like a tribe. They lived, shared and fought together. The idea of a person profiting at the expense of another was foreign to her. Viking Denmark was a harsh place where some of the toughest people he had ever seen lived. But Will knew the modern world also carried difficulties these people had never faced.

"What is your wife's name?" Heleena asked.

"I'm not married. My girlfriend left me about a month ago."

"Girlfriend?" she asked, brushing a lock of hair away from her face.

"A woman I lived with, almost like a wife I guess, but not quite."

"You people are strange," Heleena chuckled.

"Yeah I know, anyway she pissed off, had enough of me being away I guess. What about yourself?"

"Myself? I am not betrothed to another."

"I find that hard to believe," said Will, drinking in her beauty. "Why so?" she asked, her brow once again creasing.

"I dunno, it's just I find it hard to believe."

"You sound like father!"

"You're beautiful," he blurted out, embarrassed by his words but satisfied he had spoken them. "That's why I find it hard to believe. You're a beautiful woman, Heleena."

Her brow softened and she smiled. "Thank you, Will."

"No problem, just an observation," he muttered. He could feel his face burning.

He was about to suggest they leave, but felt a soft hand on his face. Heleena turned his face and kissed him. She tasted sweet, like a peach. He fell into another world as his lips pressed against hers. He pulled away and looked into her eyes; it seemed they were the only people here on earth. No one else existed. No one else mattered. He kissed her again, longer this time. He could smell the faint perfume of her hair and as his arms moved around her, he could feel her soft, yielding body. He quashed his desire to rip her clothes from her and push her down beneath him. A faint voice broke them away from each other.

"Did you hear that?" she asked.

Will's blood was pumping. He had not heard anything. He conjured horrible thoughts to overcome the battle of the bulge that was occurring in his pants. When the battle had been won, he climbed to his feet beside Heleena.

The voice was louder now.

"Heleena!"

"It is Father!" she said.

"Ho father!" she called out.

"Never have I known you to disappear like this!" he called, his voice with an edge of anger in it.

"Hi Foothark!" called Will as the elderly man strode into view.

"You are not alone either I see!" he called, although he did not seem perturbed by Will's presence.

"I was showing our guest around," Heleena said, as Foothark came closer.

"That is good, this is an important place to know," called Foothark.

"My oath it is," grinned Will.

Heleena stifled a giggle.

"If you have finished your tour, your mother has cooked a handsome meal to break your fast."

The three made their way back to Ulfor. At one point when Foothark had made some headway, Will pulled Heleena aside and pressed her up against a tree. He kissed her before the couple stumbled back out onto the path laughing and giggling.

"What's that you say?" called Foothark not bothering to turn. He spoke in Anglish out of respect for Will.

"It is a fine day!" replied Heleena stifling another giggle.

"That it is. That it is," her father replied.

When they returned to the village, Foothark held the door open for them. As they entered, they smelled cooked bacon, seared beef, boiled corn and fried egg.

"This is the life," said Will, sitting down to the hearty breakfast.

"I agree," smiled Heleena winking at him.

CHAPTER 10

The next morning Berag invited the Australians for a tour of the village. It was larger than they thought. To the east were acres and acres of corn, wheat, rye, barley and a selection of vegetables. They also kept colonies of bees, from which they extracted honey to make their mead. The ploughs were kept under protective shelters ready to plough the earth, once the harvest had been completed in the summer. Berag explained the horses and oxen that pulled the ploughs were kept in the homes of the owners through the winter months. Once spring arrived, they were turned out to pasture. Far to the south, Berag showed them the burial grounds of his village. Before he led them forward, Berag paused. He closed his eyes and kept his hands by his side. After a moment, he nodded at them and walked on. Each grave was marked by a series of stones laid around the grave in a long oval shape. At the head of each grave was a stone larger than the others, into which was carved a series of runes. Presumably the name of the deceased and perhaps a testimony to their life. Berag explained that the long oval shape represented a bird's eye view of a longship. Some of the stones were dark with age, others had sunken into the ground over time. But that there was an air of reverence was unmistakeable.

"Our people," said Berag, gesturing towards the graves around him. "Our story. Some have died of old age, others far before their time from sickness. A few died as they were born. Others as they gave birth. Many of our warriors lie here too. We farm to live, to survive, but always," Berag touched his chest, "we are warriors. Before hair grows on our faces, we can wield a sword, skewer a boar with a spear and form the Skyaldaborg."

Berag paused when he saw the confused faces. "The shield wall," he said. "The shield wall or the Skyaldaborg is the formation we make when the enemy are upon us. We form a line with shields overlapping. Warriors stand behind the front rank ready to take the place of a warrior should they fall. The warriors who are buried here died as they would have wanted, as every Norseman would want. In battle."

Berag led them back to the village. The homes each had runes carved into the wood surrounding the entrance. Berag explained they were protection runes, to bring safety to the household. The walls of many of the homes displayed weapons, chainmail, helmets, colourful shields and animal hides.

The village was surrounded by thick forest, so they were never in need of wood, for building or firewood. The firewood was usually cut at the beginning of summer and allowed to dry over the months leading to winter. The wood used for building was allowed much longer to dry, sometimes years. As the wood dried, it bent and warped. It was better for the wood to do this before it was used than for it to warp once it was part of the integral structure of a building, Berag explained. It was easier to cut straight a piece of warped wood, than to tear down a building and begin again from the ground up.

Once the tour was complete, the soldiers thanked Berag, who excused himself. He had other matters to attend. The soldiers made their way to the Great Hall, which was empty now. The massive fireplaces at each end of the hall were dark with ash, but amongst the darkness hot coals glowed. The soldiers placed kindling in them. Once the flames had started, they placed thicker pieces of kindling and wood to warm the room. The soldiers sat for several hours, discussing and laughing at their incredible misfortune. They talking about their families, their loved ones and the people they most wanted to see. Will was the first to leave as sun was beginning to dip in the sky. He explained that Marie, Foothark's wife cooked dinner early. It was to be venison, pork or bird served with vegetables. In fact, none of the Australians complained about the food they had been served. The Norse ate well, they consumed a lot of meat and some fish, although that was harder to come by this far inland, and many vegetables. The meals were served in large wooden bowls or plates, the cutlery crafted out of either wood or bone.

"Pretty keen to leave hey, mate?" asked Steve.

"Just hungry, almost dinner time."

"Yeah, right," grinned Steve.

"What?" asked Will.

"I saw you two yesterday," said Steve, "walking off together into the forest."

"It's not what you think, mate," said Will.

"Bloody oath it is, Will!" Steve chuckled. "Now piss off and go get her!"

Will grinned and disappeared.

He found Heleena at home. She was sitting near her mother talking. Foothark was nowhere to be seen. Will closed the door behind him and watched Heleena's face light up when she saw him. He grinned at her. Marie, to her credit, pretended not to notice their reactions. She cast a log onto the fire over which hung a large black, steel pot filled with a hearty smelling stew.

"We will see you soon, Mother," called Heleena.

"Do not be too long," called Marie. She smiled at Will. "I want you both back by the time the sun touches the mountains."

"We will not be long," replied Heleena, closing the door behind them.

The pair walked towards the forest, talking and laughing. Within minutes, they were once again sitting inside the cave Heleena had shown Will the day before. They looked out upon the surrounding forest for a moment. As the afternoon ended, the cool air descended, falling upon them heavier than the thickest chainmail. Heleena hugged her knees and smiled at Will. He pulled her close. He could smell the perfume of her hair. Her dark eyes were soft, like deep pools of light, her skin smooth and healthy, and her lips, Will swallowed hard, her lips were inviting. He leaned into her and their lips touched. She kissed him then pulled away for a moment to brush a strand of hair away from her face. Will kissed her neck, as his arms moved about her. As she moved into him, he could feel her soft breasts pushing against him. This was not just lust, Will thought. He kissed and licked her skin. She moaned. He cared for this woman.

She pushed him down and he looked up into her face, as she straddled him. He tried to sit up but she pushed him down. She was stronger than she looked. She pulled Will's shirt off, her hand stroking a tattoo of a flaming skull above his left nipple.

"What is that?" she asked.

"It's a tattoo, ink impregnated below the skin, they use a needle to do it."

"I have heard of body pictures before. A native people far to the West engrave their bodies blue."

"Enough of them," whispered Will, pulling her to him and kissing her with passion.

She knelt up and unbuckled his trousers, pulling them down, followed by his underpants. She giggled, clasping his hardness in her hand and squeezed. Her hands stroked along his length and he suppressed a groan as he released the belt around her waist. He pulled her shirt up and over her head. Her breasts were firm and full. He kissed and licked her nipples. She cried out when he bit down on a nipple, the soft warmth of her breasts in his hands. She pulled away from him and stood, untying her forest green pants, letting them slide to the floor in an untidy heap. Straddling him, she smiled, grinding her hips down on his stiffness, but without allowing him to penetrate. He could feel her wetness on his shaft. He touched her womanhood, a finger slipping inside her. Her eyes closed, her face raised to the cave ceiling as he touched her, his fingers glistening as they probed her clitoris. Sliding over the sensitive flesh, gently at first and then harder and faster, making her cry out. He could feel her stomach muscles tense. Continuing to stimulate her, Will leaned forward and kissed her belly, licking her belly button. When he could take no more, he clasped her under the thighs, lifted her up and brought her down upon the head of his shaft. He closed his eyes as he entered her. He stopped, and lifted her up again. Her hands were either side of his head and her breasts were close to his face teasing him. He slipped further inside her this time. Sitting up, she lifted herself off him and then let the weight of her body press down upon him. This time the full length of his penis entered her. He groaned as he felt her soft skin upon his. He clenched his teeth as he felt his manhood moving within her warm, velvety wetness. She thrust down hard, groaning, her breasts swaying back and forth. He clasped hold of them, kissed, and licked them. Her hair fell on his face, but he brushed it aside and pulled her down, kissing her. She pulled away and gasped. Her movements becoming more urgent, her hips thrusting against him until she cried out. Her hands pushed against his chest and her back arched up as the orgasm washed over her.

He clasped her hips and pulled her down upon him, thrusting himself into her, his skin slapping against hers. Her eyes were shut tight as he ground against her. She was moaning. Will could feel the pressure building at the base of his manhood but tried to hold it back. Her soft skin slid upon his with wet slaps as she forced herself down upon him in rhythmic thrusts.

The pressure continued to build and he let out a groan. Her movements quickened, she gasped and bent down to kiss him. The wetness of her mouth pushed down on his lips. Will pulled away from her kiss and groaned as the pressure he could no longer hold began moving up the length of his shaft. Heleena arched her back again, her glistening breasts thrust out before her as a second orgasm rocked her. Pushing himself into her depths, Will thought an artery in his head would burst. He cried out, feeling himself ejaculate with force inside his lover.

They lay together holding each other close as steam rose from their sweat soaked bodies. They were no longer aware of the cold.

"Wow," whispered Will.

Heleena kissed him.

They lay together in silence for a long time before Heleena moved.

"We should walk back, Mother will begin to worry," said Heleena.

"I'm more worried about your father being pissed off when he finds out. I don't like the idea of an axe lodged in my head."

Heleena laughed. "Father likes you, besides there's no need for them to know. Yet."

Will pulled her to him and kissed her.

They stood and dressed. Holding hands, they walked back to Ulfor.

Marie's stew was one of the best Will had eaten.

"You have an appetite there boy," noted Foothark, as Will scraped his bowl clean.

"Bloody nice feed," said Will, wiping juice from his chin with the back of his hand.

Foothark gestured for Will to have more. Without objection, Will refilled his bowl. Sitting down beside Heleena, he began demolishing his second bowl.

"What happens now that you two are lovers?" asked Marie.

Will almost choked.

"Mother?" asked Heleena.

"I saw you walking out of the forest, hand in hand."

"I do not know what you mean," Heleena maintained an air of innocence.

"Look at your clothes," insisted Marie.

Their clothes were wrinkled and dirty.

"Your clothes were not that filthy when you left earlier," said Marie.

"And you boy," added Foothark, "I see you have grazes on the back of your legs. You were on the bottom I warrant," he guffawed.

"Father!" admonished Heleena.

Marie gave Foothark a warning glance and the older man continued to eat his meal in silence.

"We are not angry," spoke Marie.

"You aren't?" Will asked.

The older man winked. "Boy, my daughter has been looking for a man for many years, it pleases me that she has finally found one."

Will felt Heleena relax beside him. "I thought you would be full of rage," spoke Heleena. "And his name is Will!" she admonished her father.

"Of course we are not angry. The Gods have presented our daughter with a husband."

Husband. The word did not intimidate Will. As he looked at Heleena's beautiful face, he knew that he would have no qualms in proposing to her.

Even though she had admonished her father, Heleena knew he called Will "boy" because he saw the young man as the son he never had.

"But what if I leave this place?" asked Will.

"I would go with you!" said Heleena.

"But your life's here," said Will. "I'm from another place, another time."

Heleena's eyes glinted with anger.

"Don't get me wrong, I want you to come," Will whispered to her, placing his hand around her waist. "I want you with me, but what would your parents think?"

"You speak as if we do not hear your words, boy," chuckled Foothark. "The Gods give and they take away, our fate, our skane, is woven by Odin's will. If our daughter leaves, then her skane was bespoken long before Marie and I were born. Who are we to question the will of Odin? And besides which, I know that she is in good hands." Foothark smiled at Will.

These were a people whose lives were ruled by the Gods they worshipped with devotion, realised Will, and it made them all the stronger. It even made them dangerous.

The warriors could enter battle without fear, in the belief that if they died then not only was it the will of Odin, but they would also be rewarded. And if they lived then Odin had other plans for them.

* * * * *

The next morning, the Australians were woken by shouts and the clash of steel. The soldiers had gathered on the outskirts of an open field near the village, deerskins wrapped about their shoulders. They watched in confusion as warriors, some dressed in chain mail, others in hardened leather, fought mock battles. The noise was overwhelming. Amongst the shouts, battle cries and occasional laughter was the clash of steel. The dull thud of sword blows being blocked by shields and the clatter of shields slamming against one another. One man cursed, threw his sword to the ground and held his hand over a wound on his forehead.

A large group of women were on the opposite side of the field practising throwing knives, and fighting daggers, bows and spears. The soldiers, thinking the worst, had their weapons with them in case they were needed to defend the village.

"Four days between each full moon, the village practices with weapons," explained Berag.

"So this is normal?" Scott gestured at the distant fighting.

"Four times between each full moon, yes," Berag said as their looks turned from worry to interest.

As the minutes passed, the Australians noticed they were not alone. The elders of the village had gathered close by and were watching the proceedings. They pointed and commenting about certain individuals either for their skill, courage or clumsiness.

"Skyaldaborg!" the distant voice roared.

The Australians watched as warriors sprinted to one central point. A dull rattling was heard as shields slammed together as the warriors formed a line, twenty warriors wide, and two deep. A man of medium height but wide shoulders stood before the shield wall. Even from a distance, it was clear that he was instructing the warriors. Although the boom of his voice could be heard, the Australians could not make out his words.

At one point, he ran forward and launched a kick into the shield wall sending one man sprawling to the floor. The two men behind him stumbled backwards.

The instructor loomed over the downed man and roared at him. Then the instructor took hold of the warrior's mail shirt and pulled him to his feet.

The Ulfor villagers dispersed into pairs, practising their sword skills again. Again, they were interrupted when the instructor called for the shield wall. The warriors sprinted back as before. This time the instructor seemed satisfied, because although he could be heard bellowing, he did not attack them.

The Australians watched the warriors practising manoeuvres in the shield wall. Will was engrossed in the group of women on the other side of the field. He was watching Heleena throw small knives from a leather belt across her body. She had thrown six knives with aggression and precision at the face, throat and chest of a straw- filled dummy stood twenty metres from her. Heleena also carried two larger daggers on each hip.

When the women began to spar, Will watched the knives with foot-long blades in Heleena's hands. She held the knife in her right hand with the blade towards the sky, but the knife in her left followed the angle of her forearm. Will watched her with interest. Within seconds, her actions were explained. Heleena's opponent concentrated on avoiding her right hand as it stabbed towards her belly. This left the knife in her off hand open to slash across and cut into her opponent's shoulder, arm or throat.

None of the women were hurt. The blows that would have killed an enemy stopped short, so blades touched skin to show they had been beaten. As far as Will could see, Heleena was never beaten. She was perhaps the fastest and most deadly.

The battle practise went on for most of the day. As they walked back towards Ulfor, the villagers tired and dirty, were in good spirits. Matt tended to the more serious abrasions and lacerations.

Within an hour, the village had returned to normal. While the rest of the Australians ate with Berag and his family, Will had excused himself so he could be with Heleena. She was like a drug, and he was addicted.

Once they had eaten Marie's beef stew, of which Will had three helpings, the couple walked outside. They each wore a deerskin, which as Will discovered kept him warmer than any space blanket.

"Remind me never to get on the wrong side of you," smiled Will, as they sat down in the cave refuge.

"So you saw me today?" she asked.

"Yeah, I saw you, you're a regular bloody knife fighter."

"I prefer the bow. I have only had to kill a man with my knives once before and that was because my arrows were spent."

"What happened?" asked Will.

Heleena shrugged. "It was a Viking raid. They came in the early dawn, before the sun rose above the mountains. Our men met them outside the village, but they had little warning. The Vikings broke into the village within moments. Our men regrouped and the fighting began, sometimes within homes. It was the worst raid we have ever experienced. I was firing arrows from the roof of my parent's house. I had felled perhaps ten raiders but ran out of arrows so I started climbing down. Someone grabbed me from behind and I thought it was father until I smelled the stink of the man. I was either about to be killed or raped. I twisted in his grip, knocked his sword away and stabbed a blade into his throat. As he fell, I stabbed his midriff too. I watched that man die. He died a slow agonising death."

Will watched as she hugged her knees and stared out into the forest, reliving the hellish moment. He stroked her hair and drew her to him, She wrapped her arms around him and snuggled into his chest.

* * * * *

The sun was hidden behind thick clouds above the mountains the next morning. A dull grey lit the village at daybreak. Will's boots crunched and sank into thick snow. He wore a woollen cap, his uniform, a deerskin and a thick woollen blanket over that. He had not slept well. The forest nearby was tinged white, and snow fell. He had left his weapon in the house and felt naked without it as he walked towards the forest. Within minutes, he was urinating against a tree. Steam rose from the warm liquid as it trickled down frosty bark. He zipped up his trousers and walked on, looking up at the silent forest canopy. Even in the cold of a winter dawn birds welcomed the new day. He took a deep breath and let it out. Will was aware that in cold weather to inhale through the nose as it filtered, warmed and humidified the air before it reached the lungs.

Will detected distant footfalls and turned. He watched Heleena approach with a smile. He took her in his arms and kissed her.

"Let us walk," she said.

They walked hand in hand for several minutes. Whilst the path through the forest was visible, it was covered by several inches of snow and several times Will almost tripped on roots or rocks.

"You are clumsy," laughed Heleena.

"You're not wrong."

They walked in silence for another few minutes before Will sensed that Heleena was melancholy.

"What's wrong?" he asked.

"I have had a wonderful time with you," she said. "I have never met a man like you. But that just reminds me that soon the Kadark and his men will be amongst us. War will be upon us. It will be like no Viking raid we have ever seen."

"Then we'll fight them," he said.

"What if they are too many? What if you fall?"

"I guarantee as long as I've got ammo, we'll hold them at bay," Will reassured her.

She frowned. "I am not sure you understand the threat, Will."

"I'm sure your village will pull through. You've never seen our weapons before and I think you'll be surprised when you see them in action."

"Let us hope so," Heleena said, coming to a halt. She was peering down the path, her head cocked as if listening for something.

"Someone is coming," she said, grabbing Will's arm and leading him behind a thick bush. She pulled off her cloak and dropped it. Now she was wearing a loose fitting dress that barely covered her body. Over that was her throwing knife belt. She pulled one of the razor-sharp knives out, her eyes still on the path.

Will was trying to keep his mind off her seductive body. There was a crack like a twig snapping. Soft footfalls approached. His mind became blank. He moved so he could see the path through a gap in the bush. The top of a man's head came into view, then his face. Relaxing, he watched Heleena re-sheath the knife and put her cloak back on.

"Ho, Thormdall," called Heleena.

"Ho," the berserker replied when he saw them. "There is a problem. The pigs coming inland to our village a-viking are here, well at least their scouts are. Three of them."

"Where?" Heleena asked.

"I killed them," he replied.

It was then that Will noticed the blood on the Berserker's clothes.

"I killed their swords too," the berserker added. He turned and pointed down the path from where he had come. "I came across them just down the forest path." He seemed unruffled by the incident.

"Were there any others?" Heleena asked.

"Not that I could see. But there will be more later today. By this night we will see battle, of that I am sure."

Heleena took a deep breath and closed her eyes, as if to blot out a terrible vision. "We had better tell Romeeros and Berag."

Will was about to asked how ones kills a sword, but thought better of it. He could always ask later.

The trio ran through the forest towards Ulfor, the blistering cold sweeping past Will's face and filling his lungs. Before long, the village appeared through the foliage as they emerged from the forest. They hurried to Berag's house and Thormdall rapped on the door. As the heavy door opened Helga and the smell of frying bacon and egg confronted them.

"They are here," said Thormdall.

Those three words were like a bolt of lightning to Helga. She gasped and her eyes widened. For a moment, she said nothing. Then she turned and called Berag, before inviting them in.

Will shivered as the warmth enveloped him. He put his arm around Heleena's waist and drew her close. Berag rose from beside the fire where he was playing with his daughter, Tina. He smiled at the newcomers. When he had heard Thormdall's news, the smile disappeared from the big man's face. Berag strode past them and pulled a large goat horn from the wall. The horn was ivory white with thin bands of gold etched into the surface that formed intricate patterns.

He walked outside and a long, deep, booming blast sounded around the village. The horn blew again.

"To arms!" roared Berag. "To arms!"

Will could hear distant shouts as Berag came back into the house and spoke to Will.

"We go to war," he said. "Gather your friends and your weapons and meet me outside the Great Hall."

Will turned to leave, noticing that Thormdall had already gone. Will and Heleena ran back to her parent's house, where Foothark, her father, was waiting. He already had his sword belted to his waist and an iron helmet clasped in his hand.

Will smiled at Marie. Heleena's mother looked worried, but she returned an anxious smile. Will grabbed his weapon, assault helmet and his webbing and rushed outside.

"No, I forbid you to go!"

Will thought Marie was talking to him but he turned to see Heleena trying to following him, a bow and a quiver of arrows in hand.

"I will not stand by, while our village is attacked!" Heleena argued.

Foothark joined his wife. "No you will not. You will stay and defend the village with the others. If they break through us, we will need you here."

Anger washed over Heleena's face. "I am a better fighter than all the women and half of the men of this village! I will come. I am of age and can think for myself! Besides there is nothing for you to worry about Father, I can kill a man from fifty paces," she said, holding up the bow.

Marie pleaded with Heleena, but the young woman would have none of it. She gave her mother a brief hug before taking Will's hand.

"Come, let us go," said Foothark leading them to the Great Hall where people were gathering.

"Took your fuckin' time didn't ya?" Scott grinned. The soldier looked at Heleena with appreciation and noticed they were holding hands. He winked at Will.

"Yeah, been hangin' round you too long. What's the plan, Boss?"

Will asked Steve. He could see Matt jogging towards them amongst a group of warriors.

"Dunno yet. Let's see what Berag wants first. We'll work round him," Steve replied.

They could see Berag running towards them. He was dressed in a knee length chain mail coat. On his head he wore a silver helmet that covered his whole head save for the eyeholes, his mouth and chin. It reflected the light like a beacon and was well cared for. In his hand, he carried a battle-axe with a haft at least four feet long. Will noticed small intertwining vines carved all over the metal axe head. He also saw a word written in the runic language on the wooden haft.

Silence fell when Berag arrived. He strode into the centre of the Ulfor men who had now formed a circle around their chieftain.

"You all know why you have been summoned!" he said, his voice deep and strong. "The enemy is upon us! If we can move to the Valley of Ikthallon before they advance there then we have a good chance at victory. That is if their numbers are not strong. We must move!"

"Make haste. This is a war party. They come to kill and to rape and to burn. Even if they break through us, which, Odin willing, they will not, it will be a difficult task for them to locate what it is they seek." Berag coughed and spat on the ground. "Are there any questions?"

"Just one," Steve said. All eyes turned to him. "I notice that you have most of the men in the village here. Shouldn't some stay back and defend the village and protect the women?"

Berag let out a loud, genuine laugh that was accompanied by chuckles from the other warriors.

"Our women are equal or better warriors than ourselves! In fact, many of the women will fight with us today. Odin help those pack of cowards if they do break through us, they will wish they had not been born!"

As Berag spoke, Steve looked around. He noticed a blonde haired woman leaning on her bow. She was watching Steve with an amused expression. Several other women held swords, long knives or spears. Not one looked like a hapless maiden. In fact, Steve noticed, there was perhaps one woman for every four men here. Heleena was stringing her bow next to Will and had a cluster of lethal looking knives sheathed in a belt across her chest. She leaned into Will and whispered. Will laughed.

"Point taken," Steve nodded.

"We leave now!" Berag shouted. "Our forward scout is already long gone, let us march with speed and may Odin watch over his children!"

A great roar went up and the group of warriors ran towards the forest. As he ran, Will made sure that Heleena remained in front, not to be a gentleman, but so he could watch her body from behind.

Scott noticed that the women of Ulfor were standing outside, watching them leave. But they were not sobbing and waving goodbye as they did in Hollywood movies.

They were standing, knives and bows in hand, ready for battle. This was a warrior race, bred not only to fight, but to win.

CHAPTER 11

Trees whipped by as they ran, the scent of fresh snow filled their nostrils and the sound of birds taking flight stirred the forest silence. The warriors ran in single file along the forest track, determined to close with their enemy. Steve was somewhere in the middle of the pack. He could see neither the front nor the rear of the travelling column.

Even weighed down with armour and weapons, they maintained a fast pace. These were a fit, strong people. The path ascended for several minutes, and their feet sank into the blanket of snow.

Steve heard shouting and laughing ahead. Another roar of triumph sounded and the men close to Steve pointed to the left, laughing.

"Thormdall has already begun his work!" a gruff voice shouted.

Steve saw that fresh blood had stained the snow scarlet. Three bodies had been dragged into the scrub and half buried in snow. He could make out the foot of one man and the half-buried, pale face of another. They must have been enemy scouts. The main force would not be far now. It would not be a good thing, Steve thought, to meet the enemy on a narrow path like this.

Will, who was behind Steve, looked at the corpses as he ran past. They had been buried. They must have been the warriors Thormdall had intercepted earlier that morning. Will noticed that beside one of the bodies was a sword that had been bent in half and dropped on the ground. Will remembered Thormdall's comment about killing their enemy's weapons. It was a question he would ask Thormdall when this was over.

Heleena was jogging but not even breathing hard. Although Will was fit and able to maintain the pace, he knew that at this speed he would only be good for another ten or fifteen kilometres. Heleena, with longbow, quiver of arrows, throwing knives and leather breastplate, looked as if she could hold the pace all day.

Steve almost lost his footing as the path descended. He righted himself. Ahead there was shouting and laughing. A man had fallen and rolled off to one side to avoid being trampled as his comrades ran past. He climbed to his feet, brushed himself off and continued running.

Matt was beginning to experience tightness in his chest and could already feel the lactic acid burning its way into his thighs and calves. A heavy hand slapped him on the shoulder.

"How goes it?" asked Berag, running alongside.

"Good," replied Matt, wiping his forehead.

Berag was running up the line slowing to talk or encourage individual warriors before moving on. Berag himself did not show signs of weariness, even though the chain mail he wore looked to weigh more than ten kilograms. He was a strong man.

Matt ensured he was at the action condition for the third time. The safety catch of his weapon was engaged so the rifle would not discharge by accident. He had plenty of spare ammunition and the first aid pack, the most important pieces of equipment, on his back.

Scott remained several warriors behind Matt. The Minimi he was carrying clanked and rubbed against his webbing as he ran. He was looking forward to this encounter. He felt they were at last taking a step towards returning home. More shouting rang out from the front of the line, only this time it was different. This time they sounded aggressive. They resembled drunken shouts heard outside dodgy nightclubs in the city, just before punches were thrown.

A deep horn blast echoed through the forest. The blast came again and the warriors quickened their pace. Scott could see an opening in the forest ahead and a blue, cloud-dotted sky beyond. They moved clear of the snow-covered forest and joined the large gathering of warriors ahead. Berag stood at the front of the group.

The valley was one big firing lane. Sheer, snow-capped cliffs rose to the left and right. The only way out was the way they had come, or where their enemy had appeared from the forest on the other side. From what Steve could see there was nowhere to go and the battle about to be fought would be messy. Steve turned and caught Scott's eye. He signalled for him to come to him. He shouted out to Matt in the near distance. Nodding, the balding medic made his way over. Steve spotted Will who had already seen him and was making his way over, shadowed by Heleena.

"Okay, I assume these guys will charge each other," said Steve. "Now when the—"

"Who?" Scott asked, sweat trickling down his forehead.

"Them!" replied Steve, pointing to the other side of the valley where the enemy stood. They seemed demoralised and weather-beaten, but that could well have been how they looked rather than how they felt. It was obvious they were keen to fight.

"Shit, they're here already. Sorry, go on," said Scott.

"Anyway, as I was saying, when they do charge each other, Will, Matt and myself will be positioned right here."

"We will take single shots where, and when, we can. Try not to hit Berag's warriors. Scott just short bursts on the gun, mate. Conserve your ammo and make every shot count. We haven't got the luxury of resup here."

Steve paused. "Now Scott while this is happening, I want you to steer wide of the battle and make your way round to the other side, where the enemy is standing now. Once they have charged, the enemy will be down in the basin of the valley so you should be safe up there."

Scott liked that word "should"; it always added an element of spice to life. That was one of the reasons he had joined the SASR.

"You will be our cut-off party. Any of the enemy come back your way looking to retreat, brass 'em up. You've got a claymore?"

Scott shook his head.

"Yeah I have," said Matt opening a pouch on his webbing and taking out a claymore mine and handing it over to Scott.

"Good," Steve said. "Get that set up, Scott. And stay out of sight once you've found your position. And wait." "Got ya boss," said Scott.

"Good," Steve said. "Now ammo, how much have each of you got?"

"Three full mags," Matt said. "Same," replied Will.

"Two belts of two hundred rounds," said Scott. "One belt in the mag," he said patting the camouflage canvas magazine attached to the light machinegun. "The other's a loose belt in my webbing."

"Right. I've got two full mags. Today we'll use just one mag each," Steve said to Matt and Will. "Scott, use as little as you can, but enough to be effective. You'll be in more danger than we will up here, so if you run out and need the extra belt, use it. Okay?"

"Don't need to tell me twice," said Scott.

"Right, any questions?" Steve asked. They all shook their heads.

The four soldiers moved towards the larger group of warriors. Down in the valley stood Thormdall, facing the enemy with his sword in hand.

"Berag," called Steve. "We will be killing the enemy from up here, but it's important that when the enemy break to retreat that your warriors don't follow them!"

"Why?" asked Berag.

"Because we'll have a man on the other side of the valley and he'll be shooting into the enemy as they retreat. Our weapons are powerful." He pulled out a bullet from one of his spare magazines. "This is what the weapon fires," Steve explained. "It may look small but it is many times more powerful than your bows. Most of these little… arrows," it was the only way he could think of explaining it to Berag, "that we fire, will pass through the bodies of the men we kill. So if your warriors follow the enemy as they retreat and my man begins firing, his arrows will also hit your men. Do you understand?"

Berag looked at the bullet. "I do not understand how this works," the chieftain said, "but I understand what you are saying. I will call my warriors back once the enemy have retreated."

Steve nodded. "Good."

Silence reigned throughout the valley as the Ulfor warriors eyed their enemy. Steve moved back to the other soldiers. They watched Thormdall raise his sword above his head and walk towards the enemy warriors.

Now that the brief was out the way and his soldiers knew what they were doing, Steve had time to take in the force opposing them. They seemed to be made up of young men and teenage boys. Few of them had armour, and those that did wore half-rusted, cheap- looking chain mail. Most of them wore iron helmets that shone in the morning sun. There was a big difference between the two forces. Berag's warriors seemed larger and fitter, although that could well have been the distance playing tricks on his eyes. Their equipment was also better maintained. Their chain mail was oiled and helmets polished. Their weapons were immaculate: each sword, axe or bow gleamed in the sun. The Ulfor people had something to fight for and something to defend, even if it meant giving their lives in the process. That was the difference.

"I do not see the Kadark," said Berag from the front of the Ulfor gathering. He sounded concerned.

Steve guessed the reason why. The Kadark may have a second force, so this rag tag group would be a diversion. The main force might be making their way around the mountain ranges to attack their village. Either that or this was an advance force sent forward of the main pack. If this were the case, then the main force would be a large one indeed.

A deep voice bellowed out. It was Thormdall, who had advanced half way between the Ulfor people and their enemy on the other side. The berserker still held his sword above his head. He shouted again, plunging his sword into the ground in front of him. Raising both his arms, he threw back his head and roared in a language foreign to Steve.

"What the hell's he doing?" asked Steve to himself more than anything.

"He is offering them a challenge," replied Heleena. "This entire battle can be settled between Thormdall and one of their Berserkers if they have any. Either that or it will be between Thormdall and their leader. It saves a lot of bloodshed and does not take as long," Heleena explained. "But it does not look like that will happen on this morning."

"What is he saying?" asked Steve, as Thormdall boomed once more.

She shrugged. "We do not know. It is a language that only Berserkers are taught. Before you ask, one can only become a Berserker when one kills a full-grown bear or wolf, single-handed at, or before, the age of twelve summers. Berserkers are warriors chosen by Odin. If the boy is killed by the animal or lives but fails to kill the animal, then the Father God has not chosen him. Thormdall killed an adult brown bear just before his eleventh summer. Word spreads around the land when something like this happens. When other Berserkers heard of Thormdall, they came to Ulfor to make sure what they heard was correct before taking him away for his training."

She fell silent as she watched the proceedings.

"No Berserker has responded or stepped forward to take the challenge. Thormdall will now issue the challenge again in our language."

Steve assumed that if this second challenge went unanswered then an open battle would follow. Heleena interpreted for the Australians.

"Hear me, those who stand against us!" Thormdall's voice called. "Let us settle this now!" He went silent for a moment. "Come forward your leader, I will send you on your way! This fight is one of honour! You can be welcomed to the Hall by the Father God! Why die for nothing when you can die a hero!" He roared the final word.

Silence followed and for some time no one moved. Then Steve noticed movement at the back of the enemy. Their leader seemed to have risen to the challenge.

"Blasphemer!" roared a voice amongst the rabble and a bowman pushed his way clear. In one fluid motion, he brought his weapon up and released an arrow. The projectile screamed as it cut through the air towards its target. Thormdall did not move as the arrow missed his face by a narrow margin and slammed into the earth behind him. Will realised that the enemy warriors were Christians, or as Heleena called them Chreest Men.

"So it begins," said Heleena.

"Ready yourselves!" shouted Berag to his warriors.

"Odin still watches you," roared Thormdall to his enemy. "Today he will make you regret you ever turned away from him!"

This was met by a deafening roar and the Ulfor warriors burst forward like water from a broken dam.

"You blokes right?" shouted Steve to the other soldiers. "Yeah, all sweet," Scott shouted with a grin.

"Take care ay?" Will shouted, grabbing Heleena's hand.

The young woman laughed as if she would not for one moment be in any danger. She pulled away, running at the rear of the Ulfor charge alongside the other bowmen and women.

The enemy warriors charged towards the motionless Thormdall, who waited, sword in hand. For a moment, it seemed that the Ulfor people would not make it to Thormdall in time. But a moment later they charged around him and stopped, forming a tight shield wall.

"Righto, Matt and Will spread yourselves out, ten metres apart. Remember make your shots count. Scott, you know what to do, mate?" called Steve as he got down on his belly.

"Yup, she's sweet boss, don't worry about me."

Steve looked through his ACOG scope and applied gentle pressure to the trigger as a soldier ran into the middle of his target reticule. The faces of his wife and children leapt into his mind.

He wondered how they were and what they were doing. This was a familiar occurrence for Steve before he went into combat. He hated taking life but unfortunately, like the other soldiers next to him, he was good at it. Taking another breath and forcing his family from his mind, Steve released the shot. He watched the man crumple before moving on to another target. From this distance and over the noise, he was sure none of the fighting warriors would be able to hear the rifle shots. They would be confused if they heard the gunfire.

He heard a rifle bark from his right. Meanwhile, a large axe-bearing thug of a warrior was charging into the fray and was about to take an Ulfor man. Steve squeezed the trigger again. The rifle bucked into his shoulder and the familiar sound of an empty brass shell bouncing onto the ground gave him comfort. He watched the warrior's lifeless body slam into the ground.

The charge on both sides came to a halt as they searched the valley for the source of the gunshots. Terror rippled across both the Viking force and the Ulfor villagers. Some dropped their weapons and fled screaming, thinking the gods themselves were attacking them.

The familiar, distinct bark of an M4 came from Steve's right again. It was immediately followed by a string of swear words.

"Ya bastard! You shot my target!" yelled Matt.

"Yeah well, first in first served," replied Will, firing again. "Right, I'm off!" shouted Scott, loping off to the left.

The Ulfor villagers re-joined combat, but many threw worried glances over shoulders with each gunshot. Almost a quarter of the Viking force had fled as the soldiers opened fire.

"Okay," replied Steve. He paused and raised his head to look over the scope. "Bloody hell," he said.

At the back were about fifteen bowmen and women, Heleena amongst them. More than half the archers were women and they were pouring arrows into the fray with amazing accuracy. But this was not what had drawn Steve's attention. He had seen many war movies with the two opposing sides charging into each other hacking and slashing. But this was different. This was unlike any movie he had ever seen. Another rifle burst into life and a bowman at the back of the enemy force fell to the ground, lifeless.

The Ulfor warriors were skilled fighters. Their swords and axes carved the air in graceful patterns and spatters of blood spewed from their weapons in thin arcs of red. They fought behind the shield wall with discipline. Several warriors in the second rank carried four-foot axes, which they chopped down over the heads of those in front smashing shields to shards. The men in front would then skewer their unprotected enemy. The aggressive shouting and piercing sound of metal on metal filled the valley, but it mingled with another sound. The sound of the wounded.

The wounded did not hold in the pain with quiet gasps as Steve had seen on videos pumped out by the film industry. These men were wounded. They screamed in agony and writhed on the ground in their own blood, urine, faeces and intestines until death took them.

He could see Thormdall at the centre and finally understood what people meant when they discussed his battle exploits. The Ulfor warriors were good fighters, but Steve could see that their movements were fuelled by anger, aggression, even fear. But Thormdall seemed completely relaxed and moved with grace. His sword seemed to float through the air with fluid precision. It looked like a fast version of a Tai Chi meditation. Thormdall never stopped moving, nor did the steel grey blur of his sword. Even from a distance, Steve could see the enemy bowing backwards as men tried to avoid Thormdall. The man was unbeatable. Unstoppable.

"Cover Scott!" yelled Will.

Dropping his head, Steve stared through the ACOG scope. He watched an enemy warrior sprinting towards Scott who was running on the outskirts of the battle towards the opposite side of the valley. Giving the man a slight lead, Steve released the round, which tore through the warrior's chest and exited in a fine spray of blood. He was dead before he hit the ground.

Scott did not look around, but raised his hand in thanks as he ran. Whilst the three men continued their murderous work from above, Scott disappeared into the tree line on the other side.

The soldiers continued releasing well-placed shots until the enemy began streaming for the trees. Ulfor warriors began chasing them wielding weapons above their heads. With relief, Steve watched Berag gesturing for them to fall back to the other side of the valley. With reluctance, they did as they were told. Steve watched as two hundred enemy warriors ran towards Scott's position. He had not expected the enemy to flee so early in the battle. Now Scott could be overrun by the sheer weight of numbers. Berag waited until all his warriors had past him before heading back to where the three soldiers lay.

What the Ulfor warriors did not see was a dark cloaked figure on horseback that had burst from the forest. It was galloping towards the withdrawing Ulfor group. The mounted dark garbed figure, who Steve assumed must have been the Kadark, drew a sword and slashed his way through his own men. Before any of them had a chance to think, the rider had smashed the flat of the weapon across the back of Berag's head. As the chieftain fell unconscious, the rider leaned down, grabbed him. With inhuman strength hauled the limp Ulfor chieftain onto the horse in front of him.

"Has anyone got a clear shot?" roared Steve.

"Get out of the way!" yelled Matt, climbing to his feet to see if he could shoot over the heads of the returning Ulfor warriors milling around in front of them. He pulled the rifle into his shoulder, but a clear shot was impossible.

"Shit!" Matt shouted. "No!"

* * * * *

After checking the claymore, Scott returned to his position and lay down. Pulling the Minimi into his shoulder and flicking the safety catch off, Scott stared down the ACOG sight at the men charging towards him.

There was a thundering crash to his left and what sounded like a horse galloping off into the forest. He shook his head and decided he must have imagined it.

Scott returned his attention to the warriors who were running towards him. There were far more than he imagined. He had expected perhaps fifty, but there appeared to be more than one hundred enemy warriors fleeing towards his position.

They looked frightened, many of them casting glances over their shoulders as they ran. He had positioned the claymore some distance in front, near the tree line. The wire connecting the detonator to initiating device, known as 'the clacker', lay on the forest floor. 'The clacker', near Scott's right hand was a device that sent an electrical pulse along the wire and into the detonator. The detonator caused 700 grams of C-4 to explode, sending 700 small steel balls screaming towards the enemy. It was a primitive weapon but effective.

"Here we go," said Scott to himself. He opened fire with the Minimi machinegun. The first burst echoed out over the valley, tearing several men from their feet. The second burst exploded from the light machinegun. Scott noticed the Ulfor warriors stopped and turned to watch proceedings. The enemy warriors themselves panicked but did not know where the new enemy lay. So they continued to run straight for Scott's position. Some veered off to the left.

The machinegun continued to bark out long bursts, killing and wounding. Scott fired another burst, and another. Repeatedly he dealt out death until the barrel was smoking and the enemy was almost on top of him. He fired again, but after two rounds, the gun went dead. He swore. He was out of ammunition. Scott did not have time to reload and he was about to be overrun. Standing, he stamped on 'the clacker' with a snarl and a mountainous BOOM exploded as warriors were cut down. The metal ball bearings slammed into their bodies, bouncing off bone and exiting in a bloody swathe. He stooped, picked up the belt of ammunition from the ground and tucked it between his webbing belt and body.

By now, almost half the men who had retreated were down. Seeing Scott stand, some of the rest let out a victorious whoop, and charged towards him. The others yelled in terror and ran into the forest out of sight. Scott pulled out his 9mm pistol and shot the first man who reached him in the face.

Sprinting out Scott ran in a wide arc to avoid the group of enemy seeking him. He broke clear of the trees, turned mid-stride and releasing a shot into the chest of a man on top of him. Shooting another two warriors, he turned and began running again.

"Cover me!" roared Scott, sprinting towards friendly ground.

Before the words had left his mouth, the familiar zip of a bullet at close range tore past his head taking out a warrior running to catch him. Scott was running too fast now to turn and take an accurate shot. He hoped that with each hiss or crack of bullets at close range, would encourage the men chasing him to give up and turn away.

They did when Scott had reached the half waypoint. The rifle shots did not stop. They continued firing and each time that familiar rifle bark resounded around the valley, an enemy warrior died.

Scott saw Will push himself into a kneeling position and fire his 203 with a hollow thunk that sent a small black round in a steep arc towards the enemy. Scott watched the progress of the 40mm grenade as it hammered into the ground. It exploded with devastating effect amongst the small group of retreating warriors. It ripped half of them from their feet, while the others made for the safety of the forest without daring to look back. The Ulfor warriors flinched as the grenade exploded, their faces registering shock and disbelief.

"Yeah not bad, eh?" asked Scott as he arrived beside the conglomerate of Ulfor warriors. He bent forward to recover his breath.

"It's called a gren—"

Scott fell silent as he noticed that Steve wore a shocked expression.

Even Thormdall's face seemed tense.

"What?" Scott asked, looking across the valley.

"They captured Berag," replied Steve, applying the safety catch on his rifle. "Must have thought he'd have the crystal, being the chieftain."

"Christ, I completely missed that," said Scott. "How the fuck did they manage that?"

"Some weird looking bloke in a dark robe, couldn't see his face. After the retreat, he came charging out of the forest on horseback. Knocked Berag out with the flat of his sword and pulled him up on the horse before taking off."

"The bastard used one hand to do it as well," added Will. "Berag is a big bloke, but this robed fella reached down and picked Berag up like he was a child. Bloody unbelievable."

All was quiet save for the distant screams and groans of the wounded in the valley below.

"Come now," called Thormdall regaining his composure. "Let us gather our dead and be gone."

"But we must take Berag back!" shouted one of the warriors.

"Yes," replied Thormdall. "But not now! We must regroup, we will return to the village and seek Romeeros out. He will be able to help. You think we could help Berag in this condition?"

It was not hard to see that the warriors were exhausted. Many of them were wounded, the blood soaking through their clothes or sliding over their skin to drip to the snow below.

"We would be more of a hindrance than a help, trust me," assured Thormdall, but his eyes shone with pride. Even exhausted, Berag's people were willing to hunt for him and fight their way into hell to bring him home. Steve knew that it would not have been any different if any one of them had been taken. It was born of honour and courage, an ethic that was endemic to many special-forces elements in the modern world.

"We will return as soon as we can." Thormdall turned back to the valley and the bloody mess that was left there.

"We must take the bodies of our heroes home. Their families will wish to say farewell before they are buried."

Matt was tending to the wounded. He dressed and cleaned wounds, stitched deep lacerations, and administered morphine to a man with a wound down to his bone.

Some of the enemy warriors still lived although they carried serious wounds. Instead of killing them, the Ulfor people dragged them off to the side and left them there. The weapons of the wounded warriors were brought to them and pressed into their hand. The weapons of the dead enemy were bent or broken before being cast into the snow.

Will seized his opportunity.

"What are you doing?" he asked Foothark. The old man turned to face him and Will noticed he had a deep gash on the side of his face.

"I am killing this man's sword," the old warrior said. The deceased man was on his back, with his dry, dead eyes staring up at the sky. Blood had dried as it had trickled from the side of his mouth. Around his neck, attached with cheap looking string hung a wooden crucifix carved with little skill.

"Chreest man?" asked Will. The old man nodded. He held the dead man's sword with the tip in the ground whilst he placed his foot onto the middle of the blade and pushed with all his weight. With a metallic groan, the sword began to bend and then snapped.

Foothark threw the weapon onto the snow where it lay beside the other broken half. "Cheap metal," he said with disgust.

"Why do you kill their swords?" Will asked.

"I should not be offering you this knowledge as it is sacred, but seeing as you are not of our culture I will explain." Foothark touched the wound on his cheek. Wincing, he cleared his throat. "When a man dies in battle, he is looked upon as a hero. But to be a true hero, he must have his sword in his hand to be welcomed into the Hall of Heroes. These….men," he spat, "are not heroes, nor do they deserve a hero's welcome. When we kill their weapons, they are left without anything. Any credibility they had in life…if any is lost to them. They will wander the afterlife lost and weaponless. They will be shunned by better men and disowned by the Gods. The weapon is also imbued with the spirit of the owner. When our weapons are created, we cut our master hand and let our blood drip onto the blade when it is created by the blacksmith. The name of the weapon is spoken as this happens, breathing life into it. When a weapon is killed, this spirit is also destroyed."

Will nodded. "What about them?" he asked, pointing to the wounded enemy warriors lined up one beside the other, weapons in hand. Some were whimpering, others screaming or writhing in agony. Still others lay down with their eyes screwed up and teeth clenched in pain.

"Will you help them or kill them?" Will asked, as Foothark made his way to the next dead warrior, taking up the deceased man's axe. "Neither. It is not for us to know the will of the Gods. We leave them for the wrath or forgiveness of the Gods. If they fought well, then Teer the War God will convince the Father God to give them back their life. They will heal, take their weapon and be gone where they will. But seeing as they have cast aside the Gods, denied their existence and placed their belief in falsities then I doubt any of them will walk away from here. Once they are dead then we will kill their weapons too. But not before." Foothark threw the broken axe away and moved onto the next lifeless body.

It took several hours before the Ulfor people had finished. Nine of their number had been killed. Their bodies were carried from the valley with their weapons strapped to their arms so as they were not dropped. Thirty-one warriors were wounded, six carried critical wounds. These were helped out of the valley. Matt had done what he could for them with the limited supplies he had. The enemy dead were stacked and left to rot. None of the dead bodies had been looted, nothing had been stolen. Taking a man's possessions in life or in death was against the will of the Gods, Foothark informed Will.

In the time it had taken the Ulfor warriors to gather their dead and wounded, three enemy wounded had died. Their weapons were also killed and their bodies dumped on the pile in the middle of the valley.

Steve felt a pang of guilt as he followed the large group of Ulfor warriors into the forest. He turned one last time to look out over the valley. A light snowfall had started and the wind had picked up, masking the cries from the dying enemy warriors left lying on the ground. The snow stained scarlet around them. A boom of thunder rolled across the sky and a light snow began to fall.

CHAPTER 12

The journey back to Ulfor was slow, and quiet. Gone were the laughter and jokes, gone were the light heartedness and excitement. Several of them, like young Kettle, were men who had just come of age. They had never seen a battle before, but like any young men who returned from the front line of battle, they would be changed forever. Never again would they be as innocent as they were before.

The dead warriors were passed around often amongst the group as men became tired. It would be a long day and an even longer night. Never had they lost this many warriors in a single battle. When the raiders came to Ulfor a-viking the battle was fought around, and sometimes inside, buildings. Small groups of Norse warriors fought fragmented sections of Viking raiders. The casualties were usually light, but this had been different. This had been a pitched battle. Although it was something for which they had all trained, none of the Ulfor men had fought behind the shield wall in a real battle before.

"Catch it," someone cried. Will turned to watch a sword begin to slip from the arm of a dead warrior. One of the men steadied the sword while another tightened the belt that attached it to his arm. There was a mixture of bitter sweetness in the air. It seemed that the warriors of Ulfor were both happy and sad if that were possible.

They seemed happy that all the men who had died today had done so in battle, as they all hoped to do one day. They had not died falling from a horse or at the hands of some accident. These men had died defending those they loved. There could not have been any greater honour. But the Ulfor warriors were also sombre that these men had departed to the halls of the Father God, leaving their families behind.

At last, the warriors emerged into the open and looked out over the Ulfor settlement. Scott had never taken the time to look at the village before. It was a powerful sight. The houses resembled upturned longships, so even this far inland the ocean played a significant role in the psyche of the villagers.

Behind the houses rose a monstrous mountain that was blanketed in thick white snow. The lower half was covered in forest and sections of bare rock partly hidden under a fine layer of snow.

"Mount Skane," said Thormdall, coming alongside. "She is beautiful is she not?"

Scott had never thought of mountains as beautiful, but admitted it was a powerful sight.

"She watches over us," Thormdall said.

It was always difficult for Thormdall when he saw the family of warriors who had died in battle. They rushed out of their houses, to greet the returned. As they moved through the warriors and could not find their loved ones, a disbelieving yet defiant look washed over their faces. But they continued to search. Then at last, in desperation, they looked over those who had fallen.

The dead were laid in a neat line, one beside the other, with their swords across their chests. Thormdall could see women and children running from their houses. He heard relieved voices and shouting, and watched as families reunited.

But there was one woman, now two he realised, who had not yet found their husbands. A third had found her husband amongst the dead and a small group of people had gathered around to comfort her.

Thormdall closed his eyes. "Father God lend me strength," he prayed.

The searching women refused to look at the dead warriors. They were instead pushing their way through the throng of reunited families, their faces cold with panic. One of them began calling.

"Thorkill!" she shouted. "Thorkill!"

Thorkill had been a great warrior, a man dedicated to his family and his village. Thormdall remembered four summers past. Thorkill and Thelga had been bound together in companionship under the gaze of the gods. It had been a happy time. Today was not so happy. Thorkill had killed his opponent, but at the same moment had taken a sword through the side from a nearby enemy warrior. He had fallen and died moments later on the cold ground.

"Where is father?" asked a young boy.

A warrior knelt beside the boy and pulled him into his chest.

"Your father has gone to a better place," said the man, "a much better place."

Thormdall made his way towards Thelga, who was now wild eyed. The Berserker could see that other men were doing the same for the handful of women who could not find their husbands. She pushed her way through and walked into the arms of Thormdall. He pulled her to him and held her tight.

"I am sorry Thelga. I am sorry," he spoke holding her to him.

She made a defiant noise and tried to struggle out of his grip. Relaxing, she buried her head in his cloak and began to cry.

Berag's words drifted into Steve's mind. "Even today it is possible to see the burial ships under which Orises and his father lie." The words made sense now, for these must be the burial ships that Berag had been talking about. There must have been more than one hundred of them, long and short. Some of the rocks that formed the shape of the ship were old and weatherworn. Others seemed only weeks old.

Steve's eye fell on a grave that was just three feet long. It told of the terrible pain a young couple had gone through, maybe even were still going through.

The dead warriors were each wrapped in their thick woollen cloaks. Spades were brought out and the villagers began to dig. After several hours, the graves had been dug and Romeeros arrived with a sombre, respectful purpose.

The ceremony took some time. The Australians could not understand what Romeeros said. Steve asked the people standing near him what language it was, but he was ignored; it was a sacred moment he realised.

Romeeros stood at the front of the gathering with his hands held high. It was almost as if Romeeros was speaking to the gods themselves, for he did not seem to be addressing the people at all. After a long moment of silence, Romeeros turned to the people of Ulfor.

"Today, my friends, the men and women who set forth on this morning did so with the knowledge that they might not return. Battle was done and the enemy was turned away." He motioned to the dead warriors. "But at a terrible price. Today we have lost nine good men, who were great warriors, but who were also great husbands, good fathers and skilled farmers. They died protecting that which they cared most about. Theirs was the single most powerful action of self- sacrifice. It will, let me assure you, not go unnoticed in the Great Halls of our Father God. Odin takes kindly to those who offer up their lives to protect the ones they love."

Romeeros knelt beside each dead warrior and placed a necklace around each of their necks. On each necklace was a piece of polished wood. Into each was carved the same rune: an 'A' with the crossbar running diagonal instead of horizontal.

"What does it mean?" asked Steve, hoping he would not be berated.

"It is a symbol that will distinguish these men from the others in Valholla, the Hall of Heroes," replied a warrior. "It is one of the greatest gifts a dead Norse warrior can receive."

The dead men, with their weapons in their hands, were lifted into the graves one by one. Soil filled the graves and then rocks from the base of a small nearby hill were arranged around the graves in the shape of a longship.

Over the next hour, the crowd began to disperse. As the sun began to sink, only family of the dead warriors remained. Once they had said their goodbyes, they also began to drift away. They would now have to reconstruct their lives, which had in the space of a half-day, been pulled down around their ears.

* * * * *

That night a meeting was called in the great hall.

"We lost a lot of good men today," said Thormdall, who was standing by the door. The people around the great table fell silent. The families, including the children of the men who had died, sat silent, their eyes bloodshot and rimmed with red.

"But we did what we set out to do. We turned the enemy back."

"And will there be vengeance against those who killed our people?" asked Kerlon. His voice was deep and angry.

"Aye," replied Thormdall, who knew Kerlon had lost a son today.

The Berserker turned, looked outside at the light snow continuing to fall. He could see children standing in their doorways, straining to snatch a glimpse of the meeting.

When Thormdall turned back, his eyes were filled with controlled anger. "That is why we are here," he said. "Tonight, I want all to give gifts to the gods, for there is a long journey ahead for some of us. We are here tonight about a matter we have not yet discussed."

In a fluid motion, Thormdall bent down and threw an axe that had been leaning up against the wall beside him. The weapon landed on the table with an enormous crash that made several people jump. Matt inspected the mighty axe. It had not yet been cleaned or polished and dried blood could still be seen on the blade.

"The matter of Berag. Early tomorrow morning a group of us will track his captors, kill them and bring him home. Once he is safe," Thormdall turned to Kerlon whose eyes were still misted, "we will launch a revenge raid into enemy territory."

"Now we need to decide who will go on the journey tomorrow," Thormdall said as he walked around the table.

Steve's voice rang out. "Wait," he said as people raised their hands. All eyes turned to him as he stood up. "Thormdall," he said, "this is the kind of mission we are trained for. It is what we do; it is how we make a living. The people of Ulfor are great warriors, there's no mistaking that, but most of the year you're farmers."

"So what are you suggesting?" asked Thormdall.

"Let me explain. As I said you guys are farmers, but," he held out his hands, "I take nothing away from your skills in battle. My friends and

136

I, we are soldiers, we are warriors, it's all we do, we train for nothing else than to fight."

The people around the great table looked impressed. The ability to fight or to do battle was something they respected. It was a hard life and the ability to defend oneself, one's family or one's village from threat was a good thing, even a noble thing.

"Having said that," Steve continued, "my soldiers and I work in a specialised unit. We don't always fight. In fact, a lot of our work is observation. We sit at close range and watch the enemy then pass this information back to friendly forces that wait to advance or attack. But another of our specialties is hostage retrieval."

"What do you mean by hostage?" asked Thormdall.

"A hostage is a captive, like Berag. We are trained to deal with situations like this. We can find him, get into wherever he is being held, neutralise his captors, retrieve him and get out fast. The whole thing would be over in a matter of minutes. It is something we are particularly good at."

"Then it is settled. You will lead the raid! Now who will go with these warriors?" asked Thormdall.

As hands came up again, Steve cut in.

"Hang on, Thormdall, I'm not sure you understand. You see we work in small numbers. We make less noise that way and reduce the risk of being seen. But I would ask one thing. To pull this off, we will need clothes that will help us blend in." He pointed to his own multi-cam uniform. "This will not do. We need clothes that will not arouse suspicion in villages or towns. Clothes that people will not take a second look at, old crappy clothes if you have them."

"I do not understand what you mean when you say crappy, but I am sure we can find some old clothes for you. Are you sure you do not need anyone to go with you?"

"We're sure," said Steve. He could see the disgruntled looks on the faces of some of the warriors. "Remember, once you've got your chieftain back, a revenge raid will be planned. You'll get your chance for revenge," Steve said, hoping this would subdue them.

*****

When the meeting was over, people moved back to their houses and began to prepare for the night. Many of the Norse families visited those who had lost a loved one in the battle. It would be a long night for those who would never again see their father, husband or son.

Will watched with interest as food, hunks of meat and bread, was carried out and tied to the branches of a tree near the great hall. He watched Heleena pass a loaf of bread to a man up the tree. The food dangled and swung in the breeze like giant wind charms. These must have been the offerings that Thormdall requested them to make. Sadness touched him as he thought of the men who had died today. It made him remember Dave. He had been a fine SASR trooper and was a great loss to the ranks of the regiment.

Will went inside to find Marie fussing over Foothark as he sat with a thick cloth bound to his head. He had been lucky. Had he not slipped and stumbled, the sword would have cloven into his neck.

"You are sure that no hurt was done to you?" Marie asked Will, as she tightened the makeshift bandage.

"In the name of the gods, woman, leave me alone!" complained Foothark. She slapped at his hand.

"No, I'm fine," smiled Will.

"Do you have raids every year?" Will asked, sitting down with them. "Sometimes as many as five in one year, although that has not happened for many years. Why do you ask?" said Foothark.

"It's just that you people must fight them off each time, and I don't see any serious injuries. I mean no one with missing arms or legs."

A dark look crossed Foothark's face. "Yes, to lose a limb is the worst way to die. If one is lucky then he will bleed and die within moments. But if the wound is held closed and he does not bleed out then he usually dies slow, in days, weeks or even months. Anyone who loses a limb in battle dies in agony. For some reason, their wound goes bad and begins stinking worse than a rotten carcass. It is a horrible way to die. It seems the gods do not see any use for us if we lose an arm or leg."

This made sense to Will. He thought the lack of limbless warriors was because the people of Ulfor were extraordinary fighters. But he knew that soldiers died of gangrene infected wounds as recently as WWII, let alone a thousand years ago.

"It sounds like a horrible way to die."

These were a people who lived and died by the gods. A simple case of gangrene in the modern world was different to this, where a warrior's death was foretold by deities. Even so, Will explained about basic cleanliness. The need for regular washing, lancing pus, sewing wounds as if they sewed clothes. He described why it was important to air wounds on occasion. How rubbing oil onto scars helped the healing process. Using mead as an anaesthetic and applying pressure to arteries to reduce bleeding.

✲ ✲ ✲ ✲ ✲

Steve was heading back to the house of Tharof and Sheelga. The villagers still seemed wary of the Australians. One mother, leading her three children back home after they had taken their gift to the great tree, gave him a tight smile and a wide berth. It seemed no matter how many times they had denied it, people still saw them as the Tuatha- Day-Dannan.

"Steve," called Thormdall through the darkness. "How goes everything?"

"Yeah, great thanks," he replied. Pausing for a moment a concerned look passed over Steve's face. "Listen, I wanted to raise this at the council but I thought enough had been said. They've gone through a lot today."

"Yes they have," said Thormdall, waiting for Steve to continue.

"I cannot help but think that we're in some way responsible for the deaths of those men today. We've brought the crystal into this world so it's our fault that all this trouble has started. I was thinking that if we have a small group of Norse come with us tomorrow, then once we've got Berag out, they can take him home to Ulfor. Meanwhile me and the boys, with the crystal of course, will leave this place and search for the main portal Romeeros mentioned. That way the crystal is gone and your village is no longer under threat. We may need a guide to come with us though."

"Nonsense my friend! Do not think that you are responsible for this trouble. Everything has its place, nothing happens by accident. Terrible as it may be, those men who died today had fulfilled their skeen." He hesitated, as Steve looked confused. "A person's skeen is their life story, if you will. It is a tale woven by the gods long before they are born. No matter what they do, they cannot deviate from their skeen. As they do not know what their skeen is in the first place they could hardly deviate anyway. But those warriors, those heroes who died today were intended to die even before their mothers gave birth to them, strange as it might sound.

"Nothing happens by accident. It is why you were meant to enter this world and come to our village," he said. "But there is a problem with your second suggestion. Romeeros does not know exactly where the main portal lies. He has heard legends of it being in a land called Badawark, but is not sure. Even if it were in Badawark, where exactly? We do not know. So until we know more, you will have to bring Berag back and wait here until we can make a definite move towards the gateway."

Steve was not sure he liked the sound of that. "But when will we know exactly where this gateway is?" he asked.

"I know not, but I spoke to Romeeros after the meeting and there is a man of Byzantium, a warrior-cleric who is travelling here. He knows about the crystal and where the gateway lies. He will be happy to guide you, my friend. But we do not know when he will arrive. All that we know is that he is on his way."

"With any luck he'll be here when we get back with Berag," said Steve.

"That may well happen," spoke Thormdall.

"We will need someone with us tomorrow who knows the lay of the land, which areas or villages to avoid in case of robbery or attack and so on."

Steve was about to suggest Thormdall himself, but the Berserker cut in, "I have just the man for you, my friend. I will speak to him now. His name is Tharkol. He is a good hunter and an expert tracker. He will be of much help to you."

"I appreciate that, mate," said Steve.

The two men bid each other farewell.

* * * * *

"I say bring them on!" Korgoth roared, slamming his hand onto the table.

"That's your last warning!" said Leeka as she cleared away Scott's empty plate. Scott was billeted with this bull of a man called Korgoth and his wife.

"Sorry, my dear," replied Korgoth passing a hand through his beard.

Scott thanked Leeka as she took the wooden dishes away. Their dinner of roast pork, cabbage and corn had been exquisite.

"But I agree with you there, mate," he said to Korgoth. "We should go and wipe them all out."

"Damn right!"

It was obvious Korgoth felt passionate about teaching the Vikings a thing or two. Scott was amused by the older man's sudden outbursts.

There was a sharp knock at the door.

"That could be them, damn their eyes!" shouted Korgoth jumping to his feet and reaching for his axe.

"Oh, sit yourself down, you great oaf!" said Leeka. She opened the door to find Steve and Will standing there with snow in their hair.

"G'day there! Could we borrow Scott?" he asked.

"But of course, my dear. Hang on." Scott climbed to his feet. "You can't go out dressed like this, it's too cold," Leeka said disappearing into the end of the long house.

"But mum!" Scott said.

Korgoth snorted. "Don't worry lad she treats me like a child too."

Scott chuckled, grabbed his weapon and accepted the cloak that Leeka handed him. He put it on and fixed the broach in place. He waved his hosts goodbye and closed the door behind him.

"Reminds me of my parent's house," said Will.

The trio walked to the other side of the village where Matt was living with a friendly young couple. They walked in single file with good spacing between each other. The stars were hidden from sight by the thick clouds above.

Once they were all together, the SASR soldiers went to the Great Hall. The fires had gone out. Matt poked around in the ashes. He re-stoked the fire with some kindling to give them some light more than anything.

Will brought the fire at the other end of the hall to life and within minutes, the four soldiers were sat around the far end of the table.

"Right, why are we here?" began Steve. "Okay, well tomorrow we set off on our mission to get Berag. It shouldn't prove to be too dangerous, but I still want you all to keep your eyes open. No, there won't be people shooting at us but we don't know what's out there. The forests could be full of raiders for all we know. This brings us onto the next point, we're being assigned a guide and he's also a good tracker. He's known as Tharkol. He will know the lay of the land, where the local thieves are hiding, and so on. Should Berag have been taken to one of these coastal Viking towns, Tharkol should know which area he will be held and which areas to avoid." Steve leaned back in his chair.

"I also think we should prepare ourselves for the fact that Berag might not be alive when we find him." "Why d'ya say that?" asked Matt.

"Cos Berag didn't have the crystal, I did. I'm assuming Berag was captured because they thought he'd be carrying it as the village chieftain. Once they find out that he doesn't have it, what possible use is he to them?"

"You mean apart from holding him as hostage to make sure their demands are met?" asked Scott.

"Fair point," grinned Steve. "But we have to agree that the fact he might be dead is a distinct possibility. I hope that's not the case, but we need to cover all possibilities before we go in."

"How good is this Tharkol?" asked Will.

"Don't know for sure, but Thormdall swears by him. We'll find out tomorrow I guess," replied Steve. "Now, any other questions?"

"Yeah, I've been thinking about this a lot," said Matt. "We're the bloody pricks responsible for what happened this morning, man. Those nine blokes who died, we're responsible for that!"

"I don't think you're the only one who's thought that, mate," said Steve watching the other men nodding.

"My point is: wouldn't it be logical to take the crystal with us when we go? That way we can pull Berag out, let Tharkol take him back to Ulfor and that leaves us free to go on to this gateway that Romeeros was talking about."

"The crystal is going to stay with me no matter what," said Steve, "if it gets lost or stolen we're screwed. Having said that, Romeeros doesn't even know where this gateway is."

"Say that again?" Scott asked.

"Hang on, hang on," said Steve. "Romeeros said there was some kind of Byzantine priest on his way over who knows all about the crystal and how to use it. He also knows where the gateway is and how to use it."

"When does he get here?" asked Matt.

"Dunno yet, mate, we'll just have to sit tight and wait for him. In the meantime, forget about the gateway or Byzantium priests. Concentrate on our mission tomorrow, clean your weapons, and make sure everything is ready to go. You all know the drill. Okay? Any other questions?"

The men were silent. "Right then, well get goin', try and get a good night's rest because we'll have a long journey ahead of us. Berag could be bloody anywhere."

The other men left, leaving Steve sitting at the table with the light from the fires flickering over his face and giving him a demonic look. He had not wanted to tell the soldiers what Thormdall had told him for fear of taking their minds from the mission. As the cold air closed in, Steve walked out of the Great Hall, letting the fires at each end of the hall to die in peace.

He closed the door behind him. Tharof and Sheelga were already asleep. They lay on an earthen shelf, which ran around the perimeter of the room about three feet off the ground.

The earthen shelf was wide enough for two people to sleep side by side. Tharof and Sheelga were snuggled together on the far side of the room under a thick woollen blanket. Steve saw a blanket for him to lie on at the other end of the room. At the end of the blanket, a black dyed, thick woollen blanket had been folded. It had been placed there for him to cover himself with once he retired to bed.

Steve held a cough back as the smoke from the fire irritated his throat. He kicked off his boots and sat staring into the fire for some moments. Lying back, he pulled the blanket over him and watched the fire devour the thick logs. Pulling the crystal out of his pocket, he stared at the unremarkable object. It felt warm in his hand, almost comforting. He tucked it back in his pocket.

Steve wondered what time it was in Australia right now, and what Judy and the kids were doing. Brent always enjoyed a story before bed. Spot the Dog was a favourite, but most of the Mister Men books also received rave reviews from Brent. Kathy enjoyed being read to as well. Before Steve had been sent on deployment to Iraq, he had been reading The Lion, The Witch and the Wardrobe to her. Judy's face filled his mind, he missed her, loved her, and wanted her.

In this ancient land, Steve had started to realise that as hard as this life was, their family was everything to them. The Norse were good, caring parents with a strong sense of community and loyalty. The men, and some of the women, were the finest, most fearless fighters Steve had ever seen. But given a choice, they would always choose family first. Family was everything.

"Stuff this," Steve whispered. It was time to retire, from the army anyway. He had been working, training and fighting with the SASR for more than a decade. With each passing day, he was beginning to realise just how much his family meant to him. If he lost them, it would break him and he knew it. It was time to be a father and a husband full-time. None of this part-time bullshit. Sleep enveloped him in a gentle embrace and he dreamed of a family that needed a husband and a father.

CHAPTER 13

The soldiers set off early the next morning. The horizon to the east glowed deep orange and bright pink as the sun made its presence known. After arguing with her father, Heleena had left that morning with Will. Foothark knew she was in safe hands, but he hated that his little girl was growing up so fast. Marie kept reminding him that she was not growing up, she had grown up. But to Foothark she would always be his little girl.

Tharkol had gone ahead of the men. The soldiers had their chest webbing strapped on, assault helmets fastened and weapons at the action condition. They had a bullet in the chamber and the safety catches on. They also carried handmade rucksacks given them by members of the village with their warm weather gear and food inside. The soldiers had cleaned and oiled their weapons the night before, water bottles were filled and ammunition tallied. Nothing had been left to chance. The old clothes the villagers had supplied them were also stored in their rucksacks for later use.

"Fuckin' cold," commented Scott as they entered the forest, snow crunching under their feet.

"Yeah it is a bit," replied Matt.

A bird took to flight, soared above the forest and disappeared from sight. Steve knew this would be a dangerous mission, but it was also an opportunity to win the hearts and minds of those villagers who did not trust them. If they returned with their chieftain unhurt then perhaps those few would finally come to trust them. Thormdall had told them it was not distrust; it was that the people still regarded them as gods. Steve was not convinced.

Distrust was a dangerous thing. In a situation where a foreign military force was occupying a town or city, the humble medic was its most potent weapon. The Australian and British defence forces in particular knew how to utilise this fact to their advantage. They had done so with great success on countless occasions.

Steve was not undertaking this mission to please the villagers, he was doing it to try to win trust. In this dangerous world of long ago, it would be nothing for one of those who mistrusted them to cut their throats while they slept. He was sure this would not happen, but Steve wanted to rectify the situation before it became a probability.

He could see Tharkol in the distance with his back to them. Steve could see that they were approaching the clearing where the battle had taken place yesterday. As they approached the valley, the Norseman turned.

"The gods have taken no mercy," he said.

The soldiers surveyed the scene. None of the wounded warriors laid out the day before had survived. One had managed to crawl about twenty metres or so, but had died from the extreme cold. The others had been buried almost to their chests in snow. The large pile of corpses in the centre of the valley was tinged white. Tharkol moved down into the valley and took up the weapons of each of the men who had been left at the mercy of the gods. He destroyed them all, bending the swords, breaking bows and snapping axe shafts. With the help of the soldiers, he dragged the corpses into the centre of the valley to join their deceased comrades.

Once this had been done, the group moved on. Scott had wrapped a shamag around his face to keep the cold at bay. The other soldiers wore hats or beanies to keep in the warmth. They all knew that heat escaped fastest from the head.

Tharkol jogged ahead once again, disappearing into the white landscape in the distance. So far, he had proved to be a valuable guide, but once they reached the Viking towns, his real worth would be tested.

They could still see faint hoof marks in the snow, indicating the direction Berag had been taken. The distant howl of a wolf echoed across the forest. It was followed by the cry of another wolf to the east, which sounded closer, then another to the south. The sound was powerful and haunting. Little to Tharkol's knowledge, the wolf would be a species on the brink of extinction in a thousand years. Steve assumed the animals had picked up the scent of dead bodies and were moving in for a feast. They continued along the forest track, following both the faint hoof prints as well as Tharkol's. Sometimes Tharkol's footprints disappeared altogether, where he climbed a tree for a better view. They walked for almost two hours before Tharkol ran back to them.

"We must be quiet now," he said. "I have spotted a small group of enemy nearby. They have a wounded man with them. They are trying to help him although it looks to me like he will make his journey soon."

They could detect the distinct aroma of wood smoke and agreed it would be a wise move to go around them and continue on.

It took them an hour to bypass the campsite. With the smell of smoke gone and their enemy behind them, their pace quickened again and Tharkol disappeared ahead. As dusk approached, he returned with four rabbits slung over his shoulder.

"We rest for the night," he said. "I have found a well-hidden place not far from here, with good wind protection. It seems the Gods are with us," he added. "This is a good thing. If Lokee minds his business, then we will have a fine journey there and back."

The soldiers were puzzled but decided not to ask. The Norse culture ran deep and was not easy to fathom in a matter of weeks. But the site Tharkol had found was good; it was a small alcove, with sheer rock walls on three sides and thick forest covering the fourth. There was plenty of dead wood buried in the snow and it took some effort to dig up. Within an hour, they had enough to start a fire. Tharkol began building one against a rock wall that would reflect the heat. Meanwhile the soldiers searched for more fuel to keep the fire burning throughout the night. By the time the light was almost gone, they had enough wood. While one sat on watch near the fire, the others slept, or tried to.

Will lay with his hands behind his head looking up at the stars. He listened to Heleena breathing beside him under a shared blanket. He looked across at her and took in her beauty. She was curled up beside him, the warmth of her thigh draped across his legs. The dim light of the moon shone from her skin. A tuft of hair partly hid her face, but her lips and slender shoulders were exposed. Her full breasts pushed against him and arousal washed over him. Staring back at the sky, his mind was filled with her presence. Her soft, warm skin, her engaging smile and gentle voice. She was a goddess. But lethal too, he thought. The Norse world was as violent as it was beautiful, more violent and lawless than the modern world to which he was used.

Sleep took him in the early hours of the morning. Shortly after, Will awoke to a soft kiss and looked up into Heleena's face. She was smiling. He pulled her to him and kissed her again.

The morning arrived and as the sun rose, Steve cleared the campsite, extinguishing the fire and destroying any evidence they were there. They put on their cloaks, gloves, beanies or shamags, threw their webbing on, strapped on their assault helmets and headed out. Tharkol took the position of scout up ahead and out of sight.

It was a hard journey, but by the middle of the tenth day, they found themselves on a small hill overlooking the city that Tharkol called Skrethorg. Heleena explained it was a shipping town. In the harbour, long flat-bottomed barges could be seen making their way up and down the river, some were empty and others cluttered with wares. Larger ships were sailing out of the fjord towards the ocean and distant lands. Trade held Skrethorg together.

"Those are war ships," said Heleena, pointing at five long, narrow longships of great beauty. Their prows and sterns rose out of the water like rearing snakes, banks of oars drove them through the calm water of the fjord.

"Vikings?" asked Will.

'Rich ones, yes. A single chieftain, a Hersir, will be in charge of them. He is wealthy enough to pay them for their ongoing employment. All the warships belong to him. They will prey on inland and coastal villages."

A faint, grey cloud hung over the city created by the smoke spewing from each house. The dwellings built from hard wood and nailed together with little care. Some were falling apart and others looked abandoned. The city spoke of a gross lack of care and culture. The impression was that these were a lost people, they had forgotten what it was that had once made them Norse. Before the Chreest men had visited these shores, the city would have been as welcoming as Ulfor. But in the space of one-hundred years that had all changed. They had changed their culture and entire way of life.

"I remember my great-great-father speaking of Skrethorg. He lived here as a boy. It had been a kingdom, a jewel resting by the sea," said Tharkol, with sadness in his voice. "Gone are the long houses. Over to the east there," he pointed to an open field in the distance, "is where the summer gathering was held each year. People from all over Skandinavia would come. They would compete in many things. At the end of the week, which was the duration of the gathering, there would be ship races. All the great warriors from all over Skandinavia would race in their longships. Some vessels were so large that they could carry eighty warriors. There was a king in those days, and he would present the winning ship with a pouch of gold."

Tharkol fell silent. Whether the people of Ulfor would admit it or not, their culture was dying. In another hundred years, Ulfor would resemble Skrethorg. They were an island and the ocean was rising. It was hardly surprising they fought against the coastal dwelling Vikings. To do otherwise would mean the death of their way of life.

"There is nothing left in Skrethorg now but darkness and treachery," said Tharkol moving down the slope. "Stay alert, for danger can come from anywhere in these places," he added.

Before they approached the town, the soldiers changed their clothes. They looked strange with their chest webbing strapped over their woollen shirts. They took off their assault helmets and fixed them to the chest webbing. Finally, they pulled large thick cloaks around their shoulders to hide the webbing from view. They attached the cloaks with a wooden brooch at their throats.

Steve could see people on the outskirts of the city felling trees. The wood was being sold as firewood. Large horse-driven carts were moving back and forth. Some empty, others packed with huge tree trunks that would be cut into planks and used for building. There must have been two hundred people cutting into the forest. It looked like a huge industry and would bring in a lot of money.

The city was a-buzz. It stank of human filth and the townspeople eyed the newcomers with curiosity, indifference or open hostility. Most eyes were drawn to the four soldiers and their short hair. Even though the SASR patrol had thick beards and unkempt hair that touched their necks, it was still considered short in this ancient place.

"Sorry, mate, but where exactly are we going?" Matt asked Tharkol.

"Have patience, my friend," the warrior replied. "I know a man and I will ask him if he has seen or heard anything out of the ordinary. He may even know where Berag is. I doubt it, but he is a good place to start."

Matt noticed two women on the other side of the alley, walking up and down, trying to gain the attention of each man that passed by. Finally a man stopped. With a smile, one of the women took him by the arm and led him into a house. They were hookers.

He nudged Scott. "Wouldn't touch that with a barge pole," he said, gesturing towards the remaining woman. She looked at Matt and, motioned him towards her.

"Dunno, looks pretty tempting," said Scott with sarcasm.

The woman broke into a coughing fit, and spat onto the ground before wiping her mouth with her hand.

"Oh yeah, that just turns me on baby," said Matt.

The group took a left turn and the smell of the ocean reached them.

After a short time, Tharkol led them into a pub on the docks. The bitter, almost unpleasant, smell of Viking beer hit them. The pub was crowded and there were no spare seats. Tharkol talked to a burly man behind the bar.

"It seems Berag has been taken to the southern end of Skrethorg, which is not good," he informed the soldiers. "South Skrethorg is a violent place. The dwelling in which he is held is three times the height of a normal dwelling. It should be easy to find. Let us go," said Tharkol making his way back to the smelly street.

It was indeed an unpleasant neighbourhood. All the locals wore tattered clothes. This was a place to avoid. Every city had an area like this. A drunken man called out to them. He held a clay jug in his hand, which he raised, making him trip and almost fall.

Ignoring him, the men moved on. The soldiers had their weapons hidden underneath their cloaks, but they were ready to use them.

Outside each house was a hole for urine and excrement. The place reeked and it almost seemed as if all the diseases of the world had been born in this place.

A mangy dog padded past, its ribs visible. The animal's head hung limp as it moved and was not far from starvation.

"Spare some money?" asked an old woman in a doorway. The dress she wore was stained with dirt.

"Come now, such well-dressed men such as you must be able to offer a poor old lady some coin?"

The men pushed past her.

"A pox on you," she called out.

Soon Tharkol turned to the soldiers and pointed at a three-storey dwelling ahead. There was a man out the front standing guard. He had an axe in his hand, and a round shield strapped to his back. He wore no helmet. His chain mail had begun to rust on the right shoulder and it had a large hole around his stomach. Dressed as the man was, the soldiers noticed his axe blade was pristine; it had been sharpened and cleaned with care. Such details told a lot about a person. This man was a good soldier and would fight well. Steve saw the guard was watching them.

"It's just down here," said Tharkol, pointing off to the left.

The soldiers followed him down a side alley. Once they were out of sight, the men stopped and formed a tight circle.

"There's bugger all of 'em," said Scott.

"Yeah, I noticed that," Matt said.

"Wonder where they all are?" asked Will.

* * * * *

Foothark got out of bed earlier than usual. He stretched, wincing as a shoulder cracked and a sharp pain shot down his arm. Marie was still sleeping. He knelt by the fire and prodded it back to life before stepping outside.

Yawning he thought of Heleena. He berated himself for letting her go, but as Marie had reminded him, she was of age and was in the care of a fine man.

He had only known Will for a short time, but trusted him. Many young men had approached Heleena and he had trusted none of them. But Will was somehow different. He seemed to care for Heleena, something Foothark had not seen before.

"Odin keep you safe," he whispered into the cold.

The sun had not yet risen, but a gentle light was touching the sky to the east. Foothark strode through the fresh snow towards the forest. He urinated against a tree and passed wind. But a noise made him turn. It was a loud snap like a fallen branch breaking underfoot. At first, he supposed it was a deer, unaware of his presence. He looked into the forest where a large band of men was creeping through the trees. The instant they saw him they broke into a run.

Foothark swore and stumbled as fast as he could towards his home. "To arms!" he yelled. "To arms!"

* * * * *

"Okay, Matt, I want you on the rear exit," said Steve watching the soldier pull out the M110 sniper rifle and clicking the safety to fire.

"Heleena, you stay here," said Steve.

She scowled at him and a knife appeared in her hand. "You do not command me, I go with Will."

Steve held his hands up. "Okay, no arguments from me, but you stay well behind me and Will okay?"

She nodded.

"You all set?" he asked Will.

"Yup," Will replied with a grin.

"Right, Scott, I want you to neutralise the guard. Once you've done that, find a location and cover our approach. Will and I'll clear the building. We'll locate Berag and pull him out. With any luck he's here and still alive."

"Okay, not a problem," said Scott, moving away.

"You good to go?" asked Steve.

"Where would you like me?" asked Tharkol.

"Just stay here for the time being," answered Steve. "We shouldn't be too long."

Steve moved around Will and watched Scott talking to the guard. The man laughed at a story Scott was telling him. Then Scott made a small hand gesture. He was asking if they were ready to move. Steve nodded and Scott picked up the movement in his peripheral vision. Without hesitation, Scott took a step back and brought the Minimi up, firing a short burst into the man's chest. The guard dropped to the floor immediately and before the sound of the gunshot had echoed into silence, Will had kicked the front door open. The two soldiers, with Heleena close on their heels, began clearing the building as Scott took cover behind a building. He

150

would ensure that no enemy could enter the building behind them or that Berag could be brought out and taken elsewhere.

The first contact could be heard as a short burst exploded, followed by another. There was shouting and several more gunshots. The distinct loud crack of an M110 sniper rifle sounded from the back of the house where someone had tried to make an escape.

Four enemy were down. Steve and Will moved fast through the dwelling. Steve was about ten metres behind Will, who was moving forward fast, his weapon pulled into his shoulder watching for enemy. Will disappeared around a corner and another loud burst exploded a moment later.

Steve rounded the corner to be confronted by a body. Three or four rounds had torn through the man's chest. Steve moved alongside Will and signalled for him to move forward.

Will nodded and then held his hand up, telling Steve to wait. Heleena knelt behind them facing rearward, a knife drawn in case an enemy came from behind. Will pulled the magazine from his rifle and slapped in a fresh one before bringing the weapon to his shoulder again.

* * * * *

"To arms!" Foothark roared, as he reached his door. With relief, he noticed that many of the younger men had appeared swords and axes in hand. Foothark barged through the door and saw that Marie was awake. She was holding his sheathed sword, which she passed to him before kissing him on the cheek.

"Be careful husband," she whispered.

He slung a round shield over his shoulder and nodded, striding out before slamming the door behind him. A small group of village men had formed a shield wall and were already in battle. The ring of steel and angry shouts cut through the morning air.

"To me!" the distant roar of Thormdall's voice rose above the battle. "Ulfor to me!"

Foothark ran through the thick snow and towards a large group of armed men around Thormdall.

"Skyaldaborg!" the Berserker yelled and the warriors instinctively formed the shield wall, as they had been trained.

"Follow me!" commanded Thormdall, and ran towards the battle.

The warriors moved fast, but not as fast as the Berserker. Their close formation hindered movement. Long before the shield wall could close with the enemy, Thormdall was amongst the raiders. No matter which direction they came from, Thormdall blocked, parried, stabbed, slashed and kicked. No matter how many there were, or how concerted their effort, the raiders fell before the Berserker like wheat before a scythe. Only two Ulfor warriors remained from the original shield wall. They ran back to join the larger battle approaching. Foothark found himself in the second rank, and within moments, battle had been joined.

Thormdall had broken clear of the fight to allow the shield wall to press forward into the undisciplined ranks of the Viking raiders.

One Ulfor warrior darted clear of the shield wall protection and was immediately killed. The man behind the felled warrior stepped forward to take his place. The raiders almost broke through the wall, but were pushed back.

"Hold the wall!" roared Thormdall.

Two raiders broke clear of the fight and charged the Berserker, but Thormdall killed them with ease. He made it look like a game. But this was no game.

The raiders were held at bay by the Ulfor shield wall for what seemed an age. The Ulfor warriors in the second row, and some in the third, were making great effect of long spears and long hafted axes. They stabbed and hacked out beyond the front rank, shattering shields, swords or skulls. The Viking raiders were being decimated, but instead of retreating, they chose the coward's path. They broke ranks, streamed along either side of the shield wall and sprinted for the village of Ulfor.

"After them!" roared Thormdall. The raiders were after Ulfor's most valued commodity: the women and children.

* * * * *

Steve kicked the door hard. It flew backwards. A startled half-dressed man with a dagger in hand ran towards a room to the right. A single shot rang out and the ejected cartridge bounced off the wall with a dull clink before coming to a rest in the dirt at Will's feet. The limp corpse ploughed into the ground, blood pumping from a hole in the man's skull. The trio moved forward, clearing the rooms to the left and right as they went.

* * * * *

For Welf this had turned into a bad day that had grown worse. The torches, held in place by steel brackets, flickered against his face. They threw shadows, which danced across the walls like distorted creatures from myths. At sixteen summers, he had been proud to be accepted into the ranks of the Vikings. He came from a poor family and saw the Viking raiding parties as a way to support his family. There was plunder aplenty or so he had been told, and if he could send some home then his mother and his younger sister would not go hungry.

His father had left them when he had been six, he remembered the day well. There had been a shouted argument between his mother and his father, followed by a sharp slap. Welf had run from his room to see his mother hit the floor hard. His father had turned and left. It was no bad thing Welf had often told himself. His father had been a pig, and hoped he was dead by now.

There was a groan from the other side of the room. The prisoner was awake again. The hostage was a chieftain of some small inland village and they were hoping to be paid for his return. Inland villages were wealthy, which is why the men often went inland a-viking. With some luck, Welf might have come out of this venture with more coin than he had entered it. Now he was not sure. Loud thunderclaps came again and there was a dull thud above him, almost like a body hitting the floor.

"They are coming for you, boy," came the prisoner's soft voice. "Shut up, old man!" shouted Welf, fear coursing through him.

The prisoner's left eye had closed Welf noticed with pleasure. A group of them had beaten him yesterday afternoon, punching, kicking or stomping until all movement had ceased. After that, the man had become delirious, moving often from a waking state to sleep. Each time he awoke, he groaned or cried out in pain.

* * * * *

They were on the second floor and about to move to the third. Many of the enemy were dead now, although they had still not found Berag. Steve ran up the stairs ahead of Will, moving around the large room. It was empty. Moving through buildings was a skill. To fire with accuracy, the weapon needed to be held steady as one moved, and this was achieved by walking from the knees, not the hips. Walking from the hips meant the individual bobbed up and down so could not shoot with any accuracy.

Walking from the knees was also much quieter than walking in the normal manner. The soldiers rushed to a closed door opposite them. Steve swung it open and they were confronted with a steep, dark staircase. Keeping his weapon pointed into the blackness, Will flicked on a small mag light and moved forward. The stairs were chiselled from stone and seemed to go down a long way. Down they went, further and further into the musty gloom. Steve guessed they were now under the surface of the ground.

There were only two things found this deep: a prison or a torture chamber. It was the only place Berag could be. At last, they came to the bottom and cool air enveloped them. They found two old wooden doors. One led straight on and the other faced left. It reminded the soldiers of the old stories where life resided behind one door and death behind the other.

Will pretended to flick an invisible coin into the air. Steve grinned and pointed left. Will positioned himself. There was not enough room for them to move in together, so Will would have to kick the door in and clear the room himself. Will kicked out hard, the door flew open and a startled warrior crumbled sideways as several bullets tore through his chest and throat. Four other warriors scrambled to their feet. One managed to draw his sword and charge, shouting in fury before he was taken down by a short burst. Another received a bullet to his head.

The other two backed away with fear in their eyes. They too were torn from their feet. The soldiers had been guarding a small prison. Prison cells lined the small corridor, each separated by a thick stone wall. The place stank. Will and Steve looked into each barred cell. Heleena remained outside the prison a look of disgust on her face. Half the cells were empty. One contained a dead man, another housed a filthy young woman who was living in her own excrement and three other men who had been beaten. One was dead. Steve forced himself not to dry retch.

Berag was not here. They turned back to the second door.

* * * * *

Foothark had joined the headlong rush towards Ulfor in pursuit of the Viking raiders. He pushed through the mass of Ulfor warriors and sprinted towards his home. The raiders had spread out so that enemy warriors were streaming in all directions. Foothark watched four Vikings barge through his front door and disappear into his home.

"Marie!" he screamed. "Marie!"

Fury fuelled him, hatred coursed through his veins dissolving his fear. He flung the round shield away, almost slid over in the snow, righted himself and carried on. He heard distant shouts as battle was re-joined elsewhere in the village, but ignored it. Marie was the only person that drove him on. The power of the fury coursing through him served to drive him forward at an inexhaustible speed and for a moment, he knew what it was to be berserk. Launching a kick at the front door of his home the hinges ripped free and the entire door hit the ground with a crash. He stepped through and saw the invaders in his home. His home. One was already dead, Marie's knife still embedded in his throat. Without thought, Foothark brought his sword down hard on the head of the closest Viking. Blood exploded from the mighty wound and the enemy crumpled without a sound. Marie was dead. She was lying on the ground near the fire, her dead opponent nearby. Her throat had been cut, blood soaking into the ground. The Viking closest to her had untied his breeches and was about to rape her deceased body before Foothark kicked down the door.

"Marie!" roared Foothark.

Levering the sword clear of the Viking's skull, Foothark felt a sharp pain explode in his belly. The Viking closest to him had stabbed him almost to the hilt. The blade of the sword had exited near his spine. The Viking was grinning at him.

Foothark grinned back. His eyes were wide with madness. His teeth were stained claret and blood dribbled down his chin. Swinging the sword with all his strength, he watched his opponent's eyes widen moments before his head departed his body.

The third Viking darted forward and brought his sword down on Foothark's shoulder. The blade cut deep, shattering the collarbone.

The old man crumpled to the floor, but kept a firm grip on his sword.

"This is where you die old man," growled the Viking over him.

"It is," agreed Foothark. With one last mighty effort, Foothark drove his sword up and into the Viking's groin. He felt the blade sink deep. His opponent screamed and dropped to his knees, clasping his blood-drenched breeches. With a snarl, Foothark stabbed the sword into the abdomen of his enemy. He twisted it before ripping it free and hacking the blade into the Viking's throat.

"This is also where you die boy," Foothark said, as the Viking collapsed to his side.

✶ ✶ ✶ ✶ ✶

Welf drew his sword as the thunderclaps sounded again, this time outside his door. They were loud and piercing. There was something inhuman about them. He could hear a man shouting a war cry before more thunderclaps rang out. Within seconds, all was silent again. It was as if the gods themselves were roaming through the house, slaying as they saw fit.

"There's nothing you can do, boy. You chose the wrong side," chuckled the prisoner.

"I said shut up!" Welf shouted. "Shut up! Shut up!"

A loud crash made the boy jump. The door opened and two tall men appeared with metal pipes pulled into their shoulders. In the half second he had, Welf noticed that neither of the newcomer's eyes registered anger, hate or fear. But they did radiate a purpose he had never seen, and it frightened him. Welf saw a bright flash. He was dead before he hit the floor.

Steve went straight to Berag and hauled the man to his feet. "How do you feel?" he asked.

"Not well, they may have killed me."

Will and Heleena forged ahead, providing them with cover. In the second room they searched the dead bodies until a set of keys were found. They swung each cell door wide to allow the prisoners to escape. They did not have the manpower, or the time, to drag prisoners out.

"Let's go," Will said, his right arm supporting his rifle. His left trailed behind him with the mag light so that Heleena, Steve and Berag could see where they were walking. It was a long slow climb to the top, but no more enemies were seen during the ascent. Outside they saw Tharkol and Scott waiting nearby. Loping past them, Scott called out to Matt. It was time for them to leave.

Returning the way they had come, the soldiers left the corpse-filled building standing silent.

* * * * *

"Can you hear the mountain's song?" whispered Thormdall. The Berserker had found Foothark and dragged him outside so he was facing Mount Skane. He had carried Marie out and laid her beside him so they would be together in death. The snow around Foothark was stained red with blood. Foothark tried to shift himself into a more comfortable sitting position, but winced as pain from the sword wound flared.

"No," replied Foothark. The older Norseman was holding his sword tight and looking at the distant peaks of Mount Skane and the smaller mountain ranges nearby.

"It is the mountain. She is singing, be still, you will hear," Thormdall's voice was almost inaudible.

Mount Skane stood like a mighty oak within a forest of saplings; it was like a bright beacon amongst candles. The rising sun gave it an immensity and beauty that was incredible to behold. Foothark noticed the awesome beauty of the mountain for the first time and a realisation hit him. The mountain's song was not audible; it was a feeling, an appreciation of nature's power, of her beauty.

"I can hear her song," said Thormdall. "Be still and you will too," the Berserker looked at Foothark.

The old warrior's dead eyes stared at the mountain and his face was content. The man had died a hero, a warrior who had died fighting for all in which he believed.

It was said that a mountain remembered all that had occurred upon its slopes. In a thousand years when the faces of the present generation were gone, the memory of a single man's sacrifice would be carried on the breeze. His epitaph would appear on Mount Skane as the sun rose in the sky.

CHAPTER 14

Heleena screamed when they returned to Ulfor. It was a low growl, which ended in a long, high-pitched shriek filled with anger and loss. Her parents had been washed and dressed in clean clothes before their burial. Others who had died during the raid had been buried nine days earlier, but Heleena's parents had been left in the hope of her return. Crushed herbs and flowers had been rubbed into their skin and clothes to ward off the smell of death. Heleena knelt by them for hours, sometimes in silence and others in shuddering grief. Her tears spilled on their cold, dead skin. When the sinking sun met the horizon, Will knelt beside her and helped her to her feet. He hugged her to him, listening as she sobbed into his chest. He stroked her back and held her, wise enough to know that no words would ever make up for her loss and soul-rending grief.

They also learned that a young girl by the name of Hilda had been stabbed in the stomach during the raid. She had survived the wound, but had been clinging to life ever since. Matt tended to her at the parent's house as soon as he heard.

Foothark and Marie were buried as darkness claimed Ulfor. Thormdall recounted Marie's bravery and Foothark's skill. He told of the last moments of Heleena's parents, of two elderly Norse farmers who had taken on and conquered four armed Viking raiders. It was a story that would never be forgotten.

"I will kill them," said Heleena in the forest cave later that night. "Every one of them."

"Who?" asked Will.

"The Vikings. Whenever, wherever I find them, I will kill them."

Will nodded.

"They have started a blood feud by killing my family, and so I will send them to their demon god," Heleena snarled, a tear dripping from her chin.

Will pulled her to him and kissed her. Part of him wanted to try to persuade her otherwise. But he knew if his parents had been murdered, he would be head hunting the culprits as well.

"We'll find them," he said.

"I want their heads," Heleena said.

He could feel her body shaking, out of shock or rage, he did not know.

"Tell me about them?" asked Will.

"Father," Heleena fell silent for a long time then giggled. "Father was always mother's servant. He did everything she asked. Father loved her. As a young man, father had accompanied his merchant father. They visited Ulfor to trade their wares perhaps three times a year. It was on one of these visits that father spotted mother. From that moment on he could not be kept away. Father was seventeen summers in age and mother fifteen, when they were bound in marriage. Mother was eighteen summers when she gave birth to me. They were always happy together. Although they bickered a little, it was never over great matters." She stared into the fire. "I miss them," she said.

They sat in silence for a long time, listening to the nightlife and the gentle crackle of the fire. Outside, a thick blanket of snow had fallen.

"What of your family?" asked Heleena.

"Not much to tell," said Will. "Dad was a boiler maker for a company contracted to a local coal mine. Mum was a secretary at a law firm. They met, got married, had me."

"There must be more," she laughed.

"Oh there's more," he smiled, but without warmth. "Dad was a drunk, got pissed every Friday and Saturday night. Sometimes he was good, most times, he wasn't. Me and mum could tell what mood he was in by the way he walked down the road, you could hear him from the end of the street. On the bad nights he'd beat Mum up, even put her in ICU once." Will saw Heleena's confused expression and explained. "A place where only sick or hurt people are sent to get better. Or to die. On the good nights he'd just shout at Mum and then fall asleep on the couch in front of the TV and snore." Will explained what a couch and television were. "Shit he could snore," he chuckled.

"When I turned thirteen, Dad came home drunk and started beating Mum up. He had her by the hair and threw her against the wall. She was pleading for him to stop but he was drunk and wasn't going to listen. Anyway, I was ready for him that night. Earlier I had hidden a piece of wood under my bed. I clubbed my dad to within an inch of his life. I only stopped when he stopped moving. I wasn't there when the coppers or the ambulance arrived."

"Coppers, ambulance?"

"Think of Thormdall for coppers and for the ambulance, well think of Matt," he smiled.

"What happened to him, your father?" Heleena asked.

Will shrugged. "Who knows. Who cares? Mum and I left after that and never saw him again. She met a half decent bloke who treated her well. She deserves that. She's always deserved that."

Heleena was silent for a long time. Will knew there were some things in his story like the TV that she would not understand. But that was not what caused her silence. She was stunned. Stunned that a man would strike his wife. A man was expected to care for his family, to fight for them, to protect them and sometimes die for them. That was the culture she knew. For a man to hurt his wife was alien to her.

They sat talking into the night, before sleep took them. Twice Will heard Heleena crying in her sleep. Instead of waking her, he whispered to her and stroked her face, which seemed to calm her. Hours later, he rekindled the fire before retiring under the blanket beside Heleena.

* * * * *

Two days after Heleena's parents had been laid to rest, Hilda died despite Matt's best efforts. Whilst several women of the village comforted the grieving parents, Matt left. He was angry with himself.

"I did my best," Matt said, trying to console himself. But his best had not been good enough and he hated himself for it.

The entire village was at Hilda's funeral. They sent the girl on her way to the gods. Steve was oblivious to those around him. His eyes were locked on the pale face of the dead girl that reminded him so much of his daughter, Kathy.

They could have been sisters, thought Steve. Hilda's eyes were closed, but it was easy to see she was not asleep. She had been washed and dressed in new clothes that hid the terrible wound that had killed her.

What am I doing? Steve asked himself. He was missing some of the best days of his children's lives. He should be there to guide, teach and protect them.

* * * * *

Berag had a pronounced limp and large bruise around his chin and right eye. But he was otherwise in better health than he had been when the soldiers rescued him. He called a feast in the Great Hall. The entire village was invited. Three wild boars and two deer had been hunted and cooked for the occasion. The steaming meat was cut and placed on huge wooden platters, garnished with cabbage, corn and mashed barley mixed with honey. Barrels of mead had been rolled in and positioned around the great hall. Most of the villagers carried their own drinking horns. Some carried wooden or leather cups as well. The vessels were plunged into the open barrel and the drinking began. Not the most hygienic custom, Steve thought, but the alcohol would kill any germs.

160

Berag pushed a drinking horn into Steve's hand. "Drink," he said. Some of the villagers were already eating and talking amongst themselves. The majority of the village were standing around the hall, drinking, laughing or recounting tales of the raid. There was a mixture of bitter sweetness in the hall, of sadness and loss, of happiness and triumph. The village had lost almost thirty people in the raid. It was the worst raid in Ulfor's history.

"Shit house," observed Scott. "Fuckin' shit house. Those villagers are dead because of us."

"Yup," muttered Matt. Steve was nodding, but Will was watching Heleena talking with a group of women.

"It is not your fault my friend," Berag slapped a hand on Scott's shoulder. "A raid like this would have happened," he added, gulping down some mead and refilling it from a barrel.

"No it wouldn't, man," said Matt to the Norse warrior, "and you know it. The Vikings came here looking for the crystal. Once they knew you didn't have it, they had to come back here for it."

Berag shrugged. "It might have been much worse. They might have killed everyone. Thank the gods my wife and child are untouched."

"Yeah, that might be the case, mate, but they only mounted a large raid like this because of us and what we carry. They weren't after food or money. We've gotta leave, mate. As soon as that Arab priest, or whoever the hell he is, gets here, we're gone." Steve took a gulp of the mead. "Not that we don't appreciate your hospitality," he continued, "but you and your people will be much safer without us here."

"I cannot deny that," said Berag, "but raids will always occur against us. We are a wealthy farming village, and when food runs short on the coast, Viking raiders appear. It is the way of things. Do not think the village blames you for their losses, for nothing could be further from the truth." Berag grinned at the soldiers. "You are one of us now. Even when you leave, stories will still be told of you. Generations from now, children will fall asleep to stories of the Tuatha."

"Keep tellin' ya, mate, we ain't gods," said Scott.

"I know," said Berag. "I believe you, but you will be remembered that way. Do you understand?"

Soon the whole village was seated and the feast was well underway. The mashed barley had been boiled in honey and water, imbuing the food with a sweet taste. A thick, beef flavoured gravy was poured into small bowls lining the length of the long table.

"A mighty fine meal!" roared Korgoth, wiping grease from his beard. The man was drunk. When the raiders attacked the village, Korgoth had been asleep and his wife, Leeka was visiting friends several houses away. Korgoth had actually slept through the raid. But when two raiders kicked in his door and entered his home, the Norse giant met them with a bleary-eyed war cry and fell upon them with his battle-axe. Korgoth suffered a superficial laceration to his arm, but the Viking raiders had been slaughtered where they stood. Scott heard that one had been decapitated, and the other had been hit in the face with the butt of Korgoth's axe, which staved in his skull.

Korgoth downed the last of his mead, and sang and swayed in his seat. Most of the villagers around him, ignored him, but a voice at the far end of the table joined Korgoth's slurred, mistimed song. Korgoth roared and raised his empty drinking horn at the person singing along. Leeka hissed at Korgoth, but he ignored her. He concluded the song with a loud belch and went in search of more mead.

"The man can sing." Matt smiled at Leeka.

She smiled and rolled her eyes as she heard Korgoth start up again at the far end of the hall, this time accompanied by several other drunken men. By the end of the night, most of the village had returned to their homes, well fed and for the most part drunk. Not once was there any show of aggression or violence, it was just a good-natured gathering.

The village had been through a horrific event and now they had let off steam. Steve and the soldiers were talking with several villagers. Heleena had her head on Will's shoulder. A few villagers were sprawled out asleep on the floor near the fires. Korgoth was one of them. The giant Norseman was snoring and at one point passed wind with such noise, the conversation ground to silence. They chuckled and continued their conversation long into the early hours of the morning. Berag was right. The villagers were no longer wary of them, nor did mothers steer children away from them. They were now a part of the village. Steve knew that in some strange way he would miss Ulfor and her people.

*****

Over the following days, the soldiers took instruction on archery and swordsmanship. They accompanied hunting parties, using their rifles to stock up the village supply of meat. Scott took a particular interest in learning the dialect. Matt advised the villagers about sanitation. He explained washing hands before and after eating and relieving themselves was important. Matt also explained to the women about how flies and other insects could spread disease, especially if meat was left out for too long. Steve helped improve the village's defences.

He explained how hidden traps and deep ditches could slow and demoralise an enemy, giving archers time to move into position and fire on the enemy.

Two weeks later, Ulfor was once again thrown into excitement with a group of five newcomers. Four of them carried huge axes over their shoulders. Swords were strapped at their waists and round shields were slung on their backs. They wore gleaming helmets of steel and huge vests of chain mail that reached to their calves. Their boots were made of deerskin turned inside out, thick leather soles stitched to the underside of the boots. The chain mail shirts were split to mid-thigh height at the front and back, so they could wear the mail on horseback. The fifth man looked tiny in comparison. He stood just over five feet tall and wore a brown robe that covered him from his shoulders to his ankles. A cream coloured material with a dark leather band covered his head. Attached to a belt around his waist was a curved tulwar. He reminded Steve of a high-ranking Arab.

Berag called a meeting in the great hall.

"This is Ahmad Ibn Fadlan," said Romeeros, introducing the short man. "He is a warrior priest in the Order of Mahaazad and has travelled from the kingdom of Byzantium at the request of his king, Kosraw."

Ahmad nodded. "Please call me Ahmad." He spoke in Anglish and his accent was thick. The hall was filled with quiet conversation as people guessed the meaning of the Order of Mahaazad.

Romeeros called for silence. Steve noticed that at no time did the four guards stray far from Ahmad. He knew that whilst their massive axes were polished, these were not show pony warriors. They would be able to handle themselves well in combat.

"Please also make welcome the four members of the Varangian Guard sent to protect Ahmad."

"Only four accompanied me from the coast," Ahmad said. "Eighty travelled across the ocean with me."

"My son wishes to march with the host one day," called a voice from the far end of the table.

One Varangian grinned at this. "He may well have his chance if he holds to that," he replied.

"What is the host?" Steve asked.

"The Varangian Guard," answered Berag as if that explained it.

It meant nothing to Steve. Realising, Berag added, "Norse warriors arrived on the shores of Byzantium a hundred years ago. Byzantium warriors accosted them. Later that day, as word spread throughout the Byzantium kingdom, the Norse warriors were subject to a full assault by the king's army. The Byzantine army beat them but they accounted for themselves well. So impressed was the king by the Norse that he dismissed his bodyguard and offered a much gold to the Norse newcomers to act as his personal bodyguard. The king's guard, six thousand in number, became known as the Varangian Guard and only Norse warriors can be accepted into its ranks. They use the long-bearded axe as their main weapon, but can make the shield wall and fight with swords if necessary."

"How do you know so much about them?" asked Steve.

"I once served amongst them," replied Berag.

The meeting continued for another two hours and villagers began leaving the great hall. The four Australians were asked to remain.

"It does my heart no good to talk behind the back of my village, but in this regard it must be done," said Berag. "Ahmad is the man who can lead you back to where it is you need to be."

"Back to where we came from you mean?" asked Matt. "It is exactly what I mean," answered Berag.

"The portal through which you came is on the outskirts of Byzantium land," continued Romeeros. "When you first entered this world, Ahmad felt your presence and began his journey to us. The crystal you brought with you is the same crystal cast into the future by Mahaazad."

"Mate," Steve said holding up his hands," you're gonna have to start from the beginning."

Ahmad nodded and stepped forward. "I am a warrior priest of the Order of Mahaazad. But, this sect was once called the Order of the Flame, and Mahaazad was a member. Mahaazad was a warrior priest like myself. When the Badawarks, warriors from a neighbouring land, forged their way into Byzantine land, he was involved in the last battle of the war. The Badawarks invaded our land because their king came into possession of a crystal of incredible power. The crystal's power made it easy for him to convince them to his point of view. He wanted control and ownership of the neighbouring country, Byzantium. Our land. The war that followed raged for over a decade and was bloody and costly for both kingdoms. Finally, the Badawarks, routed from the field, fled unpursued back to their country. The Badawark king ran for the hills and Mahaazad gave chase, finally cornering the monarch at the entrance to a cave high up in the mountains. There were two soldiers with the Badawark king. Mahaazad fought them and killed both the guards, but in the process he received a deep chest wound, the kind from which one does not recover." Ahmad declined a drink.

"Even as he was dying, Mahaazad killed the Badawark king and took the crystal. Carrying a mortal wound, he walked into the cave and found a small entrance at the back. It led into the bowels of the earth and a huge chamber. Realising that his life was ending, Mahaazad performed an ancient rite that sent the crystal many hundreds of years into the future. It is said in the legends that he threw the crystal at the wall, where its shape was forever burned into the rock. The crystal was now where the Badawarks could never touch it again. It is, of course, the crystal you newcomers have brought back into this world."

"Fuckin' great," said Scott.

"The cave sounds exactly like the one where we found the crystal," said Steve, more to himself then anyone.

Ahmad ignored them. "It would be helpful if we were to rid ourselves of this crystal once more, perhaps even destroy it completely. But do you not also seek to travel home?"

"So if we take the crystal and go back with you to your homeland, you can send us back to where we came from? And destroy the thing it at the same time?" asked Steve.

Ahmad nodded.

"Christ, that suits us," said Scott. "When do we leave?"

"Would it be remiss of us if we left in three days?" Ahmad asked Berag.

"Not at all," replied the big man. "I will send Thormdall with you."

"That will not be necess—"

"It is, and it will be," Berag interceded. "Trust me Ahmad, you might need him."

The Arab nodded. "Thank you, although I have had little experience with your Berserker brethren."

"I should hope not and with luck you never will. It is your opponents who you will want to live that experience," Berag grinned. "With a little luck we will have a clean run without any encounters, but I am certain the Kadark will give chase."

Berag nodded. "His numbers have been depleted, but he will find more. It will not be an easy journey," Berag said. "Three days then," the Ulfor chieftain announced. "And fear not, Ahmad, if the Kadark does give chase he will wish he had not, you have not seen these Tuatha-Day-Dannan in a fight yet."

"Yeah, but we're almost out of ammo," added Matt.

"I will see you all in the morning," Berag said, hefting his axe over his shoulder.

* * * * *

"It is hard to lose loved ones," said Berag. "Have you thought this through? Have you called upon the gods?" he asked.

Heleena nodded. She was sitting between Will and Berag in her parent's house.

"I have," she replied. "There is nothing here left for me now. My parents are gone and I have found the man I will one day call husband." She smiled at Will.

"I know your parents have departed this place," said Berag putting a hand on her shoulder. "But know that you are part of Ulfor and we consider you a part of our family."

"I appreciate that Berag, but it is not the same. I love the village, I love her people, but I am the last of my kin. Whilst I am a part of a larger community, I am the last of my blood. There is nothing left for me." She struggled to keep the tears at bay.

"I cannot stop you," said Berag. "I wanted you to know that you are loved here."

"Oh Berag," she placed her hand on his. "I know that, and I will never forget Ulfor or her people. Not whilst I breathe. But my time here is at an end."

"You are a lucky man, Will. See to it that you look after her."

"Mate, she doesn't need looking after, trust me. She's the most lethal woman I've ever seen," he pulled Heleena to him and kissed her. "She's a Norsewoman, of course she is lethal," grinned Berag. "You will be missed Heleena Footharksdotter," he said.

* * * * *

The night before they departed, a feast was held in the great hall. A feast held in honour the Australians, and the people of Ulfor who had given their lives. No one spoke the words, but Steve knew the Norse people continued to regard them as gods of light. To the people of Ulfor, the soldiers were physical beings sent from deep within their mythology. Berag delivered a speech early in the evening, when people were still sober. He spoke of the Australian soldiers, and of the battles in which the people of Ulfor had been involved. No one uttered a word. The chieftain talked of the first great battle in the valley, and how well the village had fought. He mentioned the soldiers rescuing him from his Viking captives and how so near to death he had been. Berag recounted the final Viking assault upon their village. He mentioned the many individual acts of heroism that brought defeat to the Vikings. He talked of Heleena's parent's last. How Marie, outnumbered four to one, managed to fell a raider with nothing more than a short carving knife.

Berag climbed onto the far end of the table and called out the names of each warrior, man or woman, who had fallen to enemy blades over recent times. There was no doubt that the people of Ulfor had suffered. During a heavy raiding season, they might lose between five and ten people. But they had lost many more during the Australians' stay here. More than they had ever lost at one time in living memory. To begin with there was muttering following each name. But as the roll of honour continued, the noise became louder. Villagers thumped the table, stomped their feet. They called out details about the person, like the name of their sword, how many enemies they felled, or the year of their birth.

"Let us not forget them!" shouted Berag. "Never!" he roared. The Great Hall exploded with cheers.

Stepping down from the table, he gestured for the food and mead barrels to be brought in.

"Let us eat, let us drink!" Berag yelled.

* * * * *

On the third day, the snow had eased and the white blanket covering the land was thinner than it had been for two weeks, but it was still cold. The villagers stood on the outskirts of Ulfor ready to farewell their guests.

"You have no easy journey ahead of you," said Berag, gripping Steve's shoulder. "But the Varangians are some of the greatest warriors on earth."

The chieftain spoke to each soldier and wished them well on their journey.

"Heleena Footharksdotter," said Berag. "No matter where you find yourself, never forget that you will always be a daughter of Ulfor. We will never forget you and will always miss you."

"Thank you Berag," she replied. "Even though I travel with Will, I'll never forget what it means to be a Norsewoman. Not ever."

Berag pushed a bone carving of Thor's hammer into her hand. The small amulet attached to a thin leather cord that she placed around her neck.

"May Thor always watch over you and keep you safe," said Berag.

The Ulfor villagers lined each side of the footpath into the forest. As the group moved through the honour guard, villagers offered their farewells. They slapped the soldiers on the back, shook their hands, banged swords on shields, and shouted their names and their praises. Others invoked the gods to protect them.

"Fight well boy," growled Korgoth, dragging Scott into an embrace.

Scott's face wedged into the smelly armpit of the giant Norseman.

Scott coughed. "Yeah, I will," he spluttered. "Thanks for everything, mate."

Leeka hugged Scott. She smelled much better too.

"May you always be safe, Scott. We'll not forget you." Her eyes were glistening with emotion.

"I won't forget you guys either," said Scott. He kissed her cheek, squeezed her hand and followed the others.

Within minutes, Ulfor had disappeared from sight. They followed Thormdall into the forest towards Skrethorg. The Berserker was not dressed for cold weather, but walked on oblivious to the biting air. Ahmad and the four Varangian guardsmen, with massive axes over their shoulders, followed behind.

Several hours later, Thormdall told them to stop. Without offering an explanation, he drew his sword and loped off into the distance. He was gone for some time and when he returned he was breathing hard. Steve noticed there was blood on his sword.

"We are not for luck on this journey I fear," began Thormdall. "The Kadark is back, but he leads a small group of ragged men who haven't been fed in a week. I intercepted their advance guard and killed them before watching his troop from a distance. They are moving slow, but they are coming this way and they outnumber us perhaps five to one."

No one spoke for a moment.

"Is there another way to Skrethorg?" Steve broke the silence. "Unfortunately, no," replied Thormdall. "We must fight them."

"It seems this will be a long journey indeed," Ahmad said.

"Fear not, priest, we'll have little problem going through them. Except for the Kadark, these men will flee at the first sign of a disciplined, confident attack," replied Thormdall.

Ahmad nodded. "We'll see."

The group moved off the track into the surrounding forest so their footprints were not so obvious. After half an hour, Steve called them to stop.

"Okay, me and my blokes'll setup an ambush here. When they walk through, we'll brass 'em up. Thormdall, when the firing stops you lead the charge. Kill as many as you can. In fact kill 'em all if you can."

Thormdall knelt by a large pine, his sword drawn and a calm expression on his face. The four guardsmen were spread out, squatting, kneeling or sitting behind trees or bushes. Ahmad was between the guardsmen with his tulwar drawn. Steve and his soldiers were lying down out of sight, in positions where they could bring accurate, lethal firepower to bear. Heleena knelt near Will, her bow strung and quiver full of arrows strapped to her right shoulder.

Minutes went by and the silence was absolute. The cold burrowed into their bones and before long, everyone except Thormdall was shivering. A distant laugh broke the silence, followed by a hiss of admonishment. Their footfalls grew louder, and the troop of warriors came into view. Thormdall was right; they looked hungry, they were ill equipped and did not look particularly determined. At the rear was the Kadark. As before, he was dressed in a black robe with a hood that obscured his face. A long sword sheathed in an animal skin scabbard hung by his waist. He seemed to carry an almost demonic aura. Steve noticed the warriors under his command gave him a wide berth.

Steve let the first quarter of the group wander past the hidden soldiers. As the centre of the group came into view, he pulled the pin from a grenade and heaved it into their midst. The handle separated from the grenade with a sound that seemed almost deafening, and the grenade dropped into the snow at the feet of the warriors. Several of them stopped and looked at what they thought was a pinecone. They looked up at the trees, and as one of them knelt and reached out to pick it up, the grenade exploded in a deafening roar that tore away half his face. Three others were killed and the grenade left another six screaming and bleeding in the snow.

The Minimi barked into life, followed by the M4s and the intermittent crack of the M110 sniper rifle. Before the Viking war party knew what was happening, more than half of them were either dead, dying, or wounded.

One warrior ran towards them. Steve shot him in the head. Another turned to flee, but the Minimi tore him from his feet in a murderous roar. Fear was upon the Kadark's warriors and several fled in terror. Another grenade exploded amongst them with a deafening roar that ended four lives and threw several men to the ground in agony.

Almost as soon as the firing had started, it ceased. Amongst the screaming of the wounded and dying came another noise. It was a terrible, inhuman wailing that sounded like a mix between a wolf howl and the roar of a furious bear. Before the band of warriors could regroup, the

Berserker was amongst them. Slaying, hacking and murdering in a rampage, Thormdall was more animal than human.

Further up the faltering skirmish line, four axe-bearing warriors slammed into their flank. The huge newcomers dealt a massive toll amongst them, leaving men decapitated, missing limbs or with deadly wounds.

The Varangian guardsmen were exceptional warriors. They battled with almost the same cool, killing power as Thormdall. The Berserker had cut through the ranks of the Kadark's warriors with as much efficiency and cold malice as a demon from the gates of hell. The Berserker killed and maimed in a quiet savagery. Gone was the demonic wailing. Thormdall was now silent, which was more terrifying than if he had been roaring furious war cries. Men either fell back in terror or died before Thormdall's cold, silent fury. The few warriors who remained standing and able, fled into the forest. Not far behind them, sword in hand, was the Kadark who followed his men into the safety of the trees. Heleena sprinted forward and was releasing arrow after arrow in methodical, rapid succession. Only six seconds passed between the release of each arrow and only one missed its mark. The others hammered into soft, yielding flesh, killing men, or bringing them down in screaming agony.

Matt knelt up and took a clear sight picture of the Kadark. He released a shot straight into the base of his neck, but the Kadark continued running and disappeared behind a large tree.

"Your eyes are going in yer old age," Will grinned.

"Bullshit, I hit that bastard," Matt replied. "I swear to Christ."

"That's why he kept running?" asked Steve. "I bloody hit him." Matt was adamant.

"We move now," Thormdall announced. His face was splattered with blood and gore and his eyes shone with controlled rage that gave him the look of a man bordering on insanity.

They moved along the path at a jog, putting distance between themselves and the Kadark. Before long, he would regroup his warriors and make a counterattack. Behind them were bodies scattered and bleeding. The cries and screams of wounded and dying men echoed throughout the forest.

The group continued at a fast walk or slow run all day and partly into the night. Then Thormdall called a halt.

"A cave lies this way," he said, leading the group off the path and into the safety of the cold, unwelcoming forest.

Steve had trained in Norway during winter, but they had high quality clothing and advanced technology on their side. Here in the hellish cold a thousand years before his time, they relied only on shelter and huddling together to maintain body heat.

The night ground past. Thormdall sat by the cave entrance, sword across his lap, ever watchful. He remained there all night long and when the sun began to rise, he kicked the group awake.

"Let us move," he said.

They shook themselves awake and moved straight out into the morning. They maintained a blistering pace towards Skrethorg. No more was seen of the Kadark and his men, which was not surprising, as the war party had been almost wiped out by a much smaller force. This must have been galling for the Kadark, and it did not take a wise man to realise that he would come for them again. The Kadark was a determined adversary, and he would continue to chase them until he was cut down. Thormdall could kill most living things, but he had never killed a Kadark. As they moved through the still, silent, freezing forest, he was not sure he could.

After ten freezing days, the group reached the outskirts of Skrethorg. Thormdall led them to the same pub as Tharkol had brought the Australians several weeks before. The familiar, overwhelming, pungent smell of Viking beer hit the Australian soldiers once more.

"Thormdall my old friend!" Hadrad welcomed the Berserker with a slap on the back. "Hello again!"

"Mead!" Hadrad shouted, bustling back to the bar.

The drinking area was empty apart from some people seated near a window and two men in a corner at the other side. All turned to stare at the newcomers.

"Look like mean fuckers," Scott said about the two men.

"Yup, won't argue there," replied Steve. "But at least there're no rules of engagement here. If they give us trouble we can just shoot 'em and no one will bother asking questions," he laughed.

Hadrad sat them at a table in the middle of the room and handed out mugs of mead.

"They call it a mug!" Hadrad laughed. Thormdall and the Varangian Guards had picked up their vessels and were viewing them with some suspicion. Thormdall had drunk from the horn of a beast all his life and was not used to this new container.

"From a land across the sea. I paid good money for them, but you can at least put them down without spilling your drink."

Thormdall remained sceptical.

"Bloody good drop," said Will, slamming his empty mug down.

Hadrad refilled Will's mug. Not long after the Varangian Guardsmen had also finished their drinks.

"It is strong," warned Heleena, "Drink slower or you will be kissing the floorboards soon."

"Not a chance," replied Will. "I can hold my grog."

Heleena shook her head.

Steve drank with less speed, savouring the taste. The mead had an unpleasant aroma, but the taste was far beyond his expectations. He savoured each sip, and as Hadrad talked about the day-to-day happenings of the town, Will smashed his empty mug down again. Hadrad, the ever hospitable host refilled his mug. Once again, almost in competition, the guardsmen finished their drinks and smashed their own mugs down on the table.

"You do not want to try and outdrink them," Heleena warned Will.

"Don't I? I can outdrink anyone," already his words carried a mild slur.

"So what brings you all to Skrethorg?" asked Hadrad.

Thormdall explained where they were heading.

"I have a boat waiting at the southern dock," said Ahmad when Thormdall fell silent. "We leave first thing in the morning."

"Winter is my least popular month. Almost all my rooms are spare, so you can have as many rooms as you like, free of charge," offered Hadrad.

"I would hear of no such thing," said Thormdall. "We will pay."

"Don't be silly, my friend, you are welcome and always will be." Thormdall grabbed Hadrad's hand and pushed a small purse of coins into it. When Hadrad began to protest, Thormdall pushed him away. "Go and put it somewhere safe, you will take it and you will keep it."

Thormdall then excused himself and disappeared into the night.

"Where's the dunny?" asked Will.

"I do not understand?" said Hadrad.

"The shitters," replied Will. "Where are they?"

"He wants to know where to relieve himself," explained Steve.

"Out there," Hadrad responded, waving towards the street.

"Righto," Will stood. The two men in the corner looked up as Will past them.

"Look Snorri," said one of the men, loud enough for Will to hear, "a man birthed by a monkey." Both men burst out laughing.

Will conjured up his best look of fear, so the men thought they had intimidated him. He walked out onto the street.

Matt saw what had happened with the men and knew how Will used reverse psychology to overcome even the toughest of opponents. Those two are about to get their arses kicked, he thought.

As Will made his way back into the inn, the two men were unrelenting.

"There's that monkey again, Snorri," the men laughed.

Will approached them. "Look, I don't want any trouble if that's alright?" Will kept his eyes to the floor, feigning fear.

One of them laughed and punched the table. Seeing his opportunity, Will leapt forward, his eyes glowing with fury. His fist cannoned into the face of the first and before the second could register what had happened Will hammered an uppercut into his chin. Blood and teeth exploded from his mouth. The second jumped to his feet, but Will kicked him to the floor.

"Keep your mouth shut next time," Will said.

Will turned, but the two men had risen to their feet with their knives drawn.

It happened faster than lightning. Heleena knocked the first man to the ground with a punch to the temple and as the second turned, she held a knife to his jugular.

"If you threaten him again," she said.

"What if I do?" asked the man whose life was in Heleena's hands.

His voice was wavering, but he was trying to make it sound as if he were in control of the situation, even though he knew he was not.

"Then I kill you," snarled Heleena.

"Let it go lads," said Steve, stepping forward.

Heleena's knife was pressing hard and had opened a small wound, which released a narrow stream of blood. The other was still unconscious.

"We can all sit down and enjoy a drink, there's no reason to pick a fight. But if you continue to bait my friend here," Steve fired his rifle twice into the ceiling. The sound deafening in the small space, "then believe me, we will kill you and drag your bodies out into the street."

Heleena withdrew the knife and stepped away. The man stared at Steve, his ears ringing and his drink long forgotten.

"When he wakes," Steve gestured to the unconscious man, "you tell him the same. That's your last bloody warning. Next time there won't be any words of warning, we'll just kill ya."

Without a word, the man grabbed his friend by an ankle and dragged him out into the street.

"Stupid pricks," said Steve, slapping Will on the shoulder. "Come on, mate," he said, "let's get pissed eh?"

"You were awesome," Will hugged Heleena around the waist and dragged her to him. "Wow!"

She cupped his face in her hands and kissed him.

"I would appreciate it if you did not scare my customers away with your magic," said Hadrad. He looked at their modern weapons with suspicion.

"Sorry about that. No magic, mate, just gunpowder and steel," replied Steve. "I could have shot the prick in the head I guess," he said.

But the humour went unnoticed.

Frowning, Hadrad turned back to Ahmad Ibn Fadlan. "At least it will be a non-eventful crossing. The Norwegians have been raiding all summer and autumn, but with the winter being so hard this year, there have been no ships a-sail. I doubt you will have a problem crossing the ocean to your home land."

"All things going well, I hope you speak the truth," replied Ahmad Ibn Fadlan. "But there can be some troublesome storms this time of year."

"You are right, my friend, but you have a Norse crew, and you could not have better if you come across misfortune on the ocean," Hadrad grinned.

"That's nice," said Will downing his drink and looking into his empty mug. "Too slow fellas," he said as the guardsmen smashed their empty mugs down.

"Depends," said one with a grin. "I think you will be under the table before us."

"You're bloody on!" replied Will.

Taking the hint, Hadrad snatched up the mugs and went to refill them.

Once Hadrad returned, Ahmad watched with distaste as Will gulped down the new beverage.

"He's a thirsty man," said Scott noticing Ahmad's displeasure. As a man of Islam Scott realised that the consumption of alcohol was against his religion.

"So it seems," replied the Arab. "Thank you for your hospitality Hadrad, but I must retire ready for the morrow," and with that he left.

"You're soft!" shouted Will, swaying in his chair.

But Ahmad did not hear him, or did not acknowledge him if he did.

The guardsmen laughed at Will. "Ready for another," one asked. "Yeah righto," replied Will.

Steve, Scott and Matt looked on in amusement. It was obvious to them that Will was outgunned. The guardsmen were hard-core drinkers and although they had kept up with Will drink for drink they still seemed sober.

"Bloody smash ya," Will slurred.

"Dunno about that, mate," said Steve.

"Huh?" asked Will, holding onto the table.

"Nothin', mate. So Hadrad how's business?" asked Steve.

"Hard. It is the worst time of year for us, because the whole city comes to a stop in winter. No one wants to drink anymore. I save what money I make in the spring, summer and autumn months to get through winter. Any surplus I spend on either renovations or on new wares for my business."

"A hard life."

"Yes and no. It is a life that sustains my wife and me. We are no longer subject to seasonal Viking raids, as we were out in the country where Thormdall comes from, for instance. But we are also expected to maintain, or at least to pretend to maintain, the belief of Christianity. All the major cities are now Christian, whereas most of the people who live in the country still believe in the old ways. Christianity is still bewildering and weak to me; it is not a belief that I would follow. But whilst I live in Skrethorg, I must show I follow the man they call Christ." He showed them the small metal crucifix he wore around his neck.

Steve remained silent as Hadrad continued to talk. As a young man who had chosen history as one of his elective subjects, Steve had been taught the Norse believed in a similar fate to Armageddon. But they called it Ragnarok. Ragnarok was a time when their gods were overwhelmed and destroyed by giants and opposing gods. In a way, they were right. Their beliefs and way of life, that others considered to be barbaric or somehow subhuman, was being eroded. Year by year it was being replaced by Christianity. As were so many other native cultures, religions and sacred ways.

As the night ended, the soldiers helped Will negotiate the stairs and they made their way to their beds. Tomorrow would be a long day and they would need the rest.

As Steve thought of Judy and the kids, and tried to blot out Will's loud snoring, he slipped into sleep. Within what seemed only an hour or two the door was thrown open and in strode Thormdall.

"Awaken, we move now," he yelled, waking the soldiers. Will groaned and rolled over. Scott stood up and kicked Will out of his bed and onto the floor.

"Wakey, wakey, sleepy head," he said.

Within an hour, all except Will had eaten breakfast and made their way down to the docks. Ahmad and his guardsmen were already waiting beside the longship that would carry them to their destination.

"How do you fare?" a triumphant guardsmen asked Will. "Not good," Will winced.

"Wait until we enter the open ocean," said another guardsmen. "It gets worse," he added, grinning.

"Great," said Will.

The ship was around fifteen-feet wide in the middle and about one-hundred feet long. It had around twenty oar ports each side and a massive canvas sail that was currently stowed away. The ship looked more like a Norse longship than the Arab ships Ahmad would be familiar with.

It seemed for good reason too as he watched the rest of the crew walk out onto the dock in a ragged mob. There were close to eighty of them and they were all guardsmen. They all carried huge war axes, or bearded axes as Berag had called them. They also carried long swords and round shields. These men protected Ahmad and crewed the ship. The dock was loud with chatter now as the warriors talked and laughed amongst themselves. The large group of guardsmen laughed as they watched Will on his knees vomiting over the jetty to the ocean below.

"We are not even ship bound and you have started feeding the fish, my friend," laughed one of the guardsmen Will had challenged the night before. He helped Will to his feet and offered him a skin of fresh water. Will rinsed his mouth out and then took a long swig. With a groan that meant thanks, he handed the skin back to the warrior.

"You'll be right, mate," said Scott.

"Dunno about that," replied Will, sitting down on the wooden jetty.

A word of command was shouted and the large group of warriors began walking to the ship. The Australians and Ahmad remained on the jetty, watching the warriors prepare the longship. They checked and adjusted riggings then formed a human chain. Passing provisions of food and water along the line, it was stowed away with military precision. Then the ship was ready and everyone climbed aboard.

Steve watched as the Varangian Guardsmen took their positions, ready to row out into the harbour and towards the open ocean in the distance. For each oar there were two warriors sitting side by side on a large wooden chest, into which they had stowed their oiled weapons and armour. Now they were dressed in much lighter clothing, which would make it easier for them to row. Some of them wore leather gloves to prevent blisters.

A Varangian Guardsmen, the commander, stood in full battle gear at the rear right side of the ship. In his hand was a large, horizontal wooden bar at waist height shaped at right angles at the gunwale and disappeared over the side into the ocean below. It was the rudder. After several commands from the warrior who steered, the vessel was untied and pushed from the jetty. Within a few short minutes, they had turned and were making their way out towards the open ocean. The oars pulled the ship through the water as the rowers worked in unison. They were often calling out to each other in a friendly challenge or laughing. One man told another his grandmother was stronger, to which the victim boomed into laughter.

More laughter echoed around the vessel as Will leaned over the side and emptied his stomach into the ocean below.

"We are still in the mouth of the harbour, my friend," called one of the rowers. "Give us a little while longer and Thor will make you wish you had not been born." This was met by more laughter.

"They're a good humoured lot," said Steve.

"Yes they are," replied Ahmad, "but do not be fooled. The Norse are the greatest sailors in the world. I have not yet seen any who could better them. Rest assured we are in good hands."

"Yeah, I believe you," said Steve, watching the Varangian guardsmen pull the longship through the water at close to fifteen knots.

Within ten minutes, they had hit the open ocean and the wind was blowing into them. This made deploying the sail impossible.

Instead, the warriors continued to row. They remained in high spirits and sometimes burst into song.

Will was not in such high spirits. He had emptied what little he had left in his stomach long ago and was now vomiting bile into the rough waters. Heleena had her hand on his back and was talking in soft tones to him. The longship was being thrown and buffeted by the waves and the wind, and still the warriors rowed, shouted, sang or joked.

"You all right?" shouted Steve, with the wind in his ears.

Will just shook his head.

"Oh well, you know never to take on a Norseman in a drinking contest again," Steve said.

"How is he?" asked Matt, as Steve sat down with the others.

"Not good," Steve said. "He's lost a lot of fluid. I'll break open some water soon and get a bit down his neck. He'll need it."

"Getting' pissed before a boat trip is bad news," Scott added.

"Bullshit, mate," said Steve. "My old man was a fisherman. I don't remember many times when he was out on the water sober. He was a bloody pisshead. He also had an iron gut!"

"There ya go," laughed Scott. "Old Will's guts are about as hard as puppy shit."

As the hours passed, Steve forced water into Will. Half of it was vomited into the ocean, but it helped. The wind died in the late afternoon and the anchor was thrown overboard. The sail was unpacked and stretched over the middle of the longship to shield them from the elements during the night.

CHAPTER 15

Steve woke at daybreak, relieved to find the ocean calm and the wind had disappeared.

"A fair morning to you," said one of the guardsman as Steve stretched. The Norseman was on the gunwale of the ship and clutching the wood. He had his trousers around his ankles and was defecating into the ocean below. He was downwind noticed Steve with some relief.

Steve nodded then went to the edge and urinated over the side. Two or three of the Varangian guardsmen were climbing back on board after washing in the ocean. They dried themselves and dressed. Others munched on preserved meat, staring out to sea. Others rubbed animal fat along the blades of their axes, swords or chain mail.

The sail had been rolled back up and stowed away. Ahmad was at the bow of the ship, kneeling on a small rug and praying. Steve noticed the guardsmen did not go near him or talk to him during this ritual. Likewise, none approached Thormdall either. The Berserker was facing the rising sun, with his legs crossed and sword across his lap. It seemed he was in a meditative trance. After five minutes, Thormdall rose, sheathed his sword and went in search of food.

The ocean boiled near the left side of the ship. Small fish jumped and darted across the surface of the water trying to escape some larger predator.

"Here," said Thormdall handing Steve a lump of meat. "Eat."

Moving around the sleeping soldiers, Thormdall shook them one by one and handed them breakfast.

"Smells like shit," said Scott.

Steve chuckled. The meat was a bit like beef jerky, only it was fish, and he could taste a faint hint of wood smoke.

"It's not bad actually," he said, taking another bite.

"Breakfast in bed," said Matt, with a grin. "Now that's service."

As the sun rose over the ocean, guardsmen took their seats and the anchor was drawn up. Oars were pushed through the ports and out into the water. Once more, they were underway and almost immediately, the banter started up amongst the guardsmen as they rowed.

The longship itself was a thing of beauty; it was sleek and crafted with great care. The bow arched like the neck of a swan. The wooden structure groaned as the planks flexed and bent to accommodate the ever-changing ocean beneath them. Steve had been told the planks were lashed to the frame rather than nailed or screwed so the wood could shift half a foot out of true without snapping. The quality was so meticulous that the longship remained watertight.

"What day do ya reckon it is?" Will asked. He seemed to be feeling much better today.

"Dunno, mate," replied Steve, gazing into the distance. "What colour's your piss?" he asked turning back to Will.

"Clear," he said, starting to clean his weapon. "You're as bad as my bloody mother," he said, opening the oil bottle.

The soldiers had been cleaning and oiling their weapons at least four or five times per day to combat the sea salt blowing in.

"How much ammo has everyone got left?" asked Steve.

"About 150 rounds left on the belt in the gun then I'm dry," said Scott.

"One mag and two 40 mil rounds left," said Will, holding the rifle barrel up to the sky to make sure there was no dirt in it.

"About one mag," said Matt, "and one grenade," he added.

"I've got just under a mag," said Steve finally. "So we're pretty close to empty. Might have to get our bayonets out before long."

"It won't come to that," said Scott. "I prefer nailing the bastards from a distance. Don't think I'd knock off a bloke at close range with a one-foot bayonet, when he's running at me with a three- foot sword."

"Me neither," agreed Steve.

"It is not quite as difficult as you make it sound," cut in Thormdall who had been listening to the conversation. "There is some skill in fighting with a sword, but the absolute basic core of sword fighting comes down to three simple things. The ability to stand, see and breathe. If you lose any of those, then you are finished."

"You're making it sound a bit easier than it is, mate," said Matt.

Thormdall shrugged. "Sometimes when battle begins, the younger warriors experiencing their first real fight freeze. They become an easy target. The first skill of sword fighting is the ability to conquer your own fear. You must be able to breathe. Breathing slow can help relax your body and mind. You must be able to see, and I do not mean being able to look. There is a difference. You must be able to see that the screaming warrior sprinting at you cloaked in animal skins with snarling face and bloody sword is a man. Nothing more. This conquers fear and makes one a more fluid fighter. Finally, to be able to stand, not just stand up, but being aware of your footing. If you fall or lose your balance, you will be dead faster than you think. The young Norsemen are good swordsmen do not mistake me. They know all the fancy sword tricks that impress the women, but when the reality of death is in the air, they tend not to be so cocky or skilled. A good swordsman takes the time to master his mind before he attempts to master the blade."

"Sounds like it's gonna take a long time. Maybe we shouldn't bother," said Scott.

Thormdall shook his head. "I have seen you all fight before, and although I might be incorrect in my thinking, I do believe you have all mastered your fear. The next step is to take up the sword."

Scott looked at the others. "Fuck I'll give it a go," he said grinning.

So as the longship cut through the waves, Thormdall took the soldiers through the basics of sword fighting. A few Varangians who much preferred their great bearded axes to swords donated the weapons. The first level of swordsmanship was learning how to block, parry, stab and slash. The three most important targets at this basic level were the throat, belly or groin. Thormdall drilled the men for several hours and it was much harder than it looked. With shoulders burning, arms tired and sweat drenching their clothes, the soldiers finished for the day. Thormdall had promised more of the same the following morning.

"The next step is to read your opponent," said Thormdall, taking a seat near the soldiers. "You will learn his habits, his strengths and his weaknesses. For instance, one man might raise his eyebrows before he attacks. He might flick his eyes down, but you will learn to read your opponent and in this way be able to counter any attack. For now the basic attack and defence will be enough to see you through many of your fights."

Dusk approached and the wind picked up behind them, so the sail was deployed. The oarsmen cheered and withdrew their huge oars, stowing them in a neat pile at each side of the longship. Steve watched the massive sail fill with wind and for the first time noticed the thick red and white stripes that decorated the canvas.

Night settled in and silence enveloped the ship as each man was drawn into his own thoughts, the rhythmic sound of the ocean sliding by. Some hours after they had eaten dinner, the wind changed and the sail was recovered. The anchor was thrown overboard and the crew made ready for another evening.

As always, Steve's mind was drawn to his family. He tried to remember the sound of their voices or the smell of their hair, but it was difficult. He chuckled to himself as Brent's cheeky face filled his mind. He told his son how much he missed him and to look after his mother and sister. Kathy's beaming smile was next, but before he could contemplate his daughter's face, it was replaced by an image of Hilda's pale, dead body. But the corpse wore Kathy's smile. The dead child's eyes opened and she turned her head towards him, "I miss you, Daddy," the smiling corpse whispered. Steve sat up and took a deep breath.

"Christ," Steve whispered.

As the longship rocked back and forth, Steve slipped into the arms of sleep. He woke to several alarmed shouts. It was still dark although there was a hint of dim light coming from the east. The ship was surrounded by a thick, invasive mist. The sail had been packed away and the guardsmen were bustling around the ship.

"What's happening?" he asked Thormdall who was sitting close by.

"Mist," answered Thormdall. "The mist hides water demons and monsters from the deep that will attempt to thwart our journey, throw us off course, or sink us."

"So what're they doing?" Steve asked.

"They will attach protection to the prow and aft of the ship," said Thormdall, pointing to a guardsman on the highest part of the prow of the vessel. In his hand, he held a huge dragon face carved in detail from hardwood. The carving was hammered into place, then at the rear of the ship, he did the same with a curved dragon's tail.

"We attach the power of the dragon to frighten the demons and monsters that hide in the mist. Whilst these wardens are attached to the longship we are safe, but they must be removed before we make harbour in a friendly port."

Once the dragon was in place, the guardsmen quietened again, and some even managed to slip back into sleep.

About an hour later, they were up again. The soldiers followed Thormdall into the centre of the ship where they once again practiced their sword skills. Steve's right shoulder still ached from the day before, but he tried his best. That the Berserker was a master was beyond doubt; his swordsmanship was impeccable.

A stop was called when Scott became too enthusiastic and caught Will on the face with the flat of his sword.

"Sorry, bro," Scott said, inspecting his cheek.

"What the hell are you doing?" roared Will. He charged Scott, stopping himself inches from the tall soldier. Will's eyes smouldered with violence, but he had gained control of himself at the last minute. A red welt was already forming on his cheek.

"Shit, I said sorry!" said Scott. "Shoulda knocked ya out!"

Thormdall gestured for them to take their places again.

"The best way to learn," said Thormdall, "is to feel pain, because after that the chances of repeating your mistake are halved. Another thought to keep in mind is that the shortest, most powerful attack in a sword fight is a straight line."

"Fuck's sake, mate, in English ay?" said Scott, resting the tip of his sword on the floor. Thormdall gestured for Scott to take up his sword.

"Do not allow Olaf to see you do that. He will skin you alive," said the Berserker.

"I will explain," Thormdall continued. "If your opponent has his sword above his head and is readying for a beheading stroke, or to hack into your shoulder, you have two options. You can block the attack or you can step into him and stab him in the midriff, the groin or the throat. Stabbing takes less time and is more effective than a chopping stroke. But countering an attack with an attack is not always a bad option."

After they had been practising for several hours, Thormdall suggested they rest for lunch. Their shoulders were sore, but they had learned that sword fighting was more than the simple hack and slash as depicted in movies. After they had rested, Thormdall taught them how deception was more valuable than hours of skilled sword fighting.

"If you feign total exhaustion or extreme fear, then your opponent will believe he has the upper hand. More often than not, he will let his guard down and he will believe you are an easy kill. This is the best way to deceive an enemy, and if done with precision you can kill an opponent fast."

Thormdall pointed at Will. "This is a tactic you know well!"

The lessons continued, but the soldiers stopped when they heard a voice calling. It was the ship's captain, Olaf, who was in control of the steer board, which steered the ship.

The wind had been at their backs now for the best part of the afternoon so the oarsmen had enjoyed a well-deserved rest. They were playing some kind of board game on a piece of silk cloth that had squares painted on it. It looked like chess, only the squares were arranged in a large cross, instead of a square.

"What do you see?" called a guardsman, glancing up from his game. "A longship, she is closing on us. It seems she means to catch us," replied Olaf.

The games stopped as the guardsmen looked out. They could see a tiny black sail on the horizon through a brown haze.

"I do not know a black sail," said Olaf.

Soon the longship was close enough for them to see a large white eagle painted against the black.

"It seems we are in the presence of a Kadark," said Olaf.

"That bloody bastard doesn't give up," said Scott. "Didn't you kill him, mate?" Scott asked Matt. "Yeah, twice!"

"I reckon your eyes are shot," said Will.

"Yeah, but I'd rather be an old bastard with bad eyes than a young dickhead," Matt replied.

Will burst out laughing. "Yeah, righto, point taken," he said.

Another hour passed and they could see the oars on the Kadark's ship. Combined with a full sail, the oars were propelling the ship along at a blistering speed. This was good, Thormdall explained to the soldiers, because by the time the ship reached them, his crew would be exhausted. Steve hoped this was the case. But experience had shown these people were tougher than the television watching, fast- food eating people of his world.

Deciding to use what might turn out to be the last of their ammunition the soldiers prepared for the fight. The guardsmen donned their chain mail and polished their axe blades. Ahmad was praying at the bow of the ship, but Allah did not seem to be listening. The ship was closing in. It was now possible to see individual oarsmen, and in the centre of the longship, the Kadark himself.

"Stay here, you'll be safe here," Will said to Heleena who was standing at centre of the ship. She wanted to argue with him, but she knew her throwing knives and short daggers would be useless in a sea battle. He kissed her.

"Be safe," she said.

When the sun had almost fallen below the horizon, there was a call for oars. The guardsmen took their seats, fed them through the ports ready to begin work.

"Pull!" roared Olaf, and the oars dipped into the ocean as one.

"Why are our blokes rowing?" asked Steve. "They are wasting energy, when they could be getting ready to fight!"

"I have only been in two sea battles," replied Thormdall, "but I know that speed and manoeuvrability are the key to success. If we get too close to the Kadark, his crew will throw grappling hooks onto our decks or rigging and try to drag us into them. Once we have been hooked, it is difficult to escape so we will be forced to defeat them. But if we try to outrun them, they may give up the chase. The other alternative is to fight a running battle with arrows and spears so the enemy can be picked off from a distance. But given the determination of the Kadark, I do not see us escaping without a full sea battle."

"Bloody great," said Scott. "We're having some fine fuckin' luck!"

The guardsmen were shouting as they worked the oars. But this time they were aggressive, urging each other on. After about twenty minutes, the Kadark's longship had only caught them by a hair's breadth. But the chase continued.

A moment later, an arrow plunged deep into the mast, followed by another. The small figure of a man balancing against the prow of the Kadark's ship leant out, longbow in hands. He prepared to send another shaft towards them. Heleena was quick to collect the arrows and place them in her quiver.

"Can you end him?" Thormdall asked Steve.

"Yup," said Steve. "Go ahead, Matt."

Matt had received endless taunts from the other soldiers for failing to shoot the Kadark. But Steve knew that he was their best shooter, and if Matt had said that he had hit the Kadark, then his aim had been true. Few men, if any, would walk away from a bullet through the base of the neck.

Steve watched Matt kneel down at the rear of the longship, supporting his body and weapon against the wood of the gunwale. Another arrow sped towards them, but it ricocheted off the deck and disappeared into the sea. Matt remained still, as the longship rocked and weaved through the ocean. After almost a minute, and as the enemy archer was about to lose another shaft, Matt fired the shot. The man's face disappeared in a spray of bone and pink mist and his bow disappeared into the water.

"Oi, Steve!" yelled Matt. "You can see a few of the oarsmen from here."

Bringing his rifle up and looking through the ACOG scope, Steve could see the Kadark's oarsmen as they leaned into their work. Sea spray hid them from view for a second.

"Nice," he said, lowering the rifle. "Make your shots count," he said.

The guardsmen continued to row. Every minute the crack of Matt's M110 sniper rifle cut through the roar of the wind and sea. Each time they heard a shot, the soldiers knew another enemy warrior had died.

"Got about twelve of the bastards," said Matt, his clothes soaked through.

"Bloody good work, mate," said Steve.

As Matt cleaned his weapon, Steve watched the crew on the chasing longship. The warriors who had been shot were thrown overboard, one after the other, as if they were nothing more than broken implements.

Even with a depleted crew, the chasing ship closed the gap. This confused Steve until he turned to see that their guardsmen had stopped rowing and were waiting for Olaf's instruction. The sail was still full and continued to pull the longship through the sea at close to ten knots, but the Kadark's ship continued to gain.

"What the hell does Olaf think he's doing?" asked Steve.

"I know not," replied Thormdall. "According to Ahmad he is a veteran of many sea battles, in fact he has fought more battles at sea than he has on land. I would not lose trust in his judgement."

"Bring in the sail!" roared Olaf.

Five guardsmen ran to the mast, pulled down the sail and stowed it away at blistering speed.

Meanwhile Steve watched the Kadark's ship gain on them.

"This is it, I guess," Steve said to his soldiers, who spread themselves out and made ready to start firing into the opponent vessel.

"Oars at full!" shouted Olaf.

The guardsmen began heaving on the oars, dragging the ship through the water. They gained speed, but not near enough to see them to safety.

"I thought you said sea battles were about speed!" Steve shouted at Thormdall.

"And manoeuvrability!" yelled Thormdall. "You cannot manoeuvre a ship well at speed, as you are about to see."

"What d'ya mean?" asked Steve moving closer to the Berserker so that he did not have to shout.

"I think Olaf means to cripple her," Thormdall replied.

"Don't worry about it Steve, we ain't got enough time, mate!" Scott yelled. He had the Minimi resting against the gunwale, ready to fire at the approaching enemy vessel.

"Bloody madness," said Steve, shaking his head.

"Turn hard steer board side!" roared Olaf.

The longship had picked up a little speed. He watched as the right side of the ship began to reverse row, whilst the left side continued to row forward with as much power as they could muster. It struck him that perhaps the word "steer board" to name the right side of the ship would become the word "starboard". But he dismissed the thought as the enemy approached fast.

Olaf's guardsmen began to turn straight into the wind towards the oncoming vessel. Thormdall was standing at the bow now. He had unsheathed his sword and waited for the onslaught to begin.

"Forward full!" shouted Olaf and the right side stopped reverse rowing and began rowing forward.

The ship edged forward into the biting wind. By the time individual planks of wood could be seen on the enemy longship, they were approaching five knots. The enemy vessel must have been travelling at almost twenty knots. Olaf's guardsmen continued rowing with full strength, shouting and psyching themselves up. Then almost as the enemy ship was on top of them, Olaf steered the longship on a collision course.

"What the hell?" shouted Will.

"Oars in!" shouted Olaf.

Almost as the last oar was withdrawn, the two ships collided. Scott's Minimi immediately opened up. Shouting erupted from both vessels and the Varangian guardsmen were on their feet. Some swinging their massive axes across at their opponents, dealing death and carnage.

Their ship grated and groaned against the side of the enemy vessel. He could hear loud cracks and looked to see that the bow of their ship was snapping off the oars of the opponent vessel as they passed each other.

Steve brought the rifle into his shoulder and opened fire. He did not need to aim. Men were torn from their seats by the bullets. Seeing movement from his peripheral, Steve looked to see Thormdall jumping across onto the enemy ship. The berserker stabbing, slashing and slaying as he ran between the rowers' benches.

Avoiding the Berserker, Steve and his soldiers continued to send bullets across into the enemy. Some had dived for cover, but most remained seated and died before they had time to react.

After killing and maiming almost quarter of the crew, Thormdall came to a halt before the Kadark. Thormdall was grinning and snarling. As he drew back his blade, his head filled with pain.

"You cannot kill me, you fool," the voice whispered in the Berserker's mind.

Fighting through the pain, Thormdall opened his eyes and brought his sword to bear again.

"How much would you like to wager?" he asked, and plunged the sword into the Kadark's chest. Instead of cutting into muscle, sinew and bouncing off or grating against bone, the sword passed through thin air.

Laughter erupted in his mind. Thormdall stepped past the Kadark and ran on. One warrior stepped in to meet him but died with a deep cut to the throat.

The soldiers continued firing into the enemy, making their shots count. As the enemy ship had almost slid by, Thormdall threw himself over and landed on the deck of the longship. Blood stained his face and hair claret. He grinned and sheathed his sword.

Steve looked up. Several pieces of metal carved into the air as the enemy passed them. Some of the Varangians had cast grappling hooks to snare the enemy ship and drag her into them, but they splashed into the ocean. With half their oars snapped and useless, the Kadark's vessel was dead in the water.

"Oars at full, turn hard steer board side," roared Olaf.

Then Olaf gave the order for the sail to be deployed.

The crippled enemy longship redistributed the remaining oars and attempted to escape. But Olaf's ship was upon them within minutes. Throwing the grappling hooks with success this time, the guardsmen pulled the fleeing ship to them until it was alongside their own.

The Varangian Guardsmen followed Thormdall's headlong charge onto the enemy ship. Steve, Matt, Scott, Will, Heleena and Ahmad stood back and watched as the slaughter ended. Not one of the enemy warriors survived, and they lost only one guardsman.

The Kadark remained untouched, even though Scott saw guardsmen hacking into him during the height of the onslaught. The dark robed figure now stood at the bow of the longship. Thormdall strode towards the Kadark, his sword sheathed. As he approached, pain erupted in his mind once more, but he ignored it and stopped within one pace of the Kadark.

"Know this," Thormdall said, "I know not yet how to end you, but when I do, I will hunt you, I will find you and I will kill you. Now be gone."

The Kadark stood watching the Berserker. This time there was no mocking laughter. A breeze drifted over the silent longship, ruffling the Kadark's hooded cloak. Still there was no hint of a face, which for most men would be unnerving. But Thormdall was not most men.

"Be gone!" Thormdall roared, taking a step forward.

Without a word, the Kadark turned, stepped into the water and disappeared beneath the waves.

"He is dead?" Olaf asked.

"I fear not. This is no mere mortal. I will think on it, but I wish Romeeros was here, maybe he would know how to end him. He breathes and walks, so he can die, I am sure of that."

"I hope you are right," said Olaf. Olaf knew that Thormdall was a Berserker, the ultimate warrior in the Norse world. If the Kadark could be killed, then it would be at the hands of one such as Thormdall.

"Let us leave," Olaf spoke again, making his way back to his own longship where Steve and his soldiers waited.

The Varangian Guardsmen carried the body of their comrade back onto their own longship. Untying the grappling hooks, they pushed the corpse-ridden enemy ship away. As it drifted away, Matt pulled the pin from his last grenade and threw it in a high arc. The small dot landed dead centre and exploded in a dark cloud. The grenade shattered a hole in the bottom of the ship, sending the stricken vessel on a slow journey to the bottom of the sea.

With first aid pack beside him, Matt knelt over a wounded, unconscious Varangian. The man had suffered a deep wound to his leg and was losing a large quantity of blood.

"What are you doing?" One of the Varangians growled at Matt. "Let him travel to the Gods in peace!"

"We can save him, mate!" Matt replied. "We can keep him alive!"

The Varangian walked away.

"He's gonna die if we don't control the haemorrhage," said Matt.

"He's hypotensive, systolic's 70, tachycardic at 130, no radial, but a good strong carotid. Tachycardic's good, means he hasn't started decompensating."

"Shit, mate, that's all gibberish to me, just tell me what you want me to do," Steve said.

"Put pressure on this," Matt pointed at a thick pad he had applied to the warrior's thigh. "Push down hard, mate, don't be afraid, you ain't gonna hurt him any more than he already is."

While Steve applied pressure on the wound, Matt placed a cannula into a large vein on the inner aspect of the warrior's elbow. He connected a litre bag of fluid to the cannula, but kept the valve shut for the time being.

"Didn't wanna do this," said Matt seeing that the pad alone was not controlling the bleeding. Applying a tourniquet to the wounded man's upper leg, circulation to the lower leg stopped, controlling the bleeding. With the haemorrhage now under control, Matt passed the bag of fluid to Steve.

"Hold that up," he said, and opened the valve to let the fluid pass into the body of the unconscious warrior.

"Will, get over here, mate," called Matt, "raise his legs."

Will obliged, lifting the warrior's legs and placing them on his webbing.

"Scott, come 'ere," Matt shouted. "Mate you're gonna have to cut his leg off below the tourniquet."

"Sorry, you want to fuckin' do what?" asked Scott.

"Take your bloody sword, mate, and cut his leg off. Swing hard to make one clean cut, make sure you hit below the tourniquet. This bloke's dead otherwise."

"Christ almighty," whispered Scott, taking a deep breath.

The soldier paused, swore and swung his weapon hard. The blade severed the warrior's leg just below the tourniquet. Without hesitation, Matt snatched up the amputated limb and threw it overboard.

"Happy eating," he muttered. "Someone go and get me a wooden plate," ordered Matt.

Scott was wide eyed, the blood drenched sword hung by his side.

"Scott, you hear me!" Matt said.

"Huh?"

"Go and get me a wooden plate, now!" said Matt.

When Scott returned, Matt took the plate. Pushing five bullets from a spare magazine, Matt began separating the bullet from the cartridge with a knife. Then he emptied the gunpowder from each bullet onto the plate. Matt asked Scott for his lighter.

Matt held the naked flame to the plate. When the gunpowder flared into life, Matt picked it up and held the burning surface to the stub of the warrior's leg. The sickening aroma of burning flesh soon permeated the air.

Within seconds, the stub of the warrior's leg had been cauterised. The blood vessels and arteries burnt closed and flesh purged of germs and impurities. For now anyway. Matt maintained a close eye on the vital signs of the warrior, who was still unconscious, but improving. The wound would need to be cleaned and redressed at least three times per day.

The wind drove the longship on for most of the afternoon. Many of the Varangian Guardsmen had removed their chain mail, cleaned and re oiled their weapons and stowed them away. They sat in small groups, talking in quiet murmurs. It seemed the loss of two of their number, had hit the guardsmen hard. One lay out in the centre of the vessel with his huge axe on this chest. To them, the other that Matt had tended, was as good as dead.

The soldiers' thoughts were drawn back to Dave, who had died at the beginning of their compromise in Iraq. It seemed like a lifetime ago, in a different world. If they ever made it back home, Dave would be mourned and farewelled and the soldiers of the regiment would feel much the same as these guardsmen did now. They had lost a brother, a fellow warrior and his name and memory would never die, not as long as they walked.

As the sun sank, Olaf called a halt and the anchor thrown overboard. They had stopped sailing earlier than usual. As the Varangians gathered around their fallen comrade, it was obvious they intended to farewell him before evening fell.

"We lost a good man today," said Olaf. "Therolf was one of the finest guardsmen I have ever had the pleasure to serve alongside. It is unfortunate that today was the day that Odin beckoned for him. But he died as he would have wished, as a warrior, as a brother. I knew Therolf's wife, Helda, so it is I who will bear her the news. It will be hard for her to hear. I believe he also taught one of our newcomers how to drink."

The guardsmen looked at Will and roared with laughter. Therolf was one of the guardsmen he had challenged to outdrink. In fact, it was the same man who had offered him the water skin the following day.

"Christ," Will said. Guilt washed over him for some reason.

"I believe Therolf won," continued Olaf. His remark was followed by more laughter.

"Therolf could outdrink a horse!" called a voice from the back.

They spoke of their memories of Therolf before lifting his body and carrying it to the side of the longship. With axes drawn in salute, Therolf was placed over the side, his massive battle-axe still clasped in his hands. Then he was gone, falling into the black depths of the sea.

"If Odin wills it, Therolf is the only man we lose today," said Olaf, looking at the unconscious warrior next to Matt.

The wounded Varangian was kept warm overnight underneath a blanket Will and Heleena shared.

"Now that's dedication," whispered Scott. He nodded at the couple sleeping beside the unconscious, wounded Varangian.

"What's that?" Matt asked.

"He lost his leg just to sleep with Heleena!" laughed Scott.

"Dickhead," chuckled Matt, "I'll have to tell Will that one." The grin vanished from Scott's face.

CHAPTER 16

After twenty days, land was in sight. The first sign were sea birds wheeling and diving in the distance. Within hours, they perched in the rigging, calling out to each other in a noisy conglomerate of sound. Sometimes they took flight and dived into the ocean, coming away with fresh fish clamped in their beaks. As for the soldiers, there was only so much dried fish they could eat. For the Varangian Guardsmen it was all they knew, they had been travelling and fighting at sea their entire lives. Twenty days with nothing but dried fish was a short, pleasant voyage for them.

The man, whom Matt now knew as Gudrik, was recovering well. By using his sword as a walking stick, Gudrik was mobile again. Olaf complained half-heartedly about the marks his sword point left in the floor of the longship. There was also a single, mighty scar on one of the benches where Scott had amputated Gudrik's leg, but Olaf did not seem concerned about that.

The wind had been at their backs for the better part of five days, so the guardsmen had enjoyed the rest. Many of them either slept, or played the board game the Varangians explained was called King's Table. But as they came closer to the coast, they prepared to row once more. Steve noticed that Ahmad stood at the helm, keeping a close eye on the coastline.

"Well, we're finally bloody here," Scott broke Steve's reverie.

"Yeah, wherever here is," replied Steve. "But it definitely isn't Turkey."

"We struck out east from what I reckon was Denmark," said Matt, "could be Lithuania, Latvia, Poland, even Germany, I guess. One thing's for sure though, man, I'd rather go east from Denmark by sea and get to Turkey by land from the north. Otherwise we'd have been bloody months at sea sailing all the way round to Turkey."

"Still might take months, mate," said Will.

"True, but at least we're on solid ground, man," replied Matt.

"Yeah, good point," grinned Will.

"To the steer board side! Steer board side!" shouted Ahmad.

Olaf was standing on his toes, leaning over the side to see beyond the sail.

"I see it!" Olaf shouted back, and began turning the ship to the right.

Steve could see a distant flaming arrow reaching its apex before descending and disappearing into the ocean. Someone was waiting for them on the coastline. Another fire arrow followed the first.

"Where are we?" Steve asked Ahmad.

"Polsk," replied Ahmad. "Still cold, but not quite as cold as the land from which you have travelled. I look forward to Byzantium, much warmer there."

"So it's Poland," said Matt. "That means we'll head south through Romania, Bulgaria and then over into Turkey. They're pretty nice countries."

"Yeah, great little tourist destinations in the twenty first century," said Scott. "But back in whatever fuckin' year this is, we'll end up getting tracked down by bloody head hunting maniacs. They'll have filed their teeth into fangs."

"Maybe," shrugged Steve, "but at least we're a bit closer to home."

As the longship neared the coast, Steve could see a small contingent of people at the water's edge there to meet them. As the minutes passed and they drew closer, he realised that the congregation was another group of Varangian Guardsmen.

"They were to await our return," said Ahmad. "They have guarded and cared for our horses. We travel from here on horseback."

"Did you say horseback, man?" Matt asked.

"I did," replied Ahmad. "Is there a problem?"

"Never ridden a horse before," said Matt. "First time for everything ay?"

"You have not ridden a horse before?" he asked in disbelief.

"Nope," said Matt.

"Neither have I," said Steve, "but it can't be too hard?"

"Famous last words," chuckled Scott.

"So you have ridden before?" Ahmad turned to Heleena.

"Many times," she replied. "I will show them what I know."

"That is something," said Ahmad. "And what of you," he asked Scott. "Can you ride?"

"Me? Fuck no! Closest I've been to a horse is Melbourne Cup," laughed Scott.

"I have," said Will.

"Well then," said Ahmad, "you and Heleena can explain good horsemanship to the others."

"You didn't let me finish, mate. I rode a horse once when I was a kid and the bloody thing tried to buck me off. Never been near one since and I tell you what Ahmad, if the one I get tries to buck me off, I'm gonna shoot the bloody thing!" Will said.

Ahmad silenced them. "Horsemanship is not as difficult as it sounds," said the priest. "It is a skill that comes fast to some, but most need teaching. We have a long journey ahead of us, so Heleena and I will endeavour to teach you what we know. First, you must not make any sudden movement around the animals," Ahmad said moving away.

When the priest was no longer in earshot, Scott chuckled. "We're fuckin' screwed."

Soon the longship was beached on the shore and the crew had disembarked. The Australians were happy to be on land once again.

"Any trouble?" asked Olaf as he approached the waiting warriors. "None at all, we saw some Polsk tribesmen out hunting from a distance, which was maybe five days ago now. I doubt they saw us," replied Rafneer, Olaf's second in command. "All the horses are sound and are well rested ready for the journey." Rafneer looked over Olaf's shoulder, "I see you are missing one."

"Therolf fell at sea, it was a minor skirmish."

Rafneer nodded. "Gudrik is a little lighter I see," he chuckled watching the Varangian making his way up the beach towards them. His gaze fell upon Heleena. "Nice," he said.

"She belongs to one of the newcomers," Olaf explained.

"Ah, the newcomers," Rafneer said, watching the four men walking towards him. They all moved with a purpose, and although their faces were not cruel, they displayed strength.

"Therolf will be missed," Rafneer said. "We have fresh pig, it is cooking as we speak," he called over his shoulder.

"That is good to hear," said Olaf. "The day is drawing to an end, and we are famished. We will set out at first light."

The night was silent. Steve's brain was expecting to hear the creaking and groaning of the longship as it slid through the ocean. Perhaps the snap of the sail as it caught in the wind or the noise of the sea. The silence prevented him from falling asleep, and his body seemed to be rocking back and forth, almost as if he were still at sea. Sleep would not come.

A thick morning mist blanketed the ground and soaked the men to the bone. They woke shivering and swearing. Steve thought he had slept for perhaps two hours at best. Even on land, the Varangian Guardsmen were wary of the mist, ever watchful and on edge. After a short breakfast, the large group gathered their horses, saddled them and made to leave. It took the Australians some instruction, a few chuckles and some patience before they were mounted and ready to travel.

"What about them?" asked Scott, looking at the small group of Varangian guardsmen, which included Gudrik.

"They will stay and sail the longship back around to Byzantium. We will go by land, as it is much faster. They have a journey at sea of perhaps three moons ahead of them."

"Shit, lucky them," replied Scott.

The mist lifted, although it was still cold as they moved in a large column through a sparse section of forest. Thormdall rode in front, talking and laughing with Olaf. Ahmad, Heleena and the Australians were at the centre. Steve realised the Varangian Guardsmen were treating them in the same way as they would the King of Byzantium. If they were attacked, those in the centre could be defended and if necessary, led to safety.

"Is this area dangerous?" Scott asked Ahmad.

"Polsk is a strange land, the tribesmen are friendly more often than not, but I cannot differentiate between the tribes. Some of the tribes are fanatical horse people. If all the tribes united under one ruler, they would pose a great threat to neighbouring countries. Some of the tribes guard their hunting grounds and will track down any who encroach on them. I have never experienced this myself, but I have heard of such things happening."

"Well, let's hope we don't meet any of those types," said Scott, wincing in the saddle.

"Okay, what ammo have we got left?" Steve asked.

"I've got about twenty rounds left on the gun," said Scott with a chuckle. The Minimi would go through that in several short bursts. It was decided to break the machinegun link into individual bullets and distribute them to those with rifles. The machinegun would be of no more use, yet. If they made it back to Iraq it would be a different story, but for now, the weapon was slung.

"Back to the old trusty sword," grinned Scott, drawing the weapon in one swift movement.

Scott's horse half reared at the sudden noise and movement. The animal galloped off, barging through the Varangian line. Scott disappeared into the forest like some possessed warrior of old on his last charge. He was holding on for dear life, with the sword held above his head as if he were about to take on the evil of the world single-handed. The distant horse powered up a rise and was then swallowed from view by the forest.

As the laughter died down, one of the guardsmen cantered off after Scott. "I'll find him," he called over his shoulder.

"Shit, that happened pretty quick," said Will.

Almost ten minutes later, Scott was led back to the group. They laughed and cheered.

"Behold, the mighty warrior returned!" One guardsman yelled.

Scott was white faced as he came alongside Steve. His hands were shaking.

"Christ, I'm never touching that fuckin' sword again, I swear my life flashed before my eyes. I tried to get him to stop, but it was like he thought I wanted him to go faster."

"What was the advice I first gave you this morn?" asked Ahmad.

"No sudden movement," responded Scott, his face still white with shock.

"No sudden movements," agreed Ahmad.

"Right, now the entertainment is over, we'll start again. How much ammo has everyone else got?" asked Steve.

"About half a mag," said Matt, "enough for one more fight."

"About the same," said Will.

"As for me, I've got about ten bullets left," said Steve, "so pretty soon it'll all be up close and personal," he said, touching the hilt of the sword.

The troop stopped once during the day and ate lunch. The soldiers groaned as they dismounted.

"This is fuckin' killin' my legs. It feels like I've pulled a muscle in my groin and I think my arse is starting to chaff," said Scott.

"Yup, and we're only half way through the first day," laughed Matt. "Don't fuckin' do that again," said Scott, stroking his horse's face. The animal nuzzled his chest.

Soon they were under way once more, the horses moving at a fast walk. They remained at this pace almost until night fell. They set up camp near a small creek. The soldiers were shown how to remove the saddles, rub their horses down and let their animals to graze.

It was not as freezing here as it had been in Denmark, but the cold still closed in around them. Steve pulled his thick woollen cloak tight around his body.

Morning came and after breakfast, they moved through the forest in single file. Once again, Ahmad, Heleena and the soldiers were at the centre of the column. The forest was thicker here, forcing them to duck low in their saddles to avoid branches from time to time. They stopped at one point to drag a large trunk clear of the path. The path did not widen. So rather than being forced to stop in single file and open themselves to a flank attack, the group ate one the move.

"My arse is fuckin' dead!" said Scott, shifting in the saddle.

"I'm sorta getting used to this," said Matt, leaning down and patting the neck of his horse. "What the hell's gotten into you?" Matt asked, as the animal sidestepped towards the forest. Matt brought the beast back onto the track.

There was the thunder of hooves and Thormdall galloped around a bend in the path.

"Be ready to fight!" he called to the soldiers. "Polsk tribesmen are paralleling us. They are watching us for now, but may attack, and if they do we will take heavy casualties."

Turning in his saddle, Steve could see nothing off to their left, but to their right he caught a glimpse of movement in the forest. But he could see nothing. He continued to watch and noticed the silhouette of a tall man moving between the trees then another, followed by a third. The men were on foot and moving fast.

"For fuck's sake, this is getting a bit old now," said Scott, his useless Minimi slung across his back. Without ammunition, he would be of no use if the tribesmen paralleling them offered a challenge. He was tempted to strip the weapon down and bury the pieces. But he knew if the patrol ever made it back to Iraq and the Land Rover, and copious amounts of ammunition, the Minimi would regain its use.

"Yeah I hear ya," said Steve, unslinging his rifle and watching the distant tribesmen. "You blokes get ready," he said over his shoulder to Matt and Will.

"Ahead of ya, man," replied Matt, his sniper rifle ready.

Will flicked the safety catch off and noticed Heleena had unsheathed a throwing knife. She caught his eye and smiled.

Thormdall galloped past them again to the head of the column. The Berserker was ready to fight, almost willing it to happen. His sword was drawn and he was glaring towards the tribesmen.

A moment later there was shouting from the front and the column broke into a fast trot in an attempt to outrun the tribesmen.

"This is fuckin' shit!" said Scott bouncing around in his saddle, his reins dropped and long forgotten. Luckily, the horse followed the animal in front. He was holding onto the saddle in an attempt to avoid slipping off and being trampled by the horses behind.

"Try and rise, mate," called Matt. "When the horse's back rises, try and rise with it, it'll be more comfortable for you and the horse."

"I'm sorta getting' the hang of it," said Steve, pushing his feet into the stirrups and trying to move with the horse.

"I'm fuckin' not!" shouted Scott, half sliding from the saddle before righting himself at the last moment. "Maybe we could fuckin' walk for a bit!" Scott yelled.

Steve noticed Will seemed completely comfortable in the saddle.

"Where the hell did you learn to ride? I thought you said you only rode a horse once?" Steve called.

"My sister," replied Will, "she represented New South Wales in dressage."

"Whatever the hell dressage is," said Steve.

After about half an hour, the column slowed back to a walk. The tribesmen had long gone.

"Thank Christ for that," said Scott. "I'm definitely no horseman."

"Makes you respect the Light Horsemen in World War One," said Will. "Those bastards charged Beersheba at full gallop with nothin' but bayonets. And they took the town."

"I'd be flat out charging at a walk at the moment," said Scott standing in his stirrups, trying to take pressure off his buttocks. "This is a goddamn work out."

"You're not wrong," said Steve.

The path had widened so they could ride three abreast now. As darkness began to descend, they found a small clearing. Dinner was cold but they ate with relish. The Varangian Guardsmen posted out four sentries, one at each side of the encampment. The Polsk tribesmen might come upon them during the night, and the guardsmen were not taking any risks. Keeping their weapons close, the Australians fell into a fitful sleep.

Steve woke during the night. Unable to fall asleep, he stood and walked a short way into the forest to relieve himself. As Steve began walking back to his comrades there was a shout in the distance followed by a clash of steel, piercing scream and then silence. Moments later more yelling erupted, another sword fight broke out. The Varangian Guardsmen, rolling from their sleep, began shouting.

"What the fuck's goinin' on?" asked Scott, rubbing his eyes.

"Dunno mate, but I've got a feeling those tribesmen have caught up with us," replied Steve, checking his weapon.

"Don't those pricks sleep?" asked Matt.

"I'm goin' for a slash," said Will, moving off amongst the surrounding trees.

"Be careful," warned Heleena. "I'll be fine," he winked at her.

More shouting echoed throughout the forest and this time it did not die into silence. As far as Steve could make out, the battle was taking place about one hundred metres to their north, but he could not be sure.

"That's better," said Will when he returned.

"We are under attack!" Thormdall had appeared from the forest.

"You're a goddamn genius," said Scott. "That's enough," said Steve.

"We need to outflank them if we can," continued Thormdall, unaware of the joke at his expense.

"Righto, well, you lead the way, mate, and we'll follow you," Steve said.

"Stay right behind me," said Will, stroking Heleena's face. "I will," she replied, squeezing his hand.

Without further discussion, Thormdall moved away. Steve followed, squinting to keep the Berserker in view. He learned long ago that to see well in dim light, direct vision needed to be focused above and to the side of the target. This engaged the peripheral vision bringing the object into better view. To look at a target in the dark tended to help it blend into the surrounding darkness. At night, peripheral vision was man's most powerful tool.

As they moved, the noise of battle drew ever closer. There was a loud thud from behind and Steve looked around.

"For fuck's sake!" said Scott, "that hurt like a bitch!" Scott had tripped on a fallen trunk. "You okay?" asked Steve. "Yeah," Scott replied.

They ran for a short way before Thormdall turned, bringing the group onto the flank of the fight. The shouting, screaming and clashing of steel was much louder and clearer now. As they fought their way through thick shrubs, they stumbled upon the battle. The Varangian Guardsmen were outnumbered, perhaps three to one. Though they were better armoured and fought with more ferocity than the tribesmen.

"You do not need to kill them, just scare them," said Thormdall, gesturing to Steve's rifle.

"Will, Matt, pump three rounds each into 'em," said Steve, bringing his rifle up into his shoulder.

The deafening rifle cracks echoed through the forest, tearing several of the tribesmen from their feet and ending the fight. Terrified by the sudden unknown noise the tribesmen ran into the forest leaving their dead and wounded behind. Giving them time to regroup and think, the Varangians decided to ride until morning. They needed to put distance between themselves and an enemy that could overrun them. After a lot of swearing and some help, the soldiers saddled their horses and climbed into the saddle.

Moving as quiet as possible, the column filed out into the blackness. The horses seemed uneasy, their rest disturbed. Some of the younger horses tried to buck their riders but were brought under control with a firm voice and a soft hand. The hours passed and as the first hint of sunrise spoke in the eastern sky, the soldiers felt dead in the saddle. Their legs, backs and backsides ached.

The guardsmen were confident they had left the tribesmen behind for good. They had moved out of their hunting grounds, but they were not sure how the next tribe would receive them. Many of the Polsk tribes were friendly, willing to trade goods or share produce. Some, as they had learned, wanted no part of foreign people passing across their lands. The Varangians had been taken by surprise and Steve knew that it was not likely to happen again. These were fierce fighters, employed to defend the royal blood of Byzantium; they would not tread without care again.

"I feel like rat shit," said Scott, yawning.

"Know how you feel," replied Will.

"You're feeling that good?" muttered Matt, dark rings under his eyes.

"You are all weak," chuckled Heleena. "We'll have plenty of time to sleep."

"I don't think it'll be long before we stop for a rest and a feed," said Steve, stifling a yawn.

"Hope not," commented Will.

Steve was wrong. They travelled most of the day, eating in the saddle and struggling to remain awake. Scott almost slid from the saddle several times, exhaustion swamping him. Finally they made camp amongst the trees about one hundred metres from the track. Once more, a guard was placed throughout the night, watching and waiting. If the enemy did reappear, the Varangians knew they would bring more warriors and their attack would be relentless. Although the voyage was faster than the journey they might have undertaken by sea, it was more dangerous. Speed was important, but with it came great risk.

The Varangians and Norse people of Ulfor had a steely resolve, for no matter how grim a situation, they would persevere. The knowledge of death made them fearsome warriors who fought with a demon like ferocity, for if they died in battle it was the will of Odin. These were a fearless, strong people. They were not caught up on the complexities of life like the society to which Steve and his soldiers were accustomed. They lived their lives to the fullest, loved with passion and worked long days for themselves, their family and their community. After living amongst them, this was something Steve wanted to emulate. He was a good soldier, but Steve wanted to be a better husband and father.

Scott began to snore. Matt kicked him.

"What?" asked Scott.

"You were snorin' like an old bastard, man," Matt muttered. "Bullshit," he said, rolling over. "Goddamn rock in my side," he sighed, and rolled onto the other side.

"For Christ's sake, man!" said Matt, "what are you trying to do, bloody spoon me?" he asked.

"Sorry," said Scott, "you didn't mind last night."

"Piss off," said Matt.

After ten minutes of banter, they finally drifted to sleep, exhaustion claiming them.

"What?" Scott's voice woke Steve. A Varangian Guardsmen crouched over Scott, shaking his shoulder. The other two were awake and Heleena was on her feet.

"You must awaken, we move soon!" the man said.

Scott muttered. "How soon?" he managed to say.

"Now!" growled the guardsmen.

Steve grabbed Scott by his shirt and dragged him to his feet. "Time to go, mate. Here ya go," he said, pushing his saddle into his chest.

Within twenty minutes, the column was moving through the forest once again.

"How long d'ya reckon we'll be riding?" asked Scott, who had been standing in his stirrups for the better part of five minutes.

"Dunno," replied Steve, "I think we're still in Poland, so for another week, maybe two at least."

"Christ almighty, no wonder those horse fanatics walk around bow legged, this is gonna bloody kill me!"

"Ah, ya girl, it's not that bad," said Matt, "just think, with each day we're closer to home."

"True," agreed Scott, settling back into his saddle with a wince.

They stopped for lunch. A group of Varangians were sent out on a hunting party and they returned with a headless deer, which was prepared and then roasted over a fire. The aroma of roasting meat wafted through the forest.

"No dried fish today!" grinned Will, "bit of venison for lunch'll go down all right."

"Too right," agreed Matt.

When the beast had been cooked, it was cut into portions and handed out. With warm grease dripping from their beards, they devoured their food. After they finished eating, the fire was extinguished and the remains of the deer thrown into the undergrowth for wild dogs. Within minutes, they were on their way.

As the sun began to die, the group made camp near a small cave located a short distance from the path. Heleena and the Australians were to sleep in the cave that night. If they came under attack, the Varangians could locate and defend them with ease.

It was amusing, thought Steve that a Special Forces soldier needed to be defended and protected, like some lost schoolchild.

They found the darkness of the cave comforting, almost as if they were shielded from the world. Keeping their weapons close, they faded into sleep, exhaustion claiming them once more.

Steve woke with his heart thumping in his chest. In the far corner, he could hear Scott snoring, and outside the cave was silence. Relaxing, he closed his eyes and tried to drift back into sleep.

As his breathing deepened, he heard a distinct noise outside that brought him awake. It was the soft movement of cloth on stone and loose pebbles tumbling to the ground below. Someone or something was outside the cave. Whatever it might be, it was more than likely no threat. But the sound of cloth on stone was no animal. Just a guardsman going for a slash. But the noise came again, this time louder. Steve's eyes snapped open and there in the cave mouth was the silhouette of a tall man. He was not dressed like a Varangian Guard. The silhouette looked up and made a silent gesture with his hand. Steve watched more warriors appear behind him, from the undergrowth above the cave. There must have been almost thirty now and their numbers swelled. When they gathered in full, the majority moved away from the cave towards the sleeping guardsmen beyond. Two remained at the cave mouth. After a short whispered exchange, they drew short, curved skinning knives and made their way forward.

Steve lifted his rifle. He sat up and waited, making certain that they were not Varangians. When he was sure, he fired two shots, the first taking one of the warriors in the chest. He was dead before he hit the ground. The second bullet ripped through the throat of the second. The man dropped to the ground, gurgling and thrashing his legs. He was trying to yell or cry out.

"Stand to! Stand to!" yelled Steve, on his feet now. "Wake up!" Steve roared. "Get up! We're under attack!"

There was a cry of pain in the distance, then silence. Movement followed as warriors began running through the undergrowth. They yelled and screamed in a language Steve had never heard. There was the clash of steel on steel and more shouting.

"Was havin' a good dream too," whispered Will, coming alongside, peering out of the cave and bringing his rifle to bear. Heleena knelt beside him, sharp knives held in each hand. Steve's warning was taken up.

"To arms!" the deep Varangian voice roared. "To arms! They are upon us! They are upon us!"

Matt stopped behind Will, brought his weapon into his shoulder and without a word fired three shots in quick succession.

"Thirty metres, slight right, base of that tall dead tree, three enemy," Matt gave the target indication. "I knocked two of 'em off, the third is," his voice trailed away as he fired a shot, "well the third is dead too." He grinned.

"Let me at 'em," said Scott, his sword in his hand, "I'll carve 'em up."

Steve chuckled. "You gotta be kiddin', mate, you're not going down there with a sword, you wouldn't last two seconds."

Scott muttered but no one took any notice.

"Let's get down there," said Steve as the fighting intensified. "Be careful, stay low and pick your targets, we've got bugger all ammo left." "Righto," said Matt, pushing passed them and taking cover behind a tree nearby. Lifting the sniper rifle he took aim, paused for a moment then lowered the weapon. It had been a Varangian.

"Let's go," Steve hissed.

"Stay here," whispered Will to Heleena.

"I'll follow," she insisted. "I fight better than all you soldiers combined. It is only that," she pointed at his rifle, "which makes you a good warrior."

Will shrugged. "Fair enough."

The group left Scott behind and made their way through the forest. They pushed through some thick foliage and walked into a small group of enemy warriors. Matt brought his weapon to bear and fired without hesitation, killing all but one who had dropped to the ground, clutching his stomach.

Nearby, two Varangian Guardsmen lay dead. Their throats cut as they slept.

"Bloody bastards," said Will, firing a bullet into the wounded enemy.

They ran on and when they came upon the main battle, they took cover behind a thick stand of trees. The Varangian Guardsmen were surrounded and had formed a large circular shield wall. They were fighting with their normal ferocity, which served to keep their enemy at bay for the time being. One of the Varangians roared a challenge and broke free of the shield wall, sprinting into the throng of enemy. His axe cleaving through flesh and bone. One particularly large enemy warrior stepped forward and took on the Varangian by himself. He died with an axe buried in his skull.

"They're fighting well, but they're outnumbered, man," said Matt. "Won't be long before they're overrun."

"This'll be the rest of our ammo," replied Steve.

"Yeah I know, but you want to get home or not?" Matt said, and began firing.

Steve and Will joined him, firing into the enemy mass, killing enemy warriors one after the other. Thormdall was fighting at the left side of the circle. He had battled his way clear of the Varangian shield wall and was walking in amongst the group of enemy warriors. They tried many times to kill Thormdall, but each attempt was blocked with blistering speed. The silent murderous rage with which the Berserker fought was something they had never seen before and they backed away. Even out by himself and surrounded, Thormdall could not be killed.

Matt fired his second last bullet, which took an enemy warrior through the temple, dropping him like a rag doll. The enemy warriors broke and ran. Hoping to surprise the Varangians and slaughter them in their sleep, the enemy had been mistaken. Instead, they fell victim to a well-organised counter attack.

With a great roar, the Varangians charged after the warriors, leaping over dead logs and snapping branches as they ran. Battle resumed as the Varangians caught their adversaries. The enemy warriors tried to break and run again but were surrounded and butchered. Their last man stood in the centre, his face speaking of the terror that coursed through him.

Stepping forward Olaf grabbed him by the arm and threw him to the ground. The tall Varangian looked down at the man, his bloody axe held by his side, a large clump of gore dripping from the axe head. He pointed the weapon at his downed opponent.

"We seek safe passage through your land, and apart from our little disagreement tonight, we mean you no harm." Olaf did not know if the tribesman could understand him, but he was past caring.

"We travel home," continued Olaf, "and we do not seek your pitiful crops or the lumps of dirt you call a currency. We are not interested in your disease-ridden women and want nothing of your emaciated livestock. We are just passing through." Olaf stopped. He was struggling with his anger. Several of his warriors had been killed in their sleep, and that was no way for a warrior to die. Taking a deep breath he continued, "Do not come upon us again, not ever! For if you do, I'll gather my forces and return to your land. And I will not return with the puny number you see here. There will be thousands of us. Thousands! We will wipe you all, every one of you, man, woman and child from the face of this land! We'll burn your buildings, desecrate your holy places and poison your crops. We will butcher your livestock and sow salt into the ground, so that nothing, not even weeds know life. Go from here and do not return. Do I make myself clear?" asked Olaf, crouching over the warrior who was staring up at the Varangian.

"Do I?" roared Olaf, grabbing the man by the throat. The warrior made a feeble attempt to nod.

"It will be as you say," said the man, struggling with the words.

"It will!" said Olaf, his voice still angry and hostile. "Go! You convince your elders of what I have told you here, or else your tribe's entire existence is at an end."

The warrior stood and nodded. He made to speak.

"Go!" shouted Olaf, bringing his axe up for the killing stroke.

Needing no further persuasion, the warrior loped off into the forest. He did not look back.

CHAPTER 17

They passed through the rest of Poland and entered Romania. The forest paths had widened so they could walk their horses four abreast. The bitter chill of winter's bite remained.

The Australians had now spent all their ammunition. Now they had to rely on Thormdall's brief instruction on sword fighting and the sharp blades that hung from their hips. Their rifles were stripped and the parts distributed throughout their chest webbing. The barrels and larger parts were pushed into their belts. It would be hard to defend themselves with a sword and a rifle or machinegun slung on their back hampering their movement.

They travelled across Romania for three weeks without incident. Leaving Romania behind them, they crossed into another land where thick forests gave way to scattered clumps of trees. The undulating, healthy land became flat and they were exposed.

"We are in the land of the Bulgars," replied Olaf when Steve asked him.

"Bulgaria. A country steeped in bloodshed and violence," added Matt.

"Great!" said Scott.

"The Bulgars we do not trust," said Olaf. "They are at war with Byzantium. If we cross Bulgars there will be no talking, we kill them. We kill them all."

"Fantastic," said Scott again.

"And I thought the twentieth century was violent," muttered Will.

"How long will it take to get across Bulgaria?" asked Steve.

"If we travel well, perhaps ten days. If the snow turns bad, it may take three times as long," replied Olaf. "Fear not my friend, we are nearing the end of our journey and we will slaughter any Bulgars who attempt to stop us. You'll see." Olaf tapped his axe.

As the day grew dim, a fireplace was cleared against a particularly large rock and a group of warriors were sent out to find firewood. Another group, of which the four soldiers were invited to be a part, were sent out to hunt the evening meal.

"I will await your return," smiled Heleena.

"Won't be long," Will said.

They moved amongst the scattered trees.

"We stay to the path," the warrior whispered. Steve nodded. "If you stray from the path you could be up to your armpits in snow and you will make the journey to the next life fast."

206

"Yup, gotcha," replied Scott.

The Varangian moved forward like a wraith in the darkness. He carried a longbow the length of a tall man and the arrows were almost a metre in length. The weapon could knock over a wild boar with ease. Ten minutes later the Varangian crouched near a thick shrub and gestured the soldiers to him.

"There is a chance that circumstances might turn foul. You do not have experience with the sword, so if it happens, the most effective defence is a retreating offence."

"A what?" blurted Will.

"Block every attack your enemy makes, make no attack of your own. And for every attacking stroke, take a step back, but be mindful of where your foot lands. When you feel your opponent has become confident of the win, attack as hard as your heart will allow. Hack, slash, stab, and fight as fast and with as much fury as you can. You will not only surprise them, but at least one of your first few attacking strokes will wound or even kill your opponent. This tactic works well in dim light, but not well during the day."

"We're just out hunting dinner aren't we?" asked Matt.

"We are. But if there are Bulgars about, they will attack and want to kill us for no other reason than entertainment. A harsh, vicious people are the Bulgars. So stay on your guard and remember what I have said." About twenty metres away they saw a full-grown pig, it was digging through the earth with its snout, unaware of its foe. The Varangian crouched by a tree and signalled for the soldiers to stay still and silent. The animal froze and it sniffed the air. When it was sure, it pushed its snout back into the earth and continued to dig for roots. The Varangian strung an arrow, brought the bow up, pulled back on the cord so the string was close to his ear and released the projectile. The arrow hissed through the air and thudded into the beast behind its front left leg, skewering the heart. The animal dropped without a sound.

"Jesus, what a shot," said Scott.

The group crouched around the downed animal whilst the Varangian guardsman cut up the carcass.

"We take the legs, some of the flank and the cheeks, the rest we leave for the forest. It is full of disease and decay," the Varangian handed a hind leg to Will. He could see flees and lice crawling through the hair.

"The cooking fire will kill them," spoke the Varangian, noticing Will picking at the hair.

"The Moslems have no idea what they're missing out on," said Steve, taking another heavy hind leg from the Varangian.

"Too right, man," grinned Matt.

Steve made a dismissing gesture at the quizzical look the Varangian gave him.

"You know," said the Varangian. "I speak Anglish well, and I understand most of the words you say, but there are some things you speak of that I do not understand. I believe it is easier not to ask," he handed the foreleg to Matt.

Within half an hour, the best cuts had been taken.

They ate well that night, the comforting smell of cooked pork lingering amongst the forest long after the meal had been eaten. The silence of the forest was absolute. Apart from several snorers, nothing could be heard save the buzz of nocturnal insects and soft wind moving amongst the canopy. Steve noticed the Varangians slept in a large circle, heads closest to the glowing embers. Their legs faced the dark forest, axes drawn and ready to fight if required. Four sentries had been posted around the encampment and these were rotated through every three hours.

Steve closed his eyes and felt the weariness in his body. The quiet buzz and hum of the forest wildlife disappeared into black nothingness as he fell into sleep's arms.

* * * * *

The sun gave off a blistering heat that stung the skin and made Steve's thirst almost unbearable.

"Hold your position!" a man snarled to his right. He found himself sword in hand, in a shield wall. He had seen the Norse use this tactic, but this time he was no spectator.

There were two rows of warriors behind the shield wall ready to step forward and replace fallen comrades. Steve was in the front rank and was walking forward with the rest of the shield wall. Dark skinned warriors dressed in black robes, carrying crescent shaped swords sprinted towards them. They screamed foreign battle cries.

They were still maybe two hundred metres away, but they were closing fast. As Steve glanced about, he saw that the Norse warriors around him were seasoned veterans, without fear or doubt in their eyes. All to a man, held the shield wall straight, without falter. Their swords were hungry to bite into yielding flesh. These were a tough, violent people born to war, but as Steve watched the approaching enemy, he knew that the Norse had met their match.

"They will die like any other man," grinned the man to Steve's right.

His face was scarred, so that when he smiled it looked like a snarl. Steve had fought as an elite soldier on many battle fields, for many years. He had killed, been wounded and watched some of his comrades die on the modern battlefield. He had no fear. On the modern battlefield, he could fight his way out of most situations. Or slip past his enemies without them ever knowing he had been there.

But this was not the modern battlefield and fear ebbed through him. They were less than a hundred metres away now, still screaming their hatred and wielding their weapons. The shield wall continued to advance. When the enemy was less than fifty metres from them, Steve saw a blur of arrows hiss from the back of the shield wall. The shafts thudded into the charging mass sending many of them in the front rank tumbling to the ground.

"Odin!" shouted a voice at the centre of the shield wall.

"Odin!" the Norse warriors roared and surged forward into a counter charge with the shield wall intact. They slammed into the black clad enemy. The screaming, black clad enemy shuddered to a halt as they met the shield wall. Inch by bloody inch the shield wall crept forward, pressing the enemy back, killing men where they stood and taking no prisoners. Some of the Norse warriors fell, but were replaced by those behind.

Steve's arm shuddered as the tulwar slammed against his shield. He rammed the shield into his opponent's face then stabbed his sword into the man's mouth puncturing his throat and touching the spine. Steve ripped the sword free and brought it down in a murderous arc that shattered the man's skull. The Arab was dead before he hit the ground and Steve stepped over him as the shield wall continued to advance.

The Arabs were a fierce, warlike people, but they had met their match in the Norse. For the Norse were just as savage and skilled. They were more determined and confident than any invader who had come ashore. The Norse pursued the Arabs, killing those whom they caught and promising those that they did not that Odin would send them to the underworld.

Steve crouched, catching his breath. He looked up as a warrior approached.

"We will not be beaten, as long as the shield wall is held strong and moves forward, we can break any enemy," the man said. Steve could not see the Norse warrior, the sun was blinding him. "You did well, you are not yet a Norse warrior, but you fought well."

* * * * *

Steve woke with a start and sat up. He reached for his rifle but found the hilt of his sword instead. He drew the cold weapon to him. The Varangian nearest him farted then rolled over. Steve rose, sheathed his sword and stumbled through the forest, still groggy with sleep. Leaning against a tree, he urinated into the undergrowth and yawned. Within seconds, he was back in the sleeping defensive circle and asleep once more.

A single, loud shout echoed through the silent forest and invaded his relaxed, dozing mind. He could hear movement around him, the clink of chain mail, but it seemed distant and unreal.

A hand hit his chest and he woke to find a helmeted Varangian, axe in hand, leaning over him.

"Up!" the voice said. "We fight."

Steve regained his senses. He heard blood-curdling screams around them. The huge Varangian who had woken him was stretching his arms and back, as if he were about to begin a weight session.

"Bring in the circle!" a voice shouted. "Those who are in reserve, be ready to plug a gap!"

"Back!" the Varangian said to Steve. They took seven or eight paces back so that the circle became smaller. Those who could no longer stand shoulder to shoulder in the circle moved into the centre, so they could reinforce at short notice.

It was then that they came. Steve could not see the enemy but he heard them running through the undergrowth and their voices were warlike.

"Swing your sword fast and hard," said the Varangian.

The shouting was deafening now but still the Varangians remained silent. Their confidence eased Steve's nerves. He shifted his sword into his left hand so he could wipe the sweat from his sword hand. His heart skipped a beat as the enemy burst through the undergrowth illuminated by the dull light of the moon. They were dressed in the black robes of his dream and had the same curved swords held above their heads.

"Come and die," roared the Varangian, sweeping his axe in a massive circle above his head. Steve noticed he was grinning.

"Shit!" was all Steve could utter as a war cry. As the enemy warrior sprinting for him was almost upon him, his daughter, Kathy's face flashed into his mind. His need to see her again overwhelmed him and he ran forward to meet his adversary. He brought the sword down in a mighty strike that smashed the Arab's weapon out of the way. The sharp steel clove into his skull, killing him before his body hit the ground. Levering the sword free, Steve stepped back into the circle of defence, adrenalin coursing through his body. The Varangian beside him stabbed an Arab warrior using his axe like a sword. Bringing the huge weapon crashing down, he half decapitating the assailant.

Another warrior ran screaming for Steve, and he blocked the attack in desperation. The tulwar slid down the steel of his sword, just missing his arm. Slamming the sword hilt into the man's face, Steve brought the sword back and rammed it into the man's midriff. He felt the metal grate against bone before he ripped the weapon free. The enemy fell to the ground, only to be replaced by another.

"Allah!" shouted the warrior, bringing his tulwar down towards Steve's head. Steve tried to bring his sword up, but he knew he was too late. The Varangian beside him blocked the blow.

"Odin!" roared the Varangian, cleaving the axe through the Arab's shoulder and pulling it clear before sweeping the man's head clear of his body.

Anger coursed through Steve again and the next attack he met on the front foot, stabbing his sword towards his opponent's chest. The blow was blocked, but Steve brought the weapon down and sliced the man's arm off at the elbow. As his enemy stumbled in pain, Steve charged after him and rammed the weapon into his stomach, hacking repeatedly into the falling Arab. Even after all movement had ceased, he continued to bring the sword down time after time. A hand grabbed his chain mail and dragged him back into the defensive circle.

"You fight like a Berserker!" shouted the Varangian, as he hacked the life from another Arab. "You will have to teach me your war cry!"

"What?" Steve asked, feeling the splattered blood beginning to dry on his face.

"Your war cry! Teach it to me."

Steve almost laughed. "You mean shit?" he asked.

"Shit!" repeated the Varangian.

More black garbed warriors ran from the forest, leaping over their fallen to attack the Varangian circle. The first was batted aside by the Varangian like a fly, whilst the second fell upon Steve like a demon. Steve blocked the tulwar and the clash of weapons jarred his arm. He blocked the wild-eyed Arab time after time, but the warrior was so fast Steve could not attack.

"Shit!" The scream was followed by the Varangian's axe thudding deep into the Arab's back. The Arab fell away from Steve with a severed spine, and the Varangian pulled his axe clear to meet another enemy.

"A good war cry," he laughed.

The battle lasted for a few minutes more before the black robed Arabs withdrew. They dragged their wounded into the night and left their dead where they had fallen. Several Varangians had been wounded and three who had been slaughtered were dragged into the centre of the defensive circle. None of Steve's men had been wounded. Thormdall was talking to Will, passing on some advice. Heleena was cleaning blood from her daggers.

A brief ceremony was held for the three fallen Varangians that would see them safe into the great halls of Odin. They were buried, side by side in a shallow grave near a great oak that Olaf said looked like the tree of life. The weapons of their fallen enemy were kicked from their hands, their bodies left where they fell to be devoured by the animals of the forest. If they had more time, the enemy weapons would have been destroyed, as was the custom.

That morning they travelled around twenty kilometres before stopping for lunch. Although they saw or heard nothing, the Varangians kept a close eye out for the black robed enemy and a tight grip on their weapons.

The Arabs knew of the Varangians and their battle skills. That the Byzantium king had employed them did not mean they were happy the Varangians were traipsing through their land. Quite the contrary. The journey out of Bulgar would take three days and the Varangians knew their enemy would attack when they thought them most vulnerable. Their journey would be long and drawn out.

Steve told himself that with each step he was closer to home. The thought gave him the strength to continue and the aggression to wield his sword with ferocity.

They made their last stop several hours before sundown. They were positioned on a hill, surrounded by thick foliage and protected on one flank by huge boulders. Any enemy would be forced to fight their way uphill and through the foliage, putting them at an immediate disadvantage. Firewood was collected and a large fire built at the centre of the defensive circle. Minutes later a large, bearded Arab was escorted towards the fire, where Olaf and Ahmad met him. Steve moved closer so that he could hear what was taking place.

"Welcome to my camp," said Olaf.

Ahmad translated for him.

"On my land," the Arab said.

"My name is Olaf,"

"Bakri," responded the man.

"Bakri," Olaf repeated. "Why are you here?"

"Why are you here?" Bakri almost shouted. "That is the question! Why are you walking through my land as if you own it? You disrespect my land and my people!"

Olaf held out his hands in appeasement. "It is not our intention to offer you or your people any kind of disrespect. We mean to travel through your land to Byzantium. We do not want to fight your people."

"As long as you are here, we will fight you," snarled Bakri. "You are here without permission and so you will be dealt with like trespassers, a crime punishable by death."

Olaf's face reddened. "I have told you that we mean no harm, and I stand by that, we seek safe passage through your land."

"Is that your feeble attempt at asking permission to cross my land?" asked Bakri.

"It is," said Olaf.

"I curse you!" Bakri spat at Olaf's feet.

"It is not my intention Bakri, to offend, we only mean to travel home."

"You may not walk upon my land," said Bakri.

Olaf sighed. "We will not go back the way we came. I ask you, as owner of these lands, to let us pass."

"I will not let you pass."

Then so be it," said Olaf. "We must disagree, I fear you may regret your decision."

Bakri smirked. "As we speak, your camp is surrounded. Not only will you not pass through my lands, but you will die here." "Is that so?" asked Olaf. He hefted his great war axe.

Bakri called out a single word. War cries erupted around the encampment as Bulgar warriors charged forward to begin the slaughter.

The leader of the Bulgars turned to flee, but Olaf grabbed Bakri's shirt and hauled him back.

Olaf drew his sword. "You will regret that you little turd." He slammed the sword through Bakri's body and the blade exploded through his back. Bakri slumped, but Olaf kept hold of the sword hilt, forcing the Bulgar to die on his feet. Olaf's hate-filled stare was the last thing he would ever see.

Olaf stepped back, kicked the Bulgar from his blade and turned to join the battle.

"To me! To me!" roared Olaf, batting aside a Bulgar blade. "To me!"

Olaf could hear the horses whinnying in terror followed by the thunder of their hooves. The Bulgars had severed their tie-up line and their mounts had fled. Now they were on foot. He cursed.

Thormdall was the first to arrive with his face spattered in blood. There was a slight smile on his face.

"Skyaldaborg!" yelled Olaf as a large group of Varangians arrived.

The Varangians made a shield wall against the Bulgar storm. As more of the warriors arrived, the shield wall expanded and the Bulgars found it difficult to break through the defence. A small group of Bulgars attempted to move around behind them, but Thormdall saw the threat. The berserker led a counter attack that left the enemy bleeding and lifeless on the leaf-littered ground.

Steve, wedged in several rows from the front, noticed that Ahmad, Heleena and the other Australians were not far away. The battle was deafening with war cries, screams of the wounded and groans of the dying, and the clash of steel. The Varangians in the front rank thrust their swords below or above the shields. They dealt crippling wounds to feet, ankles, piercing throats or lodging in skulls.

Varangians in the second rank wielded the great war axes, or bearded axes as they called them. The massive weapons swung beyond the front rank, landing with incredible force. They cut into shoulders, shattered weapons, mangling limbs or severed heads.

Steve stumbled on the corpse of a Bulgar. He continued to step back. Misplacing his foot on the face of another Bulgar corpse, Steve fell. The tall Varangian beside him grabbed him by the shoulder with a steel grip and pulled him back to his feet.

"Mind your footing," the Varangian said, "it could be your death."

Steve thanked him.

The shield wall, ten warriors wide and six rows deep, continued to withdraw from the Bulgar onslaught with effect. The Bulgars attacked but they fell against the shield wall like water against a rock. Many of them lay bleeding, dying or dead as the Varangians continued to withdraw into the blackness.

At last, the Bulgars gave up and melted into the forest to lick their wounds. The Varangians broke rank and quickened their pace until they found a deep cave that provided a good defence should the need arise. At dawn, the group departed at a blistering pace, determined to increase the distance between themselves and their foe. When the sun had come up, they stopped to rest.

"We left behind eight dead," muttered Olaf. "And lost our horses," added another.

Olaf nodded. "When this is over, I will seek council with the king and if he permits, we will bring the entire guard back here. We will bring our dead warriors home, and slaughter to the Bulgars. I want to destroy their villages," he snarled. "I want to kill their warriors, burn their crops and slaughter their livestock. The next time a Varangian party passes in peace across their land they will know to damn well leave them alone."

"Ahoy there!" roared a voice.

The Varangians were on their feet, swords drawn.

"Who goes there?" snarled a huge man, his bearded axe clasped in two hands as he strode towards the newcomer dressed in chain mail and a white robe. On the white robe, from his upper chest to his lower abdomen, was a large red cross.

"Crusader," muttered Matt.

"Henry of Yorik!" called the man in a strange accent.

The axe-bearing man lowered his axe and grabbed Henry by the scruff of the neck. He dragged him forward, stumbling and cursing until he was face to face with Olaf.

"What is your business?" asked Olaf.

Henry cleared his throat. "I am on God's business!" he roared. "You are on the business of the Gods?"

"No!" said Henry making the sign of the cross. "There is only one God. I am on His business, I am helping reclaim His land. His promised land."

Olaf chuckled. "Chreest man?" he asked.

"Yes," whispered Henry looking around. "I am a man of Christ."

"I am not," said Olaf. "I do not suggest that your God does not exist, I believe my Gods are stronger. Are you an enemy to the Bulgar?"

Henry spat with contempt. "Show me one Bulgar and I will slaughter him like a damn cow! A Bulgar is no different to a Moor, they should share the same grave!"

Olaf sheathed his sword, although the warriors standing behind Henry did not. "Well then," said Olaf. "You are welcome at my camp."

Henry untied a large drink flask from his belt and swigged from it. He wiped his mouth and burped. He swayed on his feet, burped again and retied the flask to his belt.

"Have you heard of Jacob's hymn?" asked Henry.

"Jacob's him?" asked Olaf.

"The hymn of Jacob?"

"The him of Jacob?"

"It is a song, a song to God," Henry said.

"Are you a mad man?" asked Olaf.

Henry burst into a loud song about a rainbow, a dove and some long forgotten promise made by God. The hymn went on for almost five minutes.

"We are travelling into Byzantium," said Olaf once the song had ended. He had decided Henry was harmless. "Will you join us?"

"I have just travelled from there. God forsook my men, leaving them rotting in the sun, but perhaps you can help me bring retribution upon the Moors?"

"Perhaps," replied Olaf.

"Then I agree," said Henry, taking another drink from his flask. "I agree," he repeated.

"We travel fast, so clear your head," said Olaf.

The group travelled on foot until dusk. By then the forest had thinned into nonexistence, replaced by sandy, barren, unforgiving land. Steve knew they had reached Turkey. There was no fire that night. There was no enemy either. By sunrise, they were once again on their way, ever watchful for another Bulgar attack.

CHAPTER 18

The sun beat down without mercy as they walked. Steve knew that once the sun set, the temperature would plummet well below zero. It was strange seeing this landscape again; it was like the land in which they had fought their withdrawal against the Iraqis. It was the same place he knew, only now they were a thousand years in the past. The thought sent a chill up his spine. He could make out some landmarks, but the sand had shifted and this part of the desert was flatter than he remembered. He swore, clasping the hilt of his sword, to keep it from slapping his thigh. He had already tripped once when the sword swang between his legs midstride.

"It is treating you like a good woman," grinned a Varangian.

"Always between your thighs."

But the good-natured banter had disappeared four days before when a large group of Badawark warriors had spotted them and given chase. Each day the Badawarks closed the gap. Outnumbered almost six to one, Steve knew the Varangians would have to fight hard if he and his soldiers were to make it home at all.

"Fear not my friend," Henry stumbled alongside Steve, clasping him on the shoulder. "The good Lord is on our side!" he slurred. Steve was sure that the alcohol would have been hot under the indiscriminate blaze of the sun, but Henry did not seem to mind. He stumbled a few steps and began into a loud song about a Lamb of God, but Steve tuned him out. Almost ten minutes later and still clasping to Steve's shoulder, Henry fell silent.

"Bastard Arabs," spat Henry, "bloody Moors, all to a man. They should be taught a damn lesson." He staggered towards a distant dust cloud thrown up by the Badawarks.

"Bloody bastards!" he roared, half running, half staggering away from the Varangian column towards the Badawarks. "Feel the wrath of God!" he shouted. Henry tripped and somehow landed on his back. He took another swig from his flask, pushed himself into a sitting position and burst into song again. Using his sword as a walking stick, Henry levered himself back to his feet and stumbled back to the Varangians.

As the sun began to set, Steve thought he could see the familiar mountain in the distance. It was dark and snowing when he drove to the cave all that time ago, but still he thought the feature looked familiar. He could not see the cave where they had parked the Land Rover. They were almost home and a surge of excitement passed through him.

"You see what I see?" asked Matt, coming alongside Steve.

"Yup," he answered. "Bloody oath I do."

"You still got the crystal?" Matt asked, "I bloody hope so!"

Steve patted his pocket. "Right here, mate, safe and sound."

Matt realised then that Steve had been pulling the group along with him, through the crystal's power. It was Steve's mental toughness emanated via the crystal that had cemented their tenacity as a group. The one-minded, stoic trek through endless enemy territory to arrive at their final destination. Despite their casualties Matt realised, it had been through Steve that the Varangians had found the strength to continue.

The temperature dropped fast as night approached. They continued towards their destination clutching cloaks or animal skins about them. To stop and rest would be defeat. The Badawarks would be upon them by the afternoon of the next day, and the closer they were to the cave, the more chance they had of survival. The Varangians could defend a narrow space well, but they were outnumbered and would be destroyed within an hour out in the open.

The warriors travelled until the cold became overbearing and they were forced to gather as a group to conserve heat. They slept for several hours, always maintaining a watchful guard. They moved off again, shivering and cursing, before sun up.

As they walked, Steve gathered his soldiers around him.

"Okay, no matter what happens up here, we need to get to the cave and get down into that cavern where we were sent back in time," said Steve.

"These guys," he said of the Varangians around them, "are gonna be defending that cave mouth with their lives. Ahmad and us have to make it down to that cavern so we can get back to our lives. But if the cave mouth can't be held we will be fighting with swords in the pitch black."

Matt and Will burst out laughing. "Oh we're screwed," chuckled Matt, grinning.

"Yeah thanks for the pep talk," said Scott, "I feel a shit load better now."

"Yeah yeah," said Steve, "I'm just sayin' be ready to fight if we need to. And also if we do get back in one piece, don't ever forget what these blokes did for us. Sure as shit, a lot of 'em will pay for the return to our families with their bloody lives."

The dust cloud, which spoke of the Badawark pursuit, was much closer now. The Badawarks themselves resembled a dark smear in front of the cloud. The Badawarks were pushing hard.

"So, my friend, are you one of these Varags?" Henry stumbled alongside Steve.

"No," the Australian replied.

"No? Tell me you are not a bastard moor?" he hissed.

"Nope," chuckled Steve.

"Then what?"

"I was baptised when I was a kid, as a Roman Catholic, but I don't follow the religion. I'm my own man if you know what I mean?"

"A Christian!" exclaimed Henry. "Another Christian!" he bellowed, but no one took any notice.

"Piss off!" Steve said, pushing the soldier away as he tried to put an arm around him.

"Brother, we must follow the grace of God," continued Henry, unperturbed that he had been pushed away. "For He will see us through, no matter what becomes of us in these perilous times. We, the lambs of Christ, will see victory brought to us."

"Oh for Christ's sake," Steve groaned.

"Exactly!" shouted Henry.

"Your God?" asked a Varangian. "Your God is weak," he spat. Steve watched as the drunken soldier examined the Varangian.

"How so?" he asked.

The Varangian shrugged. "You must approach your god on bended, bruised knees, hands clasped before you like some naughty child. You throw all your money into the coffers of your corrupt, money-hungry churches. You sing the praises of your god, for fear he will strike you down if you do not. Is that not a belief of yours? Fear god?" Before Henry could reply, the Varangian continued. "And yet you proclaim that your god is all forgiving and all loving and that he is the only true God."

"We do fear God, for He is the almighty, commander and creator of heaven and earth, and what of your God?" asked Henry. He seemed interested in what the Varangian had to say.

"My God? I do not have one."

"No?"

"No, I have many. Odin is the lord of the gods. We approach him as a child would a father, with respect, but with a straight back, looking him in the eye. We do not snivel, grovel or whimper on our knees before some altar in the hope of gaining his love and respect. Odin's respect is earned, and most of our gods watch over us like parents. We ask for their support in times of need, but if they refuse then we make do, as we must. We keep a keen edge on our blades, we keep our bodies strong and our crops well tended. If your God refuses you, you Chreestmen fall into a sobbing heap and whine about how hard your lot is."

"I do not snivel to my God," said Henry with an edge to his voice. "Do you not?" chuckled the Varangian. "The next time you sing one of your songs, you listen to the words yourself. Your god is a weakling and his followers try to bully and harass anyone who is not of their ilk. I care not that you do not call upon my gods. I do not think of you any less that you are not one of us, yet you are affronted that we Varangians do not entertain the idea of your god. Your god is weak and your religion is full of contradictions."

The Varangian strode away leaving Henry in silence.

"What say you?" asked Henry turning to Steve.

"I'm no Varangian, I don't believe in their gods, but shit, mate, I can see where he's coming from," he chuckled. "It's why I'm not religious, Henry. Too many times, I've been at a crossroads in my life, and once or twice at a dead end, and prayed for help only for nothing to happen. So my religion's myself. I treat people the way I want to be treated, but I make my life what it is. It's family that makes life worth living."

"But can you not see that it was God working through you, without your knowledge that has brought you through life?"

"No," replied Steve. "God had nothing to do with it. Where I'm from, most Christians I know pretend they are somehow beyond the rest of the non-Christian population.

They think they are better, when in fact, they live and behave exactly the same as every other member of the population. Apart from the one hour a week when they put a stage show on for their god about how devout they are."

Henry bellowed into song about an angel of God, as if Steve had never spoken.

"My point exactly," said Steve, leaving Henry to join Matt, Will and Scott.

By midday, the group were exhausted. They stopped to rest in a little shade under a rocky outcrop. When the heat of the sun felt like it could melt steel, a little shade was better than nothing. The Badawarks were still pursuing with aggression and would be upon them by late afternoon. The Varangians pushed hard during the day and made good progress. Yet the Badawarks knew the land and were accustomed to the merciless weather. Before the sun died in the sky, they would need to make a stand and fight, maybe to the death. If they could make the cave before the fight began, they would have a good chance of success.

"God favours the bold!" bellowed Henry.

"Does he?" grinned the Varangian who had argued with Henry earlier.

"He does!" Henry roared. "Who might you be, if you please?" Henry asked the Varangian.

"Thrane," replied the man, his eyes glinting with humour.

"Henry!" the drunken soldier shouted. Thrane nodded, committing the name to memory. It seemed that these warriors goaded each other with good humour, in much the same way as soldiers did on the modern battlefield.

"Henry, before you go marching off to display your boldness, make sure you kneel down and whimper to your god like a good boy. Otherwise he may not favour you at all!"

Henry did not react.

The troop moved back out into the torturous heat after about half an hour of milling around in the cool shade. They walked on at close to eight kilometres per hour. Some of the shorter warriors trotted to keep up. But they did it without effort, never complaining.

The cave was much closer now. Steve could see the black opening and knew that he was within reach of his wife and children. Their journey was almost at an end. He glanced over his shoulder. The Badawarks were closing fast. He could make out individual warriors now.

"I notice your gods have done nothing to help us," Henry slurred, stumbling alongside Thrane.

"My gods have kept us alive," retorted Thrane. "I notice your god has helped keep the distance between us and our enemy." Thrane glanced over his shoulder and did an exaggerated double take of the closing enemy. "Actually forget I spoke, it seems your god is as useful as a blunt blade."

"My God has done His duty. But working alongside such incompetence, He is attempting to keep us alive and maintain the distance between us and our foe."

Thrane roared with laughter. "I will relent that one."

Henry grinned and took a long swig from his flask.

As the sun began to die on the horizon, the Varangians started jogging through the desert towards their destination. When the wind changed, it was possible to hear the distant shouts and war cries of the Badawarks. Within the hour, battle would be underway.

The warriors ran through the sand, sweat pouring down their faces. There was no talking now, just the sound of rasping breaths, the soft hiss as boots moved through sand and the gentle clink of chain mail. Henry dropped off to one side and dry retched. Thrane grabbed the drunken soldier by his chain mail shirt and pushed him forward.

"Move, you fool!" Thrane hissed. "You stop, you die!"

Henry nodded but did not reply. His leather flask was tied to his belt now. It was the last thing on his mind. He attempted to stop again, but Thrane shoved him forward so that the Christian warrior was forced to vomit between his legs as he ran.

Steve ran alongside the crusader. "Keep going, mate, you can do it!" Henry seemed to gain strength from Steve's word. "Yes I can, and I will!" he said.

"Hold to your God," said Thrane, short of breath himself. "Hold on to his strength, and keep your sword close, you may need it before long."

"I can do this!" Henry shouted.

The spine chilling shrieks of the Badawarks were now loud. The cave was within a hundred metres. Steve cursed that they had no ammunition left. Hefting the pack into a more comfortable position, he pushed on, controlling his breathing and holding the hilt of the sword. He noticed the three other Australians struggling in the same way. Scott almost tripped over his sword.

"Get fucked!" he gasped.

Will and Matt bellowed with laughter.

The pack made the cave mouth and turned, panting, gasping and sweating to watch their pursuers. The Badawarks were within half a kilometre now. Steve dropped his pack and drew his sword.

"The savages have slowed!" a Varangian called.

It seemed the Badawarks had slowed to a walk now that they knew they could not intercept the Varangians before they reached the cave. Olaf called a meeting, which the Varangians called a Thing.

"It is certain they will fall upon us during the night," spoke Olaf. "We may bide our time here and fight them from the cave, or we can fall upon them in their camp."

"We are outnumbered. If we go out there, we may be overwhelmed and destroyed," replied a Varangian.

"We can make a better defence from here," agreed Thrane. "Their numbers will be limited by the width of the cave."

"And what if they lay siege to the cave? All it would take is a few days without water, and we would be finished," said one.

"We agreed to go with Ahmad," said Olaf. "We agreed to protect him, and to protect those who carry the crystal so they might find their way back home. If the savages put us to siege then it will give the newcomers time to leave this place, and that means our journey has been successful. When we run dry on water, we put the fight to them, and if

Odin wishes, we will defeat them, otherwise we will seat ourselves in the hall of heroes.”

“What if the newcomers return home now?” asked one of the men. “Once they have left, we can then slink away into the night and the savages would never know!”

“Coward!” roared Olaf.

Steve kept his mouth shut, because he had been tempted to ask the same question.

“We stand and fight!” announced Olaf.

“I am no coward!” Olsen yelled. “I wish to see this journey at an end! We could be gone from here without the Badawark Savages even knowing!”

Thormdall cut in.

“There is one other thing to consider,” the Berserker said in a calm voice. “They will expect us to await their attack. In this way, we are giving them time to organise and execute their plan at a time of their choosing. If we attack, it will send them into disarray and panic, or at least that is the best we can hope.”

“The best we can hope is that we do not all end up maggot food,” called another warrior from the back of the gathering.

“We do not need to kill them all,” countered Thormdall. “We just need to kill several, scatter some, sow some fear and force them to second guess their confidence. They saw us today, running, panting. They were hunting us like dogs, and I am sure that is how they think of us. We are wolves in dogs’ clothing and it is time to show them the error of their thinking.”

“What say you?” asked Olaf.

At least half the gathering nodded. There was some chuckling from the back where a private joke was shared.

“Give me a group,” said Thormdall turning to Olaf. “We will go with nothing but skinning knives. We will wear no armour, nothing that will make obvious sound. We cut their bastard throats and when enough of them are awake, we cut and run. They will pursue us, and when they do, they will attack the cave at a time of our choosing. Their blood will be up and all clear thoughts will have evaporated. We may not kill them all, but if the gods walk with us then we have the opportunity to deal the Badawarks heavy losses.”

“I like the idea,” said Olaf after some thought. “But all who go with Thormdall will be volunteers. And he will take no more than half our force. If the plan goes awry then we in the cave can go forth and fight a rear guard action to protect Thormdall’s withdrawal.”

Within five minutes, Thormdall had chosen his group, and it included Steve and his soldiers. It was decided that Steve and his soldiers would move forward ahead of the main group and scout the area. They would find the Badawark camp and observe them before moving back and leading the main killing group to their target.

After several hours had passed, the cave was silent, apart from men snoring, muttering and chuckling. Steve gestured his men forward and they spread out, moving slow.

There was a quarter moon, which threw enough light to see a short distance, but not enough that they could keep a safe distance from the Badawark camp. Steve knew they would be almost upon the enemy before they saw them.

The soldiers moved in silence. Steve stopped, clicking his tongue to signal the others to do likewise. He could see a dark blob on the sand about ten metres in front of him. Steve was kneeling now and was sure it was a Badawark sentry lying on his side. Steve closed his eyes and could hear the man snoring.

Scott moved alongside and glanced at him.

Steve nodded. "Make it quick, and make it quiet, the main camp won't be far from here."

"Righto," Scott replied, unsheathing a small knife one of the Varangians had given him.

Before anyone could react, Heleena moved away into the night to search for other sentries.

Steve held Will back, watching Scott move forward. Seconds later, he heard a soft gurgling sound. Scott did not move before he was sure the Badawark had bled out. In the time it had taken Scott to kill one sentry, Heleena had returned. She reported there had been three others who had been posted out from the main Badawark force. All but one was asleep. She killed them in silence.

The small group moved past the corpse towards the main camp. The soldiers could not quite see the Badawarks, but they could hear them. Some were snoring, others shifted in the sand seeking a better sleeping position. The soldiers could also smell the acidic body odour emanating from the Badawark camp.

"Let's go get our friends," said Steve and they withdrew towards the cave.

The attacking force moved slow. The main Badawark encampment was still asleep as they approached. With knives in hands, the Varangians went forth to deliver their grim retribution. Steve used a curved hunting knife that Thormdall had given him. The weapon was razor sharp. He knelt over his first victim and sliced through his throat where he thought the larynx should be. Kneeling on the man's chest as the Badawark began struggled. As the struggles became weaker, Steve stood up and moved on. His next victim was lying on his stomach, snoring, his acrid body odour forcing Steve to stifle a cough. Placing a foot on either side of the man's body, Steve leaned down over the victim and sliced through the back of the Badawark's neck. When he hit bone, he sawed the knife back and forth until he had cut through the spinal cord at the base of his skull. The man was dead within seconds.

He knelt over the next Badawark warrior. The man's eyes flicked open and he came up swinging, his fist cannoning into Steve's left temple. Instinct took over as Steve hammered his fist into the man's face repeatedly until all movement stopped. Then he cut the man's throat and moved on.

The Badawark camp was silent for almost five minutes as the Varangians moved amongst them, killing as quiet as wraiths. A piercing scream broke the silence, rousing the remaining Badawarks.

The Varangians were unarmoured and only carried small knives. They found themselves fighting off well-armed Badawarks and began to flee.

"Back!" roared Thormdall. "Back!"

"To us!" called Olaf, who was waiting with his men at the cave mouth. "To us!" The fleeing Varangians followed the sound of his voice.

The once silent night was now full of shouting, cursing and screaming. A small group of Varangians were surrounded and slaughtered. Steve sprinted towards Olaf's voice, fear tearing into his heart as the war cries and shrieks of the Badawarks began to close on them.

"To us!" Olaf bellowed into the moonlit darkness.

"Run hard!"

"Don't need to tell me twice," Matt gasped.

Steve grinned. The dark cave was in sight now and the entrance just visible in the half-moon light.

A small group of Varangians dropped back, turning on the Badawark tide. They fell amongst the chasing enemy with a ferocity of which Odin would be proud. They were killed within seconds but took some Badawarks with them. Their sacrifice was enough to give the fleeing force time to make the cave. Olaf's warriors established a shield wall across the cave mouth. As the fleeing Varangians approached the wall they peeled back to let them through.

The shield wall was remade as the last man ran through.

"Odin!" shouted Olaf as the Badawark charge approached.

"Odin!" roared the Varangians in the shield wall, their reply echoing off the cave walls in a deafening crescendo.

The Badawarks hammered into the shield wall with ferocity. But their charge halted as sharp swords appeared from both above and below the shields. Blades pierced throats, hammered into faces and skulls, or cut deep into Badawark calves or half-severed feet. Varangians standing in the second rank clasped their great axes.

Heleena was standing in the depths of the cave releasing arrows into the enemy mass with precision. She had not collected even half a quiver of arrows from the longship battle, but she was making each arrow count with incredible effect.

"I see you!" roared Thormdall, pointing his sword at the distant Kadark, with his arms folded across his dark robed body. "I'll end you," he shouted.

Thormdall charged forward in a wrath of bloody fury, his sword a blur of grey as he struck out at the Badawark ranks. The Berserker battled his way through the force like a knife through butter until he was standing toe to toe with the Kadark. Pain shot through his skull again like a burning knife, but Thormdall took a step forward until he was towering over the Kadark. Clamping a hand around his enemy's throat, his hand closed on empty cloth. The Kadark laughed and Thormdall's agony intensified until he fell to his knees. The Kadark withdrew and with it went Thormdall's pain. The Berseker clambered to his feet staring at the distant Kadark.

"I will end you," he vowed.

Turning away with a snarl, Thormdall made his way to the cave. The Varangians peeled back to make way for him.

The shield wall stood fast, hammering swords upon shields and shouting insults and challenges. Several warriors in the wall had fallen during the Badawark assault. Their bodies were dragged from the fray and men standing behind had moved forward to take their place.

Matt was working on wounded Varangians. Many of them were critical and bled out within a matter of minutes. But he managed to stabilise several of them.

After a brief lull, the Badawarks charged again. They fought with ferocity, anger and passion, which was enough to overcome enemies they were used to fighting. The Varangians, they knew now, fought with equal anger and ferocity, but they also fought with discipline. The cave meant it was impossible to overcome the Varangians.

With this knowledge, the Badawarks fell back in dismay. The Badawark dead were kicked and shoved from the cave mouth to make more room for the Varangians to move. The Badawarks left in defeat, but the Varangians knew that would not be the last they saw of them.

As morning touched the Eastern sky, they saw a second Badawark force smeared the horizon. This group was much larger than the first and closing on their position fast. The next attack would be larger, more ferocious and far more difficult to repel. With this sobering thought, the Varangians went forth to bury their dead.

"You should leave now. Our enemy will return, but now is the time for you to make your move," Thormdall told Steve. Thormdall's face was covered in blood and small chucks of flesh were scattered throughout his hair.

"We can't leave you in the lurch, mate," said Steve.

The other soldiers nodded.

"You must realise that the next Badawark force will be far greater, and much more difficult to defeat. If you and your warriors are killed, then our journey is for nothing." Thormdall handed Steve the necklace he wore. "This is Thor's symbol, it is myollneer, Thor's hammer. Take it, and let it bring you luck in times of darkness."

Steve studied the piece of silver moulded into the shape of a hammer. He put the leather necklace around his neck. "Thank you brother," he said, holding out his hand. Thormdall grasped it in an iron grip.

"And next time we will go by sea," said Thormdall, slapping Steve on the shoulder.

"May the gods be with you," Thormdall said as he shook each of the soldiers' hands. "Make haste now or all is lost."

"You must defeat the Kadark," said Ahmad, coming alongside Thormdall.

"Alas I have failed. Twice I have fought him, twice he has bettered me," said the Berserker.

"Let me have the crystal if you please?" Ahmad asked Steve.

"Don't lose it, mate," Steve said, dropping the crystal into Ahmad's palm.

"Give me your sword," said Ahmad to the Berserker. He took the weapon in his hand. "I thought the last we would see of him was the sea battle," said Ahmad. "I did not think to see him here, which is why I did not do this earlier."

Ahmad passed the crystal along the length of Thormdall's sword muttering incomprehensible words. When he had finished, the little Arab passed the weapon back. It was glimmering a dull blue now. Thormdall stared at the glowing blade in disbelief.

"That will make him bleed," said Ahmad.

"Thank you," nodded Thormdall. "I'll put it to the test," he said.

"Travel safe," Thormdall said, thumping Steve on the back.

Ahmad led Heleena and the Australian soldiers towards the back of the cave and ever closer to their lives and families. The Varangian guardsmen began hitting swords upon shields, or smashing axe heads onto the rock floor in salute.

"Farewell to you my warrior brothers," roared Olaf, "we will never forget you!"

The Australians shouted their own farewells, the words drowned out by drumming, shouting and cheering.

Ahmad led them down into the darkness. The Australians grasped shoulders, whilst Ahmad pulled Steve by his arm as if the small Byzantium priest had some kind of night vision. The path seemed familiar to Steve, but as the ground almost gave way beneath him, he could not be sure.

"Keep moving," growled Ahmad as Heleena hesitated, trying to regain her footing, "we do not have much time."

The descent into the bowels of the earth continued. Steve stopped himself shouting as his feet gave way beneath him. Although he forced himself not to laugh as he heard Will behind him almost lose his footing in the same way.

*****

"They come again!" roared Olaf. "Do they not learn?"

"Let them come," said Thormdall. "Let them learn that we are not as soft as their enemies! That we welcome a fight."

Thormdall was shouting now. "We do not fear battle! And we do not fear death!" He roared these last six words.

*****

"Hurry now."

Ahmad ushered the Australians into the dark open cavern where this whole adventure had begun. "Sit down and do not move," he instructed.

There was silence as the soldiers sat down. Heleena snuggled into Will. She was frightened. Heleena could kill almost any enemy, man or beast, but of magic, she knew nothing. Before they had time to fathom what was happening a dull light threw dark shadows upon the walls.

Ahmad was passing the bright blue glowing crystal along the length of a long piece of thin wire the width of a strand of hair. He was drawing the wire out of a pouch by his side.

"When we travelled back in time, we ended up in Denmark. Won't the same thing happen this time?" asked Steve. "Won't we be sent into present day Denmark?"

"It is why I make this magic. Without it, the portal will send the people within its vicinity back in time to any one of many portals. It is only through luck that you were sent to the land of the Danes, you might have ended up somewhere much worse." He placed the wire on the ground before putting a large rock on top of the glowing wire to hold it in place. Drawing more of the wire out, he ran the glowing crystal upon the metal.

"I also need to make this magic so that only you are sent back into the future and that I remain here. If Allah permits and the Varangians are successful, I may leave here with my life this day."

* * * * *

The Badawark advance darkened the horizon. There was perhaps more than twice the number of the previous attack.

"Stand tall," bellowed Olaf. "Hold your shields tight and your swords tighter. Let us show them how the warriors of the gods fight."

"And I'll show them how a warrior of Christ fights," shouted a feeble voice from near the front row.

"You are almost as good a warrior as the Varangians!" shouted Thrane.

"Almost?" retorted Henry, "I will show both the Badawarks and the Varangians how a warrior of Christ fights!"

This was met with good-humoured laughter.

* * * * *

Ahmad made a five-pointed star shape on the ground with the glowing wire, with a small circle at the centre. He stepped out of the star and gestured the soldiers forward.

"Come, move into the circle. Step over the wire and do not disturb any part of the shape or the magic will be lost," Ahmad said.

Heleena moved forward, making sure they negotiated the wire with care. Once they were all in the centre of the circle, they crouched and watched Ahmad move around them with the glowing crystal in his hand.

229

He chanted as he walked. Steve flinched as a distant roar hit him from above; it was the sound of shouting, cursing screaming and steel on steel. He realised that battle had been re-joined between the Badawarks and the Varangians at the cave mouth.

* * * * *

Thormdall skewered his sword through a man's face, ripped the blade clear then back slashed the blade across the neck of a foe to the right. Pushing the dying man from him, Thormdall stabbed his sword into the next attacker. He felt it plunge into the warrior's chest and towards the Badawark's spine. Kicking the warrior from his blade, he hacked it down upon another man's skull. Levering the weapon out of the bone, Thormdall turned to face his next opponent, his eyes glistening with violence and death. The Badawark stopped. He died as his head left his body.

* * * * *

Ahmad continued his chant as he walked around the group and then pushed the crystal into its recess in the cave wall. It was just where Steve remembered it. Within seconds, the crystal was glowing and writing in the cave above the crystal was emanating a deep red.

Just as Steve looked at the Byzantine priest and was about to ask him a question there was a deafening boom. The sound reverberated around the open space. Ahmad Ibn Fadlan was now nothing more than a fading shadow flickering on the wall of the cave.

* * * * *

Snarling, Thrane hammered his shield into the face of an enemy. As the man recovered, Thrane stabbed his sword into his throat before kicking him back into his comrades.

"Come, meet death!" Thrane shouted, meeting the next attack with his shield. The Badawark drove him back several steps, but he recovered his balance and stabbed his sword beyond the safety of his shield. He felt the metal bite into the man's leg. He stabbed his sword again and felt it slide into the stomach of his enemy. Stepping forward he bashed his shield into the falling Badawark and slammed his sword into his mouth, puncturing the back of his throat. Kicking the warrior away he crouched as the next Badawark ran to meet him.

230

* * * * *

All was black and Steve felt as if he was falling. His stomach was in his mouth, and he was no longer aware of the other soldiers near him.

He could hear scribbling in the blackness much like a quill on parchment. Then a voice spoke, "Never before has such terror appeared in Britain from a pagan race."

The voice faded, to be replaced by a lighter yet somehow more powerful voice. The voice proclaimed, "My will was to live worthily as long as I lived, and after my life to leave them a memory of my good works."

* * * * *

Thormdall took a blade in the thigh, which cut deep, forcing him to his knees. He dealt a massive blow to his attacker, which tore through the man's chest. As Thormdall staggered to his feet, he caught a glimpse of the Kadark. Another blade skewered his side. With a snarl, Thormdall grabbed hold of the blade and ripped it from his enemy's hand, stabbing his own sword into the man's neck. The Berserker threw the enemy's blade to the ground with contempt. He head butted the next Badawark, slammed his sword into the man's midriff, clasped his hand around the man's neck and threw the dying enemy from him. Hacking, skewering, stabbing and slashing his way into the enemy, Thormdall burst clear of the Badawark attack. Once again, he was standing before the Kadark.

"We meet again," snarled Thormdall. The Kadark did not reply.

Thormdall fell to his knees again, as the pain pulsed through his mind.

* * * * *

"A date which shall live in infamy," the American accent boomed into the darkness.

Steve still felt as if he was falling, but he could hear a loud drone that sounded like hundreds of planes at high altitude. "Take cover!" a muffled voice shouted. An explosion rocked the core of his being. It was followed by more bombs, which landed around him in devastating explosions. Silence followed and his ears rang. He felt himself falling again.

"Ask not what your country can do for you; ask what you can do for your country." The American voice boomed and Steve knew exactly whom it was speaking. As the crowd roared, silence followed and he began to fall once more.

Then a strong English women's voice broke the silence. "They have retreated, our troops have reached the outskirts of Port Stanley. A large number of Argentinean soldiers have laid down their arms. White flags are flying over Port Stanley."

Steve felt sick again, but his descent stopped. Another voice, this time Australian, spoke. "Forces have commenced combat and combat support operations." It was John Howard.

"Johnny!" said Scott. He too sounded the worse for wear.

* * * * *

"Fool, did you think you could best me?" the voice echoed in Thormdall's mind.

Anger exploded in Thormdall and he forced himself to his feet. He clasped his sword and staggered towards the dark robed enemy.

"Did you think I could not?" he growled and struck out with the blue glowing sword. The weapon did not plunge into thin air as it had before. Instead, it bit deep, sinking through skin, cutting sinew, grating from bone and lacerating organs.

The Kadark groaned and fell to his knees. Thormdall kicked him to the ground, ripped the weapon free and plunged the glowing sword into the Kadark's chest. The weapon shattered ribs and sank deep into the sand beyond.

"Who is the fool now?" hissed Thormdall, hacking his weapon through the Kadark's neck.

For an instant, Thormdall thought he could see a dark grey face, staring up at him with cat-like pupils, the maw lined with razor sharp teeth.

Cutting the head free, Thormdall watched as the black robe settled to the earth. The Kadark's body disappeared as if it had never existed, leaving nothing behind but an empty robe on the sand.

A hand grabbed Thormdall from behind and the Berserker turned. He slapped the hand away and hammered his sword into the Badawark. He blocked an attack from the left, slammed his retrieved weapon through the man's neck and turned to his next attack.

Thormdall's next blow was blocked by his opponent, who stepped forward and rammed the weapon deep into the Berserker's abdomen.

Gritting his teeth against the pain, Thormdall took hold of the Badawark and dragged him backwards. They fell to the ground.

Unsheathing the only dagger he had left, Thormdall dragged the blade across the man's throat. The berserker closed his eyes as hot blood exploded over his face and poured into his mouth. Coughing and choking back the warm blood, Thormdall pushed the dying man aside and rose into a crouch. The next Badawark hesitated when he saw the crouching, blood covered, snarling Berserker. It was all Thormdall needed. The Berserker threw himself forward, burying the dagger deep into the Badawark's midriff. He sliced the weapon up until it grated against ribs.

* * * * *

Steve came to a screaming halt, and his senses returned to him as he pulled himself to his feet. He swore he saw a blue light fade in the far corner of the cave but could not be sure.

"You guys right?" he asked in a groggy voice.

"Yeah," replied Scott.

"Think so," said Matt.

"Yup," was Will's weak reply.

Heleena did not reply. She was curled up in the foetal position in the corner of the cave, sobbing and shaking.

"You're safe, it's okay," Will said, stroking her back. He rolled her over and pulled her into his arms. "It's over."

"Such loud noises, I thought I would die!" she wiped the tears from her face.

Will realised she spoke of the exploding bombs they had heard. He also knew there would be a lot for Heleena to learn about this modern world. Some of it frightening.

"Radio's still here, thank Christ!" Matt said. He took his first aid pack off and shrugged on the heavier radio.

* * * * *

Thormdall head butted the dying warrior and pushed him away. He staggered forward into the next attack, and kneed the man in the groin before slicing deep into his jugular. Pushing the Badawark from him, Thormdall roared a prayer to Odin and waded into the Badawark assault.

"Keep together! Keep the wall intact!" roared Olaf.

The Badawarks were fighting in desperation now. They were making no ground against the Varangian shield wall. The Badawark

233

warriors broke off and ran, Henry charging after them with a mighty cry, hacking two of them down. The Christian soldier continued sprinting after his adversary and speared a third through the back. He cleaved the Badawark to death on the hot sand.

"That is for my soldiers," Henry snarled, then he spat on the corpse and turned back to the cave.

"You fight well," said Thrane as Henry walked back. "My God is on my side," replied Henry.

"How wrong you are," grinned Thrane. "But you still fight well," said the Varangian holding out his hand.

Henry sheathed his sword and shook.

Thormdall was dead. Not only had he killed the Kadark, but he had fought his way out into the middle of the Badawark charge. It was estimated that he had killed more than forty of the enemy. His corpse, along with the other Varangian dead, was taken back into the cave. The remaining Varangians began praying over the dead warriors, sending them swift and true to Odin and his hall of heroes in Valhalla.

* * * * *

They were still enveloped in blackness, but holding onto each other. They walked out of the opening and into the tunnel, which led them up towards freedom. Several times, they slid, tripped or misplaced their feet, but finally now they could see light at the end of the tunnel.

Squinting, and with Matt's hand clasped on his shoulder, Steve walked free of the tunnel. The bright sky assaulted his eyes. Holding his hand against the bright light and protecting his vision, Steve could see their Land Rover in the cave. But, leaning over the vehicle and rummaging through their bags was an Iraqi soldier.

CHAPTER 19

Steve crouched in the rear of the cave to watch the enemy soldier. The Iraqi was pulling something out of the Land Rover. He struggled with what appeared to be a belt and as he put his body weight into it, the belt snapped away and he was able to disconnect the pouch he had wanted. Realisation struck Steve. The Iraqi was not looting the Land Rover, he was looting Dave, their dead comrade. Anger coursed through him. Scott, who had also seen the event, pushed past Steve with a growl of fury. Steve tried to stop him but the soldier pulled free. Hatred burned in him hotter than any melted steel, and he drew the knife Thormdall had given him. Scott leapt forward with a roar. The Iraqi stumbled towards his rifle, but Scott was upon him before he could reach it. The Iraqi soldier grabbed Scott's knife and tried to pull it from him. The two men fell to the ground and Scott dragged the curved dagger free of his opponent's grasp. The weapon cut the Iraqi's hand to the bone. Scott plunged the sharp blade into his adversary's throat, sawing the blade until hot blood spurted from the wound.

"Fuck you, cunt!" Scott roared.

Steve pulled Scott to his feet and pushed him away from the dead Iraqi. "Calm down!"

"Fuck you!" Scott screamed at Steve. He spat on the dead Iraqi and was about to bring his boot down on the corpse's head when Steve threw him to the ground.

"Calm down!" Steve said. "I agree with you, the bastard deserved to die, but keep your noise down, we got enemy coming up on our position. Get your shit in a sock, mate, there's plenty of killin' to go around."

Steve was looking at the cave mouth and realised that it had not been a landslide that had blocked the entrance but an avalanche of snow. Outside the bright sun had worked its magic and the snow had melted leaving a muddy mess. Beyond the cave mouth in the distance, the small forms of enemy soldiers could be seen moving in their direction with a sense of purpose. Meanwhile, Matt and Will were reassembling their weapons, grabbing spare ammunition and reloading weapons. Matt also took a couple of spare radio batteries and stowed them away in his webbing.

Whoever the Iraqi soldier was, his comrades had heard the shouts and were making a beeline for the cave. They were still some distance away, but contact was not far away. The familiar rectangular obelisk with strange looking symbols jutted some five feet out of the ground near the cave entrance.

Steve reassembled and loaded his weapon then crawled forward on his stomach to the mouth of the cave to keep a watch on their advancing enemy. Scott climbed aboard the Land Rover and dismounted the mag 58. Making sure the heavy machinegun was loaded, he leapt down from the vehicle and made his way forward.

"You got any 40 mil ammunition?" Steve asked Will.

Will nodded.

"Good, see that fat bastard on the far right?" Again, Will nodded, grinning as he watched a large Iraqi soldier struggling up the incline towards the cave. "I'm gonna shoot him first, and continuing shooting. When you hear my first shot, I want you to pump two 40-mil rounds down range. Scott, while this is happening I want you to provide suppressing fire to add to the confusion. Matt, you've got a good scope on that sniper rifle, see if you can identify the officers and higher-ranking soldiers, and drop 'em. Once there's absolute chaos amongst those bastards, we're gonna start fire and moving forward to better cover. See that rocky outcrop?" Steve asked looking at the other three soldiers. They nodded. "That's where I want to end up."

"Any questions or disagreements?" asked Steve. There was none.

"Well then, let's kill them," he growled.

Heleena had both her knives ready. She was also on her stomach beside Will. The Norse woman had regained her composure.

"You're not going to need those," Will said.

"Will I not?"

"Nope, there's no way you're going to get close enough to them to use your weapons. Like us, this enemy can also kill from afar. Just stay with us, and for Christ's sake stay low to the ground."

She re-sheathed her weapons and watched the approaching enemy with curiosity. There were close to fifty Iraqi soldiers advancing upon their position. Looking beyond them, Steve saw in the time they had been gone, what was left of the Iraqi Army in the area had relocated. They had erected a small tent city on the closest side of Barzan.

The time travel had not been perfect, but then worse things could have happened. Steve cocked the M4 and flicked the safety catch off.

Taking out fifty soldiers was one thing. But with the element of surprise, it would be possible, especially with a heavy machinegun and grenade launchers. Steve knew it would raise the alarm in the small tent city. The Australians could have several hundred Iraqis bearing down on them.

"You got your radio Matt?" Steve asked.

"Yeah, new battery's in, all I can find is the British channel though," shrugged Matt.

"Better than nothin'," said Steve, watching the fat Iraqi come closer. Will pushed a 40-mil grenade into the breach of the M240 grenade launcher, which was attached underneath the barrel of his M4 rifle. Closing the breech with a snap, he flicked out the grenade sights and stared down them. Will would not miss, and whichever poor bastards the grenade landed amongst had only a short time left on earth. Both Steve and Will had 40 millimetre grenades laid out near them to ensure they did not need to delve into pouches in search of ammunition.

"Any call sign, this is Bravo One, over," Matt spoke into the radio handset.

Steve ran back to the Land Rover to pull out a map of the local area.

"Any call sign, any call sign, this is Bravo One, this is Bravo One…over."

Steve dived to the ground beside Matt, laying the map out in front of him and pointing on the map to their present location.

"Bravo One, this is Alpha Seven Four," replied the strong British accent, "go ahead, over."

"Bravo One, we are an Australian call sign at grid 2149 1720 and about to come in heavy contact with enemy. Need immediate exfil, over."

There was an extended pause, then, "I acknowledge your last Bravo One, hold your position, more information to follow, over."

"Bravo One, understood, out." Matt clipped the handset back into place and ran a hand over his face. "We'll be fuckin' dead by the time they get back to us," he chuckled.

"Ye of little faith," said Scott, cocking the Mag 58 and settling the heavy machinegun into his shoulder.

"Keep your ear out for that radio, mate," Steve told Matt, "I'm about to start the party, okay?"

"Righto," replied Matt . "Let's go home."

"My thoughts exactly," replied Steve. He stared down the ACOG scope of his rifle, nestling the overweight Iraqi into the middle of his sight.

The Iraqis were still battling up the hill towards them, but the Australians had not yet been seen. Steve stared down the rifle scope, with the target reticule ascending and descending over the chest of the fat Iraqi. Taking a deep breath, Steve fired two shots in quick succession. His target crumpled to the ground. Scott's mag 58 spoke in thundering bursts, tracer rounds showing the fall of shot. Bullets ripped through flesh, shattered bone and sent the enemy to whatever afterlife in which they believed. An explosion threw several soldiers from their feet leaving two dead, another five bleeding and screaming.

Steve was firing one shot a second, some rounds missed, stitching the earth or thudding into trees near his target. Most of the bullets found their mark. Will's grenade shrieked down to a group of Iraqis sprinting towards a large boulder. It exploded and none survived.

The mag 58 went silent. Scott flicked the weapon open and put a new length of chain link ammunition onto the feed plate. Slamming the cover down and re-cocking the weapon, he brought the weapon back into his shoulder. Scott fired into a small group of soldiers who had peeled away and were half crouching, half running. They were desperate to flee the fight.

Three more grenades exploded amongst the Iraqi advance whilst Scott had been reloading the machinegun. The Iraqi soldiers were reduced to a small, bedraggled group. They were behind cover, their inaccurate fire slamming into cave walls or ripping through the air above the Australians. Heleena pressed against Will's body, she was shaking with fear and he knew that to her, this must seem like a battle between gods. The grenades had stopped for the time being. Steve and Will were now shooting at, and around, where the Iraqis were hidden. This tactic reduced the Iraq's return fire and made them more hesitant to lean out from cover to take aim. The louder, deeper sounding M110 sniper rifle fired every so often. Within the opening minutes of the firefight, Matt had cut the Iraqi chain of command to ribbons.

Not able to take any more, two Iraqis sprinted from cover and ran back towards the tent city in the far distance.

It was the worst thing they could have done. The fire from the Australians intensified for several moments killing the enemy.

"We're just wasting ammo here!" Steve shouted over the noise. "I'm gonna move forward, cover me!"

The others nodded as Steve sprinted forward and dived to ground behind the thick trunk of a tree. Glancing out from his position of cover, Steve fired several shots, and then ran forward, disappearing behind a boulder. He gave thumbs up, signalling for the others to move forward. The remaining Australians with Heleena followed Will's lead. They took turns firing and moving forward, advancing with aggression towards their adversary. The Iraqi soldiers were still taking half-hearted pot shots.

In extended line, the Australians spread out at least thirty metres. Each of them hunkered down behind cover, their shots scarce but accurate. Spotting a group of Iraqis wedged behind a fallen tree, Scott sprinted forward, supporting the mag 58 with both hands. He leapt onto the trunk of the fallen tree and opened fire, killing the five soldiers in seconds. Two other Iraqi soldiers who had been lying behind a nearby bush spotted Scott and both opened fire. But the bullets whirred and ripped around Scott as he threw himself backwards off the fallen tree. He landed on his back.

"You all right, Scott?" shouted Steve.

"Yeah," Scott grunted. "Fuckers," he muttered.

The enemy return fire was dwindling. Some of them tried to make a run back to their camp, but were hammered from their feet by Australian bullets. The Australians fired and moved forward, fighting through their enemy position, to find them dead. Some of them were shot again to make sure. It was not uncommon for enemy soldiers to fake death as they clenched a grenade or mine in their hands, hoping for an allied soldier to venture closer. Steve was taking no chances.

Only one Iraqi soldier had survived, and he had taken cover at the furthest edge of the firefight. He stood firing his AK-47 from the hip. He was dead before he hit the ground. The Australians advanced to the rocky outcrop that Steve had ear marked as their main position. They reorganised in silence. Will was sent back to the Land Rover. The fuel tank had been pierced in several places by bullets and diesel soaked the ground. Although the vehicle would not start, Will managed to push it out the cave. Using the force of gravity, reversed it down the gentle slope. The vehicle was as close to the rocky outcrop as he could get it. They refilled their magazines with ammunition and cleaned their weapons. Steve dismounted the .50 cal machinegun from the Land Rover.

Matt had the remaining 66 rocket launchers from the Land Rover. There were eleven left and these were shared amongst the soldiers. They had no doubt that the distant tent city was aware of a disturbance and that they would soon be mobilising.

Steve had a two-hundred round belt loaded into the mag 58 and another thousand rounds nearby. They were determined to put up a strong fight, and if they were overrun, they knew they would fight in a way that would make Odin proud.

"Bravo One, this is Alpha Seven Four, over," the British voice crackled into Matt's radio handset.

"Thank Christ for that," breathed Steve.

"Alpha Seven Four, This is Bravo one, over," Matt replied.

* * * * *

"This is Alpha Seven Four," spoke Corporal Stuart Evans. "Hold your position, I say again, hold your position, we will have an exfil for you by sundown, over."

The British communications room was buzzing with noise. Some of the noise was as a result of the small Australian SAS patrol, but most concerned hundreds of other multinational units all over Iraq. Stuart was under the command of a chubby warrant officer, Scott Blamey, who in turn was under the command of Captain Jason Otter. The British communications centre room was six metres wide and fifty metres long. It was full of computers, telephones, radios, printers and faxes. Out of the one hundred and fifty personnel who worked in the building at any one time, only five were not on radios or telephones. There were also eight supervisors who walked up and down ensuring that the centre ran like a well-oiled machine.

"Bravo One, I fuckin' hope so," crackled the Australian voice. "Because our vehicle's disabled and we'll be dead by nightfall."

"Did he just swear over the radio?" warrant Officer Blamey asked.

Before Stuart could reply, Blamey was coming towards him. "Tell him to mind his ratel procedure," Blamey said.

It took all Stuart's willpower to stop himself answering back. These poor bastards were fighting for their lives and all Blamey was worried about was swearing over the radio.

"Warrant Officer Blamey!" Captain Otter called out. Otter shook his head and said no more. Blamey understood because he stormed back to his seat in silence.

"Alpha Seven Four hold fast, we'll get you out of there, out," Stuart said, noticing that Captain Otter was hovering over his shoulder.

"Their vehicle's out of action, Sir," said Stuart. "They've got no way of getting out of there."

"I heard. Is that their grid reference?" Otter asked, inspecting Stuart's notepad.

"Yes, Sir."

"Good job, Stuart, I'm going to make some calls."

Captain Jason Otter was back at his desk and dialling a number.

"This is Captain Otter, communications centre, which unit is on standby?" There was silence for a moment. "Three Commando, Royal Marines? Good, good. Can you put me through to their CO? Okay, thanks."

The phone rang several times before it was answered. "Major Breckner," said the gruff voice.

"Afternoon, Sir, my name is Captain Otter, communications centre. I understand that Three Commando is on standby?"

"That's correct," Breckner said, "but my boys are out. They're reinforcing a bit of a shit fight out west and may not be back 'til the day after tomorrow."

"Oh, I see," Otter replied.

"What's the problem?" asked Breckner.

"We've got an Australian SAS patrol in heavy contact with the enemy up near Barzan. Their vehicle's out of action and they're fighting hard. They think there's a good chance they'll be overrun by nightfall."

"Right," Breckner said and paused. "Give me half an hour," he said, "then give me a call back. I might be able to pull together a multinational team."

"Right you are, Sir," replied Otter.

Captain Otter was back at Stuart's desk. Stuart was on another call, something about a water and food resup near Basra. Otter waited for the transmission to end.

"Okay, for the Aussie SAS, the British unit on standby are out, but their commanding officer is trying to get a force together. I'll speak to him again in about twenty-five minutes."

"No problem, Sir," replied Stuart. "Thanks for letting me know."

Otter nodded.

Poor bastards, thought Stuart to himself, I hope we get to them in time.

Captain Otter was thinking the same thing, as he filled out paperwork, replied to emails and answered the phone. Just as half an hour passed, he picked up the phone again.

"Major Breckner."

"Captain Otter, any results on the multinational force?"

"Not yet, I have tried pulling rank with no joy. I have a few more tricks up my sleeve, give me an hour."

"Sir, with all due respect, another hour and we might be too late."

"Trust me," said Breckner. "I have one last option to follow before all normal protocol is satisfied. Then I'll be free to speak to whomever I please. Trust me Captain Otter, I'm not going to let these boys die. Having said that, never underestimate the SAS, British or Australian, those boys will fight hard."

"I have no doubt. I will call in an hour, Sir," said Otter.

Captain Otter carried on replying to emails and swearing at the odd person's lack of common sense. He spoke on the phone, sent faxes, made sure Warrant Officer Blamey was not bludging and kept Corporal Evans up to date about the SAS patrol. Stuart had taken the radio call and it was only fair he be kept in the loop.

* * * * *

"Fuck, I miss home," said Scott, sitting against a large boulder and searching for some cigarettes in his pack. "I could have sworn I left a pack in here somewhere," he muttered.

"Yeah, me too mate," Steve replied.

"What, you got smokes?" asked Scott.

"No, you drongo, I miss home too. Miss my wife and kids, can't wait to see 'em again," Steve said, putting the mag 58 back together after cleaning it.

Will was on piquet and was lying some twenty metres away, keeping a watch on the distant tent city. Heleena was nearby, sharpening her knives.

"Are we to die here?" she asked unexpectedly.

"I hope not," replied Steve. "I don't think we will, but," he shrugged, "there's always that possibility."

Heleena looked across at Will. Steve knew what she was thinking. They had only just met and wanted to start a life together, but that opportunity might be cut short.

"Listen," Steve touched Heleena's shoulder. "We are gonna fight long and hard. We have help on the way and if they hurry, we'll be outta here before we know it," he smiled.

Heleena seemed relieved.

"Something Will mentioned to me just before," Scott said, looking at Will who was still watching Barzan through a pair of binoculars. "If we get through this, how the hell do we get Heleena through customs?"

Steve shrugged. "I've thought of that myself. Got me stuffed, mate, if the worst comes to worst, we could try stashing her away with the weapons. But that'll be a bloody long time without food and water."

"My brother-in-law works for ASIO," said Matt. "You've never mentioned that before," Steve said.

"Didn't need to," said Matt. "Plus they're a bunch of secretive buggers, they'd prefer you didn't even know they exist."

"That'd be a cool job!" Scott grinned.

"Don't think so," replied Matt. "He's based in Canberra, which is bloody cold, and he works out of some dirty brown, multi-storey building. When he's out in the field he gets to do some cool stuff and go to some

242

interesting spots. Doesn't talk about that side of things much though. Anyway he should be able to sort something for Heleena."

"What is customs?" Heleena asked.

"Don't worry about it," smiled Steve. "Everything is okay, you won't need to worry."

"Won't be long now," said Scott.

The soldiers knew it was only a matter of time before they came under attack again.

"I'm looking forward to seeing home," said Matt, filling up his magazines with fresh ammunition.

"Ah-ha!" Scott said. He had found a crushed, sorry looking pack of cigarettes and was tearing the plastic wrapper away. He lit the first cigarette and inhaled. "Oh that feels good," he said, exhaling. Heleena shrank from the foul smelling smoke. She coughed and looked at the cigarette with disgust.

Steve stood up. Leaning on a boulder, he craned his neck and looked out to where their original observation post had been. The tiny, burned out husk of the white four-wheel drive was still there, although as far as he could make out, the bodies had been taken away. The devastated remains of the APCs were still strewn across the desert, an epitaph to the brutal efficiency of the Apache gunship.

"What you gonna do when you get home?" Scott asked Steve through the cigarette smoke.

"Get laid," chuckled Steve, still staring into the distance. Scott grinned. "Sounds like a plan," he said, flicking the spent cigarette and taking out another.

"Feels like a dream," said Matt, putting the filled magazines away.

"What does?" asked Scott.

"What we just went through," replied Matt. "I think I learned about the Vikings once in year eight or something, but don't remember much. We were told they were blood hungry thieves, rapists and murderers."

"Some of 'em were," laughed Scott.

"Yeah, true, but I never expected them to be," he went silent for a moment, "shit I dunno, so bloody courageous and hard core. A lot of those poor bastards in the cave died so we could get home. I only knew a few of 'em by name."

"Yeah," said Scott, blowing smoke out. "I know what you mean, mate, but I dunno if too many died, by Christ did those boys know how to fight!"

"Won't argue with you there," Steve said.

"We got movement!" Will's voice called.

The good humour vanished.

A moment later, they could hear heavy diesel engines start in the distance.

"Here we go," said Scott.

"APCs," muttered Steve, watching the small vehicles move out into extended line.

"How many?" asked Scott. He cocked the mag 58 and made sure he had plenty of spare ammunition nearby.

"Eight, more than likely full of infantry. Oh Christ," said Steve, "and a medium tank."

"You fuckin'n what?" asked Scott, the cigarette dropping out of his mouth. "A medium what?"

"One medium tank," replied Steve, picking the .50 cal up by the handle and jamming it between a tree trunk and a boulder. He cocked the weapon. He would be able to swivel the weapon a little, which would be enough to provide heavy suppressive fire. "I bet it's the same one that fired on us before we went on our little adventure."

"Fuck!" shouted Scott. "I thought we had a chance with eight APCs," he laughed with sarcasm. "Now we're fucked!"

"Matt, what's the answer on our exfil?" asked Steve. "It's make or break time."

The familiar adrenalin kicked in.

* * * * *

"Sir, how's the exfil coming along for the Australian SAS up in Barzan?" Corporal Stuart Evans almost shouted across the communications room.

"Excuse me for a moment," the officer said into the phone. He placed the caller on hold and turned. "Why?" he asked.

"I've just received a call from them, they're saying that heavy armour is mobilising against them. They haven't got much time left."

"Bloody hell," Otter swore. "Give me a second," he said and snatched up the phone. "Call you back in ten," he said.

He called Major Breckner again.

"Sir, Captain Otter again here, I know it's a little early, but have you got an answer on that exfil for the Australian SAS up in Barzan?"

"It's in the works. I'm waiting to hear back from intelligence. If I don't hear from 'em in ten minutes I'm going down there myself to find out."

"Okay, but can you make it five minutes?" asked Otter. "Why, what's happened?"

"We've just received information Iraqi heavy armour is mobilising against them. Time's running out," replied Otter.

"Christ almighty, I'll head down there now in that case, I don't want to let these boys die as I'm sure you don't."

"You'd be right there," said Otter.

"I'm heading down there now, Captain, keep me posted if anything changes," said Breckner. He gave Otter his mobile number, before hanging up.

"Okay, Major Breckner is going to sort it out with intelligence. Tell them that the exfil will be on its way shortly," said Otter to Corporal Evans.

Stuart nodded. "Bravo One, this is Alpha Seven Four, over."

Almost ten seconds passed before the crackling Australian voice replied, "This is Bravo One, send us good news, over."

"Alpha Seven Four, cavalry is on its way, exfil will be outbound shortly, over."

"Bravo One, if you're not here soon, don't bother, over!" came the response.

"Alpha Seven Four, we'll be there shortly, good luck, out."

* * * * *

"Good luck?" Matt said, slinging three light anti-armour rocket launchers over his shoulder. "Good luck? That's what ya say to someone going for a friggin' job interview!"

"Good luck my arse," Matt muttered, watching the Iraqi advance.

"What'd they say?" asked Steve.

"Yeah, on the way."

"They'd wanna be, and fast," Steve said. "We're not going to hold these boys off for long."

The thunder of the heavy diesel engines carried on the breeze, promising nothing but death.

"Right, Will," Steve said, "come in. You other blokes close in too." Steve waited until they were all crouched in a circle. "Right, what do you all think? Start with you, Scott."

"We're fuckin' rooted!" laughed Scott flicking another spent cigarette away. "We need to keep that armour as far away as possible. We've got eleven sixty-sixes left so it's possible we can knock out at least one track from each vehicle."

"Considering their fire power," Will butted in, "we'll need to be spread out pretty good, it'll be hard to communicate."

"Yup, good points," acknowledged Steve. "Only one 66 to fire at a time and they will be fired from left to right, if one misses its mark, the next bloke along the line will fire his at the missed target. I have two 66s, the rest of you have three, so I'll only be firing for the first two bouts." "That's workable," said Matt. "You considered smoke?"

"Yeah I have. If that armour gets too close, I'll pop my smoke. When I do, I want you all to throw or fire smoke as well, okay?" The others nodded. "So Will and me will have smoke rounds up the spout of the 203s. When the smoke has drifted across their field of view we start bugging out as fast as we can."

"Yeah okay," Will said, replacing the high explosive round from his 203 with a smoke round.

Steve did the same before half standing and glancing over the rock to watch the APCs. "Right, any questions?"

"Yeah, where do you want us?" Will asked.

"Right, Will, you duck off to the left, see that little rocky outcrop?" Steve said pointing to a small stand of rocks about forty metres from their current position.

"Yup."

"Position yourself there, I will start the contact. The bloke on my right will fire, and then the bloke on his right will fire and then it'll be your turn to engage, okay Will?"

"Yeah righto," said Will, taking a quick look at their advancing enemy before sprinting off towards his target.

Heleena followed him.

"No!" Will said pushing her back. "It's safer with Steve, there's more cover!"

"My duty is by your side!" she said. "We fight together."

Will relented and they took cover together.

"No questions from me," said Matt. "Or me," said Scott.

"Right, well in that case, Scott, see that weird looking rock?" Steve pointed off to the right about sixty metres.

Scott nodded.

"That's you," said Steve.

Scott placed the mag 58 over his shoulder, shrugged the three 66s into a more comfortable position on his back and then loped off towards his target.

"I want you to stay here, Matt," said Steve, grunting as he picked up the .50 cal.

"Why?"

"Because this is the best cover and you're the best shot out of us, so it stands to reason you should be the most protected. Plus I just spotted a better position for this little beauty," he patted the cold metal of the .50 cal.

"Where are you off to?" asked Matt.

"There's a fallen tree about twenty metres to our left, I'll be there."

"Not good cover," said Matt glancing at the trunk that was less than four foot high.

"No, but it's pretty good concealment."

"All right, mate, if you're sure?"

"Yeah I'll be right, I'd rather this than facing a couple of hundred blood thirsty tribesmen armed with nothing but a sword," chuckled Steve.

"True," grinned Matt, "righto, mate, take care, eh?"

"Yeah, will do. Listen, there's a good chance some of us might not come out of this. If that happens and you run out of ammo," Steve's voice trailed away.

"If someone gets slotted I'll grab their ammo, yeah I get the picture," Matt grabbed Steve's arm, "but that ain't gonna happen, mate, okay? We'll get out of this, now get going while they're still out of range."

"Okay," said Steve, "remember I only have two 66s so don't wait for me to fire on the third bout!"

"Yup, understood, I won't be hesitating," Matt said.

Steve nodded once at Matt, and ran towards his position. The rumble of the diesel engines grew ever closer.

The four soldiers were well spread out and would be put to the test. Only with a hard fight, luck on their side and the fast arrival of an extraction force would they walk away from this fight. But then the SASR was a volunteer force, no one forced a soldier to join, and every member of the Regiment knew they might one day be in this situation. They all accepted that possibility.

The soldiers were still within shouting distance of each other. But they knew once the fighting began, the noise would overwhelm any verbal communication. But he was confident that each man knew what he was to do and when. He watched the APCs racing across the desert at close to sixty kilometres per hour. The tank ploughed along at a more sedate forty kilometres per hour. The upside was the faster APCs were throwing dust across the tank's axis of advance, blocking the tank's targeting capability.

"One minute!" shouted Steve, pulling his 66 open and placing it on his shoulder. He intended to fire at the left track of the closest APC. If the

66 hit its mark, it would take the APC out of the fight, forcing the infantry in the back to deploy into heavy machinegun and rifle fire.

"Thirty seconds!" Steve shouted. They could feel the powerful vibrations caused by the monstrous engines rumbling through the ground.

Steve looked along the line. Each of the soldiers had a 66 on their shoulder, staring down the sites, ready to engage. He took a deep breath, the adrenalin pumping through his body. He turned back, aimed the weapon at his target and placed his hand on the trigger.

"Firing!" Steve shouted, and fired the weapon with a thunderous roar. The flight of the rocket took less than two seconds before it slammed into its target. The targeted APC disappeared from sight behind a curtain of black smoke, dirt and chunks of rock. Its main gun, a 25mm chain gun that would take any thin-skinned vehicle apart fired towards Steve. But it was inaccurate; the huge rounds screamed through the air metres above his head. Steve threw the weapon to the ground and was reaching for the second 66 when he heard another APC main gun open up. The thundering boom of Matt's rocket launcher engaged a second target. Steve released the lock button and slid the 66 out fully, the sights flipping up out of their recess. He stood back up to see that the APC he had hit was now motionless. One track had been destroyed so the armoured vehicle could not advance any further. He could see the 25mm gun, which only had a limited range of movement, tracking left and right as it sought a target. The vehicle Matt had targeted was still hidden by a dark cloud of dust. Placing the weapon down Steve crouched by the .50 cal. The first of the Iraq soldiers came spilling out the back of the immobilised APC. Steve opened fire in short bursts, watching each target fall like clockwork. A trace round hit the APC and ricocheted to the left in a white blur, slamming into a tree and dropping to the ground where it lay smouldering. Steve ducked as the 25 mm gun fired. Several rounds shattered segments of the large fallen trunk he was hiding behind. He could feel warm liquid sliding down his left arm where a tiny piece of shattered trunk had lodged in his skin. When the gun fell silent, he knelt up. Several Iraqi soldiers who were more cautious had dismounted from the APC and had taken cover behind the armoured vehicle. They waited for a moment before sprinting for the safety of cover. But Steve gunned them down, throwing himself to the ground as the 25mm gun opened up once more.

Scott fired his 66, which sounded more distant, but Steve watched the rocket hammer into another APC with a violent explosion. Although it was almost impossible to tell, he was sure it had hit the right-hand side track dead centre. Steve could feel the powerful diesel engines rumbling the ground as the APCs grew closer. The APC Matt had hit was also disabled. A second before Steve opened fire on the soldiers streaming out the back of the vehicle, he heard the distinct crack of Matt's sniper rifle. Within ten seconds, the bodies of the Iraqis were strewn around the disabled APC. The main guns of several APCs were now firing. Their large rounds buzzing, zipping or hammering into the ground near the Australian soldiers.

Will's rocket scudded towards its target but hit the APC itself. The armoured vehicle drove right through the explosion.

"Shit!" Steve yelled and stood up. Abandoning the .50 cal, he brought the 66 into his shoulder and fired. The rocket exploded in a violent roar that shattered the track and disabled the APC. Now out of 66s, Steve knelt by the massive machinegun. The APC Scott had engaged had also been disabled and as Steve brought his weapon to bear, he saw that Scott had killed the occupants. They lay around the armoured vehicle like rag dolls. But Scott had disappeared behind cover again as the 25mm main gun of the APC sought retribution.

Matt's 66 shattered another APC track, but a small group of the Iraqi soldiers were wise enough to throw smoke. They had broken contact and taken cover behind a stand of rocks some two hundred metres from the Australians' position. Scott's rocket hammered into another APC. Before the dust had settled, he opened fire with his mag 58 in a narrow corridor either side of the hidden vehicle. When the dust and smoke settled it was obvious the heavy machinegun had dealt some horrific work. It seemed the Iraqis had been taught to dismount their APCs and come streaming up the left and right of the vehicle. It was a practise that was costing them their lives. Several had retreated and return fire was zipping up towards the Australians.

Will's rocket hammered into another APC, but again he missed. The vehicle moved fast towards the Australian position.

"You idiot!" Scott shouted.

Matt's rocket hit the APC's track and the vehicle shuddered to a halt. Scott's rocket flew into another APC with a shuddering explosion that hid the vehicle from sight. But the APC appeared seconds later, its tracks intact and the 25mm gun thundering towards the Australian position. Will fired his rocket, which took the APC in the side. The track broke away from the drive wheels.

"Who's the idiot now?" shouted Will.

"Yeah, righto," yelled Scott, as massive bullets whizzed above his head, hungry to find flesh.

Steve glanced over the tree trunk at the eight disabled APCs. Their 25mm guns were still active. One tree was cut in half. The huge trunk fell to the ground in a shrieking roar, throwing dust into the air.

Steve gathered up the .50 cal and sprinted for Matt's position, hunkering down behind the cover of the rocky outcrop.

"Didn't turn out quite as planned," Steve said with a grin.

"Move in!" he yelled towards Will. Then yelled the same command to Scott.

The two soldiers gathered their weapons, left the spent rocket launchers and made a sprint for the rocky outcrop. The APCs' 25mm guns followed.

"We still got the fuckin' tank!" yelled Scott. "Yeah I know, mate, no need to yell!" said Steve.

"Shit sorry, mate, I've only had half the Iraqi army firing at me for the last five minutes! All I can hear is a high pitched scream in one ear and Will's whining in the other!" shouted Scott.

"Piss off," said Will.

Heleena was glowering at Scott, her hand hovering over a knife hilt.

"He's only joking!" Will laughed.

"Bloody hell," Scott was looking at Heleena, arms spread out in mock surrender.

More 25mm rounds zipped overhead, hammering into trees. The massive rounds shattered rocks, slashed through undergrowth or ricocheted into the air.

"Righto, we're going to use smoke, blind those fuckin' APCs. Their 25mm guns aren't doing us any favours. Once they're blinded, we move on that tank, fast as fuck. We need to be able to get under the elevation of his turret before he fires."

"Then what?" asked Will.

"Get up onto the tank, open the hatch and slot the fuckers inside," replied Matt. "One or two grenades should do the trick."

"We'll work something out," said Scott pulling two smoke grenades out of a pouch on his chest webbing.

"You should still have smoke, yeah?" Steve asked Will who had the 203 grenade launcher attached under his M4 rifle. He nodded.

"Good, so do I," said Steve.

"You stay here!" Will told Heleena. "Please! We'll be right back!"

She nodded.

The grumbling roar of the tank was far lower and much more powerful than the idle burr of the APC engines. The massive vehicle attacked the slope with dogged determination. With a burst of dark diesel fumes began climbing towards the Australian position. Its 105mm gun was still pointing skyward, but as it climbed, the huge weapon began descending towards its target.

Matt threw the smoke grenade with a grunt. Scott threw his a moment later. The two 203 grenade launchers spoke a second later with a hollow thunk. Matt and Scott threw another smoke grenade each and again the 203s fired. Within thirty seconds, the APCs were hidden from sight by various colours of smoke. The Australians were in full sprint towards the loud roar of the tank's engine. The smoke screen would last maybe ninety seconds.

"Go, go!" shouted Steve as the monstrous body of the tank emerged from the smoke, its massive gun searching for a target.

Scott screamed and slung the mag 58. He clambered up the tank, straddled the gun, and within moments was above the hatch. Steve followed him. Matt and Will ran to the rear of the armoured vehicle, covering their comrades from ground fire.

The 105mm gun fired blind, the aftershock almost knocking Steve and Scott unconscious.

"Fuck you!" screamed Scott, turning the locking latch and pulling the hatch open. The hatch could be opened on the outside for safety, so that if the crew were incapacitated, rescuers could gain access to extract them. Ironic.

Scott pushed the muzzle of the mag 58 into the hatch with a snarl and fired several short bursts. With luck, the bullets had bounced around the inside of the tank, wounding or killing its occupants. The 105mm fired again. Scott and Steve cringed as their ears rang.

"Eat that!" Scott roared into the hole. He dropped a grenade in then closed and locked the hatch.

They could feel the explosion but the thick armour dampened it. Scott opened the hatch. Smoke, groans and the smell of cordite drifted out of the hole. But despite this, the 105mm gun fired again, almost in revenge. The noise and shockwave knocked the two soldiers to the core.

Scott reached into one of his pouches.

"This'll fix 'em," he said to Steve, dropping a white phosphorous grenade into the hatch before closing and locking it.

"Bloody oath it will," replied Steve.

The grenade exploded with a dull thud beneath the thick armour and smoke began pouring from slight gaps in the hatch. They could hear the screams and smell the burning soldiers within the tank. White phosphorous was a substance that reacted with oxygen and burned as long as it remained in contact with oxygen. The only way to combat it was to dive into a pool of water, which was impossible for the crew of the Iraqi tank. The tank stopped and the engine stalled. The 105mm did not fire again. Several loud shuddering explosions echoed through the body of the tank. The soldiers realised the white phosphorous grenade was causing 105mm shells stored in the magazine to cook off.

"Shit!" shouted Steve, "get back!"

The Australians withdrew from the tank. They sprinted back to their position behind the large rocky outcrop. The 25mm guns of the APCs burst into life once more as the smoke grenades died.

Heleena was crouching with her hands over her ears. She had a look of terror on her face. Will realised that the tank's shells had exploded less than fifty metres from her. Will pulled her hands away and pulled her to him. "It's ok," he said. "You're safe." But with 25 mm rounds ripping through the air around him, he realised how stupid that sounded.

"Bravo One, this is Alpha Seven Four, over," Matt's radio burst into life.

"Thank Christ for that," muttered Steve.

CHAPTER 20

Major Breckner, 3 Commando, Royal Marines strode down the clean hallway with purpose. He had a manila folder in his hand. Making a sharp left, he stopped at the third door on the right. Ignoring the "Knock and Wait" sign, he barged through the door.

The five intelligence officers looked up from their computers. One of them, a captain, stood up and was about to remind the major that the knock and wait applied to everyone, regardless of rank.

"Shut up," said Major Breckner, "and sit down, I don't give a fuck about your little knock and wait directive. This isn't fucking primary school."

"Sir, it's just that—"

"I don't give a fuck!" Breckner shouted. The Captain sat down.

"You were supposed to return my call ten minutes ago!"

"Now," Major Breckner continued, "we have an SAS patrol in Northern Iraq, they are in heavy contact with the enemy and we need to get 'em out of there quick! What can you scrounge up within an hour?"

"Scrounge up, Sir?" asked the Captain.

"Christ boy, would you like me to draw you a fucking picture?" he snarled, "those boys are almost surrounded and fighting for their lives, they won't make it past sundown! Can you fucking well find out if we have any air assets, preference for choppers that we can send in to exfil them?"

"Right you are, Sir," said the Captain signalling for the others to stop what they were doing.

Within the minute, all five officers were on phones. Breckner sat looking around. His eyes stopped to rest on a poster near the main door. "Operational security includes you!" A stern-faced sergeant was pointing at the reader. Within three minutes, all phones had been hung up.

"Sorry, Sir, no choppers are available. The RAF have fifteen Chinooks in Northern Iraq but three are unserviceable, six are currently flying. The rest are on standby for a para insertion."

"Standby? A hot exfil'd take precedence over standby wouldn't it?" growled Breckner.

"Sorry, Sir, no."

"Anything? Do we have anything? Lynxs? Even bloody fixed wing?"

Breckner asked.

"Sorry, Sir, we rang every unit in the area and nothing is available. All units are either flying, about to fly, on standby or in a maintenance phase."

"Right, not your fault. Well at least I tried the correct channels first," Breckner said.

"Sir?"

"It doesn't matter," he said, making for the door.

"Sir, I wasn't aware we had SAS in that area of Iraq?"

"We don't," Breckner said looking back at the captain, the open door in his hand. "But the Australians do, and in a war it doesn't matter which bloody country they're from. What matters is that they're on the same side and at the moment, those boys are in deep shit. Thanks for your help."

Within minutes, Breckner was back at his office and on the phone. He had known there would not have been air assets available for an unplanned operation, but he had to cover himself. Now he would use his contacts to get what he needed.

"Captain Lock speaking."

"Locky, mate, how's the war been treating you?" asked Breckner.

"Who's this?"

"Matty," said Major Breckner. He had not talked to Captain Lock for the better part of two months, so it was no wonder the Captain did not recognise the voice.

"Matty...Matty," said Lock, trying to unlock the gates of his memory.

"Breckner, Matty Breckner!"

"Ah, Brecks! How are you old man?"

"Not too bad, been busy?"

"We had a mass casualty evacuation yesterday which wasn't much fun. Got the old heart beating let me tell you!"

"Doesn't sound like much fun," said Breckner.

"Mind you, our door gunners had a hell of a time. They got some good target practice as we came in to land. A couple of times I thought we were gone; the enemy fire was so close to the chopper."

"Shit, mate. Listen it's funny you should mention a mass cas mission. I might have something similar for you."

"Go on."

"I need a serious favour. Can you help?"

"If I can, I will."

Breckner explained his need for immediate exfil.

"I'm not scheduled to fly today. One of our choppers is being serviced which will take a day or two. But I have the feeling another is available. Hang on let me find out."

The phone went silent. Breckner picked up his mobile phone and dialled another number.

"Sergeant Williams here."

"Chris, are you busy? This is Major Breckner."

"Nope, nothing on for the next four days, but then we get inserted to you know where. Two Commando will be there too. It'll be a blast, the jundies won't know what hit 'em."

"A job just came up, you interested?"

"Maybe, Sir depends."

"An Australian SAS patrol is in deep shit in Northern Iraq, near Barzan. It's close to the border of Turkey. All we need is five good men for fire support, just to put some defence down for the choppers as the guys approach and board."

"Sounds interesting, I'll organise some blokes for you, Sir. Give me a call again in a half hour."

"Done," said Breckner said. He was about to dial another number when Lock returned to the phone.

"You there, Matty?"

"Yes," Breckner replied.

"Good. We're on. We have two Lynxs available. Keep it quiet though because none of the bosses know."

"Thanks Locky, I owe you one."

"A carton of beer should cover it, mate. Listen. Be on the flight line with whoever else you're bringing in ninety minutes."

"We'll be there."

"And Matty, because we've got two choppers we can fill the first with fire support, so don't be shy. Bring as many as you can. This sounds like a serious gig."

"I've got some Marines eager to get amongst it. I want to fill both Lynxs with fire support types and with some luck, we'll have a Chinook to exfil the blokes on the ground. I'm going to try and scrounge up some Paras or SAS boys, whoever's interested."

"Excellent! Don't be late!"

"Okay! See you soon, mate."

"Yup," said Chris. He sounded excited.

Breckner was on the phone to someone else.

"Captain Booth."

"Dave, there's a serious shit fight up in Northern Iraq. You got anyone who might be interested?"

"Yup, only one though," Booth said.

"One is better than none. Tell him to be on the flight line in eighty minutes," instructed Breckner.

"Which end?"

"The Lynx end. We've got two going up and I am trying to get a Chinook and a couple of gunships."

"Right, he'll be there." "Okay, thanks, Dave."

In seconds, he was on the phone again to Corporal Patterson.

"Wayne, Breckner here. We have a serious problem up in Northern Iraq. A few boys need extracting. I'm trying to get some fire support for the choppers."

"Shit, Sir, we'd love to help, but we're on standby for Basra." "Bloody standby's killin' me. Okay, Wayne, keep your head down."

"Give 'em hell, Sir."

Within thirty minutes, Breckner had organised a fire support team. It comprised of five Royal Marines, one British SAS trooper, four Ghurkhas, three US Rangers and two US Delta Force operatives. He had organised two Lynx helicopters and a Chinook for the Australian Special Air Service soldiers and their equipment. He had also asked for two attack choppers, an Apache and a Cobra as escorts, but he was waiting to hear if his request was successful. He had wanted a British Apache, but they were all busy, so he had contacted the Americans, who were always willing to help. If they did not call back within thirty minutes, he would have to leave and just hope for the best.

He was lost in thought when Major Douglas burst into the room.

"Just what the bloody hell do you think you're doing?" the major asked.

Major Douglas was the commanding officer of the Lynx helicopter detachment in Northern Iraq. Breckner had hoped he would not find out about his little escapade, until they had lifted off. But it seemed Douglas had heard the whisperings on the grape vine.

"What do you mean?" asked Breckner, playing dumb.

"The bloody Lynxs! You're using two without my permission for some bloody suicidal mission to support a couple of soldiers who aren't even British!"

Breckner nodded. "Oh that."

"Yes that! You can't have the choppers, they are on standby for medivac!"

"Standby," said Breckner, shaking his head. "I understand they are on standby. But being on standby for something that might happen as opposed to utilising them for a real mission is a no brainer. I reckon your pilots would be of the same opinion."

"What do you know?" asked Douglas. "You're not a pilot!"

Anger coursed through Breckner but he remained calm. "No, I am not, but I know a few of your pilots. I know they would rather go in and save these soldiers than lounge around and sipping coffee. Those poor bastards out there are getting slotted!"

"I don't care what you think. I will not have my helicopters misused like this!"

"Misused?" Breckner asked.

"Bloody misused, yes! They aren't even British. You should know better, I'm going to cancel the mission."

"I should know better?" roared Breckner. "Those helicopters are built to fly in war, to infil and exfil soldiers and those fucking guns hanging off the side are there to kill the enemy."

"To break contact," Douglas corrected him. His superior demeanour had been replaced with genuine concern.

"Fucking words, mate. 'Break contact', 'slot the enemy', it's the same damn thing! These choppers will fly today. I don't give a fuck that those soldiers aren't British, they are our allies and they are fighting for their fucking lives! I won't sit back while they are killed because of some red tape! You'd better be ready to ground your precious pilots when they get back because they have just saved the lives of their brothers. You should know better Major Douglas!"

Douglas was about to defend himself, but did not get the chance.

"I don't want to hear it. Just get out," said Breckner.

Douglas left without a word.

"Fuck!" Breckner roared. His phone rang. "Major Breckner."

"We're good to go, Sir," said a man with a strong American accent. "We got an Apache and a Cobra ready to rock. Where d'ya want 'em?"

"To the British side of the flight line. They'll know where to go, the other choppers will be taxiing in about forty minutes."

"You got it, we'll be there in thirty," the man said. "Thanks for this," Breckner said.

"No problem, Sir, we'll do anything for a scrap," he chuckled.

"By the sounds of it they won't be disappointed they came. Have a good day." Breckner hung up.

Grabbing his rifle and belt kit, Breckner checked the safety, slapped a magazine in, cocked it and slung it over his shoulder. Half an hour later and he was drinking coffee in the British helicopter waiting areas. He was watching the distant Lynx crews perform start up checks. A group of Royal Marine Commandos were chatting nearby and the Americans were lounging around on the other side of him. He assumed one of them was Delta Force because of his shoulder length, unkempt hair. The man was sucking on a potent smelling cigarette.

"Bit of a shit fight?" asked a voice. Major Breckner turned to face a well-built man with messy hair and a weapon by his side.

"You the bloke Captain Booth sent?" asked Breckner, assuming he was from the Special Air Service.

"Yup, name's Pup," said the man holding out his hand.

"Major Breckner." They shook hands.

Pup nodded and slung his rifle. "Should be interesting, I hear there's a bit of a disagreement?" he asked.

"You could say that," Breckner replied. He had grown accustomed to the non-conventional rules by which the SAS abided and accepted Pup had not acknowledged his rank. A group of Ghurkhas walked in, talking and laughing in their native Nepalese.

They were only small men and their friendly, good-natured faces often gave people the mistaken idea they were gentle soldiers. Some of the best-trained, fiercest soldiers in the world in fact populated the Ghurkha Regiment.

"Brought the slashers I see. Nice," said Pup.

Pup gave them the nickname following a rumour about two companies of Ghurkhas involved in a firefight in Afghanistan. After they were beaten, the Taliban threw down their weapons and fled. Dropping their own weapons and packs, the first company of Ghurkhas drew their Kukris and ran after them. They caught the Taliban and cut every man's throat. The second Ghurka company collected the dropped weapons and packs before linking up with their comrades.

"Thought they might come in handy," Breckner smiled.

"Always," chuckled Pup. "My grandad fought beside 'em in North Africa during World War Two. He reckons after the battle they'd go out at night, cut off the dead Germans' ears and noses, and hang 'em on their belts as trophies. Ferocious little bastards."

Pup went over to the Ghurkhas.

The deep throb of the helicopter could be heard before it was seen. Breckner watched the Chinook taxi towards the Lynxs. There were three 7.62 mm mini guns on the Chinook, one on the ramp facing rearwards and one on each side. It was a large, cumbersome helicopter, but in the right hands, it was fast and could be flown at low altitude.

The rotor of a Lynx began to turn, the velocity of the blades ever increasing until the rotors were a dark blur. A moment later, the rotors of the second Lynx began to turn. In the distance, hovering into view behind the three British helicopters were two Apaches.

Major Breckner had asked for an Apache and a Cobra, but two Apaches would be just as good. He watched the Apaches turn and accelerate into the distance, until they were black blobs on the horizon. It was possible they were not the gunships assigned to the mission so the escort he had requested was yet to arrive.

"This way please, Sir," said a young soldier dressed in British desert cams, but with a bright orange safety vest. But as they said, "safety first", thought Breckner as he eyed the bright orange vest.

"Right let's go you lot!" roared Breckner.

As they walked out onto the tarmac towards the helicopters, the soldier with the orange vest gave each soldier a pair of hearing protection.

Breckner climbed aboard the closest Lynx and strapped himself in. Once all the men had boarded and were strapped in, the two helicopters taxied out towards the main runway. Breckner noticed the Chinook clawing its way into the sky ahead of them.

Major Breckner grabbed a pair of headphones hanging from one of the seats. But they were not plugged in, so communication with the aircrew was impossible.

One of the loadmasters, pointed at a plug just above his seat. Breckner plugged the headphones in and immediately heard voices.

"...bearing of three five zero," he heard.

"Where are the gunships?" he asked. No answer.

The loadmaster indicated that Breckner needed to push a button attached to the lead to communicate.

Breckner nodded. "Where are the gunships?" he asked again.

"They've gone ahead to clear the way. Apaches are a lot slower than us, we'll catch them in no time."

This surprised Breckner. He thought the Apache was one of the fastest helicopters in the world.

"So the Apaches are slow?" he asked.

"Not particularly, just not as fast as us. Chinooks and Lynxs have been known to outrun their Apache escort on more than a few occasions. Particularly on medivac missions when they didn't have time to wait around," replied the voice.

"Is that you Locky?" he asked.

"No, Locky is on the other chopper," was the reply.

They lifted off and accelerated. Breckner felt his legs and feet growing heavy as they gained altitude.

"Eyes out, go instant," said the voice.

Breckner watched as the loadmaster on each side cocked their machineguns and flicked safety catches off.

The helicopter levelled out Breckner watching the dark bitumen of the runway disappear below them. A short time later, the base's perimetre fence zipped beneath them. They were now in open territory and were fair game. At least that is how it felt.

Leaning forward he looked out the open side door and could see the distant Chinook ahead of them, hugging the mountains. Dark fumes spewed from the engines as its rotors whipped the air. He blinked almost in disbelief as he saw all three mini guns open up on the Chinook, flames and trace rounds belching from each weapon.

"What happened there?" he asked, not enjoying the feeling of no longer being in control. If they were hit, or the pilot made an error, then he would most likely die, and he would not have any say in the matter.

"Just a test fire," came the reply.

Moments later the machineguns on either side of the Lynx opened up, their noise just audible over the scream of the engines. They were travelling at close to three hundred kilometres an hour and the ground was whipping by in a blur. It was comforting to the Royal Marine officer. An enemy soldier on the ground would need to be skilled to time a rocket to hit them or even come close. He decided he would pass the message along, when they were ten minutes out, so that they could ready themselves.

"Twenty minutes to target," said the voice.

The aircrew were all wearing helmets with dark visors hiding their faces, so it was difficult for Breckner to know who had spoken. But being so far from their destination, he decided not to pass the message on to the other soldiers beside him who could not hear the radio.

Breckner was amused to see one of the Ghurkhas had gone to sleep.

He grinned.

Breckner was still grinning when he saw a group of people on the ground. It seemed that they were running towards cover, but the helicopter was travelling so fast he could not be sure. As the group were almost out of sight, he caught a puff of white smoke.

"Rocket, break left!" roared the voice in Breckner's ear. Before he knew what was happening, the straps of his seat belt dug into his body as the helicopter was thrown left. The RPG tapered off to the right. A thin wisp of white smoke trailed behind the small warhead as it slammed into the side of a mountain.

"Nice of the escort to leave us that little surprise," a voice said.

A dark rage burned inside Breckner, urging him to go back and face the men who had almost killed him.

"Speak of the devil," said another voice. In the distance, Breckner could see the Apaches.

Within five minutes they had caught up with their escort, who were flying low to the ground and as fast as they were able. One of the Apaches ascended fast and fired a rocket that tore through the air at blistering speed. The rocket plunged into a distant, abandoned building.

"Oh to have their rules of engagement," said another voice. The British helicopters were not allowed to engage an enemy unless they were fired upon first. But the American escorts were a little less rule- bound, which in some circumstances tended to save lives.

"Ten minutes to target."

Breckner tapped the man beside him and held up ten fingers. The message was passed along. Soldiers checked and rechecked their weapons and gear. It would be a tough fight. They would be landing and dismounting in the middle of a firefight and the chance they would be shot down or killed was real. The Ghurkhas were kneeling beside the doorway, holding onto one another. Their eyes squinted against the wind created by the rotor chop.

Pup was still snoozing, with his mouth open and rifle across his lap. Breckner himself remained in his seat. If the chopper took evasive manoeuvres again, he did not fancy taking a dive out of the door from fifty feet at three hundred kilometres an hour.

The Marines were moving towards the doorway on the opposite side. They moved with speed and efficiency, kneeling behind each other and holding onto the airframe to steady themselves.

When they were two minutes out the helicopters slowed and let the gunships move ahead. Breckner unstrapped himself and knelt down beside the Ghurkhas, checking his weapon. As they accelerated after the diminishing gunships, he flicked the safety catch off and readied himself. The adrenalin was beginning to pump. They came over a sharp rise before descending on the other side. Breckner regained his balance. The gunships opened fire. Puffs of smoke obscured them as they fired rockets one after another. Before the rockets landed and shielded his view, Breckner saw a mass of enemy, including APCs and a tank. The armoured vehicles gathered about two hundred metres from a small clump of rocks. From behind the cover, a small amount of return fire was holding the attacking force at bay.

The helicopter descended, throwing sand and dirt into the sky, obscuring everything from view. Breckner readied himself to exit behind the Ghurkhas. The helicopter descended to six feet, but before they moved, Pup launched himself from the chopper. The British soldier hit the ground, rolled and came up sprinting.

At three feet, the Ghurkhas exited and ran into a defensive position. Breckner followed. About one foot from the ground and unloaded, the Lynx ascended fast, banking away from the firefight. The door gun burst into life with orange flames blasting from the barrel and empty cartridges cascading from the weapon.

With dust and sand obscuring the view, Breckner dived to the ground with a grunt and looked around.

The cloud of dust had begun to settle but was still thick enough that they could move forward fast. As they exited the concealment of the brown out, the Ghurkhas went to ground. They spread themselves out and moved towards the enemy at blistering speed. The juddering roar of the helicopters was distant now. The gunships banked towards the enemy, the methodical thump of their thirty millimetre chain guns bursting to life. He was too far away to see the damage the chain guns dealt amongst the enemy but realised some were still alive as tracer rounds began zipping over his head. Breckner threw himself to the ground. Arching his neck, he could see Pup sprinting forward like a mad man. The soldier heaved a grenade towards the enemy as he ran then disappeared from sight as he went to ground. The white phosphorous grenade exploded a moment later, hissing phosphorous streaking through the air. The WP grenade blotted the enemy from view and Pup was on his feet once more, sprinting like an Olympian. Within less than half a minute Pup was with the Australians, hunkering down beside them behind the cover of the rocks. Breckner shook his head.

"Bloody crazy," he said, following the Ghurkhas' assault as they moved to outflank the enemy.

Breckner took in the battlefield. The APCs had been disabled and could not move. But their huge 25mm forward facing guns were booming their wrath up to the small group of Australian soldiers. Every now and then bursts of diesel fumes blasted from the exhaust pipes of the APCs. They were attempting to turn and bring their massive forward- facing guns to bear on the new threat. Only one managed to move a little, before its mangled, broken track dug into the ground, stopping it from turning. Two hundred metres from the Australian position another stand of rocks stood. Behind the rocks, a body of Iraqi soldiers were firing towards the new assault. Twice Breckner threw himself to the ground as rounds whizzed or cracked close to him. Breckner could not see any movement from the tank at all. Either the crew had climbed out to escape or had been killed. The latter he doubted. The Australians would have had to be good to disable a tank.

The American soldiers were fire-and-moving fast. The Delta Force operatives in particular were moving at blistering speed. The Ghurkhas continued moving. Their weapons never silent as they laid accurate suppressive fire amongst the remains of the enemy group. Return fire was still thick and the bullets cut the air above their heads.

Adrenalin fuelling him, Breckner sprinted forward and dived behind a small outcrop of rocks. A loud ricochet ripped past his head as an enemy bullet glanced off a rock close to his face.

"Let's have ya!" Breckner shouted, as he pushed himself to his feet and sprinted forward. More enemy fire burst around him.

Everything was silent, apart from his little area of the battle. He had forgotten about the helicopters and was no longer aware of the American soldiers pushing forward on his right flank. The Ghurkhas had moved ahead of him in aggressive bursts, their blood fury driving them towards the enemy. Breckner was no longer keeping up with them. For him this had become a private war; a private war that seemed to run in slow motion.

He lined up a distant enemy in his sights and fired several shots before his weapon fell silent with a metallic click. Breckner slapped a fresh magazine into the weapon and brought it back into his shoulder. He fired again, watching the enemy soldier clasp his shoulder and fall from view. Sprinting forward, Breckner again dived to the ground, skidding for almost a metre before opening fire.

The Ghurkhas moved into his line of sight. Breckner rolled onto his side and looked up at the distant helicopters. The Lynxs and Chinook had moved away from the battle and were waiting for the extraction somewhere out of view, at least that is what he assumed. Roaring low and fast came the gunships, their chain guns singing with methodical thumps. The protected enemy were fast diminishing in number.

The Ghurkhas were almost on top of the enemy now, followed by the Americans. The Royal Marines had fought their way into a position one hundred metres behind the enemy, preparing to cut them off if they tried to withdraw. The small group of Iraqis broke and ran, some dropping their weapons and discarding their ammunition. The Royal Marines shot them as they retreated, their blood soaking the desert.

Breckner watched Pup move forward from cover with caution to survey the enemy position.

Pup moved slow, with his weapon pulled to his shoulder. He was aware there might be one or two lying on the ground who were still alive and eager to kill an infidel before they died. Pup was unsure of one man who was on his back, eyes closed and with his weapon nearby. Pup fired a shot into the side of the man's skull. Coagulated blood and brain matter oozed from the hole.

Another enemy soldier was groaning as he dragged himself away from the scene of carnage. Pup knelt down beside him, cradling his rifle in his arms and reaching down to take a hold of the man's arm.

"Hang on there, we'll get you some help," he said, ripping open a trauma bandage. Rolling the man onto his back, Pup saw he had taken a large chunk of shrapnel through his belly. Most of his small intestines were hanging from the wound. Dirt had worked its way in and Pup knew there was no chance of fighting the infection that would come. The man would die slow and in agony. Kneeling down and discarding the bandage, he rested the soldier's head on his knee.

The man was talking in Arabic.

"Any of you boys a medic?" he called to the American soldiers nearby.

None were. He was about to shout out to the Ghurkhas when one of the Australians knelt by him.

"Morphine?" the Australian asked, looking at the enemy soldier. Pup nodded.

As the Australian soldier administered an overdose of morphine, Pup talked to the soldier, reassuring him. The man's eyes, which were full of pain and fear closed as the drug, took effect. His breathing became slower, shallower, and finally stopped. Pup placed the man's head on the ground. The two soldiers moved away. Within minutes the transport helicopters had landed, sending dust and dirt skyward. The gunships hovered nearby, watching for any threat. Five minutes later, the desert was silent, apart from a soft wind that massaged the dust and fluttered the uniforms of the dead.

CHAPTER 21

Major Breckner was on board the Chinook with the Australians. The beast lifted from the ground and accelerated away. SAS soldiers often dressed in full Arab clothing when they were out on patrol so they blended in with the local communities. But the soldiers before the major dressed like nothing he had ever seen before. They wore strange shirts, long pants and heavy woollen cloaks clipped at their left shoulders by large metal or wooden brooches. Two of these were shaped like hammers, another the face of a snarling man and the third a longship. Tied to the outside of the soldiers' packs were sheathed swords, but he must have been mistaken. What he found strangest of all was that the dead soldier they had dragged on board was dressed in normal desert cam uniform. It was obvious he had been dead a long time. Something was amiss here but Breckner could not work out what it was.

Breckner sat down beside the exhausted soldiers. The comforting hint of fumes and engine heat drifted in from the opening at the rear of the huge helicopter.

Steve was beside one of the side gunners.

"Hey!" he shouted.

The gunner looked round.

"Can you tell the Apache boys to put a couple of rockets into our Rover?"

The gunner shook his head.

Steve yelled over the engine noise and this time the gunner gave the thumbs up and spoke into his microphone.

Within a minute, the Apaches had each launched a rocket into the doomed Land Rover. They laced the stricken vehicle with chain gunfire, demolishing it.

There was also a young woman with them. She was beautiful, and well developed Breckner noticed. She carried an edge of strength about her. She too was clothed in a strange manner. She carried two long daggers and three smaller ones across her chest.

Breckner leaned over to the soldier beside him.

"Matty Breckner," he shouted, holding out his hand.

"Matt," replied the soldier. "Thanks for getting us out of the shit, mate, dunno if we would have lasted much longer."

"You did well lasting as long as you did!" Matt shrugged. "Luck I guess," he grinned.

Breckner nodded but he knew damn well it was more than luck. The SAS were some of the finest soldiers in the world. Although the soldiers looked exhausted, they still carried themselves well. Their faces were weather worn, but their eyes still had that sharp glint that he often saw in the Special Forces community. No matter how tired they were, or how hard they had been pushed, that cunning gleam remained in their eyes.

Breckner worked his way to the next soldier.

"Matty Breckner."

"G'day, mate, Scotty," the soldier shouted back, taking Breckner's hand in an iron grip. "Saved our arse back there, thanks for that."

"We tried to get here as fast as we could," shouted Breckner, "but you know how red tape can be, we had to put the team together behind the head honcho's back."

"Love your work. You'll have to introduce me to your head honcho when we get back," he grinned.

Although the soldier was grinning, Breckner could see the hint of violence in Scott's face.

"I don't think that's a good idea," yelled Breckner, "he's going to be pretty annoyed we went without permission."

"He's going to be annoyed?" shouted Scott. "Want me to smack him out for ya?"

"Would love you to, but it's not worth the paperwork."

Scott roared with laughter.

Breckner became aware of the pungent aroma of cigarette smoke.

Scott lifted a cigarette to his mouth and took a long drag.

Breckner was about to grab the cigarette, but a soldier from the opposite side of the helicopter beat him to it.

"You bloody crazy?" shouted the soldier, throwing the cigarette on the floor and extinguishing it beneath his boot.

"Sorry, Steve, didn't know," Scott said.

"All this thing is," Steve yelled, gesturing at the helicopter, "is one big fuel tank. All ya need is a spark in the right place and we end up a fire ball in the sky!" Steve roared. "Can't you wait half an hour?"

"Yeah righto, Steve, point taken, mate."

"Just wait until we land, mate, and I'll buy you a pack myself, you can smoke 'til the cows come home," Steve sat down again.

Breckner sat beside him. "Breckner," he shouted, holding out his hand again.

"Steve, how are ya?" shaking the offered hand. "Not bad, are you in command?"

"Yeah," Steve said. "What happened out there?"

Steve shrugged. "Bit of this, bit of that, you know how it is. We had a bit of a disagreement with the Iraqis. Lucky you guys showed up when you did."

The response didn't quench Breckner's interest, but he was not surprised. Operational security was paramount.

Breckner made his way to the last soldier, who was cleaning his weapon. The woman, he noticed, sat close to him. She looked terrified.

"Matty Breckner."

"Will," the man shouted back with a nod of his head.

"Having a good day?" Breckner realised how stupid the question sounded.

"Bloody oath, I am now!" Will shouted. "You blokes showed up just in time. Now I get to go home!"

Breckner looked down at the dead soldier hidden beneath the ground sheet.

"What was his name?"

"Dave!" replied Will. "Good bloke and a bloody good soldier. Not too many like him, know what I mean?"

"Unfortunately I do," shouted Breckner. "A lot of good men have died under my command. Too many."

"What unit you with?"

"Three Commando Royal Marines," Breckner responded.

Will nodded. "How long you been in Iraq?"

"We've been here for over five months now," shouted Breckner. "Our rotation will stay for another two or three months before going home."

"Nice!" Will replied.

Then he noticed Breckner watching Heleena.

"She's never been on a helicopter before!" Will grinned, placing an arm around her. She gave Will a faint smile.

The Chinook banked hard right and the right-hand gun opened up. The gunner was aiming at something low to the left. He was firing in long bursts, his gun tracking to the centre and to the right as they flew past the threat. The rear gun opened up a moment later. Spent cartridges cascaded from the gun and disappeared over the rear ramp, or bounced and rolled on the floor. There were several flashes close to the rear ramp that may have been tracer from ground fire, but Breckner could not be sure. The rear gun continued to fire, falling silent only when an Apache gunship came into view. The Apache turned and flares burst from its flanks as its massive gun opened up towards the ground in a roar of noise. The Chinook banked to the left and the Apache disappeared.

Breckner clung to his seat as the chopper ascended and descended over a sharp mountain peak. This was a much different ride than he had experienced on the way in to the target area. The Chinook was just as fast as the Lynx, but even at speed was quite manoeuvrable.

They flew low and fast, the desert almost a blur beneath them. Again, the Chinook ascended, banked hard to the right and descended down into a deep valley. Leaning forward Breckner caught a glimpse of one of the Lynxs. A hint of fumes trailed the air behind the smaller chopper, but it was gone as the Chinook turned again. Breckner's stomach felt worse for wear, he looked at the Australian soldiers to see they were enjoying the ride.

Will leaned towards him. "You look sick, mate!" "I feel it!" Breckner shouted back.

"This is better than flyin' straight and slow. We've got less chance of coppin' a bullet!"

Breckner was about to respond but the Chinook ascended. This time the left-hand gun began firing and the smell of cordite filled the Chinook. The noise was somehow comforting. The rear gun came to life again and as the Chinook slewed to the left, Breckner caught a flash of the Lynx again. Behind it, just for a moment, he saw an Apache fire two rockets in quick succession. A series of dull thuds mingled with the scream of the engines and flares streamed from the Chinook. Breckner watched the flares descending towards the ground, before the chopper turned to the left.

"Wish I knew what was going on!" shouted Breckner looking around for a headset.

Will shrugged. "No point worrying. We ain't in control any more. We get hit, then we get hit, nothin' we can do about it."

Breckner nodded. What the soldier said was true; their lives were in the hands of the pilot, the weapon skills of the gunners and whoever was firing at them from the ground.

The Chinook banked hard. Dave's corpse slid across the floor and came to rest with a dull thud against the side of the helicopter. The soldiers had boarded fast so there had been no time to secure the body. Breckner struggled to hold down some vomit.

"I'll warn ya, mate, I'm a sympathy spewer, so if you go and I catch a whiff, sure as shit I'm goin' as well," he laughed.

Breckner nodded.

"Go get 'em boys!" shouted Scott from the other side of the Chinook.

Breckner saw both Apaches accelerating away from them towards a group of small dots on the ground. As he watched the dots, which must have been enemy soldiers, he saw a burst of dust, a puff of smoke and a rocket zipped into the air from the ground. It was inaccurate but a second came close to one of the Apaches, forcing the gunship to fire flares whilst swerving away. Both Apaches opened up together, four rockets screaming towards the enemy. The tiny soldiers on the ground were obliterated from view in several large explosions.

The Chinook continued to dodge and weave through deep valleys until they came to their destination at last. They landed on the tarmac at a massive base on the outskirts of Basra. The American Apaches roared past as the Chinook's engines shut down. Breckner clambered to his feet as the engines fell silent.

"You look green, mate," said Steve in the deafening silence.

"Thanks," muttered Breckner with a smile.

Breckner helped carry the soldiers' packs out of the chopper. As he turned back for more equipment, he heard a familiar voice.

"Major Breckner!" the voice shouted. "Major Breckner!"

Breckner watched Major Douglas stride across the tarmac towards him.

"I told you I'd go with or without your permission Barry," called out Breckner. "These boys were in the shit, and we had the capability to help them."

"I did not authorise this mission!" screamed Douglas.

"Whether you did or not—" Breckner began. "I did not!" roared Douglas.

"Your pilots did a splendid job, if it's any consolation," said Breckner, maintaining calm.

"I don't care what they did!" yelled Major Douglas.

"No, of course you don't," said Breckner, trying to push past the infuriated officer.

Douglas pushed Breckner back. "I'll have you on a charge!" Douglas yelled.

The aircrews from the Chinook and the Lynxs approached the altercation to back Breckner.

"Oi!" yelled a voice. Steve stopped beside Breckner. "What's your name, mate?"

Major Douglas looked Steve up and down. "Sir, to you!" he shouted. "And who might you be! You're dressed like—"

Steve stepped forward until he was nose to nose with Douglas.

The Major fell silent. "I said," replied Steve, "what's your name?"

"Major Douglas," replied Douglas, trying to stand tall.

"Not your rank dickhead, your name!" Steve said.

"Who the fuck do you think you are?" shouted Scott, striding towards Douglas with clenched fists.

"Stay outta this!" said Steve, his eyes fixed on the officer.

"Barry," growled Douglas.

"Barry?" Steve repeated. The officer nodded.

"Right, Barry, come 'ere," said Steve, moving away. When Major Douglas did not make any effort to follow, Steve turned, grabbed a fist full of the officer's shirt and pulled him along behind him.

"I said come 'ere!"

With all the gear on the ground at the rear of the Chinook, Matt and Will were carrying Dave's body out of the Chinook.

"Put him down there fellas," said Steve, still dragging the Major behind him.

"Barry, meet Dave, the fifth member of our patrol," Steve stopped beside the corpse, his eyes glowing with fury.

"Dave was divorced with two kids he saw every second weekend. He dedicated his life to the Regiment."

Steve ripped the ground sheet away, revealing the corpse. Dave was dark purple and half his face was missing. Part of his brain was visible through the fragmented skull. His remaining eye was still partly open, the dry pupil staring at the sky.

"We would have ended up liked that," said Steve, forcing Major Douglas to look at the corpse. "Had Major Breckner not had the initiative and the balls to get us out of the shit today!"

Douglas's mouth opened and closed again.

"Your aircrew flew in and pulled us out of a situation that would have otherwise seen us in wooden boxes."

"I am aware of this," Douglas said.

"I'm not sure you are, Barry," replied Steve.

"I did not authorise this mission. Disciplinary action will follow against all involved!" Major Douglas said loud enough that the British aircrew nearby could hear. "I will be in touch with the Australian army, and I will see you on a charge," Douglas said, his face red with rage.

"And we can make your death look like an accident mate," said Matt in a conversational tone.

Major Douglas flinched, but Steve dragged him forward again so he was forced to look once again at Dave.

"You just remember what the people under your command did today. They saved lives and they made sure that one of our brothers was brought home for a proper burial. If anything, you should be proud! You should be recommending medals and ensuring your unit gets a citation for this." Steve shook his head as he saw Major Douglas was still adamant about disciplinary action.

"Piss off," Steve said, pushing Major Douglas away. The officer turned back but before he could respond, Steve shoved him away. "I said, piss off!" Steve said.

"All right, mate," said Will, "that's enough."

Steve took a deep breath.

Major Barry Douglas stormed towards the large demountable building of the Royal Air Force flight line in the distance. The ground sheet lifted back over Dave's body, hiding the gruesome wound from view.

"You've got a prick of a commanding officer," Steve called to the British aircrew standing nearby. Some of them grinned or chuckled.

"You should try workin' with him," called a man with a broad Birmingham accent.

Steve knew Major Douglas would be raising merry hell with his peers and commanders. He was hell bent on seeing justice delivered to those who ignored his direct orders. He would also push for insubordination charges upon the Australian soldiers. But when it came to disciplinary action within the Western military, it was much the same as civil law. Evidence needed to be sought and provided and witnesses found. None of the helicopters had taken ground fire. No aircrew died. Within the space of thirty minutes, all helicopters were refuelled, re-armed and standing silent upon the flight line. Their 'remove before flight' tags drifting in the breeze as if the choppers had never left.

Steve knew no witnesses would be forthcoming. Major Douglas could argue with his peers and subordinates until he was blue in the face. The Royal Air Force had deployed on a daring rescue mission and had been successful. It was something of which to be proud, a story to tell their grandchildren one day. It was not a mission that required disciplinary action. This would mean Major Douglas would fail.

The Australians thanked the British aircrew before carrying their dead mate between them. Dave's body was taken away to be stored in a morgue. The aircrew drifted away in dribs and drabs, no doubt to have a debrief somewhere out of sight and ear shot of Major Douglas. Matt's brother-in-law was more than helpful in organising papers for Heleena. Carried out with discretion, within forty-eight hours Heleena was an Australian citizen. Within ninety-six, she had birth certificate, passport, driver's licence and credit card.

The Australians were given accommodation for four nights. This brief stay allowed the soldiers to wash clothes, shower, eat decent food and make short phone calls home. It was not much, but a ten-minute phone call home was incredible for morale. The adventure they had experienced with the Norse was like a dream now. Some of these ancient warriors had given their lives to see the Australians make it home and the soldiers knew that there was no greater sacrifice. That the Norse were brave was beyond any doubt. It was something none of them would forget, ever.

Will and Heleena were given accommodation where Heleena learned how a shower and toilet worked. Heleena was still showering and the smell of the fresh soap was permeating the small unit. Will walked into the bathroom to wash his hands. He stopped as his eyes drank up Heleena's naked body that was glistening, wet and soft. Arousal washed over him. She smiled and gestured to him.

"Come here," she said, soapsuds sliding between her breasts and down her slim stomach.

He needed no second invitation.

* * * * *

The day before they were to leave, Steve was asked if they would like a ramp ceremony for Dave. A ramp ceremony was a display of respect. Soldiers lined up either side of the rear ramp of the plane into which the coffin was carried. They saluted the coffin as it passed, offering their respect and acknowledgement. Steve knew Dave would not have made any complaint, were he alive. The people who mattered most to Dave, his family and his mates, were in Australia, and they would be at his funeral. The ramp ceremony was a kind gesture, but it was declined.

The Australians were waiting out on the flight line before dawn. Dave's coffin was delivered half an hour later. Within the hour, the soldiers were airborne on a USAF C-130 Hercules. They stayed the night on the massive American Base, before they were airborne once more early the next day for Dubai. Once they landed, they had a four- hour wait before they boarded the Australian flight home.

They stopped in the Maldives to refuel before continuing for Australia. Finally, they touched down in Perth.

Judy was waiting to the side, and it took Steve some time before he found her. She was running towards him. He opened his arms and kissed her hair as she wrapped her arms around his waist. They stood holding each other for a long time, neither of them saying anything.

"I missed you," Judy's voice said into his shirt.

"I missed you too," he said, smelling her perfume and feeling her body pressing against him.

"Where are the kids?" he asked, as she pulled away.

"Still at school; it's only twelve o'clock."

He smiled and kissed her. "Good. We could do with some time alone." He draped his arm over her shoulder.

"I think we could," she smiled.

Matt was on the far side talking to his girlfriend, Vanessa, who was smiling up at him through her tears. Scott was with an old girlfriend he had split from several times before. Will was standing hand in hand with Heleena, who was dressed in modern clothes that flattered her.

Steve looked to see Dave's ex-wife waiting, with her two children.

Judy had noticed too.

"I know Dave didn't make it," she said, "should we go over?"

Steve nodded.

Steve and Judy walked over to Sandy, who had been holding it together. She had not been crying, but her eyes were glistening and the children were confused.

"Sandy," Steve said as he held her to him. He could feel her shuddering before the tears came. She buried her face into his shoulder and cried for a long time.

Matt and Vanessa came alongside them. Matt knelt and pulled the children to him.

"Where's Daddy?" one of them asked.

"Your daddy has gone to a better place," said Matt, holding the boy and girl close. He could not remember their names and cursed himself for it.

"If you close your eyes tight you can see him, and if you whisper to him you can hear him. He is here with us, you just can't see him," said Matt, his voice breaking. "When you go to bed tonight, close your eyes and speak to him, you'll see," said Matt, smiling at them. They seemed reassured, for now anyway. Matt and Vanessa grabbed the children's hands and pulled them away from their mother. They led them to the spectator's window, where people could watch planes land and take off.

"Wow, look at that one!" said the girl, standing on her tiptoes as she pointed to a twin propeller plane roar into the sky. Several minutes later a Qantas jet landed, its airbrakes roaring with power.

They stood there for some time with the children until Sandy had regained her composure. Matt and Vanessa led the children back to her.

*****

Dave had been in the Special Air Service a long time, but in his will, he had still opted for a private burial. The media were not invited. Sandy would be damned if her ex-husband's funeral turned into a media frenzy as journalists pushed and jostled to get a story. Just one Australian Defence photographer was permitted to attend the funeral.

Steve and Judy arrived an hour before the church service to find Sandy talking to the priest about the coming ceremony. She was holding herself together, but her eyes were dark rimmed and puffy. She had not slept well.

Steve left Judy with Sandy and the priest, when he spotted Dave's parents. Dave's father, Al, was a hard-eyed man who had served with the Royal Marines before migrating to Australia in the late-1960s. Catherine, Dave's mother, was the opposite. It was easy to see that her heart had been broken. Al was supporting her as they walked in.

"Al," Steve shook the older man's hand. "I'm sorry."

Al shrugged. "These things happen," he said. Even though he was making out that he was dealing well with the death of his son, it was clear he was not. "I just hope the bastard who got Dave was slotted."

"Yeah we got him," Steve said.

"Good," growled Al.

Steve looked at Catherine. She was pale and her cheeks were wet with tears.

"I'm sorry Catherine, I'm sorry," he said. "Oh Steve! Oh Steve," was all she could say.

"How did he die?" Catherine asked after a long while.

"Come on, love," Al said, taking her arm.

She pulled away. "No, I want to know Al, I want to know how our boy died!"

"I don't know if it'll help," Steve said.

"Tell me," Catherine said.

"All right," said Steve, taking a breath. He took a few minutes to explain what happened.

Catherine nodded and blew her nose. "Thank you," she said looking at Steve through tear-filled eyes.

The church was now packed with Dave's family and friends. The ceremony began as his coffin was carried to the front of the congregation.

Some of Dave's friends recalled memories of the man. Sandy spoke of her memories of a husband and father. Scott recalled how on one hot day in the Middle East, Dave had beaten him hands down at a game of cards, winning almost two hundred dollars in cash.

"I still reckon the bugger cheated!" Scott said, as he moved away from the back towards his seat, eyes glistening.

The burial was at a cemetery on the outskirts of Perth. Steve, Scott, Matt, Will and their respective partners stood with Dave's family.

Steve recalled the battle in which Dave had died. They had fought long and hard, and although they tried gunning down the small force, which had moved to outflank them, the task had been impossible. He had not seen Dave die. When they had initiated the ambush on the Iraqi soldiers, no one expected one of the enemies to fire a quick, un-aimed burst. Much less for the rounds to kill one of their patrol members. But unfortunately, that was what happened. As skilled as the Australian SASR were, all the enemy needed was to fire one lucky shot at the right time to kill a man.

Judy clasped her hand on top of Steve's and squeezed. Steve gave a gentle squeeze back.

He looked down at Dave's coffin, which was ready to be lowered. On the coffin was a large, framed colour photo of the patrol just before their deployment into Iraq. Dave wore a wide, proud smile and his eyes glinted with mischief. Dave had been one of the Regiment's finest soldiers; he was not only decorated but also well respected.

Steve saw two eagles circling in the sky. They were flying near a stand of pines, most likely where they had nested. One of them soared high and for a second was silhouetted against the sun. Steve felt as if the bird was giving its own farewell.

Dave's coffin was lowered into the grave. The photograph of the patrol, once bright in the afternoon sun, was cast into shadow and a moment later disappeared from sight.

Steve closed his eyes in silent farewell and a single tear slid down his face.

The congregation filed through and threw a small scoop of dirt onto the coffin. People said their own private farewell to Dave.

* * * * *

The soldiers were called back into work for a debrief after having spent three days with their families. Judy dropped Steve off, as he knew that the debrief would take the better part of the day and she needed the car to pick up the kids from school. She and Heleena would spend the day together. Judy enjoyed Heleena's company and liked teaching Heleena all about the modern world. She showed her how to open a can of dog food and how to use a mobile phone. The young Norsewoman was a fast learner but she needed to be, there was so much to learn.

Steve walked into the briefing room. He noticed the Regimental Sergeant Major, Commanding Officer and a group of soldiers waiting. The idea of a debrief was to gather all information possible from the actions of a patrol on the ground, to learn what had gone wrong or what had worked. Within half an hour, the four soldiers were seated.

"Morning all," began the debriefing officer, a man by the name of Major Ken Griffith, who was also an Intelligence officer. "Ah, 'The Usual Suspects'," he said, greeting the four men in front of him.

"Yeah, minus one," replied Steve.

Griffith nodded. "Sir, Ma'am," he looked at the Commanding Officer and the regiment's psychologist.

"So, what happened out there?" he asked.

"We got pulled into a time warp and found ourselves in the dark ages. Man, their beer was strong!" laughed Scott.

"Enough! Sit down!" Griffith shouted.

"Sorry," mumbled Scott.

"Well," Steve began. He took the better part of half an hour to explain what happened.

"We thought something like that might have happened," said the Commanding Officer. "That's not what interests me. What interests me are the thirty-six hours of radio silence before your first and final firefights. We didn't have direct radio contact with you, but our allies were passing us details of your transmissions. There was thirty-six hours where you were silent. Nothing."

Shit! Thirty-six hours, is that all? Steve thought.

"What can I say, Sir," said Steve, "we had enemy all over us. We had driven the vehicle into a cave and camouflaged ourselves. They were hunting for us and pretty determined to find us. The bastards didn't give up. So we couldn't afford to make a break for it, or make any unnecessary radio traffic. Once the coast was clear, or at least when we thought the coast was clear, we made a move and again got compromised. The Rover took a few bullets in the fuel tank in that first contact so was out of action. We had to call air support otherwise we would have been finished off there and then."

"Okay, Steve," nodded the CO. "Fair enough, that makes sense."

"You'll be happy to know," said Major Griffith, "that General Mohammad Al-Hazareen was in the white four-wheel drive. Your patrol killed him within the first few seconds of the contact."

"Fuckin' told ya!" said Scott, nudging Will.

"The UN had flyers dropped throughout Kurdish communities. The flyers maintained UN forces had been sent to hunt down and kill Hazareen, and that they had been successful. Not quite true, but that's politics I guess. As it happens the violence in Iraq's major cities eased after that pamphlet drop. Not too sure if that's as a result of your actions or a result of UN peace talks, maybe both."

"In any case, it may not have gone quite to plan, but well done, lads," said the CO, "I would ask now for a minute's silence in memory of Corporal Dave Hill."

After the silence, the group broke for morning smoko before going into detail about the patrol's firefights. The group listened as the soldiers described their final fight against the APCs and the tank. It had been a near impossible fight and the fact that four soldiers had taken on and immobilised eight APCs and a battle tank was incredible.

The day ended just on 1800hrs. Within half an hour of Steve's phone call, Judy had dropped Heleena back at Will's house and was there to pick Steve up.

Back home, Steve relaxed in his reclining chair with his hands on his head, watching the TV. The smell of roast pork wafted from the kitchen. He looked up at the framed picture of the SASR patrol taken by Pete Massicks all that time ago just before their deployment. It felt like another life. Steve's eyes rested on Dave's face. The big soldier wore a grin like a Cheshire cat, and little wonder, he was about to deploy into a Middle Eastern desert.

I'll miss you mate, Steve thought.

He was watching the television, but he was not listening to it. He was listening to his children playing and giggling in the far room. His kids. He heard the oven door open and listened as Judy checked the roast, decided it needed longer and put it back in the oven. She was humming to herself.

Steve closed his eyes. He was thinking of their mission in the Iraqi desert. He thought back over the years, the excitement the Regiment had to offer and the camaraderie. But there were also the mates he would never see again. The soldiers who died either in training accidents or in some of the most arduous and dangerous places on earth. Some died in car accidents in Australia. He felt a hand stroke his face and opened his eyes. Judy was sitting beside him. He smiled, leaned in and kissed her. He was home.

* * * * *

Several days later, Matt, Will, Steve, Scott and their partners decided to go out together to a local bar. Will and Heleena arrived at Steve's house several hours early, so Judy could show Heleena how to apply makeup. But, the night was over shortly after Heleena, squeezed on the bottom by an older man, punched him to the floor and was about to break his neck.

*****

It was raining outside, and as the sun began to set, the air became quite cool even though it was only autumn. There was a knock on the door. The kids were in bed, so Steve was careful not to make much noise as he made his way to the front door.

"Greg," nodded Steve, pushing the door open, to welcome the SASR's Regimental Sergeant Major.

"Apologies for my sudden appearance."

"No problems, mate, want a beer?" Steve asked.

"Yeah, wouldn't mind actually," replied Greg. "G'day, Judy," he smiled.

"Hi Greg, want a coffee?" asked Judy. "No, love, he's havin' a beer."

Steve cracked a stubby and passed it to Greg, offering the RSM a seat.

Steve sat down too.

"What can I do for ya, mate?" he asked.

"I'm not gonna beat round the bush here, Steve. I heard about you guys when you came off that chopper, I heard how you were dressed. As far as I know, no patrol's ever been dressed like that for desert operations. I know that you did not lie in the debrief, but I get the strong impression that you did neglect to mention parts of what happened. I ain't here to chest poke, mate or to reprimand. What you say to me will stay in these walls, I promise. I just want to know for my own peace of mind. What the hell happened out there?"

Steve took a swig of his beer. "Mate, with all due respect, I'm not sure you'd believe me if I told you the truth."

Greg looked at Steve. "You know, Steve, my first real operation was in Vietnam. We were supposed to observe an NVA battalion that was rumoured to be operating near the Australian AO. We were out there for close to twelve days before we came across their scouts. I was only twenty-three at the time and it scared the shit out of me. We went to ground and watched them and as Murphy's fuckin' law had it, those scouts

278

picked their way through the jungle straight onto our position. I'll never forget that NVA bloke's face. His face was all shock and fear as he realised too late. I knelt up and plugged him straight between the eyes. Luckily enough the rest of the NVA battalion had little idea where their scouts were and no idea where the shots had come from. We were able to call in Arty onto their position."

Greg took a swig of his beer. "I've been shot five times, I've been stabbed twice, once in combat and once in a damn pub brawl which left me with a lacerated liver. I've been in more conflicts than I care to remember and I have killed fifty-seven enemy soldiers in my time. That's something I don't want to remember, but as you know, it's something that is burned into your memory. My point is, Steve, that there isn't anything in this world that you could tell me that would shock me."

"I hear ya Greg," Steve said. "Shit I'm gonna need another beer to tell this story," he grinned.

"I'll have anothery," chuckled Greg.

"Righto," said Steve handing another beer to Greg.

"Okay," he said. "Well I'll just say it. We opened a time portal by accident and were sent back in time about a thousand years to Viking Denmark."

The room was silent for a long time.

"I told ya," said Steve.

"Just give me a moment," said Greg. "Okay, now that you've stopped stuffin' about, tell me what happened."

"I wish I was stuffin' about, mate, I shit you not," Steve said.

Steve spent the next half hour explaining their journey.

"You've gotta be shittin' me," Greg said at last.

"I told ya, mate, this is what happened."

"What were they like?"

"The Norse?" asked Steve.

"Yeah."

"As tough as nails, mate, like nothin' you've ever seen."

"Sorry if I look stunned, I'm still taking this all in."

"Thought you couldn't be shocked," Steve smiled.

"Yeah well, you just blew that theory clear outta the water."

"The real McCoy, mate," said Steve, handing the sword over to Greg. "This is a real Viking sword, not some gimmick. This thing has killed men."

Greg held the sword in his hands. It was a one-handed weapon and the weight felt perfect in his hand. Greg could see the hundreds of individual hammer blows that had been used to shape the weapon. It was as sharp as sin and not some cheap replica. The dagger was a curved weapon, its hilt carved from bone. The crescent- shaped blade was sharp on both sides.

"Looks real enough," said Greg.

"They're real, mate."

Greg finished his beer and placed it down. "I'm gonna head off, sorry again for intruding so late. I'll give you a call in a couple of days."

"No worries, Greg, hear from you then," said Steve walking the RSM to the door.

"By the way," said Greg turning back. "I got a phone call yesterday about some insubordination incident that some British officer wanted to press against you and your men. Something about being abusive and insubordinate."

Steve suppressed a grin. "Yeah."

"Don't worry about it, I threw it in the bin," said Greg. "Will I see you back at work after your leave?"

Steve decided to square with the RSM. "Yeah, you will mate, but only to hand in my discharge."

Greg nodded. "I thought as much, you're gonna be missed, mate. I'll see you in a couple of weeks."

"Yup, righto," said Steve closing the door and padding back to the lounge where he turned on the television.

EPILOGUE

As coincidence had it, there was a program on ABC made in the late-80s. It was called "The Vikings" and outlined the spread of the Norwegian Vikings towards Greenland and Iceland. The Swedish Vikings ventured east and became known as the Russ. They pushed into and conquered lands that would later become known as the USSR. The Danish Vikings travelled south and enveloped present day England. Their influence still clear in place names such as York. The Vikings called the city Yorvik; it was the trade capital of the northern world. Steve was half asleep at this point, but something about the programme made him sit up. The presenter was explaining that the Viking influence had spread to the Middle East. He was standing outside the cave where Steve and his men went back in time. Steve was sure it was the same cave. On the inside of the cave was the familiar rectangular obelisk almost five feet above the ground. The presenter moved to the rock and pointed to it, the camera zooming in.

"Now this is interesting," he said in a strong Yorkshire accent. He ran his fingers over the strange writing. "These are Norse runes. If I'm not mistaken, it says here 'Let it be known that Olaf and his Varangians did great battle here and were victorious against the savage horde. Let it be known that Thormdall of Ulfor fell here and took many enemies with him to the Great Hall.'"

"I can only assume by great hall they mean the hall of Valhalla," said the presenter. "This is quite interesting," he continued, "but I don't understand it. Why were these Viking warriors here? And what were they fighting for? There is nothing here, no precious jewels, no coin, nothing to loot or pillage, no slave girls to be had. This," said the man with his hand on the rock, "is a testament to a great battle that took place here, and the Vikings were victorious. Why, or what, they were fighting for, or even against who, we will never know. Thank you for joining me, I'm Jeremy Summers."

Steve tried to turn the television off but pressed the wrong button. The television changed to a soccer game hosted by a loud, French commentator. Steve swore and turned the television off. He sat there for some time before finding the sword and drawing it from its sheath. The metal glinted from the light thrown from the kitchen.

"Daddy!" Kathy called from her room.

He could hear the creak of the bed as Judy rose to check on her daughter.

He put the sword down and went to the master bedroom. "I got this babe," he told Judy. She mumbled something before climbing back into bed.

"It's okay, baby, just a bad dream," Steve called to his daughter. "Just a bad dream," he said to himself.

* * * * *

Steve was keen to read as many history books as he could on the Norse. He wanted to find out if the final battle in which they had been involved had ever been recorded.

Steve sat at the desk in the library. Unaware of the time, he had been reading for the better part of three hours. He learned about the Norse culture, their beliefs and the terrible violence the Vikings brought to the world. But as he continued to read, he realised that the Vikings were no more violent than those whom they attacked. It was a violent time, an age of sharp steel and ever watchfulness. Steve did not find any mention of the village of Ulfor, although he did find a saga about a man called Berag who had been captured by the Vikings. The saga stated that Odin looked upon Berag kindly. So much so that he had been liberated by the Gods of Light. These gods did not use swords or arrows, but commanded the thunder and lightning of Thor, striking down those before them as if by magic.

"You're kidding," he said aloud.

He read another book about the Varangian Guard. A Byzantine priest named Ahmad Ibn Fadlan was quoted to have said, "I travelled across land and sea with a troop of Varags, to a small Norse village. It was called Ulfor, to seek counsel with those named Tuatha-Day-Dannan. I did not see godliness amongst them, they were mere men."

The book went on to mention a long-faded rune stone found somewhere in present day Turkey. A small host of Varangians had led the Gods of Light home, where they were sent back to Odin's hall of heroes. The author interpreted a small inscription. He wrote the inscription said, "The Tuatha-Day-Dannan never again entered the world of men as a group."

The author mentioned Olaf, one of the senior officers of the Varangian Guard. Olaf was said to have led three thousand guardsmen on a rampage into present day Bulgaria. They destroyed villages, burnt crops, slaughtered livestock and killed all in their wake. They took nothing. The attack only lasted about two weeks before the guardsmen returned to Byzantium. On the return journey, it was recorded that the guardsmen carried with them the skeletons of eight Varangians who had fallen long before.

Another book he stumbled upon mentioned tiny, hollow vessels in which women kept perfume and which they wore as necklaces. The tiny vessels had turned up in coin hordes and in archaeological digs. One had even been found welded into the pommel of a sword hilt.

"This seems such a poor analogy in the face of such an ancient people," the author of the book wrote. "But, one could be forgiven for thinking that these tiny, unexplainable vessels look like spent cartridges. It seems ridiculous, believe me. But they bear a striking resemblance to today's ammunition cartridges!"

"Bloody hell," whispered Steve.

"Excuse me," a woman said.

Steve looked up.

"We're closing soon."

"Ah okay," Steve said, gathering up the books. "May as well take these with me then."

The librarian smiled.

* * * * *

Steve discharged from the army, deciding that he wanted to spend more time with his family. Securing a managerial job at a local security firm meant that he would be home most nights. Two years after his discharge, Steve took his family on a holiday to the Middle East. They visited the pyramids, the Sphinx and watched the sunrise over the beach of ANZAC cove. The war in Iraq had finished twelve months before, so he also took his family to an obscure cave on the border of Turkey. While his kids played amongst the sand, his wife keeping an eye on them, Steve placed his hand on the stone and looked out at a familiar view. The following year they booked a five-week holiday to Denmark.

Will and Heleena were married a year later; it was only a small wedding, but nothing was left to chance. It was the first time Heleena ventured out in public without her knives. Heleena gave birth to two beautiful, healthy children, a boy and a girl. They both had the strong eyes of their father, and the thick, curly hair of their mother. Will deployed twice more to Iraq, once to Afghanistan and spent one deployment in East Timor, which felt like a holiday. He remained in the army, reaching the rank of Warrant Officer Class 1. He would later become the SASR's Regimental Sergeant Major.

Matt discharged from the army two years later. He studied medicine and years later became a doctor in a busy emergency department.

Scott remained in the army, although wasn't promoted beyond the rank of Sergeant. He deployed three times to Iraq, twice to Afghanistan where on the second tour of duty he was wounded in the leg. During three weeks' leave, he travelled on holiday to Turkey, where he visited a cave on the border of the country. A cave with which he was familiar.

The Reckoning: The Day Australia Fell
The Unforeseen Series Book 1

Australia has been invaded.

While the outnumbered Australian Defence Force fights on the ground, in the air and at sea, this quickly becomes a war involving ordinary people. Ben, an IT consultant has never fought a day in his life. Will he survive? Grant, a security guard at Sydney's International Airport, finds himself captured and living in the filth and squalor of one of the concentration camps dotted around Australia.

Knowing death awaits him if he stays, he plans a daring escape. This is a dark day in Australia's history. This is terror, loneliness, starvation and adrenaline all mixed together in a sour cocktail.

This is the day Australia fell.

Aftermath
The Unforeseen Series Book 2

Mick and his family have returned home to the farm following Indonesia's withdrawal. But thousands of battle-hardened enemy soldiers remain hidden in the forests and hills, ready to strike when they are least expected. This fight will take Mick to the limit, and protecting his family will require all his strength and determination.

Jimmy and Spud lead a platoon through the Australian scrub on relentless guerrilla strikes. But when they find themselves outnumbered and outgunned, it might have all been for nothing.

A new Australia will rise again … or will it?